KILL OR BE KILLED

by Ivan Narayan

*Thanks Todd,
I hope you enjoy
the read. Thanks for
supporting
the book)*

authorHOUSE®

AuthorHouse™
1663 Liberty Drive, Suite 200
Bloomington, IN 47403
www.authorhouse.com
Phone: 1-800-839-8640

© 2008 Ivan Narayan. All rights reserved.

No part of this book may be reproduced, stored in a retrieval system, or transmitted by any means without the written permission of the author.

First published by AuthorHouse 11/18/2008

ISBN: 978-1-4343-9137-7 (sc)

Printed in the United States of America
Bloomington, Indiana

This book is printed on acid-free paper.

"I got news for you, sweetheart. Life is full of moments. It's what makes life worth living."
GABRIELLE DIXON, 1942

CHAPTER 1

I hastily scanned the half-open windows above. Each was highlighted by a pale, yellow glow that reflected eerily off the damp pavement, and moth-eaten curtains that swayed gently in the cold breeze of the night. I looked toward a corner window where at that moment laid the corpse of a 'supposed' dead man. A long time ago I considered myself a dead man. Now, the blood was flowing through me, through the old tired bones that had seen too many dead mugs and dark alleyways. I felt alive again.

Behind me, the bridge climbed out of the water like a steel and brick monster. The shadow it created stretched across much of the river. A few empty lots bathed in waste marked the edge of death like a clock stuck on midnight. Above the suspicious solitude could be heard the far-away steady hum of cars crossing the bridge. It was like watching death do the tango to the sound of raised voices, distant gunshots and blaring police sirens.

As if on cue, police sirens suddenly rose up out of the muted volume of the city, increasing in degree with each passing second. Most people, if they lived here long enough, could figure out where they came from and where they were headed. If you were really good, you even knew why. I knew they were headed here, and I also knew why.

It began an hour ago when I received a call from Mr. Nobody. That's right, Mr. Nobody. See, Mr. Nobody called and told me there was a dead fish here, in this apartment building on Henry Street, and that I needed to be here when the cops arrived. That was it. That was all. I suppose that should have been enough.

After the mysterious caller hung up I contacted Pete Miller, a friend on the force, and told him about the call. Twenty minutes later, I found myself staring down a potential murder scene, wondering all the while why I was the one that had to be here. I didn't feel like complaining until I knew what was going on and what my alibi would be. In New York, without an alibi, call yourself a bowl of soup and get served up for dinner because everyone wants an alibi. I know it sounds corny, but it makes sense to me, and honestly, that's all you got to know. The rest of it couldn't get you enough to buy a decent cup of coffee at the local burger joint.

I mulled these and other thoughts over as I waited patiently for Pete to show up. Moments later, Pete pulled up just slightly behind my car, parking like a granny set to make her way to the retirement home. I could never figure Pete out. He was tough and took no guff from anybody, but sometimes could be the biggest baby of the bunch. He looked like his mother still dressed him, and he smelled like he just got finished rolling in a rose bush. Sure, I was no Sunday picnic, but you had to figure a guy who played cops and robbers had some raw edges to him, but in Pete, sometimes, I didn't see any. Sometimes I believed I didn't want to see any. It felt good to see that someone from the old neighborhood had done well, because a lot of the guys we used to know were either in stir or in the ground. Anyone else left out would quickly join them. I suppose I was just waiting to see which side of the ledger I'd be counted into. Pete, on the other hand, had done well. He married a beautiful dame, had a couple Pete juniors running around, and was looking for a quick promotion to Captain soon. Had I stuck, maybe I'd be where he was. But all things being equal, I didn't think being on the inside worked for me. Outside is where I belong. It's where I've always belonged.

Pete got out just as another police car was pulling up. He ambled over, smoke from a barely lit cigarette wafting up and away from him like a tiny scarf caught in an autumn breeze. The flaps of his overcoat were drawn up tight against his neck, the bottom spreading slightly with each step.

"Hey, Pete, how's things?" I asked.

"I'd rather be in Hawaii," Pete hissed.

"What's wrong? You look like someone who's just had their favorite babe magazine thrown into the fire."

"I've been staring at too many John Doe's, Dix. This city is getting worse everyday." Dark shadows lined the bottom of both eyes. His face hung low, lower than I'd ever seen before. He was having one of those rough, raw moments I rarely got to see.

The job was tough, and more times than not you found yourself asking questions that confused even the smartest of University professors. It was hard to believe when everything around a guy was screaming ugly all the time.

There were times when Pete and I could count on booze to keep us level, but even that was not enough in some cases. It was all I had. Pete had the comfort of a woman who loved him, and two kids that could bring out a smile when nothing else could. Still, the job kept getting in the way, like a guy trying to bud in line at a movie theatre, or an itch that wouldn't stop itching no matter how much you scratched.

"Who said it ever had a good day?" I asked solemnly.

"Sometimes I can see it, but not often. Once in a while I'd like to look at the city and see nothing but blue skies and rainbows."

"I'm just a rum-filled private detective on his last legs, and you're a cop who thinks too much about things that aren't your business, or mine for that matter. We're paid to believe the world is as it is because someone left the sewage tap on a little too long and all the crud is just now coming to the surface." My eyes drifted toward the building again. I turned to Pete and added, "Maybe, we're looking at the world all wrong. Maybe you and I need different glasses."

"Rose-colored?" Pete asked sarcastically.

"No. Actually, I was thinking more like shot glasses."

Pete and I laughed. One joke made everything okay again, if only for a little while. Just one of those moments in a day could keep the nightmares at bay for a few precious hours. For a cop, that kind of peace was priceless.

The sound of more sirens brought us reluctantly back to the present. Our laughter died as suddenly as it was born. I scratched an imaginary itch while Pete flicked his cigarette against the pavement. We turned and examined the mysterious building that supposedly housed a corpse. The whole place looked dead, only a few morose shadows swinging lazily across small windows were any indication of life inside. I glanced around to see people staring here and there like tourists lost in their own city.

This was a largely Jewish section with ancient tenement housing filling up faster than a poured drink. You would never find anyone with money, real money, living around here. What you would find were people devoted to the ideals that America had been founded on. They believed unfalteringly in those principles, sometimes to the discredit of those born in this neck of the world. Because of these new Americans, living on Pike and Henry Street, and other similar streets, the American dream was still alive; otherwise, it would probably wind up in some five-and-dime along with all the other useless junk.

"So, where is the John Doe?" Pete asked.

"Sixth floor, corner apartment," I replied.

"And you have no idea who called you on the phone?"

"You got me. I was all ready to go and see Mahoney when my phone rings. Some guy on the other end tells me there's a John Doe here and that I should be the first one on the scene. Then he hangs up. Go figure, the guy's not even decent enough to wait until after I've had a few."

"What did he sound like?"

I thought about the voice for a minute, trying to replay it in my head like the White Sox last World Series win. "He's probably around our age. He had a smooth-sounding voice, kind of muffled, but mostly just a normal-sounding voice. I can't tell you anymore than that. There were no discernable background noises of any kind."

"Hmmm," Pete murmured. "That doesn't give us much, if there really is a dead guy up there. Do you think it could be one of your past cases coming back to haunt you? It's been known to happen, you know," Pete said suspiciously.

"I thought about that, but I keep coming up zeros. The only way to know for sure whether this is on the level is to go in and see for ourselves. What gets me is that everything around here seems so quiet, so natural, as if everything is business as usual." I surveyed the landscape, attempting to unearth the reason for my trepidation.

"Well, if everything is on the level, I'm taking you in for disturbing the peace."

"You should thank me. If it wasn't for me you're life would be one big bore. Pete, I'm the umbrella in your martini, stirring things up enough to keep your life interesting."

"Stirring up trouble, you mean."

We kept trading verbal jabs as we made our way inside. The building wasn't much to look at, but for those who lived here, it was home. The pungent aroma that flowed easily through every corridor and stairwell reminded me of the large Italian spread at Mama Cuppo's.

There were no elevators so we had to make our way up a small, rickety set of stairs that hugged the paper-thin wall to our right. Each step groaned in protest, and the railing swayed to the left and right like an overloaded freighter caught in a winter storm.

Each floor was lined with row upon row of dingy, brown doors that had probably seen better days. The hallways were small, and looked like they had been built by some guy who kept one eye closed the whole time. Oddly curved angles dominated the entire building. The walls looked bowed if you stood far away, and the floor seemed to gain a subtle incline in the middle. Even the light played strangely against the wood and paint, increasing its glare in the nooks and crannies while seemingly disappearing in the open areas.

More than a few times, as if on cue, a pair of questioning eyes followed us as we walked up. Normally, that wouldn't be a problem, but this time the look in those eyes was different. Every pair I looked into seemed to house a deep fear, as if an ominous cloud were about to settle over everything and everyone. An odd assortment of queries also followed us up, but mostly we ignored the patter, concentrating instead on what may lie ahead. We ascended another wobbly flight of stairs. By the time we reached the sixth floor, Pete and I began to wonder how we had managed to live so long while being in such bad shape. I felt like I had just gone ten rounds with Joe Lewis. My legs felt heavier than a twelve pack of Schlitz, and my eyes were starting to water like the fountain in Central Park. Pete, on the other hand, didn't show his weariness, but I could tell it was hitting him too. He talked slower than traffic through Times Square, and he hunched over, just slightly, but enough to have me believing he was the reincarnation of his old man just before he died.

We looked at each other but said nothing. We didn't have to. Had others been around, it would have been like getting caught in Times Square with our pants down around our knees.

"Where's the room," Pete said, the words sounding like they were spoken through a handkerchief.

I looked back toward the south end of the hallway where the overhead light bulb had gone out covering everything in a dismal black that seemed almost perfect for whatever we were about to see.

"That's it there," I replied, pointing toward a nondescript brown door clinging to the end of the hallway.

Pete turned and asked, "You packing?"

"Does Mahoney look like an overworked mule?"

I pulled out my gat the same time Pete pulled out his. The floor creaked under our feet, the sound crashing through the hallway like a drunken nag in a glass factory. Pete motioned for me to stand on the left side, near the window, while he stood to the right.

I nodded to Pete, letting him know I was ready.

"Open up, it's the police!" Pete barked. Other than the stray bark of a mutt from somewhere outside, the place was as quiet and still as a cemetery. Pete repeated himself only to be greeted by more deafening silence. I looked passed him and down the hall. The doors remained closed, as if aware trouble was on the menu.

"Alright, you asked for it!" Pete kicked the door open. The sound of his foot smashing into the flimsy wooden door resounded not only through the empty hallway, but through my body, almost shaking my bones to dust. Suddenly, I became as ridged as lumber, my mind emptied of everything but this moment, this hallway, this room.

Seconds ticked off the clock rapidly, as if time were a giant ball rolling down a hill. I took a few short breaths before sneaking a glance within the room. The place was lit well enough for me to see the usual things like curtains, furniture, pictures, and the not-so-usual things like bodies lying on the floor in a pool of dark liquid.

I studied Pete for a few anxious moments. He knew what was coming just as well as I did. I strode through the entrance and into the room before he could shoot me. My gun led the way, but I knew I wouldn't need it. Not here. Not now. Pete was quick on my heels, fuming like a chimney in the dead of winter.

"Damn it, Dix," Pete bellowed in frustration. His gaze fell over every inch of that apartment except me and the body lying on the floor. There was no time for a lecture on the finer points of entering a crime scene. That would come after the place was secure.

Pete searched the bedroom and bathroom to our right. I searched the rest of the place; at least what there was of it. The light in the bedroom was also on, but if there was anyone hiding within they were invisible. Behind me, the kitchen, clinging stubbornly to a half-darkness, was also devoid of life. The entire place was. Pete walked slowly back into the living room and studied me with eyes that could have raised the dead. Light coming from an ancient-looking lamp in the corner of the living exposed the awful truth that laid there.

"Damn it, Dix! You should know better! The room wasn't clear! We don't know what's in here!"

"We do now. Looks like you have another one of those corpses you were talking so happily about before." Pete looked down at the body. The John Doe was young, possibly in his early twenties. He was dressed in a white dress shirt that looked like he was still trying to grow into it and black dress pants with more creases in it than a discarded paper bag. His arms were bound behind his back with thick, gray cord that was more red than gray. His legs were also bound. Other than that, he was all red. You know; the kind that has blood written all over it.

"Whoever shot this guy must have been using him for target practice. He's got half a dozen bullet holes in him, at least," Pete offered solemnly.

The dead body was marked by numerous entry and exit wounds, as if some blind man had used him for target practice. The light also exposed a long, haphazard trail of blood and dirt leading away from the body, as if trying to escape the scene of the crime. A small smattering of crimson also decorated the wall directly to the right of the corpse, just under the window.

"Looks like someone also used him as a punching bag," I said.

Pete looked down at the guy and winced. It wasn't a pretty sight. His face was a mixture of red and black welts with streaks of dried blood slashed across his mouth like badly-painted lipstick. Some of the wounds looked fresh. His face still had a dash of warmth left in it, but not much. Rigamortos had begun to set in.

"I'm going down and get some more help up here. How about you try to not ruin the crime scene until I get back?" Pete said.

"C'mon, Pete, give me some credit," I interjected, placing my rod back in my holster.

Pete just shook his head and walked out, leaving me alone with the stiff.

I circled the body a few times, trying to reconcile the scene in my mind. I knelt down to get a better look only to have the face of an angel return my gaze. His hazel-colored eyes seemed to retain some miniscule spark of energy. I couldn't stop staring at them. A quick glance at the rest of him shook me out of my trance.

An expression of puzzlement decorated his battered face, as if he were in deep thought regarding the slightly unkind circumstances surrounding his fate. His was the type of face I'd seen a thousand times on kids delivering newspapers, reading comic books, or watching big ships sail in and out of the harbor on lazy Saturday afternoons. Out of respect, I reached out and closed his eyelids.

I was alone with him only a few minutes, but in those few minutes I saw a kid who hadn't had a chance at life. I wasn't a psycho doctor with a degree, but it didn't take one to see the deep regret etched eerily into every inch of his angelic-looking face. He had rough edges to him, that was certain, but they weren't so rough they cut. For a guy like me the rough edges were what made life worth living. They brought out the danger the same way a piece of cheese lures a mouse or a sweet-smelling dame brings out the vultures. I found myself enjoying the danger, all the while pretending outwardly that I despised it. That same danger kept Pete on the force and away from my area of town. He sandpapered off the rough edges, reveling in the newfound smoothness, hoping it would transform the Hell's Kitchen kid that lived inside into a sweet-smelling rose that said his prayers three times a day and never wiped his nose unless it was with a handkerchief and not the sleeve of his shirt.

Pete walked back in a few moments later with a couple of droopy-eyed coppers in tow. He examined me for a moment. It was the kind of stare you gave someone hungrily knocking on the door of insanity. "Are you trying to have a communion with the dead?"

"Couldn't hurt," I replied quietly.

Pete looked at me like I had two heads. "I leave you alone for five minutes and you turn into some kind of magician. You need help, Dix."

"He's one of ours, Pete."

"You mean a cop?" Pete asked warily.

"No, I mean he's from where we used to be."

"Hell's Kitchen?"

"Maybe, maybe not, but I don't think he could recognize a silver spoon if it hit him on the head."

"How can you tell?"

I looked at him again. All the clues were there, begging me to pick them up like a deck of cards scattered across a floor. Even the shadows that stretched away from the kid didn't belong. It was like looking at an expensive painting hanging in a burger joint. The whole scene was wrong.

"Well, for one thing, a corpse doesn't shrink this quickly. The clothes this kid is wearing are two sizes too big for him. On top of that, look at his shoes," I said, pointing to his shoes.

Pete walked around the body slowly, crouched near the shoes and just stared. Sometimes, looking at Pete, I wondered how a guy so slow could become a detective. It wasn't like he had a rock for a brain, but sometimes the simplest of clues rushed by him like a horse at a racetrack. He must have had pictures of someone doing something they weren't supposed to be doing, otherwise, had I stuck with the force I'd probably be President by now.

I tried not to laugh and found that looking at the dead kid made it fairly easy to keep from laughing my guts off. Pete looked on, wondering what was wrong with me.

"They're scuffed up and dirty. The souls of his shoes have bits of mud, gravel and grass on them. The tops have a decent layer of dust and dirt as well. You might want to check some of the empty lots around here. Maybe check some of the abandoned buildings too. The scuffmarks on the heels tell me he was probably dragged. Look at the amount of dirt and mud on them," I said, pointing toward the back of his shoes. The trail that led away from the body was a mixture of the same sand, gravel and grass. "Probably the only pair of decent shoes he had," I muttered. The heels were thin, and the tread reminded me of the tires on my car, only cleaner. I stood up and looked around at the apartment, taking in everything in one big sweep. The dead body and the apartment seemed a study in contrasts. The scene wrapped around the kid about as well as a gunsel in a church.

"I don't think this is his apartment either."

A mixture of distrust and impatience decorated Pete's sage-looking mug. I couldn't entirely blame him for not falling at my feet every time I saw a clue; however, there were times when that look tested my own patience, and this was one of those times.

"I know that look, Pete, and I know what it means, but trust me on this one?"

"Dix, if you're crazy, then I'm going to have to lock myself up as well." He scrutinized me for a few more tense seconds then looked at the body again. Outside the apartment, a sudden flood of voices told me more of Pete's boys in blue were on their way in. Mixed into the sudden onrush was an exotic mix of verbs and syllables that meant the peeping toms were also out in full force, informing anyone who would listen that they'd seen nothing, heard nothing, but knew everything.

"You don't really think this is his place, do you?" I asked.

"I don't know anything yet. I'm just wondering how you know so fast."

"Simple. There are too many doilies and watered plants in this place for me to think this kid lives here. On top of all that, the cross on the kid's neck doesn't quite match the star of David hanging on the wall over there," I said, pointing toward a small silver star that hung from the wall near what served as a kitchen. The star was about the size of a dinner plate, and the clean, shiny surface reminded me of the buffed nameplates that hung off the sides of the mansions on Park Avenue. Someone had taken great care to keep it in good order, and it was a good bet that someone wasn't this kid. "The fact he's still wearing it means we can probably eliminate robbery or mugging. Whoever killed this guy wanted him dead for a reason."

"Hmmm, good point. He probably wasn't shot here. Someone would have heard something, especially with that many holes in him."

"You're right there. He's been shot too many times. That kind of business would have left a mess everywhere. The only mess is the blood on the body and on the floor. If he'd been dragged in, we'd see a long trail of blood all the way to the door, but there isn't one. I think he was carried in here and dumped on the ground. That might explain the spatter marks against the wall," I said, pointing toward the wall just behind the corpse. "Most of the blood has pooled around the body." I scanned the droplets of blood and detritus that stretched erratically to the door. I walked a few steps toward the door, examining the floor as I went. "There are drops and small smears. The smears are probably our handy work. But, there isn't enough there to tell me he was dragged in."

I studied the walls and ceiling, noticing nothing but cracked, dirty plaster that looked like old, rumpled newspapers. The curtains had also seen better days. Small, rickety furniture hunkered here and there like skeletons in an open-pit burial. The whole scene was as pretty as New York in July. I wanted to leave, but something about the phone call made me stay. I'd been in tough spots before and had managed to miraculously escape with most of me still intact. This time things seemed different. It was like looking through a bottle and into a world distorted beyond all rhyme and reason. After a few seconds you pulled the bottle away only to see another distorted view.

Which one was better to look at? I wasn't sure, but in this case I saw two worlds: one world that centered on this apartment, and another centering on the kid. The truth lay somewhere between.

"If that's the case, how does someone get a dead guy all the way up here without anyone seeing anything?" Pete asked.

"Maybe they brought him up the fire escape."

Pete walked out into the hallway. Before walking out, I looked back at the kid one more time. A thick veil of darkness obscured his true identity. All I could do was stand there and make assumptions. The whole thing made me want to hit something. Something about that veil of darkness made me realize that whatever happened to this kid wasn't over yet. Stuff like this never ends. It rumbles forward like a train on an endless journey, going nowhere, but going there with a purpose.

Had I been ten years younger, and ten cases of scotch lighter, I'd probably be more upset; however, things were different now. The past year had seen me fall in and out of love as easy as draining a beer glass. My mind returned to a lady named Rose every time I walked by a lonely-looking apartment building, or drove by a cemetery in the middle of the night. I had become a backward-looking wreck ever since. It wasn't the sanest thing in the world to do, but I was on my own and had no one else to worry about. Looking at the kid seemed to change all that. I was starting to care again, and that was a dangerous thing. I had to get out and away from this place before it choked the life back into me. I understood what Pete meant when he said he had seen too many dead bodies. So had I. I had seen too much. The weight of it pushed me to the ground until I was no longer above it anymore, but below it, joining the same sorry souls that had haunted my dreams for so long.

I closed my eyes then opened them again. The room shrunk until it was just the kid and I. Beyond me, the world existed only in fragments. Someone wanted me to know the kid was dead. The real question was why? It was that part of this scene that existed beyond me, in fragments. The part that was close was the kid. I had felt that death before, in a place much like this one. Seeing him lie there brought back memories of another time, another place. They were moments that didn't matter anymore. At least I kept saying that to myself in the hopes I would start believing it.

I stood up and started for the door. In the hallway, more cops were making their way to the scene of the crime. Pete was standing near the window, flashlight in hand, looking out at the fire escape. He turned to me just as I walked out.

"There's blood on the window pane, and some more on the landing. There's some dirt here too. Looks like whoever punched this kid's ticket dragged him up the fire escape, through the window then carried him into the room. The only problem is figuring out how they did it without making more of a mess."

"Well, that's a problem you can figure out on your own because I'm out of this one for good." My shoulders sagged along with the rest of me, leaving me looking like a mummy in an Egyptian sarcophagus.

Pete eyed me suspiciously but didn't press the point. There was no reason for me to be there anyway. I had done my one good deed for the week and was looking to balance the equation with a little tonic at Mahoney's. Truth is, if Pete could, he would've been right behind me. That's the beauty of having no responsibilities. You never have to worry about looking over your shoulder to see who's looking for more scraps than you. I had no one, and no one had me. It sounded real simple when you said it real fast, but you had to make sure you didn't think about it too long or else the truth came out tasting flatter than last night's beer. A part of me couldn't help wondering who was better off: me or the dead kid.

Pete started to say something then thought better of it. We knew each other too well to press each other's buttons and get away with it. He didn't want to be there anymore than I did.

We turned away from each other and walked in opposite directions. He walked toward a new darkness while I, with closed eyes, stumbled clumsily against the same old nightmare.

I heard a baby cry as I walked down the stairs. A cold, sharp chill crawled up my spine.

CHAPTER 2

The days after Henry Street passed quickly. It was as if someone had downed too much coffee and decided tearing the pages off the calendar two and three days at a time was a good idea. I kept myself busy taking whatever jobs came along. Most of them were pretty thin, especially where dough was concerned. The worst ones were always the tail jobs. In the private detective gig, a tail job is considered the dog's breakfast, meaning it's somewhere near the bottom of the to-do list as far as work is concerned. Some dicks hate it so much they'll even pass out other dicks' phone numbers just to get out of them. It's never a good way to do business, especially if the mug on the receiving end finds out who sent the mark.

Anyway, I took the cases not so much for the money, although it did help take a small slice out of my bar tab at Mahoney's, but because they kept my mind occupied, or at least I fooled myself into believing they did. I could feel a large hole where thought, feeling and action should have rested. Nothing I did could bring the kid back from the dead. And the fact I didn't even know who he was didn't make the emptiness any more palatable.

I hunkered low in the driver's side, the cigarette warm against my face, its amber glow bright against the deep darkness that enveloped me. I tried the radio, hoping the smooth chords would be sweet enough to wash away the self-pity coursing through me. It didn't work. I couldn't get away from the truth of what I'd seen. His face and eyes fell over me like rain. It was like standing in a room surrounded by mirrors. I saw my reflection everywhere, eyes wide open and uncertain, as if waiting for something or someone to come along and open a door that had kept me locked out most of my life.

Sitting in my car, I suddenly wondered what Pete had found. It would be an easy call to make, and with a little fancy talking I could back out of the situation without Pete having to know I wanted in. But, did I want in? I felt like a guy in a one-man tug-of-war. I closed my eyes, but the shadows remained.

It was dark by the time I arrived at my apartment. It was cold and I was in no mood to do much of anything except sleep. I had been tailing some fat guy who seemed to have a penchant for dancing girls. Normally, that wouldn't be a problem; heck, I probably would have joined in. The problem was his wife didn't like the idea of having to share his husband with a bunch of floozies. I followed the guy all day, jotting down everything I saw. I thought about calling the broad and giving her the bad news, but listening to a dame scream and cry tonight didn't go over too well. I went by Mahoney's and got a half bottle of Jack Daniels along with a few words of unasked for wisdom from the big man himself before heading to my apartment. I sat down on the bed, opened the bottle, poured out a glass and downed it fast. It tasted wet, cold, and good. I shut my eyes, letting the booze wash through my system. It helped clean out some of the memories that had polluted my mind for the last week. Brittle shadows spilled across the cracked plaster walls of my room. I thought about the kid again. I poured another glass, downing it faster than the first. This time, it didn't go down so well. The kid's memory hovered over me like an unwanted vulture hoping for some small scraps of flesh from an already barren soul. I finally put the glass down on the table and casually picked up the receiver. I gripped it tightly for a few seconds, wondering whether this was a good idea or not. Somewhere in the city a murderer was enjoying his unearned freedom. The image burned into my skull like a forest fire. I started dialing Pete's home number. A few seconds later, Pete's wife answered, her always-pleasant voice echoing above what seemed to be Crosby warbling some new tune.

"Hey, Doll. When you gonna leave that sourpuss husband of yours and run away with me to Hawaii?"

"Oh, Dix," Wilma said laughingly. "That sounds great, but what are we going to do for money? After all, a girl has got to eat."

"We'll live on love, sweetheart," I replied, my heavy breath seeping through the receiver like a slow wind passing through Times Square.

Wilma laughed forever. It was a good laugh. It made me feel like I was home again. I was happy that Pete had such a swell lady for a wife.

"Are you ever going to straighten out, Gabrielle? Pete and I are worried about you."

"I'm okay, Wilma. I just haven't been getting enough sleep lately. Is Pete around?"

Wilma sighed for a second. She knew me as well as Pete did. She also knew I wasn't ready for counseling. "Yes, he's listening to the radio. I'll go get him for you."

"Thanks." It was hard to tell a lie to someone as nice as Wilma. It was also harder to tell the truth.

A few moments later Pete was on the phone. He was probably grinning like a kid who just found a nickel. He started easy enough, "What's going on, Dix?"

"What did you find out about the kid?" I asked immediately.

"You wouldn't be talking about the kid we found at Henry Street, would you?" The sarcasm dripped off him like too-much mustard on a hot dog.

"Yeah," I replied sheepishly. We both knew he had me.

"His name was Joseph Baker. He was nineteen and worked part time at a grocery store in Queens. He also worked three nights a week at a club called the Pheasant Lounge. By the way, the apartment we found him in belonged to his step-mother."

"What about his real parents?" I asked.

"Apparently the kid's parents died when he was young so an old Jewish lady adopted him. Talking to her was like talking to a brick wall. She wouldn't give us the time of day."

That didn't surprise me. Criminals and gangs imposed a gag order on newly arrived immigrants that, if broken, led to severe repercussions. They didn't have to do much. One death was usually enough to keep people from talking. And for many of these immigrants, trust was a commodity that was hard to come by and even harder to spare.

"Did she tell you anything interesting?"

"Why the sudden concern, Dix? A week ago you didn't want any part of this scene, and now it sounds like you might actually care what happened to him."

"Somebody wanted me to see the kid for a reason. I have a hundred different guesses as to why, but only one fits." It was a great line, but I wasn't sure if I meant all of it. Fact is I wasn't sure what I was doing or why. All I knew was that since the phone call my world had gone from a nasty little breeze to a nightmarish tornado.

"Are you telling me you want in, Dix?" Pete asked.

"Yeah, Pete, I do. Maybe I can get information you can't. Let's face it, cops going in with badges flashing doesn't always work. Stuff like this needs tact, and I'm all about tact."

Pete laughed quietly, almost absently, as if forcing laughter that wasn't quite there. "Alright, Dix, but you still got to play by the rules. You can't go in like the Lone Ranger, like you did at the apartment. Stuff like that only looks good in the movies."

Pete's concern was almost touching. If he was in the room, I might have even bought him a drink, after I borrowed two bits off him. "What's the old ladies name? Maybe I'll go see her first. See if she'll talk to me."

"Her name is Shanny Warchinski. She sells fish off a pushcart in the open market a couple blocks south of Henry Street during the daytime."

"Did she say where she was that night?"

"She said she was out collecting junk. She got there a couple of hours after you left. The coroner took the body an hour before she came home. Still, she didn't look right. She was real calm when she found out, but you could tell it was breaking her apart inside."

"She identified the body as her son?" I asked.

"I didn't show her the body, but one of the boys showed her a picture of his face the next day and she confirmed the i.d."

"Hmm," I mumbled. "Anything else I should know?"

"Yeah, stay away from the Pheasant Lounge."

"C'mon, Pete; you know words like that give me an itch I just have to scratch."

Pete's tone suddenly took on a somber cast. Ever since I could remember, Pete had always tried to scare me off in his own special way, but rarely did he get an edge this sharp in his voice.

"I mean it, Dix. This isn't an ordinary dive. Big Pete owns it, unofficially. You go sticking your nose into his business and you're liable to wind up at the bottom of an endless hole. I've kind of gotten used to having you around, so steer clear of it."

We both knew his warning was falling on deaf ears. I was going there and nothing he could say would stop me. If the kid worked at the lounge, and the biggest gangster in the city happened to be his boss then something somewhere added up to more trouble than you could shake a stick at.

"You know something, Pete?" I asked sarcastically.

"What?"

"It's been a long time since I went dancing. Maybe I'll go tonight. You go check out this grocery store and I'll go cut a rug."

"Dix!" Pete yelled.

He didn't get a chance to finish. I hung up the phone.

The shadows that surrounded me had become bigger, erasing more of the apartment wall since I last looked.

Outside, the night had taken on the color of death.

CHAPTER 3

The city moved slow and easy. The steady confidence in that flowing tide reminded me of the ticker-tape parades that wound through Times Square for soldiers returning from the First World War. The beat wasn't as quick, and the noises weren't as festive, but the movement seemed similar. It looked good once, but now only a few inelegant, misshapen trees the color of mud dotted the few streets where people still cared about stuff like that. The rest was all concrete, glass and brick, and even that wasn't a given.

I arrived at the Pheasant Lounge where big money was the name of the game and where small-timers were as welcome as the plague. Although it was no bigger in stature than the buildings that surrounded it, it still seemed bigger. The street it rested on was a long one, with crisp angles that straightened about as much as they could, especially when you considered the money that went to build them. Big Pete had a lot of money invested in streets like this. His philosophy rested upon the supposition: You own the streets and you control what happens on them.

I took a good look at the lounge. It was decorated with the kind of glitz and glam one expected from a place owned by one of the biggest mobsters in the city. The inside was rarely experienced by anyone not in the high-income crowd. Before Big Pete took it over, the Pheasant Lounge was strictly third-rate as far as action. Now, the place was on the top of the to-do list for every fat cat and kitten in the city.

I pulled up to the curb and waited patiently for the door guy to come over and shoo me away. I took out a few bills as he approached and handed them over. The guy, maybe in his thirties, looked like a chiseled statue. He could've been a handsome mug at one time but now looked like a guy late for a fancy dinner and hoping for the leftovers. He stood like a locked gate, hoping his somewhat-solid presence would be enough to scare me away. It wasn't. I took out a few more dollars and pressed them deep into his white-gloved palm until he ultimately gave in.

I was nothing more than a germ in his eyes and that was okay. I had bigger fish to fry. He tossed me one last angry stare then drove my car away. Instead of walking through the front doors I strolled casually along the front of the building until I came across an alley to the right. It was dark, wet, and looked like something out of a Jacob Riis photo.

I waded through the murky darkness until I came to the backside of the building. It was tall, with a grayish-brown cast that seemed more painted on than real. The best of the place clearly faced the street. The rear looked like it belonged in a Cagney mobster flick. A few solitary lights hung perilously above a pair of solid metal doors, and rusty fire escapes climbed up the sides like lizards trying to escape the deluge. Toward the far end, a five to six foot long fence separated me from the street and from prying eyes attempting to see what a bum dressed in a ragged suit was doing behind a swell joint like the Pheasant Lounge.

The rear entrance to joints like this were always locked, but I wasn't about to let that stop me. I reached inside my coat pocket and pulled out some lock picks and was all set to start another round of illegal activity when one of the doors suddenly opened.

The dame looked about as surprised as I did, maybe more.

"Say, what are you doing back here?" She sounded like a Victrola set at twice the normal speed, and with a volume that could have shattered crystal from here to California. I mentally stuck my fingers in my ears.

"Hi, sweetheart, I'm from the electrical company. We got a report of overuse of electricity at these premises. I'm here to investigate. I might be able to leave your name out of my report, if you cooperate." I threw a seductive smile in her direction.

The Trigger Method

A few seconds behind her was a tall brunette with a smile like a bag of coal and eyes as sharp as daggers.

"What's going on, honey?" the brunette asked. She had deep hazel eyes that sunk into my lie like a tiger biting into raw meat. I pretended not to feel the pinch.

"Just checking the power, doll," I said.

"I wasn't talking to you," she hissed. She placed her hand gently around the first dame and pulled her away from the door. "Who is this chump, and what does he want?"

"He says he's from the electrical company. We've been using too much electricity or something. He'll keep us out of his report if we cooperate. I think we should do as he says, don't you?" She tossed a look between the brunette and me as she spoke; her hair bobbed, weaved and bounced along with the rest of her. I bit my tongue just to keep focused. The brunette eyed me with a contempt reserved only for murderers, thieves and other lowlifes. I could've become angry, but something about her made me pull up just short. I picked up my tools and shoved them back into my overcoat pocket. I followed my gaze up then back down until it rested firmly on the five miles of leg that connected her to the ground.

"My face is up here," she hissed.

"Nice lights," I smiled.

"Excuse me?"

"I mean the lights above you. They make you look like an angel. And right now, I'm in desperate need of some divine inspiration."

"You look like you're in need of more than that," she said as she turned to the blonde. "Honey, why don't you go into the dressing room and get ready for the next number. I'll take care of this so-called power guy."

The first dame eyed me with suspicion, her eyes narrowing into fine slits. I couldn't tell what she was thinking, but quite honestly, I don't think she could either. After a few more seconds, she looked back at the brunette: "You mean he's not from the electrical company?"

"Honey, if he's from the electrical company then I'm the Queen of Siam."

'Honey' turned and studied me quizzically. Another queer look passed across her face after which she turned to the brunette and said, "You never can tell about people nowadays." She turned around and slinked back into the building. I was left with the chore of sweet-talking the warden.

"So, what's your name and number, doll?"

"Drop dead."

"Is that your first or your last name?"

A thin smile played at the corner of her lips before quickly retreating to the rear. Shadows hung over everything in the alley, eventually clinging to the brunette like cigarette smoke. Her dark, penetrating eyes were like the eagles of a hawk, her face as hard as stone, but a gentle innocence hovered here and there like butterflies just after the first spring rain. She was more than she was letting on, and I was less than I was trying to be, leaving us both in a position of weakness.

"You think you're real cute, but I know all about mugs like you. A few choice words from me will bring a world of hurt down on you so you better scram if you know what's good for you."

"You're tough, doll. I'll give you that. But you're not that smart. Any dame working in a joint like this for a no-good like Big Pete should have her head examined."

Her look changed. The name 'Big Pete' shook her out of the perfectly balanced world she had been living in. Most people knew who Big Pete was, but very few knew that the Lounge was his place. That I knew about him brought a new fear into the equation, shrinking her ego to the size of a spent bullet casing.

"I don't know who you are, but you better leave," she said nervously.

"I'm not going anywhere, sister. Not until I find out who killed Joseph Baker." I stood and watched her shift from one gorgeous foot to the other. She was nervous and anyone with a decent pair of peepers could see it. She wrapped her arms around her delicate and right-in-so-many-ways torso. I saw the weakness and exploited it. My words grew taller, acquiring an edge that could've ground the hardest rock to powder. I threw an icy stare in her direction. "The name means something to you doesn't it? What's going on? Does Big Pete have something to do with Baker's murder?" It was a lot to throw at someone I'd only just met and hadn't really hit on yet, but then I was never big on pleasantries.

She cast a glance back through the doorway before turning to me one last time. "Just go, before it's too late. You're asking for nothing but trouble."

She turned to leave, but I threw in a few loose words as a chaser. "My name's Gabrielle Dixon. I'm a private dick trying to find out who killed Joseph Baker. Tell me what it is you're so afraid of. Maybe I can help you."

"I…I… can't. Not here, not now." She left, closing the door behind her. I stood in the alley, alone, the cold biting into me like a bad memory.

CHAPTER 4

She didn't sing like a canary, but then she didn't have to. She was scared of something or someone, and whatever that something or someone was, was connected in some way to the murder of Joseph Baker. I could feel it. I didn't need to go inside to notice the evil that stunk up the city worse than rotting fish at low tide resided knee deep in Big Pete's fancy digs. I couldn't pretend I was above it all, because I wasn't. But, I also wasn't about to just stand around and breathe in the rising swell of corruption threatening to pull the city apart. Big Pete was a large part of that corruption; however, most officials just looked the other way. The chief reason for their ignorance was the way he greased the right wheels, keeping many politicians and judges in the black and hip high in broads that would make most of us normal schmucks eat our hats. It was enough to make me want to laugh myself to death.

After exiting the alley, I got my car out of hock and drove back to my office, the lights decreasing in size and intensity with each passed street and avenue. I made it back with a couple Scotch to spare. The elevator wasn't working so I trudged slowly up the feebly-lighted stairwell until I reached my floor. I opened the door and walked out into a dark and quiet hallway. Only a light or two from offices down the hall kept me company.

Two minutes later I was in front of my desk. I sat down and pulled open the upper drawer. A half-empty bottle rolled to the edge and stopped, a shallow clinking sound reverberating through my dusty office. I retrieved an almost-clean glass and poured myself a drink, downed it swiftly before pouring another. It went down like a desert.

I put the glass on the desk and shut my eyes. Just then the phone rang. The first ring sounded dull and distant, as if someone had managed to stifle the noise by shoving it inside a large pillow. I didn't answer it. It rang again. Although it didn't feel as far away this time, I still didn't answer, rolling my head back until it rested on the edge of the chair back.

I picked it up on the third ring: "Dixon Detective Agency, Gabrielle Dixon speaking."

"Hello, Shamus. How's your night going?"

It took me a second to place the voice, but only a second. A week ago, it was just a voice. No different from any other. It meant nothing, except maybe the chance to make some quick, easy dough. This time, the voice was a link to a murder.

"The Scotch is a little warm, but at least it isn't empty."

"Yeah, I suppose it does taste better full, doesn't it?" The voice replied.

"Yeah, now what can I do for you, or, should I ask what can you do for me?"

"You went to the Pheasant Lounge, didn't you?"

"If you know, why ask?" Unease hung between each word like an ice cube between rivers of gin. Only a few trickles of the truth seemed to be getting through.

"You've got to meet a man where he lives if you want to knock him out. I've been studying you for a long time. You're a man of action, a take-no-prisoners kind of guy. A guy like you doesn't sit on the sidelines and watch the game pass him by, he stands on the field and gets his mitts dirty."

"Listen, bud, I don't know what kind of game you're playing, but if I ever get my hands on you, you'll be singing lullaby's at ten fathoms."

"You're angry. I can appreciate that. I know what it's like. Shake off that mushroom feeling you got, because you'll be appreciated when it's over."

"Is that the dope you gave the kid?"

The voice on the other end went quiet. The only sound I could hear was the sound of passing cars on the street below.

A few more seconds passed and still nothing. There was no dial tone so I knew he was still there.

"What's wrong? Cat got your tongue?"

"I did what I could for the kid, but it wasn't enough. I know that now, but I didn't know that then. He was a good kid who got a bum steer. He deserved better."

"So why tell me? What do I have to do with all of this?" I asked.

"Nothing and everything," the voice replied. There was a sudden peculiarity in his voice that told me something wasn't right. I felt like I was standing in the middle of a firing range waiting for the inevitable bullet to turn my head into an exploding volcano.

"You're speaking in riddles, bud. I'm getting started on a pretty good hangover, but you're chatter is ruining any chance it might have of getting off the ground so get to it or I might just hang up and forget the whole stupid mess."

"You're in a real jam, shamus. Big Pete knows all about you. He knows you were at his place tonight. He doesn't know you talked to the dame, but he knows you were there."

The dame didn't seem like the type to sing to the first guy that shook her tree. If she did, I could've got much more out of her than just a few falling leaves. I could suddenly feel part of the case going toward Henry Street while another part headed toward the Pheasant Lounge. I was fighting a war on two fronts with nothing more than insinuations for ammunition. I mused over an appropriate rebuttal. If this guy was calling me again, it meant he was either on my side or he was trying to set me up. I had to be careful, but I also needed to know who this guy was and what angle he was playing.

"Alright, I'll give you the Big Pete thing, but how do you know that he saw me? For all I know, you could be blowing smoke just to cover your own tracks."

"You don't think I'm on the level, do you?"

"Nothing about you is on the level, bud."

"How about I give you a little something to bite down on? For starters, the dame you talked to goes by the name Holly Chalmers. She's nice as far as dames go, but the important thing is she knows something, and it's up to you to find out what. Don't worry about the blonde. She couldn't tell you the time of day. But the Chalmers dame, you find her and you're that much closer to the truth behind the kid's murder. Good luck, shamus, and watch your step. The first one is always murder."

He was funny, in a cleaver-to-the-head kind of way. He also didn't give me a chance to get in the last word. It was probably a good thing because the next words out of my mouth would more than likely have been 'thank you'.

I replayed the conversation in my mind, twisting and turning the words like a kid with a new toy. Outside, a low rumble passed innocently by my window. Inside, I was a ball of confusion. I couldn't be sure who this mug was, or why he was calling me. He could've easily been the murderer, stringing me along until he got bored and decided to give me the airs, permanently. He knew I'd gone to the Lounge and talked to the dame. I suddenly felt a dark, heavy shadow clinging to me, and eyes as sharp as knives watching my every move. I had overplayed this mug's interest and felt back on my heels. A slow, dull throb burrowed deep into my head. A quick shot of something might cure it, but being sober right now felt like a better idea. If I was being watched, I would need all my marbles in order to survive. The empty glass on my desk stared mutely back at me like a juror, waiting for some sort of truth to spew forth. I wasn't sure if I had the time.

I sat there for a few minutes before the darkness and my headache finally got the better of me. I got up from the desk, grabbed my jacket and hat and walked out. The hallways were dark. The lights from the other offices had also gone dark. I was alone.

The first thing I noticed was the smell. It was as if someone had butchered a steer in the hallway. I dismissed it to exhaustion and continued to the elevator only to remember it wasn't running. I grunted my disapproval and headed for the door leading to the stairs. The scent was stronger here than anywhere else. I cocked my head and listened intently. The hallway was unusually quiet. It wasn't something I would normally notice or care about, but in this case, the quiet was too quiet. If I was a reasonable man I would have put the whole thing off to nerves, but this was different. Besides, I wasn't close to reasonable, especially tonight.

I pulled out my gat, put my hand to the door and pushed. Nothing happened. I pushed again, this time adding a little more chutzpah to my efforts. Still, the door wouldn't budge. The only reason a door wouldn't open, if it had not been locked, was that something or someone on the other side didn't want it to open.

I pushed one more time with my gat in my right hand and my shoulder wedged into the middle of the door. I pushed hard enough to move heaven and earth, but the door held, budging only a measly inch or two, the resulting sound reminding me of a mutt with a mean case of hunger. I figured most of Jersey must have been on the other side pushing back. I gritted my teeth so hard my gums ached. The grip around my gat tightened until my hands felt like a moist towel. After a few more tense seconds the door gave, slowly at first, but slid back to allow faint, yellow light to filter through the resulting crack. I stopped pushing for a few seconds when a smell, like sour cheese, also filtered through. I looked back, but there was just the sound of silence echoing through the halls. I was alone and vulnerable. If someone wanted to pop out from behind a door or hallway corner and give me one in my gut for stupidity he wouldn't have to sweat it for too long. I thought about all the other times I knocked at death's door only to get a painful, yet welcoming, reprieve at the last moment. I knew one of these days that reprieve would come a little too late, but I hoped today wasn't going to be that day, because dying here, in this lousy excuse for a building, would be the kind of joke that coppers tell at funerals to pass the time until the good brandy comes around. I didn't intend on being that kind of joke.

I pushed harder, each successive thrust nudging the door open a little more until I was finally able to position my body between the door and the frame. I pushed one last time with my left hand on the frame and my elbow and right knee wedged against the door. A few seconds later, I was able to inch my left foot inside the slowly widening gap. The smell emanating from beyond assaulted me like car exhaust fumes in a garage. I cringed slightly, but continued.

A small light hung from the ceiling just above the termite-infested railing that lined the edge of the stairs. I looked past the railing and down then threw a fleeting glance upwards, toward the ascending stairs. Both ways seemed devoid of life. I pulled away momentarily from the door and peered back into the hallway, my body half inside and half outside the stairwell. The hallway remained empty.

I had walked up these stairs only twenty minutes ago. There are a lot of dead things in this building, ideas only being one of them; however, unless I sleepwalked during my initial expedition, I was fairly certain I hadn't leapfrogged over any stiffs.

I refocused on the stairwell, this time slipping through the space I had created. I looked down at the corpse. There was enough light for me to see that the stiff was big, pushing three bills if not a buck or two more. He was dressed in a black pin-stripe suit that had seen better days, and a black fedora that had probably also seen better days. He faced away from me, his rear end hugging the door.

I carefully maneuvered my way around until I could see his face. His eyes were closed, but his mouth hung open, as if waiting for a meal that would never come. His face resembled a big meaty lump stacked on top of a lot of other big lumps. He had probably been dead a couple of hours from the look and smell of him. His hands and legs were bound with the same type of rope Joseph Baker had been trussed up with. Rope wasn't hard to get in this city, and it was hardly the type of thing that could connect a dead kid with a dead and stinking fat corpse. If the midnight caller was to be believed, this guy was meant to be here. It might be a warning, or it might be a clue meant to lead me to the truth. If it was the latter, someone was playing the kind of joke they only allowed in insane asylums. The whole thing suddenly resembled a jigsaw puzzle thrown into the air.

I looked at my gat to make sure it was still there. It felt good in my hand, like a glove that fit just right. It had firmness to it; a weight balanced almost perfectly like weights on a scale. Without it I felt wrong. I felt like I was sinking on one side and floating to the stars on the other. It was like being pulled in two different directions at the same time, leaving only a shadow to mark my passing.

I'd been tailed a thousand times. Mugs that had no business doing tail jobs followed me as stealthily as a dog on a bone. Some mugs were so bad at it, I had to stop more than once, look back, and force them to run for cover just to teach them how to do it right. This time things were different. This new stiff was nobody to me. He might have a rep, but then he might also be some schmuck in a fancy suit and on the wrong end of a good time.

I leaned down and carefully searched the guy's pockets. I found a small card in the first pocket I searched, bent slightly, but with the name 'Benson Properties' written in bold, red script across the top. The office indicated on the front put the place in the Chrysler Building. I looked for a name but found none. I looked at the guy again. He didn't look like the property management type. I finished my search and found nothing else.

I slid my gat back into my holster and walked slowly into my office. The darkness hovered over me like bats in a cave. It siphoned your strength until you were nothing more than an empty pair of pants billowing in the breeze.

I went to my desk, picked up the phone and dialed the precinct. I was about to deliver another stiff to Pete's already exploding coffers.

CHAPTER 5

It was funny how being right sometimes felt like going to the dentist. I spoke gently, informing Pete of the dead body and how I had nothing to do with it. I told him about the card, the name, everything. I even complimented him on the stirring, energetic way he answered my call. It didn't help. I wasn't sure if he was mad because I found a stiff, or because I found a stiff so close to his quitting time. Either way, the fact the dead mug was found in my place of business wasn't going to be good for business.

I wiled away the time counting drawer pulls and rearranging the shadows on the wall. I also thought about the dead kid and why the dame at the Pheasant Lounge was so scared. Being afraid of Big Pete was one thing, but to be afraid of some kid who probably worked as a dishwasher or doorman was something entirely different. Kids like Joseph Baker were a dime a dozen in New York. They bred like rabbits and died just as quickly, especially when they mingled with the Big Pete's of the world. They were always looking for a quick buck. Earning a dime the honest way was a sucker's road, whereas smuggling, dealing or killing was the smart man's way to big dough. What they didn't see was the ending, and it was always the same. I'd seen plenty of stiffs in my time, and every one of them looked sorry to die, like they'd done something wrong. But seeing kids take the dirt knap was always tough because they never had any kind of sorry on their face, almost as if they were too young to realize that the scratch they died for wouldn't get them enough to buy a decent doughnut at any second-rate candy store.

I picked up a pencil from my desk and threw it across the room. It landed softly against the floor and rolled toward the shadows. A black anger rose in my gut and stayed there, boiling like water on a stove. Every stiff I saw gnawed at my soul a little more. Sometimes, I just stared, hoping my eyes were seeing things that weren't really there. Maybe there wasn't really a dead kid lying at my feet. Maybe it was just a shadow. Maybe I was just dreaming.

I stayed in my office on purpose. I didn't need to go out and see the guy lying there, deader than fish in a market. I also didn't need to worry about the body being disturbed since most people in this building would just step over the guy anyway. People don't want to see want they don't want to see.

My mind rested next on the card and its meaning. Most property management companies did nothing more than act as landlords for their tenants. They collected fees and supposedly maintained both the physical as well as the financial look of the property. From the look of the guy's suit and the size of his waistline, property management consultants were getting paid fairly well and living higher on the hog than most ordinary mugs. I couldn't reconcile the two images that stared back at me. I placed the bent card on my desk and just stared at it.

The building remained silent. Outside my office, the darkness crawled like a slow-moving fog. It was as an inescapable fury; the rising swell as subtle as a hurricane. I looked over at the clock on the wall like I had a hundred times before. It counted the seconds the same way it had since I first got it, but tonight it didn't seem to go fast enough.

I wanted Pete to get here and take everything off my hands. My past had always been a jumble of images that made sense only when you added everything together. When I tried to focus on one image, it suddenly blurred like a mirage. Everything was too much. The idea of knowing that the world was screwy was too much. I looked away from the window and closed my eyes, squeezing them tighter until they hurt.

At that precise moment I heard footsteps and voices. They were muffled, but there were more than one, probably closer to four. I stood up and trudged slowly to the door and opened it. A beam of bright light suddenly cut across my face.

"Cut it out. It's already too bright in here," I protested.

"Dix," Pete started, "What is it with you? Do you collect stiffs as a hobby or are you practicing for medical school?"

"Dr. Gabrielle Dixon," I started. "Has a nice ring to it, doesn't it?" Pete stood in the middle of the hallway shaking his head like an elephant trying to throw off a mosquito. Bits of light perched high in the ceiling threw stray slivers of incandescence across his face, the raw stubble coupled with fatigue reminding me of a rumpled, overused blanket.

"You have the card or did you use that to write your jokes on?"

I laughed then handed him the card. Pete stared it for a moment then said, "I've never heard of Benson Properties before. You have any ideas who they are?"

"No. It's just a hunch, but I don't think the guy out there knows too much about it either."

"Do you have any idea who good old Mr. Joe Smith might be?" Pete asked.

"I'm not the one with all the marbles, you are. You tell me who this guy is?"

"You mean to tell me in your travels tonight you didn't come across this mug, at any time?" Pete eyed me curiously, almost accusingly, as if sharing a joke that had no punch line.

"You know I don't get around much, so clue me in. Who's the stiff?" I asked.

"Does the name Durbin 'Fats' Kelly mean anything to you?"

I thought about the name. I spelled it out in my mind, each letter connecting together in a murderous alphabet soup that spelled nothing. I felt like I should've known the mug, but no matter how hard I tried I kept coming up empty.

"Search me. Who is he?"

"He happens to be a button man for Big Pete. Mostly he works out of Pete's south side joints. Sometimes he goes by the name 'the Collector'."

As soon as I heard the name 'the Collector' I understood right away. He was one of Big Pete's top guys. Not only did he make all the collections, but he also collected, besides dough, skulls. He was big, mean and dangerous, and I would definitely stress the 'was' since his vertical wasn't so vertical anymore.

"You got trouble, Dix... big trouble. A few hours after you show up at Big Pete's nightclub, one of his best shows up deader than a mackerel at your doorstep."

"If you think I had something to do with this, you're crazy. I wouldn't hurt a butterfly, unless it hurt me first."

"It's not legal trouble I'm talking about. I know you didn't do it. What you got is Big Pete trouble, and that's the kind of trouble that can leave a permanent mark on you. When he finds out that one of his best boys was found belly-up on your doorstep, that smile of yours is going to need some serious medical attention."

Pete painted a picture that I had seen a hundred times. I still didn't care.

"Alright, so one of his boys winds up dead on my porch. Anybody with brains can see I didn't bump him off."

"One way or another he's going to know you paid him a visit, and when he does, those stupid jokes of yours will fall flatter than a pancake."

"Let me worry about that," I said, slowly walking past Pete and into the stairwell. I looked down at Kelly. He was a big guy, but at that moment he didn't look all that big. I heard Pete walk up behind me. I didn't look at him. I kept staring at Kelly until everything around me disappeared.

"Alright, tough-guy, any ideas on how this guy bought it?" Pete asked.

"I'm not sure, but then I didn't really look. I figured I'd wait until you got here before I started stomping all over the clues."

"Thanks." Pete stepped past me and crouched to examine Kelly. "The body is still warm. He couldn't have died more than a couple hours ago."

"It might be a long shot, but it could be Kelly took out the kid then got taken out just for being there. The first rule of business is to always eliminate witnesses to a murder, even if they happen to be good trigger-men."

"It's a good guess, but somehow I can't see Big Pete doing something like that. It would bring down too much heat. He can probably get away with one dead body. But two dead bodies would raise too many questions. And he probably wouldn't send him gift-wrapped to you, either. He'd send him to the fishes."

I leaned down next to Pete. Kelly's suit was nicer than anything I'd ever seen. On his ring finger sat a rock the size of the Five Boroughs, a quiet glint slithering off it like a shy dollar bill. The fact he was still wearing it meant death-by-robbery or mugging would have to be excluded from the list of possible motives. That didn't leave much for a guy of my sensibilities to warm up to.

"It would've taken someone pretty big to take down a guy this size. He was no slouch," I replied.

"We won't know for sure what took this palooka down until the coroner takes a good look at him." Pete took out his flashlight and played it over the corpse. The goon looked okay, even in death. A few seconds into Pete's casual investigation I saw something that caught my attention.

"Pete, put some light on the tie."

Pete's light exposed Kelly's necktie, a black job that probably cost more than all the suits in my wardrobe. It wasn't so much the tie that caught my eye as the way it was tied around his neck; haphazardly, as if performed in a rush. A clumsy knot that resembled a deformed prune hung slightly off to the right with one lapel stuck inside and one outside. It looked like a poor man's lasso.

"Pretty shoddy job, if you ask me," Pete replied.

"Do we have to wait for the coroner and the fingerprint boys?"

"Prints, Dix."

I didn't mind rules per se, but when I saw a clue I grabbed at it like a kid grabbing the last slice of chocolate cake. I retrieved a pen from my coat pocket and gently nudged it between the collar and the stiff's neck. Pete shone his light against the area where my pen was, revealing an abrasion that looked like a dirty pearl necklace. It was a thin grey mark that navigated between the folds in his neck. Along the inside of the tie could be seen thin silvery slivers of what were probably remnants of the rope used.

"Hmmm, looks like he was strangled; some type of rough cord from the look of it," Pete said.

"Yeah, but how could someone catch a guy like this off guard, strangle him and then drag him up four flights of stairs without anyone seeing a thing?"

"Is the back of this crate still blocked off?" Pete asked.

"Yeah, it hasn't had any traffic since the landlord decided to use it as a garbage dump. There's no way anyone could have come that way. And with the elevator out of service, that only leaves the stairs." It was the answer Pete was looking for, but I was saying it more to myself, trying to come up with solutions to a riddle that seemed to have none.

"Maybe there was more than one of them. This guy was no slouch. He didn't get his reputation through the mail. He earned it. Whoever took this guy out is dangerous, Dix. You sure you still want in on this case?" Pete eyed me warily, as if afraid of the answer I would give. I wasn't sure which way his concern was blowing, but at least I could feel a little of the breeze.

"Don't really have a choice now. It's no small coincidence this guy gets bumped off probably around the same time I'm saying trying to say hidey-ho to Big Pete."

"You still think this is all connected to the kid somehow?"

"It could be. Then again, it could be just another gangland dusting. For now I'd like to think there's a reason I get a phone call about the dead kid just minutes before I find this guy."

"The same guy called you again?"

"He must have been getting lonely."

I retrieved my pen from the stiff's collar and wiped it gently on the trouser of my slacks before putting it back in my pocket. Pete left his light on the collar for a few more seconds before shining it briefly on the face. I had seen enough of the guy to last me a few lifetimes so got to my feet and looked down the stairs. The stairwell was about as clean as a henhouse at feeding time on the best of days, so any hopes of finding a decent clue would be fruitless, but I looked anyway.

"What did he say?" Pete asked.

"Told me the name of some dame that works at the Pheasant Lounge," I replied.

"What dame?" Pete asked.

"While I was trying to break in through the back door some ditzy broad with a whistle for a voice walks out. A few seconds later another dame walks up behind her. As soon as I mention the name Joseph Baker, the second dame does a vanishing act that would've made Houdini blush. She knows something, but fear of Big Pete is keeping her from talking."

"I hope this isn't like before."

Pete eyed me curiously. In the darkness of the stairwell I could see his thoughts as clearly as I could see a dirty joke in a whorehouse. The past was in the past; or at least I kept saying that to myself. In truth, I wasn't so sure. A lot had happened since then, but a dame was a dame no matter how you sliced it.

"It's not like that, Pete. Not anymore."

"You got in too deep, Dix. I can see it again, only this time it's worse. This time you're looking toward the hole, but there's nobody around to push you in. You're diving in yourself."

It was like being splashed in the face with cold water. It wasn't so much the skirt, but the situation that came of it. This time, all I had was a name. It didn't mean anymore to me than a ham sandwich, but then I'd seen mugs stress over less.

I turned to Pete, "Find out what you can about the dame. Her name's Holly Chalmers. She dances at the Pheasant Lounge. If we're lucky, she's got a history. Maybe we can use it against her."

Pete took out his notebook and wrote down the name. I'd seen that book once before and it always brought back bad memories. I looked away.

"I'll do it nice and quiet. I'll also do some checking on this Benson Properties. Maybe there's something in it, maybe there isn't. Either way I'll let you know what I find out. You might want to do the same. Remember, Big Pete has eyes everywhere. He finds out one of his employees is being investigated by the cops or a lazy private dick with too much scotch on his breath, you'll both be gone faster than either of us can down a few Tom and Jerrys."

"Don't worry about me," I said. "Just find out what that card means." I turned away from Pete and the mess I had left him with and walked slowly down the stairs. I could've looked more carefully as I followed each step down, but any clue I might find here would mean nothing. One dead mug was one dead mug. Until I found the bim, I was batting zero.

CHAPTER 6

It was morning and I was at Henry Street again. The lower East side was packed as always. Immigrants of all shapes and sizes walked, sat, and talked along many of the streets that made up this section of town. On these ramshackle streets with their densely packed tenements and filthy alleyways lived people hoping for something better. Somewhere in the middle of it all laughed Liberty, her torch held high, but slightly dimmed by the reality of a broken promise. I suddenly thought about the dead kid.

I parked my car and walked the last few blocks to the apartment building that, only a week ago, had housed a corpse. I walked to the same doorway. A few desperate steps clung to the front on which sat a couple of kids, no older than eight or nine. They reminded me of me at that age: bored and looking for some fun to pass the time.

"Whatcha' want mister?" The kid was small, on the wrong side of sixty pounds, and sported a dirt-marked face that would have made a mud pit proud. He was dressed in rags that had too many thankless years pressed down upon them, and something that resembled shoes; although, only in name. He eyed me suspiciously. I didn't blame him.

"You boys know Shanny Warchinski?"

The kid sitting next to the first looked too serious, as if a smile might shatter his already-withered features. He had the kind of dark eyes that you saw only in the eyes of ravens; they seemed able to slice through the truth. "We ain't talking to no coppers. We ain't rats, see?" He spewed out the words in two's and three's like a horse with too much feed in his mouth.

"Well, it's your lucky day, kid, because I'm no cop. I'm a private detective."

The first kid's glare washed over me like the noon tide, sizing me up, trying to determine whether I was on the level or not. "Is This about Joe?" He asked timidly.

"You knew the kid?"

"Maybe we did, and maybe we didn't. What's it worth to ya'?" The second kid would make a good shakedown man some day.

"You got the time, I got the dimes."

"Dimes, that's it? We ain't talking for dimes."

"All right, it's your funeral. You can either make a few dimes, or I can walk away and you'll get nothing." I made as if I was about to turn around and walk away. I didn't need to go far and all three of us knew it.

"All right, all right; let's see the dough first."

I fished some change out of my pocket and held it in front of the two kids like it was a gold brick. "You tell me what you know and then you get the dough; otherwise, I walk."

"How do we know you're being straight with us?"

"I'm a man of my word. You'll have to believe me on that one."

They huddled together for a minute before turning back to me, their eyes shining like jewels against the sun.

"Okay, whaddya' wanna know?" The second kid asked, abruptly.

"Everything you know about the kid, his mom, his friends; everything." I tried sounding official, if only to emphasize the necessity for truth and accuracy.

The first kid started, "He was always comin' and goin' like he was late for somethin'. His old lady was always on his back about it. I live one floor below her, and I could hear her yellin' and screamin' at him, kind of like my old man. She's old, but she's plenty tough. He kind of yelled back some, but mostly it was just her voice I kept hearin'. If it wasn't one thing, it was another. You kind of get used to hearin' stuff like that around here. Somebody's always yellin' at somebody, you know what I mean?"

"Yeah, kid. I think I do. Did you ever see him hanging out with anybody?"

"He hung with some fancy shmancy lookin' suits, but none of 'em looked too interested in anything but these crummy buildings. Him and Alby was good buddies, though. They was always together. I think they was trying to be big shots or something."

"Who is this Alby? What's his name?"

"You gonna' give us the dough, or what?"

I thrust forward two dimes. The second kid shoved his dime into his mouth like it was a cookie, bit down to make sure it was real before hiding it in his left shoe.

"Albert. He used to live in the room just down the hall from Joe's old lady, but moved out a month ago. He doesn't come around no more."

"Does he have a last name?"

"Yeah, but I don't know it."

"What about you? You know this Albert's last name?"

"Nope," the kid said quietly.

"What about dames? You ever see them with any dames?"

The first kid thought hard enough about the answer to lend his face the look of a discarded candy bar wrapper. The second kid did the same. I stood there, staring, trying hard not to laugh. I limited myself to a slow, teasing grin.

"There was this one. I only remember because his ma made a big fuss over her once. That was the time I heard her yellin' and stuff. He didn't like it because next thing I heard was the door slammin' and him runnin' out the door." I reached into my pocket and pulled out two bits. I thrust it forward temptingly. "This is yours too, but only if you can tell me her name and what she looked like."

The two kids looked at each other like they had just discovered a secret treasure of popcorn and soda. It was a stretch to think the dame was the same dame from the Pheasant Lounge, but then I'd been lucky before.

The second kid replied, "Yeah, she was swell lookin'; a real dish. I don't know what her name was, but she did come here a couple times with Alby and Joe."

The first kid looked off into the distance. "She kinda looked like that dame from all them movies. You know the one. She's in them posters they got hanging at the revue; you know, dancing with that funny, skinny-looking guy."

I hadn't gone to a show in a long time, and my smarts when it came to movie actresses was a little lacking, but I tried replaying a list of leading ladies in my mind. All of a sudden, it came to me.

"The skinny guy; do you mean Fred Astaire?" They stared at me like I was an alien from Mars. "Is he the guy with the slick-backed hair and smooth tuxedo?"

"That kinda sounds like the guy, yeah." The second kid looked past me and toward another kid, maybe twelve, standing near a fire hydrant. He was just standing there, leaning, as if waiting for the next bus to Manhattan. A rumpled cap was perched high on his head with the bill leaning slightly to the right and down, a slow-burning cigarette dangled lazily from one corner of his mouth. "Hey, stuffy, what's the name of that skinny guy what dances in all them movies with that dame."

"You mean Fred Astaire, you nitwit."

"I ain't no nitwit! I was just askin'."

I ignored the witty banter and turned to the first kid. "So, you're telling me this dame looked something like Ginger Rogers?"

"I don't know her name, but she was blonde alright. What about them two-bits you promised?"

"I got just one more question. Is the old lady in?"

"Yeah, she's here. Mostly she just goes out at night like always, but now she's a real night-owl. I think she's some sort of vampire, or something. Ever since Joe bit it, she just sits at home real quiet like; now c'mon with the two bits already. We told you what we know."

I took the quarter and handed it to the second kid. The first kid looked like someone had just stepped on his only candy bar. I took one of the last quarters I had and handed it to him. He smiled.

"Thanks, guys." I stepped by them and strolled casually into the dark foyer. I climbed up the same rickety stairs where the same groans and creaks echoed through the paper-thin walls. All the way up, I continued thinking about the blonde the kids had described to me, and about Albert. Two more names with two more stories. Evidently, the dame had made a muddy impression on the dead kid's old lady. Who the extra suits were was anyone's guess.

I walked slowly to the end of the hallway and to the same window staring out onto an unimpressive view of nothing. The place looked cleaner now. The blood stains had been cleaned up. I looked around for a few seconds then turned and knocked on the door. The light above me was on, but winked steadily like a drunken millionaire.

I heard faint, careful footsteps shuffling to the door. It opened a few inches. A questioning pair of ancient eyes examined me from behind a fear I had seen more than once. It filled the space between us.

"Shanny Warchinski?" I asked.

"Who you?" The accent was thick, yet retained an old-world elegance.

"My name is Gabrielle Dixon. I'm a private investigator. I'd like to ask you a few questions about your son, Joseph."

"Police already come. Dey ask, but I no talk. I no talk to you eider."

"I understand, Miss Warchinski, but I'm not the police. I want to find out who murdered your son, and the only way I can do that is if you help me."

A sudden, pressing silence descended over us. I turned and peered down the now too-quiet hallway. It looked and felt like a cemetery. I felt a shiver crawl up my spine.

"No. No one help me or my son. You are too late, Mr. Detective." She closed the door abruptly, but I could tell she was still there, listening intently. A closed door didn't necessarily mean a closed mind. I kept talking.

"I was here the night your son was killed. I saw his body. I want to find out who killed him." An almost overpowering solitude emanated from the other side of the door. She was still there. I could feel it. But was she listening or was she just playing out the string. "I know there's no reason for you to believe me, Ms. Warchinski; but I saw the look in your son's face that night. You're a woman who believes in her faith, strongly. Well, I'm asking you to believe in me."

"Why I believe you? I believe in police. They do noting." Her words traveled easily through a door as thick as paper.

"I'm not the police. I don't always play by the rules the way the cops do. That's probably why I stopped being one. I couldn't stand the red tape. I know you're hurting, but you need to trust someone."

"Trust is hard ting to come by now. I trust my boy once. He gone now. He gone long time."

I thought about my mislaid past. It was about more than just a few lost dollars at the racetrack or a lost dame. It was about losing a part of my past. I'd always believed once the past was gone it was irrevocably gone. Her son, Joseph Baker, was gone, but not really gone. I turned and faced the door, saying the words I thought I'd never say, telling a story I thought would never see the light of day.

"I was only seven when my brother died. The doctor said it was the flu, but I say poverty killed him. It did him in as easily as the bullet that killed your son. I got it pretty soon after, but survived. I don't know why but I did. Allan was a better kid than I ever was, and would probably have been a better man, if he'd gotten the chance to live his life. Maybe somewhere between the two of them, the two of us can find something. But that can only happen if you open the door and let me help you." The only people that knew about Allen's death were Pete and his wife. They never said anything, and they never pushed me on the details. Booze and broads were an easy way to forget what happened. It helped dull the pain for a little while, but the pain always came back, so I tried dulling it some more. But memories never die that easily, especially when a part of you doesn't want them to.

She opened the door again, this time wider. Her aged eyes looked into mine. Time lost all meaning. It was an empty thing that floated everywhere. I looked back, as if seeing something that could pull me from the darkness. The old lady eyed me suspiciously.

"Why you want help me? My son mean noting to you. Everyone treat him like just another number. No one ever care about us. Why you care?"

"Maybe I care because I hate seeing dead stiffs everywhere I go."

She pulled me in gently, like a mother taking care of a child. I let her.

I had ignored my past longer than I cared to remember. It lurked in the darkest corners of my mind, always there, always waiting. It was a hunger I fed with large portions of guilt. Seeing the old lady brought it all back. In many ways, the two of us were connected; although, not by life, but by death. She could see my past as clearly as she could see her own. It bound us together.

I stood in her living room unsure of what to do or say. The moment had crashed in on me and all I could do was stand there and look down. It was the same spot I had seen a week ago, only cleaner. The rough wooden floor with all its rough, haphazard knots and discolored inequality spread out before me like a roadmap.

I looked to my left and saw the Star of David respectfully placed against a smart portion of the wall. The polished surface starkly contrasted the darkness that dominated the rest of the apartment. For a moment, I thought I could see my reflection, a vague apparition against a barren background of brown and black. I didn't like what stared back. I looked away.

"I'm sorry to bother you, but I need some information about your son's death."

"You mean murder. Dey kill my boy outside in dirty place like dey kill pig. Dey take gun and kill my boy, my Joseph. But dey do more bad tings den just shoot him many time. Dey murder good boy inside. No, Mr. Dixon, you mean murder." She stood erect, her hands folded neatly in front of her like a statue in a church. Only, unlike the statue, the old lady looked directly at me, her eyes ablaze with a raw anger only a mother could harbor.

"Yeah, I suppose I do. It's a tough word to say, especially around old ladies."

"I am old, Mr. Dixon. I see many tings in life. Tings dat not make for good bedtime reading, but I also strong when need to be. If not strong, not last in dis country. If not strong, no get away from anger dat chase me like shadow. Yes, Mr. Dixon, I am old, but not dat old. Not yet."

I admired the old lady's spirit. She talked tough. She had to if she wanted to survive in this neighborhood, but it was more than that. She had rolled the dice on a life that came out all wrong. I had rolled the same dice, but rolled it with one hand hugging a bottle of scotch. The Scotch kept me floating above the tide, especially where dames were concerned. All the skirts that traveled through my life were nothing more than a night at the circus before a rainy Monday.

She stared at the darkness as if reacquainting herself with an old friend. This seemed to be familiar territory for both of us.

"I'm sorry. I didn't mean to offend you. It's just that in my business things get complicated when dames start the waterworks."

"I understand, Mr. Dixon. But, I have question for you?"

"What's on your mind?"

She took a few seconds to size me up, attempting to find the answer to her question before she asked it. "Why you really want case? Why you want help old woman like me? Is about past or more dan dat?"

It was a tough question to answer. I sifted through the reasons in my mind. After a few seconds I found one that fit: the truth.

"I told you a few minutes ago about my brother. It's that, but it's more than that. Life threw me a curve about a year ago. It was a tough case. Not so much because of the facts, but because of the dames involved. I walked away from it with the truth staring me in the face. It didn't go down so well, even after a few drinks. It just kept coming back."

"And what is truth?"

"The truth is I need closure in my life. I have a past full of moments I've left open, like a wound. I wondered why I wasn't the one lying there, on the floor, instead of your son. I wondered why it hadn't been me so many times before. It should have been me on any given night. I managed to make it through everything, wondering the whole time why I didn't get my ticket punched. Your son could have had something different, something better than me. He missed out on that because of a choice he made, or didn't make. I've made a lot of choices; some good, some bad. Finding your son's murderer is about my future. What I do here and now might help me deal with something that has dogged me my whole life."

The room fell silent. I turned away and wandered toward the small window that looked out onto the street, the bridge barely visible on the left. I could feel the old lady stare, wondering if I was telling the truth or not. She had faith on her side. I had lack of faith on mine.

"You like my Joseph, only taller."

I looked back to see a tiny smile play across her face. I smiled back.

"It's the shoes," I replied.

"What you need to know, Mr. Dixon?" She went to a chair in the corner and sat down slowly. With old, withered hands she tightened the black shawl that hung over her head. Her hands were the hands of a working woman. They had seen and done much. A smooth circular whiteness decorated the area around her ring finger, as if something bright and beautiful had once rested there. I looked away in embarrassment. On the floor, I could see tiny sprinkles of dirt litter the area around her feet. Another small trail led away from her chair and toward the kitchen. Obviously, Pete and his schoolyard playmates needed a more thorough lesson in house cleaning. I suddenly felt very bad for the old lady.

I waited until she was settled before I began. "What can you tell me about your son and his job at the Pheasant Lounge?"

She was quiet for a moment. She stared at the floor for a long time. She finally spoke, but the firmness she had shown just moments ago was nowhere to be seen. "Alby get job first, den get job for Joseph. Joseph say it good ting, but I not so sure."

"And why was that?" I asked.

"Joseph become different. He gone all the time, day and night. When I ask, he tell me to no worry. He tell me job have lots different hours and money he make help us live in better place. I tell him I no want better. I tell him I want peace and quiet. My feeling tell me tings not good, but Joseph happy so I say noting." A sudden sadness clouded her features. She grasped her shawl tighter, the fine gray of her hair revealed in slow, brief measures.

"What kind of work did he do there?"

"He say he do lots of everyting; when I ask more, he become angry. He say I no trust him. I say noting after that, but I tink lots. I tink he doing not so good tings. I try not to tink about such things, but tinking no help so I pray every night for my Joseph. I pray he come home safe and never do dis bad tings, but he no listen to words. He become lost to me." She was quiet for a moment. I knew what she was going to say before she said it. "Pray no do good after dat."

"I've never been one for praying," I said. "I only believe in what I can hear, see and shoot."

"Maybe dat the problem, Mr. Dixon," she replied, without hesitation. "Guns solve some problem, but dey no solve all problem. Some tings never go away no matter how many time you shoot dem." She stared at the ground again as if lost in the moment.

Maybe she was right. I never really believed in anything. For me, a church was just something I drove by on the way to the bar, and a priest was the guy that sat next to me when I downed my Scotch. Although, for all of my less-than-respectable qualities, I still saw myself as a fairly upright kind of guy. I didn't kill anybody that didn't deserve it, and I never used filthy language around anyone over the age of twelve. That had to count for something.

"Well, I'm no choirboy, but I believe in right and wrong. I know what happened to your son was wrong, no matter what he was into. I also know that whatever happened, had something to do with the Pheasant Lounge, a big lug named Big Pete Mazurski and a dame."

She straightened up for a second. I thought she was about to read me the riot act. However, the look on her face suggested something entirely different. What I witnessed was a fear that almost overlapped into terror. The first time I'd seen that look, I was face-to-face with a hundred pounds of attitude named Holly Chalmers. Big Pete's name seemed to inspire the same amount of fear then as well. That was understandable considering who he was and what he was involved in, but why a little old lady from the East of New York would fear it suddenly interested me very much.

"Dat name you say. I hear name before," she said, slowly.

"You mean Big Pete Mazursky?"

"Yes. One time, Alby and Joseph have fight. I hear fight and walk into room. I ask what is wrong. Why dis fight? Alby look at me and say no ask him, ask Big Pete."

"How long ago was this?"

"It only a month ago. Dey say name you say now. Alby say to push okay. Joseph say to push little bit. No more. I don't know what dis tings mean, but my Joseph look afraid, very afraid. I worry for him, but he tell me everything okay. Dey both go from room and to work. My Joseph become very mad because of name, so I not forget."

"They said 'push'?" I asked.

"Yes, they say push, but I don't' know more about what it mean. Dey say no more about anyting after dat."

Joseph and his friend could have been pushing anything from booze to doughnuts. On its own, the word could be construed any number of ways. However, combine it with Big Pete, and suddenly you have something that could mean 'death' in any number of languages.

"You say he have someting to do with my Joseph doing dis bad tings. Maybe he to blame for what happened to my boy? Maybe Joseph can still put man in jail." Her eyes grew large and expectant. She was hungry to find the person, any person, responsible for the death of her son and make them pay. She seemed to be rolling along on a full tank of anger and hate. I knew very well where that anger could lead her. I had been there before. I decided to throw a little cold water onto her emotions.

"I don't know that much yet. But, it's a sure bet if he worked at Big Pete's Lounge, he was probably doing something on the side. I don't know what he might have been pushing, but the only way to know for sure is to ask this Alby? What's his last name and where does he live?"

"His last name Schwarz. He go from here month ago. He move to city. I not know where."

"Detective Miller told me you were out collecting things for the depot the night your son was found. Isn't it dangerous to be out by yourself in this part of town?"

"I like dark, Mr. Detective. It good way to not see tings. My boy become bad. I no see dis tings at night. I no see bad part of Joseph. I only see good ting about my boy. Joseph in good place now. He no be bad boy no more. Bullets, I tink, do good at least dis much." She went quiet, leafing through the past like a book. I felt the hopelessness she felt. I felt the powerlessness she felt, and it seemed to attain more strength with each passing moment. I steered the conversation away from Joseph and onto other, less emotional, matters.

"Has anyone tried to contact you since your son's death, besides me or the police?"

"No. No one call or say anyting. Dey too afraid to say anyting because dey tink I bad mother because my boy dead. Dey not realize my boy go bad before he die. I tink now he at peace. Dis place very lonely now. I hear tings, but when I go outside people no look at me. No one say noting. I no go no where no more."

I saw a brief glimmer of fire in the old lady's eyes, as if there was still some truth left in between the lies. I wasn't so sure. The only thing I knew for sure was that Joseph and Albert had been doing something for Big Pete, and it probably wasn't the kind of thing you declared on your taxes. The dame at the club also knew something. I would have to find out what that was, but I also had to find the other dame; the mystery woman, Miss Ginger Rogers. She was out there somewhere, and the only person that might know was his best friend, Albert Schwarz.

"I heard that both your son and this Albert were spending time with some classy dame. She was seen coming into this building on at least one occasion. You have any idea who she might be?"

"I see only one woman come here. She come here only one time. She not like what she see so she go away. She was bad kind of girl to go out so late at night. I no like her when she come here so I go into room and stay dere. She tink everyting dirty. I never ask who girl is, but she not good girl. Maybe because of her my Joseph go bad; maybe because of her he dead."

"Aside from the fact that she was out on a school night what else can you remember about her? I mean, was she short, tall, blonde or brunette?"

"She was blonde. She have lots jewelry and she walk like dey do on fancy street. She rich, but have no class."

The old lady didn't hide her dislike for the dame, whoever she was. I wanted to put it off to spite, but if she was bad news, her connection to Big Pete would be less than tenuous. If she was a moll, I would have to be careful. Broads like that always had a way of singing the wrong tune at the wrong time.

"Hmmm," I muttered, quietly. "And you're sure she only came here one time?"

She took a few seconds to answer. "I see woman only one time."

"Did your son ever carry a gun?" The old lady went flush for a second, as if she'd seen a ghost. She took a few seconds to steady herself before answering. It was one of the few times I'd seen her rattled.

"It strange ting to ask mother: did my boy carry gun? No, Mr. Dixon, I no tink my Joseph have gun," she replied, warily.

"Kids hide things from their parents all the time. A gun would definitely be something he would not want you to see."

"No, Mr. Dixon, no gun." It was clear that was the end of that line of questioning. I dropped it and moved on.

"I have just one last question, Miss Warchinski. Have you ever heard of a company named Benson Properties?"

She paused for a moment then answered, "No, I no hear of this name. Is important?"

"I'm not sure, probably not." I finished scratching in my notepad then stood up to face the old lady. In the few minutes that I had been here the room seemed to shrink. The colors had gone from the darkness of mud to the bright yellow of the rising sun before again returning to the dismal grays and blacks of winter. In the end, everything remained unchanged; the same colors and textures hung everywhere like a ragged clothesline, while inside I could feel my world slowly expanding like an inflated balloon. When it would pop was anyone's guess.

"Thank you, Miss Warchinski. I've got everything I need for now, but here's my number if you think of anything else. In the meantime, try not to worry too much."

The old lady stood up and examined me with eyes brighter than the sun. If I were a betting man, I would have said she was letting the light of hope work its way into her heart. That level of certainty hadn't worked its way into my heart yet. Things were a long way from settled. If you didn't believe me, ask Mr. Fats Kelly.

"I know you will do your best. Find man who hurt my son. Maybe you will find someting for yourself too." I played nervously with the spine of my notebook while she spoke. It felt good to know someone who still had some faith.

"I hope so. My bar tab is starting to get out of control." I turned around and walked out of the open room, through the short foyer and out into the hallway. The light from outside stayed away from this building. I looked up at the light above my head. It was on, just barely. "You should tell your super about this light. The thing barely works."

"Superintendent very lazy. He care about noting but sleeping and eating. I stop asking him to fix. I turn off-on myself now" She reached up with her cane and gave the light one good smack. The light still blinked. She hit the light a second time. The light fluttered gently for a few more seconds before it finally grew brighter, a yellow luminescence sluggishly filtered through the corridor illuminating things that looked better in darkness.

"If I knew it was that simple, I would have done it myself," I said.

"Ting in front of face always hard to see when no take time to look, don't you tink?"

I thought about the answer to that question for a moment. "I'll ask my priest next time I'm at the bar. Be seeing you."

The stairs fell away from me like a thrown deck of cards. The steps I had walked only minutes ago seemed unpredictable now, as if the entire structure were a living being capable of thought and action. I stared at the old lady's door. It stared mutely back, revealing no secrets. Her answers helped fill in some of the gray areas, but in some ways, they created more confusion and uncertainty. I gazed at the light for a few muted moments then walked down the stairs.

CHAPTER 7

I slowly walked out into the bright morning sunshine. Things hadn't changed much while I was inside. The streets were still riddled with the filth of generations. The houses, if you could call them that, clumsily squatted along both sides of the street like beggars looking for a few stray pennies. To my left, the bridge presided over the rest of the play like a silent audience waiting for a punch line that would never come.

The kids I had talked to earlier were gone, replaced by an odd assortment of other street urchins. They glared nervously at me, their eyes indicative of a suspicious fear of authority that invaded the mind of many of the kids of this area.

I walked past them and past all the other frail signs of life until I arrived back at my car. I got in, started it up and drove away. Behind me, the buildings slowly faded like a forgotten memory.

I now had a couple of leads to follow. The Pheasant Lounge didn't open until the evening. That left me with only one choice: Holly Chalmers. If the dame had a history, Pete would be able to find it. If she didn't, I was right back where I started: batting zero.

I also had to locate the dame the kids and the old lady had seen. Finding her would be like finding a needle in a haystack, but then finding dames was never the difficult part. It was keeping them I had a tough time with. The only other lead, if you could call it that, was the card. I couldn't just walk into an office and throw Big Pete's name around without receiving some sort of unceremonious 'thanks, but no thanks' in return. I pulled over to the side of the road. A phone booth stood silently on the corner waiting to be used. A few seconds later I dialed the number to the precinct Pete worked out of. After sharing a few forgetful words with a rookie desk officer, Pete's familiar voice came barking over the other end.

"All right, Dix, what kind of trouble you in now?"

"Who says I'm in trouble; although, the day is early."

"Are you trying to make me mad, Dix? If you are, it isn't going to work. I'm in a good mood today and I have no time for your stupid games."

"Thanks, Pete. It makes me feel good to know that your day is going well. For your information, I just had a little communion with the Baker kid's stepmother. She wasn't going to spill to your stiffs, but she was all chatty with me. I tell you, Pete, dames and I got magic. One day I'll write a book and let you buy a copy."

"What are you going to call it: How to get old biddies in ten easy lessons?"

I laughed. Pete and I always had a little mutual admiration society going, the way two boxers do just before they punch each other's lights out.

"Actually, she told me about some guy named Albert Schwarz. He and the kid were friends. Looks like the two of them worked together at the Lounge, and judging from what his old lady said, were doing some fairly regular overtime."

"You think they were running for Big Pete?"

"Him or someone he knows. I can't believe that two young kids would rate with a guy like Big Pete right off the bat. More than likely they were working for someone he knew."

"Probably auditioning for a bigger spot," Pete replied.

"That would be my guess. I also found out there might have been another dame, besides this Holly Chalmers dish. The old lady remembers a real high-class broad making the rounds with Joe and his buddy, Albert."

"Someone they met at the lounge?" Pete asked.

"She doesn't remember her name or where she was from. But, from her description, the dame was loaded. The only key to finding her at this point is to find Albert. And the only way to find that mug is to make the rounds at the Pheasant Lounge."

"Maybe not," Pete replied.

"Oh?" I said.

"I did some background work on your Holly Chalmers. She's originally from California. She did a six-month stretch in Los Angeles on some public decency charge about two years ago. She's been pretty much playing by the rules ever since. The last known address we have on her is a place on the north side."

I pulled out my notepad and wrote down the address. It wasn't a ritzy area, yet was like a mansion when compared to my dive. As for the dame, the fact she had a record meant little. Sure it was a public decency charge, but that was more a public morals issue than anything else. I was more interested in what she knew than what she did.

"I'll look up this Albert Schwarz. He may have a record. If he doesn't, we're going to have to do this the hard way. That means undercover work, Dix. I know telling you not to go to the Lounge would be like telling Gehrig not to play the next ball game, but maybe if you kept your business low key you'd find out more. You could be the trailer instead of the trailed."

"You probably have a point, but they have to know I'm watching them. If they do, maybe they'll get nervous, make mistakes. The longer we wait, the more time they have to get rid of the evidence. These guys tend to scatter. You know that just as well as I do, Pete. I'm going back to the Lounge tonight. This time I'm going through the front door, shake a few trees and see what falls out."

"Well, hopefully it won't be that lame-brain of yours."

We were both quiet for a few seconds. The situation wasn't as amusing as either of us were making it out to be. Two people were dead. Only superficial evidence connected them together; however, it was no small coincidence that both men worked for the same guy: Big Pete.

"What about Benson Properties? What did you find out on them?"

"Benson Properties is a subsidiary of a larger company called Hale Financial Partners. Hale deals in financing for mortgages and loans for large corporations in Chicago, Boston and here in New York. Nearest I can figure, Benson handles paperwork for Hale and some of their other parent companies. You ever heard the name Dane Bartlett?"

"You mean the Wall Street Bartlett?"

"That's the one," Pete answered.

"Kennedy and he were running booze all over the place during prohibition. Now, he's a well respected man of business. He's so dirty he needs a shovel just to get out of bed in the morning," I replied. "Everyone knows he's linked to organized crime only there too scared to admit it. I heard through a couple of boys on the north side that Big Pete was planning something and could only get it done with Wall Street help. Ten will get you twenty Bartlett is Big Pete's man."

"If that's true it might explain the card in Kelly's pocket. It doesn't explain how he got to your front door or why he was murdered, but it does give us something to work from."

"Has the coroner figured out the time of death for Kelly?"

"He puts it at around nine last night. That's about the same time you were at the Lounge."

"Pretty close. They have any idea where he might have died?"

"Aside from the marks around his neck, the guy was in pretty good shape. We couldn't find any other marks or abrasions. You should look so good, Dix."

"What about the rope?"

"We didn't find anything particularly special about it. At least a dozen different places sell that kind of stuff. You can buy it in almost any size and length you want. We're still going over it, but don't expect too much."

"Well, maybe he knew the people that killed him. A guy like that doesn't go down without a fight. You'd expect some kind of scratches, bruises or marks."

"He wouldn't have a chance to fight if they came at him from behind," Pete replied. "One guy lassos him while one or two others hold him down. It's been done."

"You think more than one person took Kelly out?"

"I can't see it being just one person. Kelly was tough. It would take at least two guys to hold him."

"Any theories on why he was killed? He was an important guy for Big Pete. If he killed him, maybe Kelly was being a naughty boy. If someone else took him out, you may have a gang war on your hands. You remember what those are like, don't you?"

"Dix, I told you I was having a good day. Sure, we're getting a lot of stiffs, but most are just the usual dead mugs. In the thirties, they were having two-for-one sales, but those days are over."

"Are they? I wonder." I paused briefly to consider my next words. "That only leaves one thing: Big Pete. Something is going down. I can feel it. I think the kid was caught in the middle of something that was too big for him. We need to find this Albert character. If anyone knows anything, he does."

"I'll start looking for him right away, but I'll keep it hush-hush. No need to advertise anything, at least not yet."

"You do that. I'm going to pay a visit to Holly Chalmers. If my luck holds up, I'll be sitting pretty with Miss California in a little while."

"Be careful, Dix. There's no way to be sure who she is or what her game is." I repeated the same words over and over in my subconscious like a skipping record. One mistake in any game involving Big Pete would mean the world was short one shamus.

"I hear you, Pete. I'll call you when I find something. In the meantime, try to find this Schwarz guy and the other dame. The only thing I got on her is that she looks like Ginger Rogers."

"This case is looking up more and more every second. If I find her, I might not tell you after all," Pete laughed.

"Give my best to your wife." I hung up the phone and went back to the car. My life seemed to be changing like the passing scenery. Events that I could've ignored previously now tied me to places like a horse tied to a burning barn. I was now headed to another one of those places, with no idea what to expect when I arrived.

I sifted through what Pete told me as I drove to Holly Chalmers' apartment. Pieces of the puzzle had been exposed; however, their place within the larger picture was a mystery. If someone was watching me, more than likely they were afraid I would come across something they couldn't cover up, or throw in the river.

I drove past 98th until I came to the Westview apartment complex. It was nice, as apartments go, its well-manicured façade rising serenely above the street. It was fronted by a small healthy-looking garden filled with colorful flowers that in my part of the city would survive about as well as a starving man in a desert. A set of fresh, gray stairs ascended slowly to a large pair of glass doors. I stopped my car in front of the building and got out. I scanned the neighborhood for a minute, noticing the difference between Henry St. and this one immediately. It was cleaner, with ample room between buildings and a more than pleasant air embracing the surrounding landscape. I placed an image of Henry St. over the one that faced me now. The disparity was stark. Darkness lingered at its edges like a bad dream waiting to be satisfied.

I threw a cursory glance toward a row of parked cars. I figured at least one or two pairs of prying eyes would be following my every move. At this point, trying to hide my intentions would have been a waste of time. However, placing a potential source of information in harm's way was about as smart as bringing a knife to a gunfight.

I pretended to be lost, swiveling my head in numerous directions like a drunken bobble-head doll. Nothing seemed out of the ordinary. Nevertheless, I wasn't taking any chances. I walked past the building and continued down the block, passing a few smaller shops selling meat and poultry and a small hardware store that sold everything under the sun. I sauntered in and feigned interest in the shop's wares. It was your typical hardware store, crammed to the rafters with pots, pans, tools, rope, plumbing supplies and about a thousand other things you might only need once in your life. The front window faced the street, a perfect view of everything passing from the left and the right. I glanced casually at the open display and the goods it contained. With the brim of my hat hanging low over my brow I surveyed the street.

It was closing in on noon. The clouds transformed from a fixed, stubborn gray to a pasty white. People walking by were engaged in conversation of one sort or another, and every few seconds cars drove noisily past before disappearing into the distance. Between these monotonous events I surreptitiously glanced across the street. A small Ford, blackish-gray in color, was parked in front of a small Italian restaurant. Inside, a figure sat carelessly smoking a cigarette. Ordinarily, this wouldn't be a problem. This time, I knew the face and the body wearing it.

He had seen me just as easily as I had seen him. Ten years ago, Paul Brutus wasn't shy about being seen anywhere. He had been a light middle-weight with decent talent. He could jab and was in good enough shape to go the distance in any fight. He could take a licking from almost any mug, but for all his toughness he was still human. Big Pete saw Brutus for what he really was: a punch-drunk fighter looking for the quick and easy way to big dough. In his heyday, fight fans called Brutus 'the beast', but when he started throwing fights for Big Pete, they started calling him 'the priest' because he always looked like he was down on his knees praying. He didn't take that too well. He started taking the fight out of the ring and into the stands, smacking the kisser of anyone who called him something he didn't like. Pretty soon he was out of the fight game and a part of Big Pete's stable of goons.

Brutus would never be confused with Einstein, but he was smart enough to get hooked up with the biggest scum in New York, and that had to be worth something. Unfortunately, Big Pete didn't teach the mug how to perform a decent tail job. He couldn't have stuck out more had he donned a pink clown suit and shoved a big red bubble on his nose.

Brutus looked quickly away. If I had to use my brains as a weapon against the guy, he might as well have ordered his casket size now, but any direct confrontation would only leave me looking like road kill. I figured any apartment building with a front way in had to have a back way in as well. The thing was to distract Brutus long enough to get in without him seeing me try it.

I stood there thinking when a voice from behind caught me unawares.

"Hello, may I help you?"

The Trigger Method

The shopkeeper walked nimbly up to me. He was an old guy with glasses like telescope lenses and a beard that looked more at home on the end of a mop handle. He wore a long, blue freshly-pressed smock with pockets large enough to stuff bowling balls in it and shoes big enough to use as paddles for a canoe. His entire frame seemed balanced precariously, as if one stiff wind would blow him so off course he wouldn't be found unless you had a bloodhound and a dozen magnifying glasses the size of the Empire State Building. I stifled a laugh.

"Just wanted to come in from the rain," I said, in a decidedly feminine tone. It wasn't my best imitation, but I was pretty sure I wasn't being graded on style, only substance.

He looked out the window before speaking again. "But, it's not raining."

"Of course it's not raining."

"Then why did you say you came in here to get out of the rain if it's not raining? Really, this city is getting worse and worse everyday."

He opened his mouth to protest some more, but I continued on my road to insanity. "You're quite right. If it does start raining, coming in here is a good way to get out of it, don't you think?"

"I'm afraid I'm going to have to ask you leave. I have no time for the lunatics of this world. I do have a business to run."

"You mean you would toss me out into the rain? If I should catch my death of cold, you would feel quite guilty. You must allow me shelter within the confines of your quaint little shop until the deluge passes."

"But, my good man, if you look outside you'll see it is a perfectly fine day; a little chilly, but otherwise a perfectly fine day."

I turned and momentarily studied the entire length of the street across from my position until my glance fell back upon Brutus. He looked away again. He had been staring at me as I chatted with the shopkeeper. His presence meant Big Pete was more than just aware of me. He cared about where I went and who I talked to. What didn't make sense was why he cared. A single shamus running around asking questions about some poor dead kid from the wrong side of the tracks would mean little in the big man's world, unless the kid did or saw something he wasn't supposed to. That still didn't explain the corpse that wound up taking a vacation in my stairwell. But, if the guy belonged to Big Pete, it could be he was trying to send a message. Too bad I wasn't good at reading.

I turned back to the shopkeeper. "Listen here, my good man," I said, attempting my best Park Avenue accent, "this is a civilized country. We do not throw good people out into this horrid downpour. I insist you act like a gentleman and permit me a few minutes. Let me wait it out; after that I shall trouble you no more."

The shopkeeper peered out the window as if in doubt about the current weather. He lifted a bony finger to his temple and scratched for a moment; bewilderment stretched across his face in a kind of placid death mask. I stared defiantly out the window, convinced that it was raining. I looked past him and into the back part of the store. A small curtain separated the front from the back. I didn't want to use that exit yet. If Brutus didn't see me in the store, he would automatically assume I went out the back way and come after me. That could leave the Chalmers dame in a real jam.

"Now listen young man, I appreciate a good jest as much as the next man, but this has gone on long enough. I insist you leave my store at once or you'll force me to call the authorities." He placed his hands firmly against his sides. He resembled a mannequin on a diet.

"That's hardly a sporting proposition, my good man. However, if it makes you feel superior then I'll indeed leave this hovel and seek more suitable quarters elsewhere." I turned and walked out the door before the guy could say anymore. I turned right, away from the apartment building. I didn't turn to see what Brutus was doing, but I knew he was watching me. I let him watch, walking past two more stores before I reached an alley on my right. It was short and curved away at the end. I kept walking. At the end of the street I turned right and stopped.

A kid, maybe ten or eleven, walked toward me with a bat in one hand and a ball in the other. A dirty baseball cap hung precariously to one side of his head with an ample amount of dry, stringy hair sticking clumsily out.

"Hey, kid, you want to make two-bits?"

"Doing what?" He asked, stopping just short of me.

"There's a gray Ford parked a block up on the right. The Joe inside thinks I'm going to be his next date, and I ain't interested. Go find a cop and have him check the guy out. With him gone, I'll be able to make time with a dish that'd make your head spin."

"You mean your dame or his?" The kid's eyes narrowed into questioning little slits.

"She can't stand the guy anymore because he hates baseball. Any mug that doesn't like baseball doesn't rate a dame this snazzy. You know what I mean?"

"Yeah, I think I do. All right, Jack, I'll help you out."

"Thanks, kid. Here's your quarter." I handed the kid the quarter and watched as he walked around the corner and across the street.

A few minutes later the kid came back with one of New York's finest in tow. He pointed to the car. The cop looked skeptically at the kid. For a moment it seemed as if he wasn't going to take the bait. Finally, after scratching his head like a chimpanzee in a zoo, the cop walked slowly toward the car in which Brutus sat. I watched intently. He got half way before Brutus started the motor and bounded down the street. The cop stopped, scratched his head again then looked back toward the kid. The kid was gone too.

I turned the corner and sauntered down the street as if out for my afternoon constitutional. I walked past the hardware store where the shopkeeper stood by the door looking up at the sky. As I past by he looked at me and said, "Nuts!"

"Now, now, my good man, try not to let the rain get you down. Remember, it's always sunny on the inside." I tipped my hat to the old guy and headed for the Chalmers dame's apartment.

I climbed the stairs and at the top studied the apartment directory. I quickly scanned the list until I found the name I was looking for. I pressed the buzzer and waited. She answered on the first ring.

"Hello?"

"Hiya, doll, I'm here to check your meter; how's about you let me in?"

"Excuse me?"

"I'm the guy from the power company. I'm here to check your meter. Let me in and I'll let you know if your legal or not," I replied.

"Oh, it's you. I don't know how you found me, but I'm not talking to the police. If anyone sees me talking to you, it'll be my funeral and then yours."

"The cops are the least of your worries. You got bigger fish to fry and I got no time to waste debating it with you out here in plain sight. That would make great cheesecake for any of Big Pete's goons who might be standing around watching. Now, come on sweetheart, get wise and open the door." She seemed the kind of dame you could push a few inches but no further. It didn't take long for my words to sink into that part of her mind that saw living as a good thing.

"Doesn't leave me much of a choice, does it?" She replied. I heard a distinct buzz as the door lock clicked. I pushed it open and walked inside. A nest of flowers decorated a small section of wall against which also stood a waist-high, pseudo-Chinese vase. The walls were painted a soft yellow with the more intricate parts highlighted by a dark brown glaze. The floor tiles were a black and white checker pattern that stretched across the entire length of the hallway. Set further back, elevator doors, painted gloss black, faced anyone entering the building. A similar door, presumably leading to the stairs, faced the elevator doors from the right side. I walked to the elevator and found it strange to press the button to a working elevator. I wondered where I would be right now had mine been working yesterday. A few seconds later, I was flying up toward another dame and another mystery. The door opened out onto a brightly lighted foyer. Windows at both ends allowed ample light to filter into the hall, leaving very little in darkness. The whole place seemed a study in contrast. Every aspect of the building was perfect with angles that met exactly as they should have. The shadows were gone, replaced by a bright, airy atmosphere that smelled of freshly cut roses. The carpet was clean and the walls were painted in a bright creamy tone that had me thinking of a mellow Sunday afternoon in the park. Henry Street seemed a million years ago.

Holly Chalmers' apartment was located at the far end. I walked slowly to her door and knocked. A series of clicks later, the door opened. Holly Chalmers stood before me, her eyes a deep glimmering hazel against the darkness that emptied out behind her. She was a stunner. Things can change from one day to the next, but the image from last night was nothing like the one that faced me today. Her hair was tied back into a tight bun and she hadn't put on any makeup, but she still looked like the best thing since sliced bread.

Suddenly, a pang of self-consciousness flowed through me like a raging river. If there was a moment where I didn't feel good enough, this was it. Her figure curved like a mountain highway and when she spoke it was like velvet. I almost melted.

"You should carry a sign with that says 'stool-pigeon lives here'. It would save Big Pete and his boys a lot of time," she fumed.

I got over my inferiority complex long enough to pretend to be tough. "I got news for you, sister. They're watching you like hawks. I saw one of them outside your apartment. I was able to get rid of him, but you can bet your best permanent wave he'll be back."

A shadow of fear fell across her features like a cloud swimming under the sun. For a moment, she went as black as the blackest of nights. I had grown accustomed to being tailed and watched like a bug under a microscope. Sometimes, being followed made my life easier because at least I knew where the danger was coming from. She, on the other hand, was used to being followed for her looks, not for what she knew.

A few seconds passed before her features returned to their previous glow. "My hero," She laughed. It wasn't the most reassuring of laughs I'd ever heard, but at least she was trying. She continued on with, "I think you're giving me a line. You know, making it up just to get close to me. I'm flattered honey, but I don't play those kinds of games." She was acting like a child trying to run from a nightmare that wouldn't end no matter how hard she closed her eyes.

"Stop patting yourself on the back, sweetheart. You're not that special. Not to me. I'm in it for the kid. Someone did Joe wrong and I'm going to find out who that was."

"Things happen to bad people. Maybe the kid got what he deserved."

"You don't believe that and you know it. Maybe I should go back downstairs and ask Paul Brutus what he thinks. I'm sure he'd have a lot to say on the subject." More fear. It cut a jagged path between us so wide you could have steered an aircraft carrier through it. It seemed everyone wanted to play games. Unfortunately, I wasn't the game-playing type. The more time that passed between events, the more people tended to forget. "Come on, doll. You're tough, but you're not that tough. I'd hate to see a bullet ruin that canvas of yours, especially before we got a chance to get to know each other a little better. You're being watched and I think you know it. I also think you know the reason why. It's no coincidence Joseph Baker and Fats Kelly are fitted for pine overcoats around the same time you're being watched by one of Big Pete's goons. I'm the only person that can help you, but if you don't want my help then I'll just calmly walk out the front door with a smile on my face big enough to be seen from here to Mexico."

A slight nervous twitch decorated the bottom half of her smile. I made as if I was about to turn and walk away when she, figuring I wasn't bluffing, called out abruptly.

"All right, all right. I'll tell you what I know, but it isn't much." She spoke in hushed tones as if she were in a library. I turned slowly to face her.

"That's a matter of perspective, sweetheart. How's about you let me in and we discuss it in private instead of out here in the middle of Times Square?"

She slid away from the door like a yacht effortlessly pulling away from its mooring. She kept her eyes glued on me the whole time, not allowing me an inch of breathing, or peeping-tom space. The door opened just wide enough for me to step through and past her.

I walked into an apartment that wasn't too big or too small. It was decorated neatly, but not like someone overdrawn on their bank account. It was filled with the usual stuff you would find in a dame's apartment. A sofa and loveseat adorned in red and blue flowers nestled serenely in the middle of the room and off to the corner. Lamps on desks and other paraphernalia of the domestic trade filled the rest of

The Trigger Method

the living room. A kitchen just beyond and a narrow hallway emptied into what was probably the bedroom and bathroom. It was nice, but it was also a picture I had seen before.

"You want something to drink," she asked acerbically.

"I'll take anything you throw my way, doll," I joked.

She ignored my wit, choosing instead to march through the hall and into the kitchen. I took my coat off and placed it on a hook hanging from the near wall then sat down. I had my notebook with me so took it out and leafed through the pages, briefly scanning my notes from my conversation with Baker's old lady.

The scent of roses hung in the air, caressing me like a boxer's gloves. I tried to push it aside, my eyes focusing even more on the letters on the page. I had been here before. The images flashed before me like a tired movie from the past. It was another dame in another room in what seemed a thousand lifetimes ago. I tried not to see it all, instead focusing on the words; the spaces between the letters; the spaces between the secrets.

She floated back into the room with two full glasses and a smile that seemed better suited to a taxman. She placed one of the glasses on the table. It was just slightly out of my reach. It was her way of letting me know my presence wasn't appreciated, just tolerated. She sat down and crossed her legs on the chair in a way that reminded me of the Burly-Q. I looked away like a shy kid.

"You don't really believe I'm in danger, do you?" She asked.

"If you're being watched then it's for more than you're looks. Pete's boys are watching you because they know you know something. Even if it may be nothing to you, to someone like Big Pete, it's always something."

"That makes about as much sense as a mixed up crossword puzzle. Can't you try talking in English for a change?"

She had sass right up to those hazel eyes and the dark, brown curls that curved around her face like vines on a trellis. She was a natural beauty with a natural attitude. I tried hard not to like it all.

"Listen, sister, I talk the truth. It might not make sense to someone like you, but what other people think worries me about as much as an empty holster. You're in a tight spot and you're too lame-brained to see it. If Pete's boys are watching you, then it's only a matter of time before they decide to do something. You're only a walking shadow to them. When they don't need you anymore, they'll take you out faster than a sneeze in a windstorm."

My words landed in twos and threes, like punches against a mug too dead to know he's done. Was I mad? Maybe I was, and then maybe I was just mad because she didn't seem to care. She was scared. But she wasn't scared for her life. She had a California casualness to her that reminded me of a day at the beach. She was a perfect moment sculpted in the body of a Venus. She was also an angry gray cloud. The mix was as stable as oil and water.

"You can't really believe that. I'm just a dancer. I do my job and then I go home. I've met a lot of guys like you. They promise the world, but can never deliver. There's only one reason why you want to help me, and brother I ain't selling." She made a dismissive gesture with her hand like a card shark on the verge of a straight but still too nervous to bet the farm. I didn't want to need her because of her attitude, but at this point she was my only lead to Baker's murderer and maybe to Schwarz. I bit my tongue and kept talking.

"In Big Pete's club they play chin music like it's going out of style. Someone took out Fats Kelly like he was nothing. Kelly was a dangerous guy with a bad attitude. It would take someone with an even worse attitude and real big fists to kill him. If his murder is connected to the kid, this thing is big. It's bigger than you or me. I'd hate to see anything happen to that acreage, but you're nothing more than background scenery. If I think of you that way, you can just imagine what Big Pete thinks."

She looked away, her gaze dropping to the floor. I followed her stare through my own eyes to another apartment, another floor. The shadows hung larger and darker there, slashing across the room in odd angles like sharp knives falling through the air. A desperate face filtered between those lines. It was a young face, full of promise. I looked away.

Holly talked slowly. She seemed a thousand miles away. "He was a good kid. The girls all liked him. He would go out of his way to help us if we needed anything. Sure, he was naive about a lot of things, but he was nice that way. He didn't belong there. None of us do, but he was different."

"What do you mean?"

"He didn't try to hide anything. You could see poor written all over him, but it looked good. He was honest. I spit words at him, mean words, but not because I didn't like him. I liked him all right, like a kid brother, but I wanted him to leave the place. He was too good for them. He was even too good for his best friend."

"Albert Schwarz?" I asked.

"Yeah, that kid was something to see. He was wrong from the get go. Once he started making a little dough he pretended the bad parts didn't exist. He dressed himself in nice suits like he was trying to wash away the dirt and grime. Joe stayed the same. He made some dough too, but you could tell he didn't like it. I think he did it because…"

"Because once you're in, you're in," I interjected.

She nodded in agreement. "A lot of the girls in the club see, but don't see. They don't want to see the stuff. I think it's because they like that world. It's exciting, like a new toy. I've seen too much of it." She played nervously with her cup, passing it from hand to hand like a hot potato.

"Schwarz and Baker hung out with some blonde with lots of dough. Do you have any idea who that might have been?"

She was quiet for a moment. Outside, I could hear the world go by.

"Connie Bartlett. You might know her father, Dane Bartlett."

"You don't mean that old buzzard from Wall Street, do you?" It was a stupid question, and one that I wished I didn't know the answer to.

"One and the same," she answered. She stood up with her cup in one hand and everything else in the other. She took a few tentative steps toward the fireplace before turning to face me. She placed the cup slowly against her lips, took a sip then said, "You can't take a step in that place without stepping over Wall Street financiers, bankers, lawyers and every other so-called respectable profession in this city.

That dame's old man is a regular. I don't know what her story is, but she clung to Albert and the kid like they were a safety blanket."

"Did you ever see her talk to Big Pete?"

"No, but everyone knows that Big Pete and her old man are glued at the hip."

I heard the same stories. Dane Bartlett had done pretty well for himself. He had invested in everything from apples to oil. Everyone also knew he never bought anything unless it was a sure thing. He believed in walking both sides of the tracks, profiting during prohibition and then cleaning up big when the war broke out. He had his nose in the highest reaches of government and in the lowest corners of the Bowery.

I downed some coffee. I didn't taste as good as scotch, but it was pretty good. I could feel the liquid make its way down my windpipe and into my stomach. I didn't feel hungry. The moment had wiped it all away.

I stood up and paced around the room. She stood by the fireplace and watched me. My shoes made quiet, shuffling sounds on the carpet. I could call Pete, but mugs like Bartlett had their dirty fingers in every part of the city, especially the cops. Pete had been my best friend since I could remember and was as trustworthy as the day was long. But the people Pete worked for were another story. I wished I hadn't searched Kelly's body. I wished I hadn't found the card. With Bartlett's name thrown into the mix along with Big Pete, this was quickly becoming a Greek tragedy of epic proportions. If Dane Bartlett had a daughter, and if she hadn't fallen too far from the family tree, she would be trouble in any language. If Holly was right, Baker had found out that same fact the hard way. It had yet to be determined whether Schwarz had learned that same lesson. I took another sip. This one didn't go down so well.

I felt like I was looking into a dirty mirror. The reflection that stared back seemed to be cut into narrow swaths that crisscrossed at odd angles like patches of fabric cut by a man hanging upside down. Nothing seemed clear anymore.

She spoke first, breaking the silence with a voice laced in honey and ginger. "What's wrong? You don't think Connie Bartlett killed the kid, do you?"

"I don't know what to think anymore. Throwing Dane Bartlett into the picture complicates things. His name throws a spotlight on something that'll make people as nervous as a mouse in a house full of cats. There's no way of figuring what they'll do to keep things hushed up. If they think you know something, you can bet your best pair of nylons they'll do whatever it takes to keep you from singing. It won't matter whether you want to talk or not. They'll rub you just to keep from paying the premium."

"I don't understand. You're a private detective, and I'm just a dancer. There's no reason for them to think we know anything. Everybody that works at the club knows the same things that I know. They could follow them too. What makes me so special?"

"You have a past. Maybe they think that makes you dangerous. Maybe hot dames make them nervous. Maybe brunettes are bad luck. I don't know. I don't have the answers, only questions. One of Big Pete's own winds up on my doorstep. One of his boys is sitting at your doorstep shining his seat. I didn't know anything about you until I got a call from some mug telling me who you were and where I could find you. The only other person who knew I was coming here was a guy from headquarters. If I'm being setup then we're both in trouble." I stopped pacing long enough to light a cigarette.

She gulped down the last of her coffee then went back to the sofa and sat down. She looked vulnerable. All of the heat evaporated, replaced by innocence that came around as often as a politician's promise. The truth was no longer a fascinating story hidden in the classifieds. The facts screamed across the front page in stark black and white. It wasn't about grasping at straws; it was about grasping at the truth before someone decided to use me as a Coney Island target dummy.

"If those three were in some kind of crazy love triangle, I could see Schwarz killing Baker out of jealousy. Right now, he's my best bet. All I've got to do is find him."

"He was no boy scout, but I can't see him killing Joseph. They were friends. He was pretty happy when the kid got a job at the lounge."

"Sure he was. He got the job for him," I replied.

"No, Connie Bartlett got the job for him. She showed up with Joe one afternoon at the club. We were rehearsing and she walks in and goes up to the club manager, Clint Baxter, and asks him to give the kid a chance. Ordinarily, he wouldn't give the kid a second look, but because it's a Bartlett he caves in."

Holly had an edge to her that most dames probably wouldn't take a shine to. Connie Bartlett might have been one of them. Miss Warchinski's words were strong enough for me to believe she thought even less about the Bartlett dame. To believe one would mean dismissing the other. However, the truth of Joe's hiring could have been ascertained easily enough. He had hid things from his old lady, probably to avoid the grief that would come from telling her the truth. Holly, on the other hand, had no real reason to lie, other than to get back at Connie Bartlett for being a young, rich kid with too much time on her hands. I didn't know either dame, but a Bartlett's track history in New York had been well documented. Shadows clung to it like bats in a cave, and those shadows talked of under-the-table deals and dead bodies encased in the foundations of New York's most prominent buildings. Kids hide things from their parents all the time. It made sense on the surface. It would alleviate, temporarily, any bad feelings she might harbor and give him a little breathing space.

I turned to Holly, "You have any idea where Schwarz might be?"

"I don't know. He didn't show up until after the kid died. He wasn't at the club for at least a few weeks before, but then Brutus was always giving orders to the boys. Brutus is Big Pete's right arm. When Brutus said do something, you knew it was really Big Pete talking. He must have seen something in Schwarz because Schwarz started making bigger coin. When you get big enough, you can start coming in the front instead of the back. I remember one night going in the back door just before my shift, but just before I did I saw Schwarz a few feet behind me. As soon as I walked in, I looked back and he was gone. About five minutes later I see him trying to get lucky with a couple of the girls inside. When I asked him how he got in, he tells me he's a high roller now and high rollers don't go in the back way. I wanted to smack him in the grill right there and then, but I need the job so I keep my trap shut and walk away. I could feel him trying to look right through me. Something about the mug always gives me the creeps."

"Did you see him there after the kid died?"

"I saw him the next night. He acted like everything was hunky-dory. It sickened me to see him laugh. Anyway, that was the last time I saw him. He disappeared after that."

"I've got some suspicions, but right now that's all they are. So far, there's nothing tangible to link him to anything. One way or another I need him to squawk. That means finding him. As for you, you got to go back and pretend as if everything is business as usual. The moment they get wise to our little chitchat, we'll both be sharing suites at the morgue."

"Are you crazy? First you tell me that Big Pete's boys are watching me. Then you tell me my life is in danger. Now you want me to walk right back into the lion's den. You want I should paint a bulls-eye on my forehead while I'm at it? I'm blowing this town while I'm still vertical." An angry, defiant stare lingered stubbornly between us.

"You run now, you'll always be running. If I'm going to get to the bottom of this, it's going to be with you in plain sight. They'll be more trouble for you if you don't show for work. What time do you start tonight?"

She was quiet for a moment, the cloud of anger slowly deteriorating to a slight mist. "I usually show around seven," she mumbled, strengthening her hold on her cup. She could've told me to fly away in any number of ways. She could've stood up, and with her mile-long legs, kicked me half way to Cincinnati instead of mutely agreeing with my assessment of the situation. It was difficult to admit when you were wrong.

It was obvious Holly had lived a hard life judging from the battle scars that echoed in her voice. To me, she resembled a dame living her life like a race, running from a past that was always second to her own fears. Her looks alone could have gotten her a different mug for every day of the week. However, under the glitz and glamour lived a dame looking for something more.

"Fine, you go to the club. If anyone asks you what's going on, you say you don't know a thing. If one of Big Pete's boys asks you anything, you tell him some guy came around, but you told him what's what. Try and pretend like you don't care about the kid." She didn't seem to like those last few words. I didn't care.

Her stare could have frozen every lake this side of the Rockies. She took a few seconds to steady herself before returning my volley.

"You're really something. You threaten me, insult me and then tell me you don't care what happens to me. I can deal with that, because I'm used to no-good mugs like you. But how dare you insinuate that I don't care about what happened to Joe. Just because I didn't kiss him every time I saw him doesn't mean I didn't like him, or that his death doesn't make me want to kill every one of Big Pete's goons. You're a cruel man with rocks where your heart should be. If I have to spend another minute with you, It'll be one minute too many."

I let the words slide off my back like water running down a hill. I felt like I was in a shooting gallery where loud noises bounced crazily off the walls and ceilings. There was noise everywhere. This dame's words were just excess noise to me. I heard everything only didn't care what it all meant. I had bigger problems.

"You try and step out of this city and Big Pete will be the last of your worries."

She stared at me like a hungry mutt staring at a steak. Her eyes went red hot and she balled up her fists as if ready to go twelve rounds with Max Schmelling. It was then that the phone rang. We both just stared at it. It almost looked like a bomb ready to explode.

"You going to answer that or should I?" I asked.

She shot me an angry glance before standing up. With hands together and her walk slow and steady, she resembled a priest preparing for mass. She moved slowly and quietly to the phone. At the third ring she picked up the receiver tentatively and uttered a soft: "Hello?" She was quiet for a few seconds. It seemed whoever was on the other end was carrying the conversation. All of a sudden I felt guilty for what I had just said. I stayed quiet and listened.

"How did…?" she started, "Yes, he was here, but I didn't tell him anything." More quiet. Fear filled the room like poisonous gas. "He asked me some questions about that dead kid. I told him I didn't know the guy. He didn't believe me. I told him I didn't care if he didn't believe me so I threw him out." More quiet. "I'll be there at the same time as usual. Okay. Bye."

She put the phone down with hands shakier than brittle leaves in a hurricane. I had seen fear, but this was different. This was more than fear. This was terror. I waited for her to say something.

"That was the club manager, Mr. Baxter. He heard you had been around asking some questions and wanted to know what I told you. I told him I didn't say a thing. After that he asked what time I was coming to the club." She spoke as if in a church. Each word uttered softly, almost hesitantly, as if in disbelief. She looked at me again, this time with eyes as big as all the stars put together and a pleading look on her face. I dissolved into a mass of nothing.

I rapidly came to the realization my ideas concerning the status quo no longer held water. Sending Holly to the Pheasant Lounge was akin to signing her death warrant. "The only place you're going is with me. I knew these mugs were quick, but I didn't think they were that quick. We got to get out of here now. There's no way I can take you back to my place. They're probably watching that too." I looked around before speaking again. "Pack a small bag."

"Where will we go?" She stared at me like a child, her world rapidly thinning out until it became just her and I. Suddenly she became as insurable as the Titanic and it was my fault. I could feel a cloud of guilt smothering me. I fought the feeling, but it was too much. It was like fighting an onrushing tidal wave. Her eyes were so big I almost jumped in.

"I have a friend. His name is Pete Miller, a cop. He's the only guy I trust more than my local barkeep. I'm going to take you to his place. After that, I'm going to pay a visit to a couple of lowlifes. They might know where this Schwarz guy is."

"There's no way your sticking me with cops, friend or no friend. I'm going with you and that's final. You got me into this and you're going to get me out."

"What's that supposed to mean? Anyone who works for Big Pete is trouble in my books, doll. You dug the hole, not me. I'll try and get you out of it, but don't for a second think it's my fault. As for coming with me, that's out of the question. I've got enough problems without some silly dame following me around." I turned away thinking that would be the end of it. It didn't take me long to realize how wrong I was.

"You and I are going to be glued to the hip. You can take it up with the union if it bothers you," she growled.

She stormed out of the living room and into the bedroom. I could hear the sound of drawers opening and clothes being thrown about. I was preparing a list of comebacks when she peered into the room once again, her fear diminished to a tiny flame.

"So, who are these lowlifes we're going to talk to?" She asked before retreating back into the bedroom. "Do they have the same kind of manners as you? I hope not; otherwise, I'm in for a long night."

She wasn't going to be the only one. I sighed.

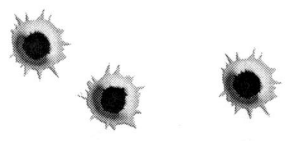

CHAPTER 8

I walked out of the building fifteen minutes later, dame in tow. I didn't have a set plan. I was pretty much making it up as I went along, and all that was fine when it was just me. But now that the dame had invited herself along, my plan seemed as effective as a band-aid on the back end of an elephant.

All the way to the car we argued. We argued getting in. We argued driving through most of New York. We even argued between bites of hamburger and fries. I could feel my gat in my holster. It would have been an easy matter. All I had to do was pull the trigger. She glared at me as I considered the idea, and for a moment I thought she could see exactly what I was thinking. I tried to hide the thought like a guy hiding a scar from a beauty pageant winner. The quiet only lasted a few seconds before we started arguing again. It had only been an hour since I had seen her and already it felt like forever. I sighed again.

Outside, the afternoon brilliance began to turn. Slow, turbulent clouds moved in from the east, slicing through the city and into the heart of every citizen. The nights were getting colder. I could feel it in my bones. She could feel it too, but it was more than just the weather. It was something deeper and it ate away at both of us.

I saw an empty telephone booth off to my left and started fishing in my pocket for change only to find a couple of pennies.

"You got a dime? I need to make a call."

She shook her head in frustration before reaching inside her purse and pulling out a couple of dimes. We both got out and walked to the booth.

"Who are you going to call?"

"My buddy works out of twelfth precinct. He might have a lead on where I can find this Schwarz character."

"Are you sure you can trust him?"

I almost thought about the answer, almost. "We grew up together. He's one of the only people I do trust." I shoved a dime into the slot and a few seconds later got Pete's precinct.

Behind me, Holly stood unfazed by the moment. She stared off into the distance, a quiet serenity evident in all her features. She could have been window shopping, or out on a walk, or during a hundred other things than what she was doing now: in fear for her life. I gripped the phone tighter.

"Hey, Dix, What have you got?" Pete sounded worn out, like a doormat that's been stepped on once too often.

"Little bit of this, and a little bit of that. You know how it is, Pete."

"I found out where that Schwarz guy lives. I've got a couple of my boys waiting for him. As for this mysterious dame you're talking about, I still don't have any idea who she is."

"I already got that part figured out. Her name is Connie Bartlett. You won't need two guesses as to who she's related to."

"Dix, tell me this is some kind of joke, because if it isn't I just might retire."

"We're knee-deep in the kind of things only pigs like. Bartlett's daughter and Bartlett both keep regular schedules at the Lounge from what I hear. Pete, this card isn't just a one-off anymore. It's a bigger player now and we both know it."

"Benson Properties is into land. Big Pete is into making money anyway he can."

Bartlett was just as crooked as he was straight. Ever since the twenties, Bartlett jammed his greedy digits into anything he thought had a buck lurking under it. Big Pete did the same thing, only he used a gat as his calling card. "The card is probably a plant. Someone wants us to know about the connection between these two. She knew Schwarz and Baker and was seen with them by at least two people. It's not much to go on, but it's also more than just a coincidence."

"Someone's getting information first hand, and I have a feeling that someone is sitting pretty close to one or both of those two."

"Yeah, and until I figure out who that someone is, my gat and my shadow are going to be my best friends." I didn't like the way that came out, but I didn't want to hold anything back either.

"What's that supposed to mean? You think I'm working for the other side, Dix?" Pete didn't sound angry, just hurt.

"I didn't say that, Pete. You know as well as I do that Bartlett is shaking hands with the mob and the police. How many of your boys can you really trust when a whole pile of dough is waved in their face? This is a dirty city at the best of times. I've already seen one goon today that traded in his pride for dough. You might remember him."

"Who's that?" Pete asked warily.

"Paul Brutus."

"The ex-prizefighter?"

"He was sitting outside the Chalmers dame's apartment. Big Pete is already keeping an eye on her. Schwarz might still be around, but he might also be about ten feet in the ground. She said she saw him the day after the kid died, but he's been pretty much persona non grata since. If Big Pete did kill Kelly, there's no reason to believe he wouldn't kill Schwarz as well. Either way, I'm not taking a chance with my life or Holly's."

"I've already got people watching the club and two or three other spots. If Big Pete makes any kind of move we'll know about it. If this Chalmers dame is with you bring her in. We'll keep her safe."

It was a tempting offer, but Holly wasn't about to have any of it. There was no use in even trying to talk her because she would probably just say 'nuts' and ask me what our next move was.

"No dice, Pete. It isn't that simple. Trust is a hard commodity to come by and right now I'm not selling. I trust you, but I don't trust those around you. Say hello to Wilma for me." I hung up the phone and turned to Holly. Her features had softened since I first stepped into the booth.

I looked away from her and into the street. The usual evening traffic was slowly descending over the city like vultures on a dead body. Brightly lighted street signs cast long waves of translucent radiance across the avenue. Every few seconds the beam was cut, the magic broken. It felt colder during those moments. When the light returned it no longer seemed as bright, as magical, as if something had been lost in the interim. I turned and faced Holly.

"So, what do we do now?" She asked.

"I want to know what Connie Bartlett has to do with Baker and Schwarz. The only way to do that is to go straight to the top. That means paying a visit to the charming Mr. Dane Bartlett. If I'm lucky, he'll get offended, threaten me with a few lawsuits then cause a few ripples by calling Big Pete. Bartlett's just a money man. Big Pete makes all the decisions that require that human touch. Either way, the next few hours are going to get interesting."

"Why do I get the feeling you don't plan on being the perfect guest?"

"I'm just a little rough around the edges," I replied. We walked back to the car. The conversation was a strange one. We could have been walking through a park, or under a starlit summer sky exchanging sweet nothings between shots of vodka and versus from a Sinatra song.

Her hair curved gently over her neck and shoulders like water over a waterfall, and her eyes seemed to cut through the night like headlights from an automobile. She was a perfect picture hung in the wrong place. I kept stealing glances at her as we walked, hoping she wouldn't notice. Her perfume was a drug; I could feel the scent swimming through me, lifting me toward the stars above. Her heels clicked gracefully on the cold, hard sidewalk.

"I don't get you, Mr. Dixon. You're infuriating, but obviously you care about something. You're like an old, dirty coin with a good side and a bad side." We reached my car but we didn't get in. I turned to face her from across the roof of my car, a low mist rising from the manholes acted like a buffer between us. It was like something out of a movie. "On one side, I see a scarred image. On the other, I see something that should be hanging in a gallery somewhere. Which one are you?"

"I'm just a shamus trying to get at the truth, Miss Chalmers. I don't always use agency-approved methods, but more often than not I get results. There's an honest Joe underneath it all, but I don't have time to let him out. Not right now. And call me, Dix. My old man's name was Mr. Dixon." I opened the door and climbed into the driver's side. She got in the other side and looked at me for a long time. I didn't look back.

CHAPTER 9

It was a nice place, by Yankee Stadium standards. It rolled over the quiet country hills like an endless carpet. The driveway alone was long enough to use as a race track, and enough trees provided shade over it to landscape Brooklyn from one end to the other. Accompanying the excess shrubbery was a small army of marble sculptures. They presided over the place like sentries. It was obvious Bartlett had sunk a lot of dough into the spread. Blood money, I thought.

We emptied out onto a large semi-circular, roughly-paved driveway. The furthest edges of it were lined with long stretches of rose bushes of red, pink and white. Beyond that lay more trees. Staring at the house was like staring at a castle, with smaller stone statues, gargoyle-like, perched atop the corners like bodyguards ready to pounce on uninvited guests. The house itself was built in the Gothic style, with large overhangs, stained glass, and brick columns that seemed to reach into the sky. A large water fountain stood in the center of the driveway. It was intricately decorated. Two dolphins with water erupting from their mouths in thin streams surrounded a cherub. All three seemed to be staring up at the moon.

I pulled up just past the fountain and turned off the ignition. The first thing that caught my attention was the lack of noise. It was quieter than a cemetery. Holly got out and looked around warily.

"This place looks like a funeral home. Where are the ghouls?" Holly asked.

She was right. The place didn't just look deserted, it looked dead. It was like standing in the middle of a ghost house waiting for the big scare. A slow, cool breeze wafted back and forth, gently nudging the flowers and bushes against each other creating an unsettling 'shush' sound that echoed across the entire property.

Holly and I turned to face each other. That brief interlude momentarily chased away the strangeness that surrounded us. Our words hung in the air; we were unable to speak, only admire the spooky view. A sudden violent rush of wind against nearby trees brought us back to reality.

"Has this mug ever seen you? I mean, would he recognize you if he saw you?" I asked as I turned to view the rest of the surroundings.

"I don't know. There are a lot of girls working in that place. He usually came in sloshed and left the same way. I would just be another pair of legs to him."

"Good. You're my assistant, Jessica Plumber. Don't say anything unless I tell you to. Got it?"

"Is that how you see me, as a Jessica?" She asked.

I didn't know how to respond to that one. I had to think for a second before I said: "I..It's just a name. You can choose a better one if you want."

"Jessica will be fine," she laughed.

I tried to not like her. It was a good laugh with all the naturalness in the world wrapped up within it. It resounded across the haunting canvas that stood before us like a newborn baby's first cry. I thought about it all the way to the front doors. They were big, almost the size of a medieval drawbridge. Two large, metal handles decorated the middle. Small eagles were carved into both. I rang the buzzer and waited.

The door to my right creaked open and a thin wisp of a man with chalk-white hair and deep-sunken eyes greeted us with a barely-audible, "May I help you?" Light from the hall behind washed over his delicate frame crafting the vision of a ghostly apparition at the expense of the man.

I tipped my hat. "My name's Gabrielle Dixon. I'm here to see Mr. Bartlett on some personal business."

"Is Mr. Bartlett expecting you?"

"I'm here uninvited. I'm afraid I'm not very good at making appointments. Things like that just seem so stuffy and I'm not really the stuffy type. I prefer to cut to the chase. As a matter of fact, I had talked to Mr. Bartlett previously about the matter when I ran into him at the Pheasant Lounge. He was fairly interested in what I had to say; so much so that he recommended a private audience with him so that we might discuss it further."

Holly stood next to me batting her eyelashes like a hand-held fan during an August heat wave. I turned my attention toward the butler. He was staring at me; yet, it almost felt like he was looking through me and at something else. It seemed at any second the large mahogany doors would be closed in our faces, but at the last moment he uttered a firm, "In that case, please follow me into the parlor."

The butler teetered and tottered his way through another large pair of mahogany double-doors. Passing through them felt like passing through the door of my seventh-grade principal's office, Mr. Featherby. Every time I walked through his door, I knew I was going to get in trouble. I hoped history wasn't about to repeat itself.

"If you'll wait in here, Mr. Dixon, I'll inform Mr. Bartlett of your arrival." The butler tottered back out, closing the door as he went. A soft, soothing luminescence washed gently through the large room revealing a large wall full of books and maps as well as a few paintings of people that had probably been dead longer than the dodo bird. A row of windows wrapped in rusty-colored drapes stared out into the evening darkness. Through the reflection I could see an image of myself, bedraggled and shrunken, more dead than alive, but alive nevertheless. I glanced at the wall behind me only to see another panel full of books and other paraphernalia. I wondered if this junk meant anything or whether it was here just for effect.

"Pretty fancy looking museum. The only thing missing are the mothballs," Holly noted. She wandered a few steps in each direction, her heels making muted clicks on the floor. She looked like a young girl swimming in an ocean of innocence, unaware of the dark tide that was quickly developing under her feet. I felt like a heel for trying to be brave, for trying to be more than I really was.

I looked away from her and toward nothing in particular. "He probably keeps those in his coffin as a late-night snack," I joked.

She laughed quietly. It was the kind of laugh that had me thinking of those rare moments in life when things seemed okay. Her hair brushed gently against her face, as if a slight breeze had just passed by her. There was no mistaking the fact that she was a swell dish, but I also had to remember the reason I was here was because of a dead kid, not my dead social life.

The moment was broken by the sound of the door opening and the corpse that walked like a man re-entering the room. "Mr. Bartlett will see you in a few moments. Would either of you care for some refreshments?"

Holly spoke up first. "Thank you, yes. A cup of coffee will be fine for me, and Mr. Dixon will have some orange juice, hold the vodka."

"Very good, ma'am," he replied before shuffling out of the room.

I looked at Holly for a moment like a guy about to cry. "Thanks, but I've been ordering my own meals since I was twenty."

"Have you been dressing yourself that long as well?"

I winced for a quick second. "You're a real piece of work, you know that?"

"Yes, I realize that. Thank you for noticing." She threw the comment in my direction absently, as if unaware of my presence.

I was preparing a witty comeback when the doors to the study suddenly opened. Dane Bartlett walked in quietly and confidently, like a man convinced of his innocence. His was a firm face with eyes as sharp as tacks and a questioning nature etched into every crease and fold of his tanned skin. His hair wasn't the usual idle gray like most in the higher-age bracket. Instead, Dane Bartlett's mane shone like the bumper on a brand new Ford. It was clear he knew why we were here before he walked in. A red and blue satin robe hung from him like a bed sheet strung across a clothesline. He tried looking like a guy who didn't care. I knew better.

Everyone had heard the stories about the old man and how he had managed to chisel his way to the top of the New York business scene.

No one dared guess the number of bodies he buried during his climb up the corporate ladder. The dark and dirty secrets that threaded through the infrastructure of Wall Street whispered of shady deals consummated amidst the remnants of others' fractured dreams; Dane Bartlett's name was always in the middle of it all.

He stopped a few feet away; a pipe was entrenched firmly in his mouth; smoke erupted from it like a volcano. He looked first at Holly then at me. After a few more tense seconds he said, "Well, Mr. Dixon, I don't recall ever meeting you before. To what do I owe the pleasure?"

"It was a quick meeting, Mr. Bartlett. You had a drink in one hand and Wall Street in the other."

His laugh was like gunfire; it came out in short, rapid bursts. "Well said, Mr. Dixon; however, Wall Street is hardly for any man who exists solely on water. It takes a man with a firm grasp of his affairs and an even firmer grasp of his glass to succeed."

"Maybe you're right. I've never really had to worry about Wall Street. See, my car always broke down a few streets away."

He laughed some more before steadying himself like a card player getting set for the first hand. "Ah, well played, Mr. Dixon." He turned to Holly and said, "And who might this beautiful creature be?"

"This is my assistant, Jessica Plumber. She's here to remember all the stuff I forget."

"Miss. Plumber, I am very pleased to meet you. Beautiful women are such a rarity nowadays. I was just thinking that I might never see a woman as pretty as a poem, but here you are."

"Thank you, that's very sweet." She didn't faint. She didn't even blush. She merely held out her hand and allowed Bartlett to kiss it. I wanted to laugh, but didn't.

"Mr. Bartlett, I'd like to ask your daughter a few questions."

"What, may I ask, will be the topic of your conversation?" He asked.

"A young man named Joseph Baker found himself on the wrong end of a gun a week ago. From what I hear your daughter knew Mr. Baker fairly well. I'm hoping she can help me fill in some holes."

Bartlett eyed me suspiciously, his look all but saying 'not today, buddy'.

"You are merely a private investigator. I don't believe there is any reason for me to concede to your request now is there?" The tension in his voice increased an octave. Suddenly we were two knights on the field of battle, our words our swords, and the truth the prize.

"You're right about that. She doesn't have to talk to me. Mind you, I'm not here to discover her guilt or innocence. I'm just here to find out what she knows about Joseph Baker. The police are the ones likely to be more interested in the former."

He didn't like that, but then I wasn't really in the caring mood. Everything about this guy was wrong. My senses were screaming like a five-alarm fire, and the look in his eyes told me he knew exactly why I was here, what I was going to ask, and the truths as well as the lies. I was behind in strikes and needed to catch up, fast.

"Your tone is rather harsh, Mr. Dixon. You come to my home uninvited, wave a murder investigation at me, and then insinuate that my daughter may have something to do with all this silly business. It is quite an affront to my hospitality." He finished the sentence with three quick puffs from his pipe, the smoke accumulating a few inches in front of me before dissipating. I smiled serenely, pretending not to notice.

Holly stood quietly, a grin the size of Nebraska painted on her face. I looked back toward Bartlett. He kept his hands wound tightly behind his back like a man being led to the chair. His eyes were open, as if trying to remember the next lines of his speech.

"I'm sorry if you don't like my tone, Mr. Bartlett. My manners aren't the greatest at the best of times. My grades at finishing school never did make mom and dad very proud, but at least I gave it the old college try."

I didn't get to finish my speech. "I apologize, Mr. Bartlett. Mr. Dixon is trying to quit drinking, and because of that has been on edge all day. We just want to ask your daughter a few questions and then we'll be on our way. We would be grateful for any assistance."

There it was all neatly laid out on the proverbial red carpet like a sacrificial lamb before the wolves. Sure it was easier being polite, but a guy like Bartlett didn't deserve polite. He didn't even deserve civil.

Bartlett smiled. "Thank you, my dear. A polished sense of propriety does go a long way."

He didn't get to finish his speech. I looked past him and toward the girl that was supposedly the spitting image of Ginger Rogers. Truth be told, Ginger Rogers had nothing on this dame. She was young and impetuous; the dress told me that. It was a high-class number that probably cost more than the GNP of most countries. It shimmered in the light and the slit in the side snaked almost up to her neck. I should have paid for the show.

The old man knew she was there but kept his eagle eyes on me. He was no longer playing the bewildered father. He had suddenly transformed into the shrewd Wall Street businessman, inspiring fear and loathing as easily as a Nazi with a moustache.

The next few seconds found me bouncing back and forth between the old man and his daughter. I couldn't figure the relation between the two. She was everything he wasn't. She was tall with legs that could have easily been confused for stilts. Her blonde hair hung gently over her neck and back with a precision that would have impressed an architect, and when she talked the consonants poured out like a Vera Lynn love song. She was wrong in so many ways. I smiled before remembering Holly. I glanced at her. She wasn't smiling.

"Is something the matter, father?" Her voice hadn't been given a chance to grow up along with the rest of her. The words and phrases spoken were Yale or Harvard, but the tone was strictly second grade.

"These people would like to talk to you about a young man." Dane Bartlett stared at his daughter like a tiger staring at morning breakfast. His composure seemed to be drifting idly between a slow breeze and a wild thunderstorm. Something about the scene told me I was on the right track.

Connie Bartlett drifted into the room like someone casually strolling through a park on a quiet Sunday afternoon. She carried a small black purse in her right hand and a lighted cigarette in her left. Small twists of smoke drifted away from her as she walked. The old man stepped away, marched to a small expensive-looking table and opened the top drawer. He pulled out a pack of cigarettes and a lighter.

"Would either of you care for a cigarette?" He asked politely.

"No, thank you." Holly replied.

"I better not. It's bad for my figure," I added, throwing a cursory glance in Holly's direction.

"A man with a sense of humor; you interest me."

"I don't really know how to take that, especially with your father in the room. We haven't exactly hit it off you see."

Holly was starting to see where this was all headed. I was never much for the fancy types that strolled down Park Avenue. My sense of propriety was as refined as a bum at a backyard picnic. I didn't care for Bartlett's world. It was as real as a fairy tale and as meaningful as a bar without booze. I wanted to walk over and shake the truth out of Bartlett, but Holly's presence formed a barrier between thought and action. I felt like I needed to be on my best behavior.

"Oh, that's a shame," Connie replied. She abruptly turned to her old man. "Father, have you been rude to our guests?"

"Of course not, my dear," Bartlett replied. He looked both angry and confused, as if he had just stepped into the place for the first time. After a few furrowed brows and angry exhales Bartlett turned to the door and finished with, "Now where is Norton with the refreshments? Let me go and see. The three of you can get better acquainted while I'm gone." Bartlett turned and walked out of the room, his satin robe trailing behind.

Holly turned to Connie who was taking a gentle puff from her cigarette. "That's a lovely dress you have on. It must have cost a fortune."

"Yes. Father insists I have the best. Our social position demands it, don't you know."

"I'm sure." I replied. "Miss Bartlett, tell me what you know about Joseph Baker, aside from the fact that he's dead?"

She studied me, trying to separate what I knew from what she should tell me. There was no way of knowing exactly who had the advantage.

"I didn't know him that well. I met him through Albert Schwarz. Albert and Joseph worked together at the Pheasant Lounge. That's where I met them. I was bored and they seemed like a good time. I mostly hung out with Albert, although Joseph would tag along quite a bit. When I heard about his death, I was shocked. He seemed like such a nice kid." She said 'kid' like she was an old matron ready for the retirement home. It was like watching a little child put on her mother's makeup and clothes and stroll around the house pretending to be all grown up. The only thing stopping this kid was the chastity belt that hung loosely around her waist.

"Aren't you a little young to be going to nightclubs?"

"Young is merely a state of mind. I'm almost twenty. In my twenty years I've experienced more than some will experience in an entire lifetime. My father views everyday as an opportunity and has passed down that philosophy to me. It's my motto for life."

I glanced at Holly to see her reaction. She rolled her eyes in plain view of both of us. Connie noticed but said nothing. Instead, she put the cigarette to her mouth, took a deep drag then exhaled in Holly's direction. The smoke didn't reach her entirely, but the message was clear. Holly simply smiled, as if oblivious of the entire exchange and its meaning in the larger context of things.

"That's great. My motto is 'seize the bottle'. Now, tell me more about Joseph. Why did you hang out with Alfred more than Joseph? What was it about him that turned you off?"

"I felt bad for Joseph." Her eyes looked everywhere but at Holly and I. She was reaching, although not very far.

"Why's that?" I asked.

"He kept telling me he wanted more. He saw Albert was making good money and wanted the same. From what I saw, Albert was good with the customers. People liked him because he was friendly and outgoing. Joseph seemed very shy and quiet in comparison."

The butler walked in with a tray full of glasses filled with various concoctions. One of the glasses held a bright, yellow liquid. I started thinking of ways to thank Holly. After exchanging a few words of apology for taking so long, he left the drinks on a nearby table and walked out. There was no sign of Dane Bartlett.

"Did Schwarz and Joseph ever argue about anything?" I continued.

"Yes. Me."

"They argued about you?" I asked.

She tipped the cigarette to her lips and drew in a quick blast of smoke. She blew it back out just as quick. Everything about her was phony, right down to the way she smoked. Her eyes narrowed into tiny slits and her brow furrowed slightly as the smoke swam rudely inside her mouth. When she exhaled it was like watching a kid try to blow out the candles on a birthday cake. She took a few seconds to steady herself.

"Yes. After Albert got Joseph the job, Joseph started talking to me a lot more. He got in trouble many times for talking when he should have been working. Joseph meant well, but he constantly had a hard time with the work."

"You mean Albert got Joseph the job? The way I heard it, you got the manager to hire him."

Connie resembled a child who'd just been caught with her hands in the cookie jar. Even in that low rusty light, I could see her face turn a deep shade of crimson. She faced away from me, feigning interest in some books she'd probably never even knew existed. She finally looked back, took the cigarette from her mouth and said, "The manger, Clint Baxter, is a friend, but I never talked to him about Joseph. He only came to my attention after he started working at the Lounge. Albert and Joseph seemed close, but Joseph was always getting in hot water over one thing or another. Albert told me several times how he had to cover for Joseph's mistakes. I don't think Albert liked having to cover for him so much."

"What kind of mistakes?" Holly asked. I looked at Holly. Her face looked overcast. All the features on her face became hard, more pronounced.

"I'm not sure. I never pursued the matter. I just took Albert at his word." Connie walked casually toward a brown leather sofa situated near the center of the room. It was the kind of walk that could make a guy's eyeballs fall out of his head. Holly stared bullets at her.

"You make it sound as if he was an incompetent fool. I wonder if there was anyone else who felt the same way as Albert." I could sense the anger in Holly's question. I got the feeling she didn't like being made to look like a fool and a liar.

"I don't read people's minds, Miss…?"

"Jessica Plumber. I'm not asking you to read anyone's mind. I just want to know if there was anyone else who felt the same as you. If he was incompetent as you say he was, why didn't the club manager fire him? The Pheasant Lounge is a high-class establishment. I would assume that a place like that would only hire the best."

"I'm not the club manager. You'd have to ask Mr. Baxter about that," Connie protested.

"We could do that. If he doesn't have the answer, do you think Big Pete would?" I asked.

She hadn't expected the mention of his name. She took a few seconds to steady herself. Her cigarette dangled carelessly from her fingers like an unwanted toy, a stray smoke trail drifted casually away from her. It had been a shot-in-the-dark to assume she might be linked to Big Pete. Most times, hunches will you win you about as much as a nickel bet at the racetrack; however, tonight, Connie seemed to be disproving that theory shamelessly. "I'm sorry, but I don't know anyone by the name 'Big Pete'?"

Her acting lessons hadn't paid off enough to impress me. She knew who Big Pete was and we all knew she knew. Everyone in this haunted house knew exactly who Big Pete was. As far as I was concerned, the apple didn't fall too far from the tree.

"Skip it. Besides the fact Baker wasn't about to win the employee-of-the-year award, can you think of any reason why anyone would want the kid dead?"

"Like I said before, he was a good kid. It was a shock to hear he was dead. I can't think of anyone who would want to kill him. Sure, he and Albert had a few issues, but it wasn't enough for Albert to want the guy dead; not in my book, anyway."

She spoke the words as if they had spilled out of the good book. To her, the insinuation wasn't just an opinion but a statement of fact. Innocent enough when taken on its own; however, when coupled with everything else, sounded like a truth that merited the immediate arrest of one Albert Schwarz. It sounded good but then Pete did always say I was a little hard of hearing.

CHAPTER 10

The old man had been gone a long time. His absence seemed to inspire an odd sense of relief on Connie's part as she disclosed her answers to our questions with an increasing amount of creativity, reveling in her newfound ability to invent conclusions the way a child invents a story to save himself from a severe paddling.

I had seen this movie before. The plot eerily familiar along with the shady characters that populated the bit of fiction I was now listening to. Nestled comfortably between Schwarz and Baker was Connie, a semi-transparent shadow of intriguing possibilities through which the truth and lies intersected.

"The kid was so secretive. He wouldn't even let me visit his apartment. He said his mother probably wouldn't appreciate my type. I asked him what he meant by that, but he was always so cagey. Even Albert couldn't understand it. Albert told me Joe's old lady tried to stop him from working at the lounge more than a few times and even slapped him once, but he kept going because he needed the money. I think he just wanted to be near me. Mind you, I didn't really care one way or another, as long as I didn't have to go back there again." She half-shut her eyes as she spoke, "The whole place is quaint, in its own way. Mind you, the lights don't work half the time, and the smell is quite atrocious. I can't see how they live there."

"They?" I questioned.

"The poor people," she said frivolously.

"They get branded like cows. After that, they just heard them through the streets, sometimes yelling, sometimes shooting, but they just heard them through until they find the dirtiest, smelliest part of New York. I think they call it immigration."

Holly smiled at that one. Connie didn't.

"I really don't appreciate your sense of humor, Mr. Dixon. If there is anything else, I suggest you take it up with my father's lawyer," she replied, contemptuously.

"I'd only do that if I was trying to arrange your accommodations for the next five-to-ten," I hissed.

She whirled around to face me, her eyes narrowing into beams of pure hate. Her manufactured and manicured mood dissolved into a fury centered on me and my insults. I had made it clear from the moment I walked in her story was about as believable as a blind priest in a women's change room. Bartlett stood next to the door, statuesque in appearance, observing the exchange like a tennis match. He looked visibly shaken. I dug into him like I had his daughter.

"You're playing a dangerous game, Mr. Bartlett. This family is hiding something that can't stay hidden no matter how hard your money tries to bury it. Your daughter knew Joseph Baker. On top of that, everyone in town knows you and Big Pete are the best of chums. One of his boys, Durbin Kelly, was found dead with a card in his pocket. Ordinarily that wouldn't mean anything. But, the card was for a place called Benson Properties. It seems you have a big stake in that company. Can you tell me why one of Big Pete's goons would have a card in his pocket for a property management company, or should I just go and ask Big Pete?" He said nothing. He stood quietly staring at me with a blank expression emblazoned across his face. His gaze, for a second, switched from me to his daughter. I thought I saw a thin film of mutual resentment embedded deep into the stare that Connie and he traded between each other. She took a few more anxious puffs from her cigarette. I finally broke the tension by adding an exclamation point to my exit. "Somewhere in this mausoleum the truth is dying to get out."

Bartlett advanced a few tentative steps before half-turning to face Holly and I. "I do hope you find what you are looking for, Mr. Dixon," he said politely.

"I'm sure I will. And when I do, you'll be the first to know. You can tell your lawyer all about it before you go on trial."

The two of us stood like gunfighters ready for combat. I had no proof to back up my claims, only feelings. However, something I said touched a nerve with both. Suddenly, their manicured and polished world seemed a little less polished, less refined. The cracks in the mirror were just starting to show.

Connie stood quietly surveying the scene like a gun before discharge. A new desperation highlighted the tension in her features, transforming her from a youthful twenty into an aged forty or fifty. I had dropped the names that needed dropping and come away with enough to tell me I was on the right track. I coughed as I walked to the door leading into the hall.

"Miss Plumber, we better take our leave of these fine people. I'm sure they have things to do."

Holly and I dived into the cool of the night. Behind us, the door shut quickly and quietly. There was no figuring the exchange between Connie and her father after our exit. Part of me didn't care. They would be just words with no real meaning because talk for these people was cheap. It was a bus that passed by while you were sipping champagne, or a stray raindrop that fell just inches from your three hundred dollar designer shoes. The stuff only touched them if they let it. The rest of us didn't have a choice.

A few minutes later we were driving down a lonely stretch of road and back to the heart of the city. Holly sat quietly waiting for me to say something. Too much had been said already. I needed time to take it all in, like a breath of fresh air to a coal miner.

"Those are two strange birds," Holly started. "She was trying real hard to make that kid out to be some sort of nincompoop or something. He may not have been the smartest kid on the block, but he was a good worker. No one had any complaints about him."

"She was reading lines from a tired script, sweetheart," I muttered. "Someone told them the wrong answers to the right questions. They're being guarded about more than just their taxes. Whatever happened to Baker has Bartlett written all over it." Holly turned and asked me how I knew.

"He knew I was a private investigator even before I had a chance to flaunt it. He might be smart, but he isn't that smart. The stare they gave each other when he walked back in definitely didn't convey warm father-daughter feelings. One or both are not happy with each other. Benson Properties might have something to do with it, but I think it has more to do with Kelly's murder. They're covering for someone, or being told to cover for someone."

Holly sat silently, peering out the window at the passing darkness. In her mind, names and places stirred gently like leaves of grass in a gentle breeze. I knew what she was thinking and I knew what she would say once she was finished. I sat quietly and waited for her answer.

"Big Pete?" Holly asked.

"Someone out there knows why the kid was murdered, and knows that any investigation into his death will be traced back to Big Pete and Bartlett. Someone out there knows what everyone else is thinking, and I don't think its Big Pete." That was the only explanation for the card. Someone like Kelly would never carry anything that could be traced back to his boss in any way. The card was a sure plant meant to point a finger in one direction, and one direction only.

"Most of Big Pete's goons are as loyal as the family dog; to run around on him would be like signing your own death warrant."

I thought about that for a second. Holly was right. In the gangster business, biting the hand that feeds you would leave you with nothing more than a bullet in the brain or a noose around the neck. I thought about Kelly some more.

Maybe I was wrong. Maybe the long hours of constant thought had finally driven me batty; however, facts were facts. Kelly was dead because of something he knew or something he did. I was betting on the latter.

The road back to Mahoney's was defined by crumbling rock and rough-hewn stone; each successive jolt traveled through my body like a thunderstorm, my bones keeping time like a bagful of coins on a roller coaster. The lack of smooth passing seemed indicative of the last few days and hours. Each successive clue felt like a bump along the route to the final truth.

"I think Kelly got an inch and decided to take a mile."

Holly glanced over. "I don't believe it. It would be too hard to try anything without getting noticed."

"You might be right, but things like this have been done before. I just can't figure out why Kelly would want to try something like that. Big Pete's stranglehold on the underworld is pretty tight. He knows what happens in this city before it happens. Kelly had to have known that, unless someone tried to teach him different."

"You don't mean Bartlett, do you?" Holly asked.

"Everyone knows Bartlett is dirty. He's got his hand in almost every civic project in the city. He knows the right people and the wrong stuff they've done. All he's got to do is snap his fingers and the politicians come running like mealtime at a pig pen. If Big Pete and he are connected, it could be someone else got close to something and thought they could make a go of it by themselves. If it was Kelly, maybe he was trying to use the kid as bait to save his own can and wound up fish food anyway. If Big Pete got wind of the scam, and Kelly's involvement, he wouldn't waste any time getting rid of him. The fact it comes so close on the heels of the kid's death tells me that something is going on and it ain't a company barbecue. When was the last time you saw Kelly at the club?"

Holly turned to me. "I saw him last Friday night. He was talking with Clint Baxter. They were both headed into the back offices. I didn't see him leave but then I wasn't really paying attention."

"That would've been the night before Baker died. You sure you didn't see him after that?"

She went quiet for a moment. She looked off into the night, as if studying something that wasn't really there. It was a nice look.

"No. That was the last time. Sometimes they would walk out through the alley instead of the front. He might've gone out that way while I was on stage."

"They wouldn't kill him there. Big Pete's got dozens of hideouts all over the city. He could've easily taken him to any one of those places, had him killed then shipped his carcass to me."

I felt like a dog chasing its own tail. The kid's murder had gone from a dime to a dollar faster than a brush fire. Along the way I managed to not only endanger my own life but Holly's as well. She couldn't go back to her apartment, her job, or her life. The fears she realized began seeping into my subconscious like a slow snow drift. I needed time to think. I couldn't take Holly back to her place or mine; both would be watched. I couldn't risk going back to my office either. Taking her to Pete was out of the question. I had already risked two lives; I wasn't about to add Pete's family to that list as well. There was only one place left: Mahoney's.

"We need to get off the road and out of sight. If we follow the side roads we should be able to make it to Mahoney's without any tails. He's got a basement entrance that not too many people know about. It worked great during prohibition, but now it's just a storage entrance. He's got an apartment above his bar that he uses once in a while when he's too beat to go home. We can hide out there for a few hours."

"How do you know he's not being watched too? They probably already know everyone you pal around with."

She was right. I didn't know. I was just too tired to care. I couldn't stay on the road forever. "We don't have a choice. I need time to figure things out and I can't do that while I'm trying to duck cars, bullets and thugs with nasty tempers. After what I said at Bartlett's place you can bet he's already passed word to Big Pete."

She didn't say any more. She knew I was right. None of it felt any better since the timeline that had become our lives had shortened considerably leaving us with nothing more than a slim chance at survival. It was a reality neither of us wanted to face.

The next few minutes passed in silence, interrupted only by the steady passing of air. I surreptitiously glanced across at Holly as she sat in the passenger's side. She was a swell dish; a blind mug could see her beauty. She appeared to be gazing into an austere darkness that defined our situation better than words ever could. I didn't blame her for being angry. I was angry too. However, I didn't have the luxury of falling back onto someone else's emotions. She could sit happily by and dish out all her fears onto my shoulders and then shut her yap. I couldn't just look toward someone else. There was no one else. There was just me. Blame for the situation lay with me, but the situation had rapidly developed beyond my control. Too many shadows suddenly hung over the dead body of Joseph Baker.

"You believe her, don't you?"

I thought about my answer for a few seconds. "Should I?"

"You think I'm the one that's lying. That's why you didn't press her when she said Alfred got Joe the job at the club."

"This is starting to feel like a marriage," I grumbled.

"Don't flatter yourself, buster," Holly objected. I couldn't tell if she was angry or merely surprised by my assessment of the situation, but somewhere between lay the hint of a smile.

"How about giving me some credit? I may be dressed like an East side schmuck, but I do know a thing or two about reading people. She rehearsed that whole speech. Did you notice the way she kept looking down and away when she talked?"

She looked over at me belligerently, "Yeah. So?"

"She was trying real hard to remember her story, like a lousy actress trying to deliver lines from a play that isn't worth the price of admission; body language, sweetheart, body language. Plus, according to the kid's old lady, the dame was not only over there, but was inside her apartment. Connie said she'd never been inside, so how did she know about light bulbs that didn't work?"

"Lot's of light bulbs in old buildings go on the fritz. That's why they call them old," Holly noted.

"Maybe, but the bulb in front the kid's apartment wasn't working. That's too much of a coincidence for me. She's been there all right. There are dozens of reasons to forget and right now she only needs one: murder."

"But wouldn't she know that just being at someone's home isn't an automatic indictment for murder?"

"One witness to her being there is dead. If Schwarz is missing or dead, then it comes down to her word against Baker's old lady. And right now, Connie Bartlett has got the upper hand in that department as well. If she says she wasn't there, no one is going to try and disprove it. If I can find Schwarz, if he's alive, maybe he can tell me what really happened."

"He tries to be a real smooth fella', but he's hiding something more than just his address. Connie got the picture right, but she painted the wrong guy's face on it. Schwarz was the secretive one, not Joseph," Holly said.

Joseph and Albert were two sides of the same coin. Albert came across as the guy looking for a way out of the life he had inherited. Joseph seemed the kid just trying to make end's meat for a mother who took care of him when no one else would. In between both young men was a truth harder to find than an honest buck in a politician's office. Maybe it was never meant to be found.

The rest of the road leading to Mahoney's was filled with snake-like twists and turns. I decided to take the long way around, turning into side streets and through alleyways I had never seen before. Holly kept her head on a swivel, continually peering back to make sure we weren't being followed, simultaneously throwing questioning glances in my direction, wondering if I knew what I was doing and where I was going. I had a slim idea.

The last few blocks would normally have taken no more than two or three minutes. Unfortunately, with Big Pete's boys combing the streets the trip took ten. We parked the car a few blocks away and walked, quietly. I was nervous and more than just a little scared. I didn't want to show it, but my nerves were bouncing up and down like a cat on a trampoline. My eyes twitched uncontrollably like a runaway piston and I breathed in shorter bursts the closer I got to Mahoney's and whatever was waiting there.

I tried looking for anything out of the ordinary. Usually the same cars and the same mugs and broads walked through this part of town. Any outsiders would stick out worse than a mortician at a garden party. Locals could tell outsiders from the way they walked and the way they talked. Sure it was all New York, but mostly it wasn't.

I looked down the street toward two suspicious cars parked a few blocks south. They silently huddled against the curb in a stifling darkness that hung low against the adjacent buildings. The night sky had clouded over long ago crafting a muddled contrast between the jagged exteriors of the buildings and the darkness emanating from within. I stopped and motioned for Holly to retreat into a nearby corner.

I skirted the edge of one building until I was only a few yards from Mahoney's building and the alley that defined its boundaries. It was dark, like most alleyways, and on both sides stood barrels, boxes, trashcans and the occasional cat wondering what we were doing there before bounding off in search of more desirable prey. Small rivulets of fog ascended from the ground, like miniature clouds, looking for somewhere to go.

We continued on, slowly, approaching the corner of the alley cautiously. It broke sharply to the left and toward a second intersecting alley. Meager light from surrounding buildings, beyond the twisted fence, provided some permanence to the path ahead. Holly followed behind, her heels clicking noisily against the damp concrete. I reached into my holster and pulled out my .38.

The alleyway shouldn't have taken more than ten seconds to cross, but in that moment, the space between Mahoney's and the secret entrance looked and felt like a minefield; each step was taken with extreme caution. Every second could have been the prelude to a new calamity. As it was, we made it without being discovered.

I approached the corner and looked to where the entrance should have been. The alley was dark, but not dark enough to hide any goons. From where I stood I could observe the entrance. They were still there. Two wooden doors, parallel to the ground, were currently concealed under a large, rusty trash bin. I looked back at Holly, her face partially hidden by the darkness. Her eyes were a blaze of bright hazel. Her hair was awash in darkness, but the satiny smoothness was still apparent, even here.

"The door is over there, under the garbage bin. I'll walk over and push it. You'll need to hold the gun and be the look out. Hopefully, a few passing cars or something can cover the racket," I said.

Her soft, glowing features were highlighted by a steadily growing concern. "How long will it take? If they're here and they hear the noise, we're done for."

"We don't have a choice. We've got to take that chance. I could probably walk through the front door, but not with you in hand. It's better if they don't see either of us." I handed her the gun then slid across the alley until I was plastered against the opposite wall. It felt like a wet sponge against my back. I could smell rat droppings, stale beer and a mixture of other scents. I wanted to throw up, but the tension of the moment kept it all down.

The bin wasn't fixed to anything and would be easy to move. I looked back at Holly, her figure barely visible against the mixture of light and darkness. It was now or never. The first push did nothing but rattle my bones. I suddenly felt like a kid trying to play up to a hot dame with a pile of dead flowers. I thought about the angriest moment in my life and pushed again. This time the thing moved, but only a few stubborn inches. I pushed once more, each conceded foot sounding like nails on a chalkboard. I kept thinking any moment Big Pete's boys would race around the corner with guns in their hands and murder in their eyes.

A few tense seconds past during which I swore, spit, and cursed for everything it was worth. Finally, I felt my foot brush against one of the handles that was fixed to the doors. All I needed was to budge the bin far enough to open one door. I gritted my teeth, shut my eyes and pushed with everything I had left. Rusty, gritty wheels budged obstinately against dirty, cracked concrete until the entire surface of the door was exposed.

I slumped against the bin gasping for air like a fish out of water. I had little else to give. I managed to muster enough strength to look over at Holly. She kept close to the wall, watching me while also keeping one eye out for unwanted trouble. Her silhouette resembled a shimmering echo, glistening in smooth twists and turns like a clear, moonlit sky. From this distance her frame was solid, unmoving, like a stone statue baring its teeth against the worst of elements. I suddenly hated myself for my weakness. I beat the side of the bin with my elbow. A vicious pain traveled swiftly up and down my arm. It felt like someone had decided to use it as a skipping rope.

Holly stared at me, the dim indication of a gun glimmering in her hand. I kicked gently at the door handle. My foot brushed over the handle and the lock that hung there. The pain in my arm slowed to a dull throb. I motioned Holly to come forward. I crouched low and examined the door and the door lock. It was an old lock that had, through the ravages of time, rusted so completely as to resemble a glob of hardened dirt. The door itself was a sturdy thick piece of oak that had aged well.

The scent of roses wafted over me. I looked to see Holly crouching by my side. "Can you get the lock open?"

"Give me the gun," I whispered. It was a strange thing to do, especially considering the racket I had just made, but I did it anyway. I don't know why.

She handed me the gun. With the safety on, I held the barrel and used the grip to give the latch one swift smack. It broke off as easily as snow falling from the branch of a tree. I pulled the door open before peering into a striking darkness. I could sense Holly's ever increasing fear. An even stronger fear raced through my own heart. As Holly and I stumbled down the stairs and into Mahoney's dark cellar, I wondered if it wasn't too late to recite some prayers.

CHAPTER 11

We managed to cut through the brooding darkness, up rickety stairs that reminded me of a skeleton dancing a jig, past a couple of rummies singing some old pirate song and through a dingy hallway that resembled a funeral parlor. We were both tired. It had been a long day, and one that neither of us had seen coming.

Chaotic lights threw hasty glimpses toward empty sections of wet pavement. People ambled past; however, few looked like they were gunning for anything more than a nightcap. I pulled the shade down and turned to Holly. She stood off to one side, her eyes washing over the room like a lighthouse searching the sea. The scant light that filled the space did little justice to her features. Her hair gleamed like stars splashed against the night sky and her eyes were diamonds gleaming in the afternoon sunshine. Still, she was all done in. She looked caught between the past and the future, between the moment that had passed and the moment that was rapidly descending upon her.

"Why don't you get some rest? The bedroom and bathroom is through there," I said, pointing down the hallway, "I'll sleep in here. I'll call Mahoney in a minute and let him know what's going on."

"What am I supposed to do? What am I supposed to wear? I left my bag in your car." She sounded dejected, as if her whole life had been one big lie and she was the last one to find out.

I could've walked over, held her, assured her things would get better. Instead, I scoped out the joint, ensuring that we were its only occupants. We were. Returning to the living room found Holly still standing in the center of the room, a glut of emotions defining her elegant features.

"Listen, I'm sorry about everything. If I could have done this without making your life a nightmare I would have. Unfortunately, I've never been very good at staying out of trouble." I looked at the clock decorating an otherwise barren wall. The numbers jumped out at me. "I didn't expect a lot of things, but then I've never been confused for a swami. We're both in a jam right up to our eyeballs. The only thing that can get us out of it is the truth. Out there…" I said, pointing toward the window "is that truth, and one way or another I'm going to find it."

She said nothing. She angled toward the sofa, sat down, and began to cry. Each tear was like a knife stabbing me in the heart. She couldn't take anymore and neither could I. I had only been on the run for a few hours, but in those few hours I had seen Holly live her whole life. Each emotion she felt increased in intensity. Suddenly, nothing was simple and easy anymore.

I sat next to her. I took my hat off and placed it on the table in front of me. I didn't know if I was doing the right thing or not. I'd seen dames cry before and said nothing, did nothing. This time, things were different. Hearing her cry, watching her cry, was like watching my own past come alive.

I reached out and gently pulled her into my arms, slowly turning her until she was facing me. Her makeup had run, just a little, but her eyes still had that radiant glow of starlight. She could've fought me, rejected my shows of empathy. Instead, she accepted my embrace.

"Listen to me, baby. You're not alone. I'm not about to let Big Pete get his mitts on you. I've been around mugs like this all my life. They're strong in numbers, but get them on their own and they fold like deckchairs. I guarantee you we'll make it through this, as long as we stick together, and as long as you can keep it together. Besides, I know a few ears I can still bend, and maybe one of them can give me that one thing that could blow this case wide open."

Her tears gradually subsided until they resembled deep pools of sunlight against the quickly disappearing room. Her beauty made me shiver. She looked weak, almost ready to give up. I didn't want to accept it because accepting it would mean not only letting Holly down, but letting myself down as well. I placed my life on the line for a lot of reasons and wasn't about to let a no-good thug like Big Pete take me down, no matter the odds. I needed Holly to understand. Was it my ego talking? Maybe, but then I didn't have to time to care about little things like that. I had a murderer to catch.

"I don't know if I can do this," Holly cried. Each word came out in short, muffled spurts, emphasized briefly by tears and sniffles. I held on to her arms, afraid to let go.

"Listen, doll, I'm close and Big Pete knows it. He's trying to scare me off. First he tries with Fats Kelly, then with Brutus. That mug wasn't waiting around your place for the view. Somehow they knew I would show up. He didn't need me to be there to pay you a visit so why did he wait?" I kept talking, if not for her sake then at least for mine. "And why hasn't anyone seen this Schwarz? Detective Miller told me they were watching his place. That means he hasn't shown up there yet. Why not? The only reason is there was something going on between Schwarz and the kid. Maybe it was big, maybe it was small; either way, it was big enough to get Baker killed and Schwarz noticed by more than just his tailor. Fact is, whatever it was, Big Pete found out. And if the big guy found out about it he wouldn't waste time fitting either for concrete shoes. When old man Bartlett came back into the room he had the kind of look on his face only jailbirds on death row get. He talked to someone, maybe Big Pete. If you're right, Bartlett and the big guy were partners in some kind of crazy scheme. And now with a couple of murders Bartlett's getting cold feet. Somewhere in the middle of all this is Connie Bartlett. She knows something and it's important enough for her to try and throw us a story so bad only a judge could believe it." Holly's tears had almost ceased. She fixed me with a curious glance, like a mathematician studying an algebra problem. I wanted to kiss her, but didn't.

"That dame is no fool. She knows exactly what she's doing," she said between sniffles. "She had both those kids dancing around her like some sort of Christmas Eve ballet recital. They'd cut their arms off if she asked them to. I don't think there is much they wouldn't have done for her."

"That dame's got the same killer instinct as her old man. She put those two up to something."

"That's what I think," Holly replied.

"The three of them were playing ring-around-the-rosie, but what I can't figure is who was leading. I find it hard to believe, as smart as she is, that she would be at the head of this ship of fools."

"You think there's someone else?"

"There's always someone else. The question is: who is it?"

"Big Pete?"

"That's the logical answer, but I'm not one for logic. It could have been Fats Kelly. That might be the reason why he was bumped off. He wouldn't wind up that way because he was playing by the rules."

The relationship that stretched before me resembled a strange configuration of crossed paths and inter-lacing nightmares. Joseph Baker stood on one side of the configuration. Albert Schwarz and Connie Bartlett stood on the furthest edges; in the middle stood a fourth. That person watched my every move, standing ahead of me at every twist and turn, laughing like a clown at a circus. I grimaced.

Holly was calm now. Looking at her was like staring into the center of a tornado-the eye of the storm-and into the heart of a dame both fire and ice. I could feel the fire spreading until it reached out with its fiery digits and encircled my throat. I was already angry at being the patsy for bums that hadn't lived an honest day their whole lives; I was already angry for letting their diseased excuse for a life ruin those trying to be something more, something better. I wanted to wipe Big Pete and all the other Big Pete's off the face of the Earth.

I caught a glimpse of Holly reaching into her purse. She pulled out a handkerchief and dabbed gently at her eyes. I waited until she was finished before I started my act. "We both need some rest. You need to sleep and I need to think. You take the bedroom and I'll take the chair. Mahoney keeps this place pretty clean. In the morning we can grab some breakfast, then try and find Schwarz."

"What if we can't find him?"

The Trigger Method

"I know some people that make it their business to know where other people are. They can usually come up with something within a few hours. I also want to do some checking on old man Bartlett. Those two are up to something they probably won't declare on their taxes. If I stir the pot enough, maybe the real dirt will rise to the surface."

Her looks softened for a moment, the hard edges gone, replaced by an ease that looked as beautiful as the surface of a placid lake. It was like looking at a new, shiny dime with all the raw edges polished out. She seemed to glisten again, as if suddenly remembering that she had temporarily been given the job of being the sun.

"I suppose I could use some rest. I don't like the idea of having to wear the same outfit two days in a row, but I guess I don't have a choice, do I?"

"It ain't the ritz, baby, but it's real."

Her laughter echoed through the room like the perfect song. She excused herself and went into the bedroom. I got up and looked around after Holly shut the bedroom door. I was sorry for what I was seeing and for what Holly was living. It was a bad piece of beef that kept trying to come back up no matter how many times you swallowed.

I looked for some paper. In the corner of the apartment was a small nook that doubled as a kitchen. I went through the drawers until I found an old flyer for a circus act from Coney. I smiled for a second before turning it over and pulling out my pen. I wrote a few words. I could see Holly's anger spilling out from the apartment and into the streets. I cringed, but continued writing. When I was done I folded the paper and wrote Holly's name on it. I walked over to the table and left it standing upright.

I couldn't tell if she was awake or not, but ten bucks told me she was probably lights out the second she hit the bed. I couldn't blame her. Most of me felt like doing the same thing, but there was a murder to solve and a life to save besides Holly's: mine.

A few minutes ticked silently off the clock. I wanted to be sure Holly was asleep before I made my next move. An ear to the door and a silent backlash told me my escape route was safe from discovery. I left, silently closing the door as I went. I retraced my route down into the cellar and out into the alley.

I pushed Holly out of my mind and concentrated on the car parked along the street. I wasn't about to say anything to Holly since she was scared enough as it was. My mind worked feverishly on the next few moments and how to survive them.

I walked out onto the sidewalk and casually glanced over my shoulder. Parked a few cars down and to the left was a gray Packard with one shadow sitting behind the wheel. Earlier, my first glimpse had chased him into the passenger side like a kid whose favorite marble had just rolled under the seat.

Now, he sat calmly, his shadowy figure barely visible behind the darkness-soaked automobile. I stuck close to the wall of the building; the immense blackness shielded me from the street. I didn't know if Big Pete had left just one mug or if another was waiting somewhere on the other side of the building.

I looked up one more time, toward Holly, before retracing my footsteps back through the alley. As long as the guy in the car didn't see me, there was no reason for him to go investigating.

A minute later, and a few stray headlights later, I was in my jalopy. It was time to go searching for a killer.

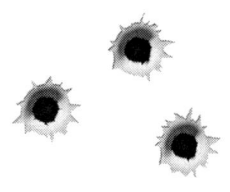

CHAPTER 12

Looking at the Pheasant Lounge now was like looking into the heart of a hangover. The darkness beyond paled in comparison to the mysteries that lay within its four walls. The marquee shone like a million fireflies dancing to a Bing Crosby tune, and the shiny silverware that strolled through the gleaming doors reminded me of a funeral procession. The same deadbeat kept the door company while those walking past noticed him like they noticed a stain on the ground. Small oval windows, like giant bullet holes, faced the street.

I hunkered behind the wheel and waited for the inevitable. From my vantage point I could see the alleyway as well as the entrance. It remained cloaked in darkness. I reached inside my pocket and lit a cigarette, the heat filtering through my body like a warm glass of beer. It didn't taste good, but it kept me from turning into an icicle. Outside the car, the temperature was drifting somewhere between cold and frigid. Inside, I felt like an icebox.

In the sanctity of those moments I let my brain work over the facts as they presented themselves. For one thing, I couldn't quite figure out Connie's connection to everything. She was involved somehow, but how? Then there was Schwarz-the man without a face. I found myself wondering whether the stiff existed at all. All I had was a name and the vague outline of a personality. He worked for Big Pete, but so did a host of other shady mugs and skirts, Holly notwithstanding. I also couldn't forget about my date on the phone. So far, all his information turned out to be on the level. He knew the players and their histories too well to be some low-level gangster wannabe. He had to be a mug on the inside.

If the big guy was having employee problems, then the next logical question was why? Someone had taken down Fats Kelly like he was nothing, and that big lug was far from nothing. Next to him was Alfred Schwarz. He was either an innocent kid or a punk with a rep to sell. His disappearance meant someone somewhere was scared.

The weight of it all pushed my shoulders somewhere down near my waist. I sunk deep into the driver's seat simultaneously blowing a large trail of smoke up to the ceiling of the car. I watched it mingle with the coarse fabric before dissipating. The facts that made up the kid's murder seemed to dissipate just as easily.

I closed my eyes for a second to think. Those were the most peaceful moments I had experienced over the last week, and the last ones for the next twenty-four hours.

As if on cue, the passenger door opened violently. Before I could reach for my rod, the goon was inside and shoving a gun, like a sharp knife, into my guts. The thing you got to understand about the private detective game is that one mistake, just one, can get you bumped off faster than a bad ham sandwich. Most shamus's only make that mistake once. I had made it on more than one occasion. I was still here, but I could probably count my remaining lives on one finger. I had been counting on Big Pete posting my picture on the current events bulletin board at the local gangster's union hall, and I was also hoping one of Big Pete's boys would join me, but I also hoped I wasn't making the biggest mistake of my life. To get at the truth would mean walking into the lion's den. I glanced at the mug casually.

"Hiya, shamus. Why don't you and I take a little ride?" He growled. A building had nothing on this guy. His frame filled the entire passenger side, and although the suit fit the mug perfectly, he looked like a guy more comfortable wearing prison pinstripes decorated in blood. His smile seemed stolen from a hangman and he blinked about as often as a statue. I had expected most of Big Pete's goons to know me, but it didn't make me feel any better about the situation.

"This ain't no taxi, bud. You want a free ride, call a cop." I studied him carefully as I spoke. He moved slowly, his baseball glove hands

The Trigger Method

maintaining a firm grasp of his rod and the situation. He had the upper hand and he knew it. All I could do was sit idly by and hope I was doing the right thing.

"You're real funny, shamus. The fishes are gonna love your jokes." A ghoulish grin spread across his mug as if he had just one the right to smack a piñata. His voice was deep, like he was speaking from twenty fathoms down, and the lack of cadence emphasized each word and its meaning to my future, such as it was.

I thought about Holly alone at Mahoney's apartment and how I needed to get back to her. In my mind I could see images, like snapshots, from a horror movie. I wanted to close my eyes, shut out the blackness. Instead, I focused on my guest.

"You think you're just going to shoot me here, right in the middle of all these people and get away with it."

"It's been done," he grinned. "Still, spilling your guts here wouldn't make the joint look too good, so what say we take you somewhere's else and teach you some manners."

"Let me guess. You forgot to pay your mobster dues for this month so they stuck you outside with the rest of the shills."

He didn't like that. Mugs like this always overdressed and overplayed the part. The Jimmy Cagney world only existed in movies, and even then it never worked out. Nevertheless, he had the drop on me, and a heater pointed at my ribs meaning that one shot and I'd be all over the Pheasant Lounge marquee. Nevertheless, I still didn't feel frightened. Something about the scene felt wrong.

"The best thing for you to do is keep your hands on the wheel, right where I can see them. Try anything, shamus, and I'll pump you full of lead."

"You're making me tired, fella. Just get to the point."

"Start driving."

I started the car and slowly pulled away from the curb, slicing carefully through traffic like a granny on a horse and buggy. I could've taken the mug right there, but I needed information. If this guy was as stupid as he was ugly I might get some important pieces to the puzzle.

"You're making a lot of people real mad, shamus. Big Pete tried to be nice, but you wouldn't listen. As for the screwy dame, we'll find her eventually. Nobody hides from Big Pete for long."

"Is this the same speech you gave Fats Kelly?"

"Naw. He was never good at listening," the mug replied sardonically. "He had a big neck that ain't so big no more," he laughed.

Score one for me. Big Pete did take out the fat guy; at least according to this mug. The more important question now was why?

"Only a gee with a yellow streak a mile long would rub out a mug from behind." It was a stab in the dark. I wasn't sure exactly how Kelly was killed, but if you don't take a few risks in this game, there's no reason to start playing to begin with.

"I ain't yellow. Things happen for a reason, shamus. The sooner you realize that, the sooner you and I can be friends," he smiled. The whites of his teeth resembled sharp fence posts. I looked away.

"You mean the kind of reason that takes the life of innocent, young kids? One wasn't enough so you had to take out two?" A thousand other questions milled around in my head, but for some reason I asked that one instead.

"You talking about that snot-nosed Joe? From what I hear, that guy got what was coming to him. A few bullets for breakfast never hurt nobody that didn't deserve it. He disrespected everyone around him. He gets a good job and decides that ain't good enough. He gets jobs out of town, but that ain't good enough neither. He wants more dough and the dames that come along with it. There ain't no point trying to earn respect as far as he's concerned. Taking his lousy carcass out would have been a pleasure. I wish I was the one on that job."

I wanted to lean over, grab that fat skull of his and open it like a coconut. I would make sure before this night was over this mug experienced what real pain was all about. I gritted my teeth and listened to him cluck some more.

"The other kid was all right. He never said nothing to nobody. He worked hard and kept to his own business. He could've taken a yard, but Kelly kept saying that he wasn't ready. Kelly never trusted nobody that was scared of carrying a gat. I couldn't really blame the kid. Them gats they was carrying were no toys. It really is a crying shame about him, but when you start playing games with the big boys, you better be ready if you lose. Whoever rubbed him out must have had ice in his veins." An eerie look crossed his face. I suddenly wondered if Schwarz was findable anymore. Speaking about someone in the past tense is always a reliable way of determining whether they are above ground or below it. It seemed any interrogation of Schwarz might have to be performed by undertaker. I gritted my teeth some more. "Dames really went for that mug."

"Connie Bartlett?" I asked.

"It won't hurt for you to know since you ain't gonna know it for long anyway. Yeah, that dame was nuts for the kid; followed him everywhere. She laughed more with him than the other one. With that Joe, it was all business. Nobody liked that sorry punk."

The tip of his gun kept a constant vigil in my side, its presence achingly obvious from the dull throb quickly working its way from my side to my head. I kept driving. Around me, traffic dwindled. I steadied my temper before asking: "Why take out Fats? Did he eat Big Pete's favorite desert, or something?"

The mug laughed, but only for a few seconds. "You ask more questions than a judge, shamus. You should try going on a diet; it's better for you. Turn right." I slowed down and took a right down a lonely street. It looked like a million other streets. I kept driving.

"You mean to tell me that fat lug took Kelly out because he had a big mouth? I thought the big guy appreciated big things, especially with that skull of his."

The mug laughed some more. It was a strange laugh. In fact, it was more like a painful sneeze than a laugh. I don't think he did it very often.

"You sure are something, shamus. It's a shame you ain't going to sing after tonight, though. I would have enjoyed having a drink with you."

"Thanks. Too bad I can't return the compliment."

"That's okay, shamus. You ain't going to be returning much after this night is over."

"That's a tired line, mug. You should try saying something new. It might get you noticed in the sucker's union." He jammed the gat tighter into my ribs. I could feel the muzzle worm its way into my guts, like a dog trying to get inside a doghouse that's two sizes too small for him. It didn't hurt, but I don't think that was his intention. He was reminding me he was there out of more than just social curiosity. I slowed the car. He didn't seem to notice. He continued spitting out threats I had heard a million times before. I listened patiently.

"You and that fancy dame ain't going to be living long so there ain't no reason to not tell you. Kelly was a sucker right from the start. Big Pete gives him a few inches, but he decides he wants a bigger piece of the pie. The problem: he tries taking a piece from Big Pete's pie. Nothing happens without Big Pete not knowing about it. Not here. Next thing Kelly sees is his tongue hanging out of his mouth like a lovesick puppy. Those two were in cahoots. Big Pete knew about the whole thing and showed them the exits, if you know what I mean," he winked, adding "A few bullets were all that kid probably needed." He glanced in my direction, black eyes so dark they looked like a miniature night sky. There was murder in those eyes.

I've seen death and spit in its face more than a few times. I know one day I'll take a bullet the way a mug's supposed to take a bullet, but tonight wasn't one of those nights. I wasn't ready to go out. Not that way. Plus, something the mug spit out between useless threats interested me.

His rod caressed my ribs like a vulture picking at a dead body. Had I looked over, I would have seen the blackest eyes matched to the blackest heart. He seemed single-minded in purpose and demeanor, as if nothing else existed except my soon-to-be-over life. If I was smart, and that was sometimes debatable, I might be able to use that to my advantage.

I kept my hands on the wheel. Ahead of me, the road split into three directions. I knew this area well. It was the kind of place people avoided at night. In these parts, the darkness was filled with hands more apt to kill than to shake. The cops hated this area because of the paperwork it created. Most mobsters liked these deserted spots because it made disposing of corpses that much easier. And they didn't have worry about nosy private eyes or honest cops looking to make a name for themselves. There seemed fewer of those these days.

"Turn up here, shamus," the gunsel grinned. I discerned a thin film of perverse amusement in his voice. He sounded ecstatic, like a bride on her wedding day. Only this guy was no dame, and he didn't seem to care too much about beginnings.

I shook the image from my mind and decided enough was enough. I got something out of him, and something was better than nothing. I turned my attention back to the road. I gripped the wheel tight. I was only a few feet from the turn when I jammed the accelerator to the floor. I turned the wheel sharply to the left with both hands and hoped for the best. The move caught the mug by surprise. I felt the tip of the gun clumsily slide away from my side. It moved only half a foot or so, but it was enough. With my right hand I grabbed his left and pushed it forward, toward the windshield. His finger still controlled the trigger. A loud smack, like a dead body hitting water, reverberated through the compartment. I closed my eyes just as the windshield showered over me. My entire body went hot, like a freshly baked cake. The whole thing seemed stupid, like a reckless stunt by a kid. I didn't need to be here arm wrestling for my life with a mug crazier than a shrink in a nuthouse. I should have been at Mahoney's apartment, watching over Holly. Instead, I was here, on this dirty street, with some mug that looked as ugly as day-old bread.

The car shimmied crazily from one side of the street to the other. Meanwhile, I tried to valiantly gain control of his left hand while he tried madly to grab me with his right. He couldn't decide what to grab: my coat, my throat or my face. He screamed words at me that sounded like nails on a chalkboard, but I kept fighting. I was sweating now, not sure whether I was alive or dead, or even whether any of this was real. Beyond my shattered windshield New York billowed like a curtain in a winter storm.

I could just make out the road ahead in between fists bouncing across my skull and tiny flakes of windshield carving love letters into my face. I could even see the grey and black of passing buildings, their windows and doors blacked out or locked up. I would find no help here. I was my on my own. I tried leaning into him, using the driver door as leverage to push him away, to gain some control over the gat, his fist; anything, but each wild turn of the wheel pushed me further away like a dingy caught in a wild storm. My palms were sweaty now, the wheel that much harder to control. I was one bad turn from being a new addition to a warehouse or dank office complex. I forgot the wheel, forgot the slick feel of my hands and forgot my life could be seconds away from dust. A gun shooting blindly in a confined space can make a guy forget a lot of things if he tries hard enough. All you do remember is how not to die. I was remembering real hard, hoping against a hope thinner than the souls of my shoes. If I didn't do something now I was a goner.

The pavement my car skidded along seemed to stretch on into eternity. I could have been driving down it for five seconds or five years, it seemed to make no difference. Each bump and thud felt like an old friend missing since forever. I could barely hear myself think above the screeching of the tires or the rhythmic spasm of the engine.

To my right, the mug continued his physical barrage, connecting more than a few times, causing my vision to blur worse than a mix of rum and tequila. He swung his gat frantically, like some psychotic ball player in the on-deck circle. Every bit of me wanted to shove him inside the glove box, but I also had to take him out without getting myself killed in the process. Suddenly, two more shots, like cannon blasts, roared from his gun. My ears liquefied like mud during an earthquake, and my eyes watered like white caps on a storm infested sea.

I was fighting against hands that belonged to the strongest guy on earth. Everything I did seemed in vain. He fought through my weak defenses like a man used to having his way. With one hand tenuously gripped to the wheel I couldn't hope to survive. Finally, with all my energy and strength near exhaustion, the goon managed to get one large hand around my neck. He squeezed real hard. My eyes bulged until I thought they would pop out of my head like marbles flicked across concrete. I was a fish out of water, gasping for air with a crazy man's mitts on my throat. I strained against the impending darkness, attempting to shake loose his hand, but everything I did was as guaranteed as even money on a sucker bet. And right now, I was the sucker.

I reached into myself and retrieved what scant reserves remained, hoping my mind would clear enough for me to see something, do something, before it was too late. A brief splash of light illuminated a brittle-looking brick wall to my right. It disappeared for a second before coming back into view. It was the only chance I had. I was running on fumes, hoping it would be enough for one last push. I let go and with both unsteady hands on the wheel drove toward the wall.

Hitting it was like falling in love. It came hard and fast.

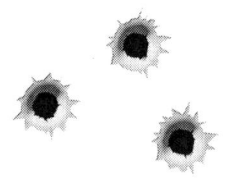

CHAPTER 13

Stars; I saw stars. They resembled small insects buzzing incessantly around me in a kind of crazy square dance meant for lunatics, nuts, and lame-brained private detectives with too much guts and not enough sense. I tried to reach into the hovering darkness and swat away those insects, but they eluded my reach, each time laughing from a new position of superiority. I thought about my gun and the good it could do me. I wanted to reach for it, but countless invisible hands kept it always just out of reach. The hands kept me from a lot of things. They seemed to enjoy covering me in darkness.

I could just make out Holly in the same gloom. I could make out her outline of white against a cluster of towering, black trees. I shut my eyes and then opened them again, only this time the vision changed. A man, all dressed in black and galloping like a thousand horses chased Holly through those trees. He seemed so close. Her hair glistened as light from a half-moon hanging precariously from the night sky fell across her hair and face. A tear, like a drop of rain, fell from her cheek but didn't hit the ground. Instead, it seemed to hang in the air, unsure of what to do. In the end, like everything else, it fell to the ground where it was greeted by a thunderous silence.

I tried moving again. This time, my body shrieked in protest. I looked up at Holly, but she was gone. She had been replaced entirely by the man in black. He stared coldly back at me. I returned his stare. I was daring the mug to hurt her.

"Try it fella," I screamed hoarsely.

He simply looked away; his smile disappeared into the night. I wanted to get up and do something, but the world just laughed at me. I could see Holly again, but she was slowly disappearing into nothingness, like a mirage that was never meant to be. I reached again for her. This time I thought I had her, but my fingers slipped through the trailing edge of her white gown. Behind her, the man in black continued his evil pursuit. I needed to move, fast, before he got his evil mitts on her. I pushed against everything, but every bone in my body ignored me, choosing instead to go for a drink. I was left to my private hell.

Every few seconds, the moon that was supposed to be above me would drift away to the left before coming back into view. My attempts to see Holly were foiled by shoddy lighting. I cursed again.

"I'm sorry, baby," I muttered. I wanted to cry like a kid who'd just lost his favorite toy, but something inside wouldn't let me. It kept pulling me away from the darkness, away from the emptiness and into the dim light that swung lazily above. All I could think about was Holly and the man in black, his ragged grin stretched across a face that possessed as much appeal as road-kill. I hated death.

A loud noise jolted me awake. My eyes greeted a mangled mess that bordered on the insane. A large, gaping hole stood where the front of the car used to be, and much of the passenger section was covered in brick and blood; most of it belonging to the now-deceased gunsel. I had managed to steer the car into the wall even with him pummeling me like a pillow. I patted myself on the back.

I tried moving, but a sudden pain danced an Irish jig over my carcass. If there was pain, then I was still alive; that meant someone somewhere was going to pay for this, and it wasn't going to be the insurance guy.

I surveyed the damage inside the car. The smell was worse than Mahoney after a thirty-six hour shift at his bar. I didn't need to look at the mug to know he wasn't joining me for a drink. Thanks to my fancy driving he had received the worst of the collision, with the wall a close second. I looked down to make sure my body parts were still where they needed to be. They were.

I don't know how long I had been out, but I could see a touch of gray slash across the horizon like a shoddy brushstroke. Daylight was not far behind. I tried moving again; more pain followed. I glanced out my shattered window. The streets were still deserted. I had to get out of the car, out of the area and back to Holly. She was alone at the apartment with Big Pete's boys sitting outside just itching for a chance to take her and me out. I had risked a lot to get the information I got. It wasn't much, but it was something. The way I saw it, the bruises and cuts were a small price to pay for the truth, especially when compared to the price Baker had paid.

I quickly looked around. The front part of the car resembled crumpled newspaper. The dash had been violently pressed into the passenger compartment until it hung precariously over my legs. Thanks to the mug's stray bullets, most of the windshield had cracked and split apart, especially on his side. Part of the glass on my side had peeled away from the frame like a dog-eared page from a book waiting to be turned.

Both my arms had come out of my little joyride unscathed. They hurt, and would hurt for a few days; however, they were still in one piece. My door was a different story. The impact had buckled the joints, causing the entire frame to push in like a beer can. With the glass hanging over me, and the door shut, there was only one other avenue of escape: over the dead mug.

The stench was unbearable. Portions of the brick wall had flown through the front and the driver's window and struck him dead center. Long slivers of sharp glass carved forget-me-nots into the base of his skull and neck leaving the guy looking like a Halloween pumpkin carved by a kid.

I looked through and beyond the front windshield. Parts of the wall lived in what was left of the passenger side and the hood. Streetlights washed down in pale, round arcs illuminating spaces between things. In the car, everything was dark.

I had a few inches leeway between my legs and the dash. Using what little space existed I heaved my body up and over, being careful not to mess up my unwanted guest. My bones creaked and hollered in protest, each inch and foot feeling like knife against flesh. With both hands, I cleared a few stray bricks from the opening. The pain had reached a point where it became meaningless. It helped me focus enough to crawl, on my belly, off the hood onto the pavement. In the solitude of that moment, the pain gained momentum over my conscious mind. I saw stars again.

I wanted to fall asleep to the sounds of Gene Krupa or Count Basie. I could hear the music bouncing off the walls inside my head. The notes had a rhythm and energy, like a freight train rumbling on a track. As kids, Pete and I would listen outside some of the East side jive joints as the music filtered onto the street. We'd sit there and listen like zombies, sometimes tapping our feet or snapping our fingers to a long trombone or high trumpet as it busted out lines that jumped like grasshoppers under a hot August sun.

I could feel that same warmth worm its way down the side of my mouth, like hot whiskey. I ignored it and the pain in my bones. I got up and stumbled down the gray street, picking up speed with each successive step until the distance between my handy work and I quickly became a distant memory.

All of a sudden, each step became torture. My bones ached with a thousand year old pain and my head felt like a broken champagne bottle. Still, I kept walking, hoping to find a phone before I collapsed. It was going to be a photo finish.

CHAPTER 14

My eyes opened to stars that shone like twinkling lights on a Christmas tree. The brightness of the moment quickly became unbearable. I retreated into the blackness once more. A thick fog twisted and curled through my mind creating emptiness where memories should have been. I couldn't remember where I was or what I had been doing.

I tried sitting up, but something held me down. Unlike the first time, in the car, this was a different feeling. I opened my eyes again, this time to a shimmering cloud of color that moved slowly, but with a definite purpose. The light around me was different, more focused. I could feel something on my head, a coolness that felt like snow. I groaned.

"Easy, me bye, you've had quite a go of it." The accent was unmistakable.

"If I'm dying, Mahoney, why are you the last person I see before I go?"

"Always with them jokes, Dix. One day, them jokes is going ta make you a permanent resident 'o this god's green earth." Mahoney would never be confused with a poet, but he always had a way of making sense, no matter the subject. "What do ya' think, lass? Should we bother tending ta his wounds, or just let him slowly bleed ta death?"

"He looked like the dog's breakfast before, but now he looks like breakfast, lunch and dinner. I say throw him to the fishes." It was the kind of voice a mug could die to.

"I may not be pretty anymore, but I carry a big gun. That's got to count for something."

She laughed. It was smooth as silk and as natural as a summer breeze. My vision hadn't cleared up completely, but I could just make out her eyes and the gentle way her hair formed around her face. If I could move I'd make dreams come true.

"After the stunt you pulled, I ought to use that gun on you. How dare you leave me on my own and just take off without a word. What do you think this is: last stand at the O.K. Corral? If something had happened to you, what would I do?"

There was something in her voice that I hadn't sensed before. It was a new emotion that lingered at the edge and stayed there. I left it alone, for now. "I wasn't too worried about Big Pete. He doesn't want me dead anymore than he wants a hole in his head. Besides, what I needed to do, I needed to do alone, and I couldn't have Big Pete's goons outside following me. If they figured we weren't here, they'd just sit there and wait. If they saw us leave, it would've made things a lot harder. As it was, I managed to get a few interesting little bits of the puzzle." I rubbed my head only to have more pain rumble through it like a delivery truck.

"What do you mean?" Holly asked.

I closed my eyes and said, "I was right. Connie Bartlett and Schwarz had something going on together. Fats Kelly was mixed up in their little triangle too and got a necktie that was two sizes too small for his troubles. For all I know, Schwarz is already a goner." I tried getting up, but the world kept pressing down on me. I don't know how bad I looked, but judging from the way I felt, I probably wouldn't be a beauty pageant winner anytime soon.

"I don't know about that," Holly started, "After you disappeared, I called up a friend from the club. She told me that she saw Schwarz leave the club around nine o'clock with someone that looked like Paul Brutus."

"Maybe he was taking the kid to a funeral," I replied.

"Yeah, his own," She said.

"What time is it?" I asked. I couldn't see the window from where I was and the clock was so out of focus it may as well have been in the North Pole.

"It's almost eight o'clock at night. You've been asleep all day. After you called Mahoney, he found me upstairs, alone, told me what happened and then went looking for you."

"It wasn't so easy getting away from them ruddy buggers, my bye. Holly told me they were waitin' outside so I got a couple of the boys too sloshed to know any better to go over and keep them distracted while I went lookin' for you. They were still waitin' there like a pair of raven's eyes, but I managed to make it into the alley without them thinking anything of it. Dirty Joe and Harry the horse dragged you up to the room and into the tender mercies of this sufferin' lass. I parked down the street and walked right through the front door. They didn't move then and still haven't moved now."

I felt like a heel as I glanced sheepishly at Mahoney. I didn't remember making the phone call. In fact, I couldn't remember much of what happened after the crash, although a few scattered visions slowly crept into my awareness. The image of the dead goon in the front seat stuck out like a shining light, and the car just before it bit into the brick wall. It wouldn't take the cops long to trace the jalopy back to me.

I crumpled deeper into the pillow that supported my sore noggin. "So, if Schwartz left with Brutus last night, why did this mug tell me he thought the kid was dead?" Mahoney walked back in with a small glass of Scotch. I could have kissed the guy had Holly not been around. It seemed like a million years since my last sip. He handed me a cup and after downing it quicker than ducks in a shooting gallery I held it out again. The fog surrounding me had dissipated enough for me to see Holly's unimpressed countenance. "It's for medical purposes, doll." Mahoney glanced sheepishly at Holly for a moment before filling my glass once more. He retreated into the kitchen, returning empty handed.

"You almost die and the first thing you do when you wake up is booze it up like its prohibition. How about thinking up a glass of get-out-of trouble juice or something? You and I could both use one, not to mention the fact if Big Pete's goons are staking out the bar then Mahoney's life is just as much in danger as ours is." She was right. I had some serious thinking and acting to do before all three of us wound up on the same East River fishing pole. Big Pete wouldn't be too impressed with me taking out one of his goons and might, one way or another, want to let me know about it. I tried to chase the gloom away with a little of my trademark witty banter.

"Did anyone ever tell you that you glow when you get angry?" I grinned. Holly blushed immediately, turning away as she rose from the chair. She walked to the fireplace. I pictured a frame surrounding her more desirable frame; she filled it perfectly. Looking at her was like looking at the perfect sunset. Her shoulders sagged slightly, her body quivered.

I could feel the pain rumbling through me like an out-of-control train; still, I managed to awkwardly climb off the couch. I thought I heard the devil laugh as I stood up.

Ignoring the screaming in my head, I shuffled like an old buzzard to Holly and place my hands on her shoulders. She turned around to face me with eyes as deep as an ocean and tears that looked like raindrops against a brilliant sun. Her eyes lowered, as if she were preparing to say grace. She gently wrapped her hands around her torso like a mummy ready for a thousand year sleep and stood silently, the breeze the only sign of life in the room. I gave in to the moment.

"Listen, baby, I'm sorry for what's happened but I couldn't bear to see you hurt. Last night wasn't the smartest move I've ever made. The truth is no one ever confused me with Einstein. If you were there, you might have ended up in the same condition as me, maybe worse. I can take chances with my life, but I can't take chances with yours. These mugs are playing for keeps and their playing with a bigger stack of chips than us." I placed my hands around her waist and pulled her close. She didn't resist. "I promised to get you out of this and I never make promises I can't keep, except maybe to bartenders," I said, looking casually over at Mahoney. "And I'm not about to break a promise to a dame strong enough to take on the whole German army by herself." I placed my hand under her chin and gazed into her eyes. They were dark pits of fire that harbored emotions of violent intensity. I looked into them like a man just before judgment day. She didn't look away. Instead, she fell into my chest like a kid falling into a pile of leaves.

I held her as she cried. She was warm and soft, my arms seeming bigger now than at any other time. Mahoney watched us for a moment before standing up and pacing around the far end of the room. It took a while for him to say anything. He breathed deep, like a man standing at the edge of a bottomless pit. The pit seemed packed with as much raw hatred and anger as any man could possibly feel.

"This be a terrible business. A man gets up every morning and tries his hardest ta live a decent kind o' life. It's not much, but it's all he's got ta cling ta. Now, these no-good buggers that you're dealing with, me bye, are the kind that think only o' death. They think about it the way a mouse thinks about cheese, or a bird thinks about a worm. It be nothing more than a means ta an end for these ruddy buggers. They don't fear death because they be around it all day long. The man who tries ta live a decent life not only fears it, but more importantly, he respects it. Me bye, I think it be time for you ta make them fear death for a change."

Mahoney was uncharacteristically gray and sullen. It was a side I rarely witnessed. He was a hundred percent Irish, and a hundred percent teddy bear. Sometimes the one conflicted with the other. Mahoney kept his eyes riveted to the floor. Had he looked up, I wouldn't have recognized the man standing before me. He was no longer the barkeep, but a hardened, embittered man who had had enough of the hooligans of New York. Revenge was a physical act, like a midnight train, that passed him by long ago. For me, it was reality.

Was he right? I peered into the murky corners of my mind and into Holly's heart to see if I was standing in the same place Mahoney was. Did I want revenge as bad as Mahoney did, or was I just in it for the kid?

I realized, quickly, the importance of Holly in the investigation, but where would she fit in my life. Before I hit the brick wall, her image flashed through my mind. When I woke up to a dead man in my car, I realized I needed her. It's something you can explain only once, because once is all it takes.

Holly buried her head into my chest and wept. She had lost almost everything that she had worked for within the space of a day. She had lost her job, her home and most importantly, her identity. It was easy for me to lose myself since I never really knew who I was anyway. But Holly was different. She was a dame that found herself in her darkest hours. She held her head up high, using anger built up through years of misunderstandings and close calls. She was hard, but she was also a dame. She knew herself well enough to know she couldn't make it through the Big Pete's of the world on her own. That's where I came in.

She raised her head until her eyes gently looked into mine. "No more running, baby. I'm sick of running. It's not what I do. I'm no peach, but then who is. Stick with me for a little while longer and I swear I'll get you your life back, even if it means plugging holes in every goon this side of the Rockies."

It was tough talk. She probably heard words like it a thousand times before, from a thousand different mugs; however, the look in my eyes told her this time things were going to be different. I knew it just as I knew the sun would rise, or that one day the next glass of Scotch might be my last.

"Wh…Wh…What are we going to do?" She asked, her eyes shimmering slightly.

"Every dog has its day, baby. This dog is about to have his." I let her go and walked over to the phone, purpose built into every stride. I picked it up and dialed the precinct. Outside, the devil was having his way with the night. Obscene shadows hung, spider-like, from every nook and cranny. I wanted to throw my heart at the night, shattering the illusion like glass. Instead, I looked away. After a few quiet seconds, the desk sergeant answered. I had no time for jokes. I asked for Pete.

"Dix, where in blue blazes have you been? We found your car with one of Big Pete's boys inside, outside, and pretty much everywhere else."

"I killed him, or at least the brick wall I ran into did. Just put it on my tab."

"We found his gun at the scene. It looks like he shot off five rounds before he kissed the wall. Did any make you smarter, or lighter?" Pete asked.

"It they did, I'm talking to you from my grave, Pete." I sounded cold. I trusted Pete, but I also trusted a dollar bill as long as it didn't leave me. "You said you knew where that Schwarz kid lived. Did you go and say hello?"

"Yeah, but no one was home. Somebody accidentally left the door open so we walked inside to make sure everything was on the level. It wasn't fancy, and it wasn't occupied. It looks like he hasn't been there in a few days. The apartment manager said the kid was a real night owl. According to my sources, he was doing something for Big Pete, besides the dishes, and whatever it is must be profitable because the rent there is more than I make in a month."

"Did the manager say when he saw him last?"

"He said it had been at least a couple of weeks."

I wondered where Schwarz had been spending his time, if not at home. A man can disappear easily in a big city after a murder, but why disappear before one? Schwarz was seen briefly the day after Baker's body showed up at his old lady's place. According to Holly's friend, Schwarz was alive and well and making the rounds with some of Big Pete's best and meanest thugs. If I believed what the gunsel said, the kid was doing the breaststroke off the New York pier. Since then, Schwarz has been as findable as a generous millionaire. "Pete, we may not find the mug. Guys like Schwarz are bad for business."

"Only if you believe Big Pete is innocent of the kid's murder," Pete replied.

It would have been easy to point a finger in Big Pete's face and say he killed the kid, but my gut told me different. Guys like Big Pete don't leave evidence lying around like Christmas presents. If someone is dusted, the only thing left of them is their social security number and their shoes. Everything about this mess spelled setup. The dead goon with the brick wall rammed up his can had been sure enough about Kelly. But he hadn't been so sure about Schwarz. He kept saying 'probably'. Gangsters giving a mug his last ride don't mind dishing the truth because it'll wind up at the bottom of the East River soon enough. But he wasn't so sure about Schwarz.

A murder can work its way through the underworld faster than the flu. Anyone who knows about it, or has heard about it, will show it off until they're blue in the face. But to say 'probably' is to say you don't know. If this mug didn't know then did Big Pete know, or was he guessing along with the rest of us?

And why didn't he mention Connie or her old man? He talked about Kelly, but left out any connection to Mr. Wall Street. The cops could bring in the Bartlett's for interrogation, but only if they didn't mind having the mayor and about a dozen other city officials on their case for it. The coppers didn't have the evidence or the jam to go after Connie or her old man. I had a gut feeling and for me that was good enough. However, no judge was about to convict anyone on a gut feeling. Big Pete was counting on Bartlett to deliver and wasn't about to let a part-time gunsel or a wayward private dick ruin the payoff. It was a set-up alright, but which sucker was setting up which? I decided to shine my light in Big Pete's direction, for Pete's sake. "I'm sick of the bum, Pete. He's had me chasing my own shadow for too long. It's time someone taught that slicker what East side fear is really about."

"Don't go being a hero, Dix. It isn't about just you anymore. You know that just as well as I do. You got that dame hanging off you like last year's winter coat. We got a lot of dead bodies, with plenty of supply to still go around. If you come in, I'll be able to protect you. But if you stay out in the open, all I'll be able to do is bring flowers to your grave."

"No dice, Pete. It started with the Baker kid, but it's going to end with my heater jammed down Big Pete's slimy throat. And the only way he's getting out of it is to talk to God."

Pete was silent for a moment. I could almost hear him swallow. "Listen to me, Dix. You don't trust me, fine. But don't take the law into your own hands. There are a lot of ways to get at the truth. You think about that before you go doing something stupid."

"Big Pete is getting what's coming to him, and I guarantee he won't like it. He won't like it one bit." My rage was a rock tumbling down a hillside. Every passing second saw my words transformed into images of violence bordering on the insane. I couldn't let Pete be a party to it, no matter the cost. Pete and his boys are about as stealthy as a fat woman in a candy store. They're a modest collection of trigger-happy rookies and veterans on the take. Enough bad attitudes were spreading across the city. I couldn't put coppers into that soup as well. "You do what you have to do, and I'll do what I have to do. Maybe we'll meet somewhere in the middle when this is all said and done. If we don't; well, it's been a slice, Pete." I hung up the phone and silently stared at Mahoney and Holly.

Holly stood watching me with a reserve that bordered on Librarian. Mahoney sat on the couch, his large arms folded around his barrel-of-a-stomach, deep in thought.

"All right, someone say something before I pass out."

Holly didn't bite. Mahoney did. "It's a dangerous game you're playing, me bye. It ain't dangerous enough that you got ta be sniffing in Big Pete's business, but do ya have ta be doing it with a cigarette and a blindfold on?"

"That statue that sits behind the judge in all those movies you like to watch has a blindfold on, doesn't she? Maybe she doesn't want to see what we stiffs do for a living. Maybe it's too hard to explain. I don't know and I don't care. I do know without the cops keeping Big Pete at least a little bit distracted, I can't get to the bottom of this mess." I met Holly's stare. "Listen, baby, I got a lot to do in the next few hours and I don't want to be doing it fighting you and the bad guys. You're either on my side or you're not. Which is it going to be?"

"Be careful how you answer, lass. Dix here is sometimes like a wind blowing in the wrong direction. He may look angry, but it's an anger that belongs ta someone else."

I hated Mahoney for knowing me like that.

"I already know that, Mahoney. Problem is he doesn't know how to take care of things. Without me, he'd probably shoot himself in the foot, or drive into a brick wall or something. I'm with you. Now, what's our first move," Holly replied, dabbing her eyes gently.

"I need to make one more phone call. Hopefully, the mug at the other end can tell me what Bartlett and his daughter might be up to. If not, then we track the dame down and find out, because whatever she was into got Kelly killed, and I'm betting that's the reason Baker was rubbed out." I picked up the phone and dialed a number I hadn't dialed in a long time. The mug on the other end was the kind of guy you only called when you needed a favor. I had performed a few for him, and did them as I was checking my morality at the door. I wasn't proud of it, but I live in a dirty world where the only thing coming out clean is a Yankees uniform.

The phone clicked for a few seconds. Finally, a voice that sounded too much like a rusty gate creaked over the line. "Yeah, waddya want?"

"It's me, Dixon. Is Lucia around?"

"Waddya want?"

"I want to buy you English lessons. Get Lucia on the phone, now."

"Hold on, wise guy." The line went silent. A few seconds later, another grating voice came on. It was Sonny Lucia. He was like Big Pete, only smaller. The only reason I didn't send the guy to the cops airmail was because he made a good stool pigeon. Any dirty deed in the city might go unnoticed by a lot of people, but Lucia wasn't one of them. He knew the day, the hour, and the minute something happened and who was involved. I never asked how he got his information and he never asked what I did with it. It was a good deal all the way around, as long as you remembered to shower after you were done. He was too small time for Big Pete and Lucia liked it that way. Information was Lucia's stock and trade. Sure he could shoot a gat when he needed to, but mostly he sold information to whoever wanted it. The way he saw it, information was worth getting as long as the one you were getting information on didn't know about it.

"Long time no see, peeper, how's things?" The sarcasm dripped off the bum like mustard off a hot dog. I played along.

"Great, Sonny. Bums like you are stilling drilling each other in the street, and guys like me are still winding up with the dame in the end."

Lucia laughed like a guy choking on a philly. "You're always good for a laugh, shamus. Now, what can I do you'se for?"

"What do you know about Dane Bartlett and Big Pete?" All of a sudden Lucia forgot how to talk. I wasn't sure what Lucia was thinking, but I was sure it had something to do with his keister. "Come on, Lucia. Even Congress doesn't take this long."

"Don't push me, shamus. Not on this."

"Why? Does he have pictures of you at the zoo breast-feeding the animals?"

"You do funny real good, shamus. Wise mugs like you always laugh until someone puts a hole in 'em the size of the Bronx."

"I'll be laughing at your funeral, Sonny. I'd hate to have to tell Faletti about how you played stool-pigeon on his numbers setup. He might not like it. Not to mention the fact I got those pictures of you and his wife. They'd make pretty good front page viewing, don't you think? Maybe I'll send those into the Times." I was pushing with kid gloves. He and I both knew it. The only thing left was to see who blinked first.

I didn't have to wait long. The whole thing seemed easy, too easy. "All right, shamus, you win. From what I hear fancy pants is dancing real good with that fat pig. They're buying up property around the East side like it's about to die or something. Lots of people are getting shoved around and the only way to keep it quiet is through fancy pants."

"Is that what Benson Properties is all about?"

"That angle is all the old man. He does the whole thing real legal, real legit. People sign over their property without even knowing it until one day a mug with ten other mugs shows up and tells them to get out. It's real easy, and it's a real money-maker." Lucia laughed, but thrown into the mix were tiny sprinkles of closely-guarded jealousy. I pretended not to notice.

"What about his daughter? Does she know about this?" I asked.

"That broad's screwy. From what I hear, she's been making time with a lot of different mugs. Her old man knows about it but can't do nothing. Kids these days," Lucia mused. "She's wants into the family business, but things ain't working out so good. She's been trying to hook up with any mug will give her the time of day and the time to make dough. She tried to get in tight with Clint Baxter, head stooge of the Lounge, but I don't think her old man liked that mug very much. Last I heard, Kelly and her was making the scene. She's a hot number, only she knows it too much." A few of the brush strokes on the canvas were becoming clearer, more precise. Big Pete could take out the dame, but not without losing the old man. That would be like shooting the goose before it laid the golden egg. But killing Kelly would be easy and relatively hassle-free since there is always another bum waiting for his turn in the rumba line. Besides, any slightly interested coppers would just see it as internal affairs and move on to the next doughnut.

I moved on to a more familiar topic. "You heard of a kid named Albert Schwarz?"

"Everybody heard of that mug, only no one can find 'em. You lookin' for 'em, too?" He asked gently.

"Yeah, but I might be too late."

He laughed like a guy choking on a banana. "Ha, ha, ha; you don't know from nothing, do ya' peeper? He ain't anymore dead than I wish you was. He's around. He's just hiding like Big Pete tells him to. He'll come up for air soon enough."

"One of Big Pete's boys tried taking me for a ride last night. He said the kid's dead."

"Word on the street is he's hiding out somewhere on the South side. You remember Jimmy No Shoes?"

Jimmy No Shoes was a shooter for Big Pete. Ten years back he tried doing his own thing. Big Pete didn't like it and told him so. He survived only because Jimmy was good with the gat. They say Jimmy took out more mugs than the flu. For Big Pete, guys like Jimmy are rare. They kill without mercy, reveling in their deeds like a kid winning a prize at a circus. I knew about Jimmy all right. "What about him?"

The Trigger Method

"He's the one watching the kid. You find Jimmy, you find the kid."

"Wouldn't it be easier just to take him out? Why waste time keeping a kid safe that isn't worth his weight in beans?"

"It all comes back to fancy pants. Keep him happy and you keep the whole set-up running smoother than a Tommy gun. Besides, there are more players in this party than Big Pete knows about, and until he's sure who's on what side, the kid stays alive."

"You mean he stays alive as bait."

"Call it whatever you want," Lucia said.

I read between the lines. Lucia was talking about Bartlett, but not the right Bartlett. If he was right, Connie was the one with the free pass. According to Holly, she was tight with Baxter, the club manager and right hand man to Big Pete. If she accidentally let it slip about her plans, it wouldn't take long for Big Pete to find out. However, her old man had power and Big Pete knew it. You don't go twenty-feet deep with a Bartlett and keep doing business as usual. The powers that be wouldn't stand for it. If the old man kicked, the numbers on Wall Street would go south faster than a bottle of Rum in an East side tenement. We'd been through the depression once. No one was itching to go through it again.

He was trying to keep things on the down low, hoping the less light shed on Baker and Kelly's murders, the more quickly they could get back to business as usual. Somewhere between that point and the distant future, Big Pete would probably find an easy way of getting rid of Bartlett. But for now he needed him. If the big two were looking to cut up the east side, they couldn't do it alone. They needed each other, but Connie seemed nothing more than window dressing. Also, I still didn't know how the Baker kid fit into the whole scene. Was he part of Connie's vicious circle and disliked as the once-alive mug in my car alleged? Images flew through my head like drunken planes, each one slipping and sliding along, once in a while bouncing against each other creating illusions that only made sense if I lived my life backwards.

"What kind of deal did Kelly and the dame have going on?"

"I can't say sure. All I know is it was big enough to make that fat pig see red. I guess it wasn't the same like Jimmy No Shoes. That mug had something to give back to society. Fats got nothing but gas to give back," Lucia laughed. "If Kelly was in on it, maybe it was some sort of protection racket or something. That mug knew lots of guns on the east and south side. He was doing lots of business with some boys down on the bowery and along the bridge."

"Which bridge?" I asked.

"The Manhattan."

"You mean around Pike and Henry Street?" I asked.

"Yeah, them places is always ripe," Lucia replied.

I felt the bottom drop out. If Big Pete found out Fats was working some protection racket without his permission, Kelly would find himself the proud new owner of a one-way ticket to six-feet-under land. But, Kelly was still a valuable asset in Pete's organization. Just like Jimmy No Shoes, Kelly was a dangerous man who knew a gat like a preacher knows a sermon. But, in the end, money formed stronger bonds than goons with a good aim. That held even truer if those bonds formed around property worth in the millions.

"Do you know if he still has that import front by the docks?"

"Yeah, he still has it. Don't know if he even knows he has it, but he still has it alright."

"All right, Sonny. Thanks for the information. I think I'll leave you alone for a while," I replied.

"You think Big Pete is gonna leave you alone anytime soon?" Lucia laughed like a kid pulling the wings off a fly, and enjoying it. Listening to his manic glee made me want to puke, but the guy proved useful. And when a mug like Lucia gives you something, being civil doesn't hurt. I might need him again.

"He won't have a choice. By the time I'm done with him, Big Pete will be the biggest con on death row. Thanks again, Sonny." I hung up the phone and moved to the window.

Holly spoke first. "Who's this Sonny character? I get the feeling he's not the kind of guy that goes to the policeman's ball every year."

"He's one of the bad guys, but in a good way. He knows what happens in this town and he knows it in spades. Only problem is he's not big enough to do zip about it, so he sticks to the edges making a few dollars here and there; not enough to get noticed, but enough to keep himself in the chips."

"Sonny Lucia is a maggot. Only thing keepin' him alive is hamburgers and beer. If it wasn't for the fact mugs like Big Pete didn't care about the fathead, he'd have bitten the dust a long time ago," Mahoney roared.

"I'm lucky he's not there yet. I managed to get some bite-sized morsels out of him. Seems Big Pete is getting into the real estate gig. Bartlett and he are in bed up to their necks, and the only way Bartlett is getting out is by hearse. Benson Properties is the legal arm of the whole deal. The card I found on Kelly is obviously someone's way of helping me connect the dots."

"Where does Connie fit in?" Holly asked.

"I don't exactly know. My best guess is Fats and Connie got mixed up in some sort of racket. Big Pete finds out, knocks off Kelly, but keeps the dame alive because she's a Bartlett, and anyone with brains knows you don't knock off the prize pigeon before the payoff."

"You think the Baker kid was in on it?" Holly asked.

"There's only one way to find out," I replied.

"And how might that be?" Mahoney asked warily.

"I'm going to go and ask Bartlett myself. If he doesn't squawk, he will when I jam my rod in his yap."

"You better think this one through carefully, me bye. That mug is too well-heeled ta be threatened and take it like a little schoolgirl. He'll find a way to get back at ya'. It might not be today or tomorrow, but he will find a way ta make your life difficult. I think you should try talking ta the man, sensibly. Making threats will only make things worse for you and for Holly." Mahoney looked like a schoolteacher lecturing a student.

"Sorry, Mahoney, but I only know one method of dealing with guys like Bartlett."

"And how might that be?" Holly asked.

I stared at Mahoney for a moment then said, "The trigger method."

CHAPTER 15

With my car out of commission, I was left with only one alternative: Mahoney's ancient Plymouth. It was parked along the far side of the building, the back end facing away from the goons watching the place, permitting Holly and I ample opportunity to casually sneak out without drawing any attention.

My body was one large sore. Each bone creaked like a rocking chair bound for the scrap heap. I moved slow; too slow. A couple shots of anything would have done the trick, but the last thing I needed was Holly laying another guilt trip on my shoulders. I couldn't really blame her. There was only one thing worse than a private dick who thought he knew everything, and that was one loaded to boot.

The thought that Big Pete might have some of his goons waiting for me at Bartlett's acreage hadn't slipped my mind. It would make sense since Bartlett was the biggest and weakest link in the chain. Part of me was hoping for company. My gat could use the exercise. Another part of me realized the grave danger Holly was in and that whatever she and I faced from here on in would test not only my courage and eagerness to get at the truth, but also my feelings for her. In truth, it felt like we were in some fouled up Hollywood movie. It seemed you were always watching some sucker with a two-dollar smile get a bullet in the gut for being too smart too late. Somehow, I felt like that sucker. I couldn't shake the feeling the world was about to drop on top of me like a hammer.

I didn't look at Holly. I took one long drag from my cigarette. A long time seemed to pass before I said anything. "Schwarz could be dead. And if he is, we're both in a lot of trouble."

She was quiet for a minute. "Yes, you might be right."

"That leaves only one thing. Either your friend lied, or she told the truth."

"Honey hasn't lied a day in her life. She couldn't tell a lie even if she wanted to." Holly looked at me like I had just stolen her best pair of nylons. It was the kind of look that had truth written all over it.

"I'm not saying she did it on purpose. If they know about Mahoney's link to me, they know about Honey's link to you. They knew you'd call her, and they knew you'd ask her about Schwarz. They probably got someone with her right now. If you showed up there they'd nab you before you got a chance to say hello. There's too much dough at stake to let two loose cannons like you and me run around lousing up the works. That's why Bartlett is so scared. He knows he's in over his head."

"We've got to go over there and see."

"They won't do anything to her as long as we're above water. Another dead employee of the Pheasant Lounge wouldn't look good on the front pages. And right now, Big Pete is trying to avoid drawing attention to himself," I assured her. I could've been right, but I could've been wrong as well. It was just one big stab in the proverbial darkness that had become our lives.

Holly turned to me with eyes as red as the sun. She didn't like my answer and that was fine. I wasn't sure the truth would go down as well, but trying to fool her was becoming a full-time job, and I was never a full-time kind of guy.

"The goons we're dealing with don't get tired; they don't give up, and they definitely won't care about one dame and one private detective. Right now it's about you, me and a kid named Joseph Baker. I can't see outside of that circle. I can't let myself get distracted. If I do, we'll both be dead. Our lives are bus fare, nothing more."

The feelings we had shared at Mahoney's were rapidly evaporating into words caked in bitterness. "You don't really think Connie's old man is going to tell you anything, do you?" It wasn't so much a question as her assessment of the situation.

"He better, for his sake," I grunted. My head ached like a drum solo that would never end. I gritted my teeth.

Silence passed the time with us the rest of the way to Bartlett's swanky pad. We were both drowning in our own thoughts, reflecting on the moments that had defined our lives for the past two days. The further I drove from the city, the larger the trees seemed to get. Looking at them, their branches swinging in the breeze, I wondered if we, Holly and I, weren't being blown around the same way. Were we swinging back and forth from one clue to another, pushed toward something only because we wanted to believe it? Was Big Pete the wind blowing through our lives, pushing us from one secret to another, from one lead to another like chess pieces? Was he the one pushing Bartlett and his daughter back and forth like nags at a racetrack? I consider the options and found none of them any more appealing than saying hello to Bartlett again. He was the kind of guy who enjoyed buying the truth since it was easier than working for it. He surrounded himself with luxury because it helped dull the senses just enough to weed out the real truth. The real truth was Bartlett stood on his pedestal because he was afraid of everyone else around him. He was afraid of the status quo because it was too raw; too perceptible, like an open window that looked out onto a garbage dump. The truth was ugly and went down about as well as day-old porridge. Bartlett knew ugly; he looked at it everyday in the mirror. Connie walked a close second in the family line.

I rounded the curb and drove up the same driveway from a day ago. The air tasted stale, as if someone had left it on the stove too long and now had to throw some of it out. With my window open I could hear the gentle breeze stirring through the tall pine and oak trees that bordered the property. They shielded the place from the noise beyond, allowing me to get a true sense for the spread, and to also see a big black spot that hadn't been there the first time. I stopped my car and turned off the engine.

The big black spot suddenly roared to life. It was a car's engine and it sounded angry and desperate, like a cornered lion ready to kill to stay alive. I suddenly couldn't hear the breeze or the gentle swishing of the leaves. The only sound came from the car's engine; a beastly rage bellowed in an uncoordinated rhythm that shook the ground and spewed forth turbulent white clouds in all directions. Stark white lights washed over Holly and me. I pulled my gun out as I took one step onto the smooth gravel. I also yelled at Holly to get down.

My heart was pounding fast, each beat sounding like a chord from Little Johnnie Jones. I gripped the .38 tight; I kept my eyes square to the target. I could almost feel the heat racing from across the driveway. The car leaped forward in one fluid motion, a small Ford awash in the darkness, like a giant, black blanket on wheels. The seconds that separated me from it vanished into an abyss of empty emotion. There was no time to care about anything or anyone. There was only time to act.

I squeezed the trigger; the bullets flew high and just a little to the right. It was just a warning shot; an attempt on my part to get the driver's attention. There would be no second warning.

Tiny shards of rock and dirt erupted from the tires as the Ford bounded forward, its lights cutting a path straight toward us. I steadied my aim and pulled the trigger again, the recoil sending pain screaming through my body like giant waves against a life raft.

I didn't look to see if Holly was okay. Another second passed; one second too many. I pulled the trigger again. This time the bullet shattered the driver's window. I pulled the trigger again: more pain, more noise. My gut told me to pull the trigger until nothing was left, but I held back. One thing you learn is to never use emotion when killing someone. You have to be cold, uncaring; otherwise, your fish food.

The fourth bullet seemed to hit the mark. The Ford swerved erratically, edging closer to me, but slowing as it did. At the last second it veered to the right, just inches away from the front fender. It slid forward a few more feet before the front tires bit into the small circle of stones that formed the perimeter for the garden with the cherub statue. The car finally came to a rest. I threw a cursory glance back into Mahoney's ride and saw Holly hunkered low in the passenger's side, her eyes an ocean of fear. "Stay down! There might be more of 'em!"

I crouched near to the ground using the car as a shield against any oncoming threat. A straight line of trees ran the entire length of the property, reaching back toward the entrance, toward the way we had come. I could see only darkness stare back. If someone was there, we were both in trouble. The house stood off to the left, thirty or forty yards up. The only light was a large lamp that hung above the even larger doors. The whole place appeared haunted.

I returned my attention to the bullet-riddled car, small tendrils of smoke billowed from the radiator. The engine sounded like a second-rate organ grinder. I tried looking past the car, into the large expanse of grass and gravel that stretched across the remaining length of driveway, but the dark continued laughing at me like a clown at a circus. I aimed my gat at the damaged car, unsure of the medical condition of the person inside. I would have to get closer if I wanted to know whether he was dead or alive. I shuffled quickly to the left, clinging to the side of the Plymouth like a man clinging to the last bottle of Jack Daniels in a bar. The gravel beneath my feet sounded like cannon fire. This would be a stupid way to die.

The tension of the moment rose above the pain in my body. I flung it away for now, like a guy discarding a dirty pair of socks. I had no time to waste on little things like cuts and bruises when two lives were hanging in the balance.

The space between the Ford and I was no-man's land. It was a stretch of six to seven feet, a virtual wasteland of impending doom. Over that open terrain anyone with half an eye could take me down faster than a shot glass at an alcoholic's convention. I slid lower to the ground, scanning the area to my immediate left and right as I went. Everything seemed cloaked in loneliness. My heart beat fast, too fast. I could feel a sudden nausea threatening to pull me under. I bit my lip to stem the rising tide.

As I neared the rear of the Plymouth, I heard coughing coming from the quickly dying Ford. I had made good on my last shot. Still, the door of the Plymouth looked a thousand years away. Every second of indecision meant more information lost. The guy in the Ford was alive, for now. Waiting any longer might mean the difference between life and death, a truth and a lie.

I lowered even further. I swung my gat in half-circles like a turret gunner, aiming at everything, focused on nothing. I held my breath and skittered across in seconds. Nothing happened.

I felt a modest warmth radiate through my overcoat as my back met the side of the Ford. A wall of impenetrable thought and action stood between the last moment and the next. A brief hint of the truth seemed to lurk just beyond that. The groan of the driver was like a version of that truth, only much dirtier and with legs enough to run just slightly out of my reach. Between even those moments was a vision of Holly. I pushed it out of my mind. I needed the truth now before the darkness encircled me like the same darkness that surrounded Baker's old lady during her nightly constitutionals.

I half-crawled to the front of the car. An entire list of do's and don'ts filtered into my mind as I crouched near the door figuring my best move. My gun was in my left hand and opening the door with my right would leave me vulnerable to any attack; although, I'd be able to defend Holly easier should someone try to surprise me. I looked down the path one more time, then looked back toward the Plymouth and further on to the front of the house with its solitary light reaching vainly into the night. Everything looked dead. I swallowed one last time, reached up and gingerly tried the handle. It creaked noisily. Other than my cursing under my breath, little else of any significance occurred.

The entire cabin was masked in darkness. A lone figure in a black overcoat and black hat seemed its only passenger. I could tell the figure was a male, maybe thirty-five to forty and reaching the end real quick. He was bent over the steering wheel. Gravity forced his body to angle slowly toward the door, toward me.

A low painful moan seeped out of the driver's side. I reached in with my right hand and helped him fall out. He tumbled to me like a sack of laundry. I scanned the rest of the vehicle. There was no one or nothing else inside.

The amount of light between the two cars could've filled the head of a pin so I took out a small flashlight and focused the narrow beam on the driver. He was in his forties judging from the streaks of grey that highlighted his slick-backed hair, well-groomed, and sported a moustache as smooth as a checkmark. Whatever color he sported before our encounter quickly faded to the ghostly pale of cemetery fame. I searched him and felt the tip of a gun poking out from his jacket pocket. I pulled it out, careful not to leave my prints all over it. It was a stylish little .28 that looked well taken care of. I checked the chamber and saw that two bullets had been fired. I took the rest of the bullets out then placed it back in his pocket. I suddenly thought about Baxter. I was set to call for Holly when careful footsteps behind me produced a woman, slightly shaken, but mostly in one piece.

She recognized him right away. "It's Clint Baxter. He's the manager from the club. What could he be doing here?"

"Let's ask him." I reached out and grabbed both lapels. "You shouldn't go around trying to run people over. It makes them feel unappreciated."

Most of what was left of Baxter lay motionless on the ground. His upper torso was wet with blood. His face scrunched up like an old rag, and his eyes resembled ice cubes just before the booze is poured in. He was dying and we all knew it.

"H…Hi, Holly, l…l…long time n…no see. You still l…look like a million bucks, baby. B…Big Pete really misses you. You ought to go and say hi to him."

I pushed my flashlight slowly into the wound. He shrieked like a girl running from a mouse. I could feel Holly's stare. I didn't look back. The next few moments had little to do with being polite.

"Talk or I'll shove it so far in you'll need a surgeon to get it out."

"All right, damn it, all right! I c…came to see the old man. B…Big Pete wanted something from him, but he wasn't in the giving mood. I scared him a little. That's all."

That wasn't all. There was more to it. "What did Big Pete want?"

Baxter laughed then spit out the words, "His life."

Only a fresh-cut rookie two weeks on the job would go for the kind of story Baxter was selling and I was no rookie. I had heard better stories on the radio. Big Pete wasn't about to send a first-rate joke like Baxter when he could dispatch a couple of real vicious dogs to do the deed. Baker was all rose; to rub out a guy like Bartlett required the services of a Venus flytrap.

"You're talking out of the side of your mouth, Baxter, and we both know it." I took the flashlight and shoved it into the wound again, deeper this time. I could feel him back away from me, but I wasn't about to give him anything but a hard time. He cried like a child having a nightmare.

I ignored the tears and tortured him some more. He finally started talking between short sniffles. "The o…old man's a daisy. He sings to Big Pete about everything including his own d…daughter. A man l…like that doesn't deserve to live. I was trying to d…do the world a little favor. Then again, maybe Big Pete ordered me to do it. Maybe he's tired of looking after Bartlett. If he ratted out his own daughter, maybe he won't be so choosy when the cops come around. M…maybe that's g…got t…the boss worried." Baxter coughed in spurts, blackish liquid forming at the edges of his lips and chest. One of the bullets penetrated his lungs. He had another minute, maybe two. He was spitting out bits of truth and mistruths, trying to cover up for someone or something.

"Where's Schwarz?"

"He's dead," Baxter replied hesitantly. He didn't look at me. Instead, his eyes stuck like glue to the ground. Deception was hard to read in the dark. It mixed easily with the gloom of the night until it almost resembled the truth.

"You're lying, Baxter."

"I d…don't care what you t…think, shamus. B…Bartlett got what was c…coming to him. He thinks he's too good for everyone, including me. I fixed that. That stupid k…kid also got what he deserved; both of 'em, and pretty soon you'll be next."

"Looks like you might beat me to it, sucker. You can make it easy for yourself at the pearly gates by telling the truth."

"Go c…catch flies. The kid's d…dead and nothing you do will make me c…change my story."

This was the second time someone told me Schwarz was dead. It was an easy answer to an easy question. The only problem with easy is it takes too many other factors out of the equation. "Did Big Pete kill Baker?"

"H...He doesn't take out anybody. That's what he's got his boys for."

"Stop speaking in riddles. Did he kill the kid or not?"

"M...Maybe he did and maybe he d...di...didn't. It doesn't really matter anymore, d...does it?" He closed his eyes, his chest rising and falling like an out-of-tune motor. I still didn't care.

"Where's Honey?" Holly asked. "What have you done with her?"

"I...I'm sure she's okay. She's with N...No Shoes. He always knows how to show the l...ladies a good time." Baxter went lights out again. I shook him awake. His eyes opened abruptly. "W...Whoops, almost went on y...you there, didn't I?"

I felt like I was fishing for the truth without a pole. If Baxter killed the old man, the only one left to tell the truth was Connie. Either it was a warning as Baxter said, or Connie called the shot on the whole deal leaving her in line to get the whole kit and caboodle. It was nice. It was neat. But I still wasn't buying.

"The only reason your soon-to-be ex-boss would take out Bartlett was if he felt he had no other choice. If he really is trying to buy up the East side, he couldn't do it without Bartlett. That's what Benson Properties is all about. If you're here, then maybe he doesn't have control. Maybe someone is trying to do business their own way, without his approval. Maybe that someone is you."

"What do you mean?" Holly asked.

"Y...You're crazy," he protested. I could sense the unease in his words. I was onto something and he knew it.

"Am I? Taking out the old man brings more heat than fatso needs. You didn't mind spilling about Schwarz, but you're not so sure about the Baker kid, are you? If you thought Big Pete did it you would have said so. Mugs like you don't get scared. You show off murder like a medal. Who you working with, Baxter? And I don't mean the dame. You won't survive the next few minutes so you might as well tell me." I was shaking the guy like a tree, trying to see what fell out. Everything he said left me with a sour taste. He was protecting someone, and I could only think of two people: Big Pete and Connie Bartlett.

"Nuts to you, shamus. I…If you think you know e…everything, you don't need me," he laughed, but the pain working its way quickly through his system only allowed him a few precious seconds.

Holly looked down at Baxter with unfeeling eyes. "Clint, tell us, please. Be a right guy for once in that thing you call a life."

Baxter turned his gaze toward Holly, his features softening for a moment. His face was an ashen white. His eyes glazed over, his body becoming increasingly still. "S…Sorry, babe, b…but I got to be what I got to be." He closed his eyes and went to sleep forever.

I got up and looked around. The place was quiet and empty. Baxter had come alone. It's not smart to try and take out a guy like Bartlett with just one gee unless you're doing it on the sly. Someone was trying real hard to upset Big Pete's applecart. Five would get me ten Baxter was in on it, but who was he connected to? Connie might have seen herself as Baxter's partner, but that was far from the entire picture. Whoever was fronting this thing had the brains and the moxy to go up against Big Pete; maybe even play right under his nose without him knowing. Finding that mug might put me face-to-face with whoever killed Baker.

I finally turned to Holly. "Don't worry about Honey. She's still alive. Otherwise, Baxter would have told us different. I don't think Big Pete knows where we are. For a while I was thinking we were all he was thinking about. After talking to this guy, maybe we're not the only ones watching our backs."

"What do you mean?" Holly said as she stood up.

I looked toward the deathly-still house of Dane Bartlett. "The only place we'll find the answer to that question, baby, is inside," I replied.

"Do we have to go in?" Holly asked.

"Yes. But don't worry. My friend here will keep us company the whole time," I motioned to the .38 in my hand. I pulled a few loose bullets from my jacket pocket and inserted them quickly into the empty chambers before starting up the driveway.

The large front doors were closed, their strength more than apparent, although, maybe not strong enough to help Bartlett this night. Holly was close on my heels, each of her steps matching mine sound for sound, inch for inch. I pulled a handkerchief from my breast pocket as I reached the door.

"Why the handkerchief?" Holly asked.

"We got to call the boys in blue in a few minutes and the last thing I need is Detective Miller chewing me out because I dirtied up the whole crime scene before they got a chance to look at it."

I tried the door. It opened easily. I wasn't so sure this was a good sign.

With my left hand I reached back and pushed Holly gently to the right of the door. The wall was solid brick and would stop any bullet that came from inside. The door might not. I looked back toward the cars. Baxter's jalopy was still smoking gently against the curtain of night still hanging over the horizon. Everything else looked empty and silent.

I hung close to the opposite door and peered inside. I could see the Butler lying face down only five feet from the door. It was safe to say the help was going to need help, and probably from an undertaker.

I couldn't see Bartlett from where I was standing. "Wait here. I'm going in to see about Bartlett. I see the butler, but he's a goner."

"No," Holly whispered. "I'm coming in with you." I felt her hands against my back, a gentle caress that told me she needed me now more than ever. The feeling was mutual.

"Okay, but stay close. No hero stuff." The butler's dead corpse greeted me as I walked into the foyer. A dark pool spread out and away from him. I checked his pulse anyway. It was about as lively as a skeleton in the Sahara.

The parlor lay off to our right. A tiny sliver of light escaped from under the door. I walked forward, one eye focused on everything away from the light. I reached it and with my handkerchief-covered hand slowly opened the door. I could've been more careful, but my gut told me there was no reason to be.

I noticed Bartlett immediately. He sat face up against a small chez lounger that squatted contently in the middle of the large room. Small streaks of blood dotted the area between the door and where Bartlett wound up. Bloody hand prints decorated the floor every six inches. He must have dragged himself back to the lounger, hoping against hope someone would come to help him before he bled to death. Unfortunately, he wasn't hit too bad; he would live. His eyes were open, his chest rising and falling in quick measures. He was wearing a dark suit, unbuttoned, that showed off his waistline as well as blotches of red that looked like brushstrokes by a kindergartener. His hair didn't look as silver or as shiny as before. It just looked gray and old. Holly and I rushed over.

"If you want air conditioning that bad just turn on a fan, Bartlett," I said mockingly.

A few short laughs escaped, but the pain in his chest killed it before it really got going. He shut his eyes for a moment and grunted. He finally spoke, but in a manner meant for bedtime rather than as a deathbed confession. "I shall remember that next time, Mr. Dixon." He sat deathly still, his eyes turning a shade of pale that reminded me of old parchment.

"At least you're smart enough to know you'll get a next time," I said as I checked him out. "So, how does it feel to be on Big Pete's sure-to-be-dead-soon list?"

"Mr. Dixon," he started, "I'm not dead, only wounded. The blasted fool that shot me couldn't hit the broad side of a barn." He tilted his head slightly and eyed me for a moment. "Looks like you've had a run of bad luck as well."

"I'll live. That's more than I can say for your help."

"Yes, I heard the shots and started toward the door. Before I knew what was happening I was lying on the floor."

I turned to Holly, "Get on the phone and call headquarters. Ask for Pete Miller and tell him what's happened. It'll take him and his boys at least twenty minutes to get here. That should give me enough time to get the information I need." Holly stood and walked to the phone by the door.

"Whatever suspicions you may have buried deep in that skull of yours regarding me are quite incorrect, Mr. Dixon. I…" I didn't let him finish. Here he was, at death's door, trying to negotiate with an overworked and underpaid shamus that didn't care. I would have traded his life then and there for a good pillow and ten solid hours of sleep.

"I'm no baby-kissing politician so you can skip the tall tales, Bartlett. Someone wants you dead. Ordinarily, I might care. But in your case I'll make an exception." I stared into his steel-gray eyes. He stared back. A solemn sanity quickly reasserted itself into the conversation. He wasn't scared of me. Not one bit.

"I do appreciate your concern, Mr. Dixon; however, I am more than aware of the danger. Since you are standing here, alive, I can safely assume you dispatched the fool whom attempted to assassinate me?"

"Don't sit there and tell me you didn't recognize the face?" I could hear Holly talking in the background. Her voice was slow but steady.

"I was too busy getting shot to notice who it was doing the shooting, my good man." Listening to him talk was like listening to static on the radio with bits of conversation mixed in for flavor. I've been shot before and it hurts like hell. It feels like someone just stabbed you with a red-hot poker. As the warmth disappears, the real pain begins. You're body shrivels up inside, consuming whatever heat is left until, in the end, you look like a cold slab of meat. Unfortunately, I didn't think Bartlett would make it the slab-of-meat stage.

"What would you say if I told you it was Clint Baxter?" I asked. If the room wasn't quiet before, it was now.

"You mean the chap from the Pheasant Lounge?"

"That's the guy. Maybe you forgot to pay your bar tab or something, because I can't think of any other reason he or Big Pete would want you dead. Maybe you can think of a reason or two." The names I spit out got his attention right away.

"Your insinuations are quite amusing, Mr. Dixon. Please continue."

"You can laugh all you want Bartlett, but you and I both know your swimming in the same pool with Big Pete. You've been with him from day one. I know all about you're little renovation project on the East side. I gave you a chance to tell me before, but you decided to play dumb. I waved Benson Properties in your face and all you did was bat your eyelashes at me and chase me out the door. But, let's just say for a second that I believe you. You're innocent and I'm a first-class sucker with a brick wall for a car and booze on my breath." I studied him intently, like a spotlight on a guilty man, each word generating more heat. "Have you seen your daughter lately?"

"Constance is a free spirit. Her life is her own. Whatever fantasies you wish to invent regarding my daughter's interests are just that." His glance chased shadows along the floor.

"Is that right? Three mugs she was real close to are now either dead or missing? All three were involved in some scam. Every time I draw the picture a Bartlett is always at the center of it. What kind of interests could cause that kind of damage?"

That made him mad. If there weren't bullets in him, he probably would've gotten up and slapped me with enough lawsuits to paper Times Square. As it was, he just glared at me like a mad bull waiting for dinner.

"Perhaps you forget with whom you are speaking, Mr. Dixon. I am not some illiterate, lifeless creature. You will do well to remember that in the future," he scowled.

I ignored him. Instead, I kept the insinuations flying fast and furious. "A little birdie told me your daughter is good friends with Baxter. You think Big Pete would trust your murder to that schmuck when he has mugs like Paul Brutus and Jimmy No Shoes around? He sends pros after nobody's like Fats Kelly, but sends a moron like Baxter after you? If Big Pete didn't send Baxter then who did? You need me to put two and two together, or do you think you can do it yourself?"

Holly put down the phone and walked back to where I was crouched. "Your friend wasn't in, but the desk Sergeant said they'd have someone here in twenty minutes. When they asked my name I hung up."

I turned back to Bartlett; his face was boiling with an almost inescapable anger. "How dare you. My daughter loves me and I love her. We are all we have. You think my own daughter would want me dead? You're a fool, Mr. Dixon. The fact my daughter is acquainted with Mr. Baxter means nothing. I'm sure Mr. Baxter knows quite a few people."

"Maybe, but they weren't all looking to pop you now were they? Think about it, Bartlett. With you gone, Connie inherits everything. That includes your relationship with Big Pete. She had a nice little angle going with Kelly and Schwarz, but before they could get started, her big mouth probably blew the whole thing to smithereens. She's in it for the excitement; the adventure; guys who can carry big guns, and dough; and not necessarily all in that order."

"I'll enjoy suing you, sir," Bartlett growled. His eyes looked colder than ice. He sat in a position he was relatively unaccustomed to. With the pain roaring through his body, Bartlett could do little but stare angry epitaphs at me and hope he would have his day in the sun. I wasn't so sure. If a guy like Baxter got this close, Bartlett's life span was contracting by the second.

I had been threatened enough times that Bartlett words evaporated into a big bowl of nothing. I threw a few more accusations in his face. "Why would your daughter want to kill you? Hmmm, let me think. The first time I was here you left the room, and for a long time. Who were you talking to and what did you say? Did it have something to do with Connie? Is that why Baxter was here tonight? Was he getting trying to get revenge for something you did?" He looked away from me. I was grabbing at air. The only problem was Bartlett wasn't sure if I was or not. That was my edge. Guys like Bartlett make paranoia their best friend because it's better than winding up with pie in the kisser if you're wrong. He knows all about Connie, I don't. My hope was he'd lead me to the truth before all the players in this drama disappeared. "You're walking on thin ice, Bartlett. The only thing keeping you alive is your contacts. Without them, you're nothing."

I looked him over one last time to ensure he'd survive. Once I completed my superficial diagnosis I got to my feet, put my gun in my holster and walked calmly away. Holly remained near the old man for a few tense seconds. I stopped and looked back.

"Listen to me, Mr. Bartlett. If Big Pete hurts my friend, Honey, I'll make sure that your life is a living hell." Holly stood up and walked away.

I looked at Bartlett one more time as Holly walked out of the parlor. "You're safe for now, Bartlett. But dollar bills can't stop bullets forever."

Baxter was still dead when we went back outside. His body lay crumpled on the ground, His face was still a mask of pain. In the end, he was just a statistic. I didn't know the bum, didn't care. A tenuous connection between Baker and Baxter existed, and maybe because of that connection Baker was dead. Big Pete's position in the picture was fading slowly. He would gain little from the kid's murder other than a few moments of peace of mind followed by endless nights of hassle from the cops. Taking out Schwarz would make more sense because of the heat following the kid around, but Baker was nothing more than a shadow in his world. Only two people would have gained from Baker's murder as I saw it. If one of those two was dead, then there was only one other viable suspect left: Connie Bartlett.

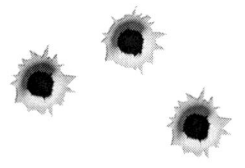

CHAPTER 16

The path back to my office was clear sailing. That was the first tip-off. The fact nothing had been touched was the second. Outside, the streets were clear except for the usual stumbling and bumbling foot traffic. Holly and I walked up the stairs to my floor and around the chalky outline of Kelly still fresh on the ground. It stood out like a beacon against the dingy gray of the stairwell. Light from offices down the hall filtered through shoddy glass panes. The rest of the place resembled a cemetery.

Things in my office remained unaltered. Dust, dirt and cobwebs hung here and there like old friends. Lou Gherig still hung on the same dusty wall and my water cooler was still empty. None of that really mattered. I was here for one thing and one thing only: the phone call. If I was right, he would know I was here. It was a long shot, by football field standards, but a risk worth taking. Besides, I missed the cobwebs.

I left the light off. I sat down in my swivel chair, swiveled a little then put my feet up on the desk. The cigarette in my mouth completed the picture. I let the light from the match burn brightly for a few seconds, exposing the dinginess of my office. I held it up high. Holly's face seemed to sparkle against everything else. I blew the match out.

"So, we just sit here and wait? That's your big plan?" Holly asked impatiently.

"Yup, pretty much," I replied as I threw the match in the garbage can. The scars on my face felt bad and the pain that scurried through my body like wharf rats felt even worse, but Holly's constant chiding was starting to feel like nails against a chalkboard. For the last thirty-six hours, our relationship had hovered between love and hate with a healthy dose of murder thrown in for flavor. I couldn't blame her for being anxious but the case couldn't be pushed. Too many dead bodies left too many unanswered questions in their wake. The answers I did get had helped, but I still wasn't any closer to the real killer. Multiple paths spread easily away from me, crafting a series of questions that created more confusion. I felt like I was in the middle of a nest of breeding rabbits. I laughed.

"What's so funny?" she asked.

"Nothing. I was just thinking about Bartlett."

"Were you right about what you said back there?"

"I'm not sure, but I don't think it really matters. What matters is what Bartlett thinks. Right now he's thinking about Connie and whether what I said is true. Baxter wanted Bartlett dead for a reason. It's like I said before: love or revenge. If I'm right, the mug on the phone will call back and help clarify things for me."

"That takes us back to my first question. We just sit here and wait for that to happen?"

"Yes and no. If he is as close to Big Pete as I think he is, he'll know exactly what's going on."

"What makes you so sure?" Holly asked, abruptly rising from her chair. She casually strolled over to the picture of Lou Gehrig and studied it in the darkness. I studied her; she seemed the eye in the heart of the storm. She was a calm wind that could blow like a thunderous tornado at any moment. She was the perfect picture of every emotion ever harbored by man or woman. I wondered whether I was looking for the perfect criminal with the perfect alibi, or something else. In that moment, I realized every opposing human nature and what that meant for this case. I kept talking to keep myself from thinking.

"Someone's chewing on Big Pete's holy numbers and it isn't his malamute. A lot of action is floating around on the streets, and a lot of people are going to be sitting pretty when the dust clears." She turned to me, her eyes full and dark. "Nobody can take down Big Pete right now, but they make him stumble a little. If someone throws enough bones out there, even the cops will get curious. Problem is they got the whole setup wrong."

"What do you mean?" Holly asked.

"You don't frame Big Pete. He's too big. That's why they call him Big Pete. He puts dollar bills in the right pockets and those pockets are always kept full and happy. The only way to really get at him is through those under him. All it would take is one or two dead bodies to get the cops interested. It wouldn't hurt him for long, but it would hurt any chance he might have of pulling off this east side property grab."

Holly was about to say something, but the ringing of the phone stopped her. I answered it on the fifth ring. I knew who it was before I even picked it up.

"Hiya, peeper, long time no talk. You were gone so long I was starting to think you didn't care." It was obvious from the sound of his voice things were different. I could feel the tension.

"Don't worry your pretty little head about it. After all, you still got your gat to keep you company."

"I'll give you that one for free, but you'll have to earn the rest, big boy."

"Is that right? Seems I've been doing pretty okay on my own. All you've done is get me shot at, beaten up and chased around like a clay pigeon at a shooting range. You're not even in it for justice. You're just feeding me to pad your own bottom line. You're playing me for a patsy and I'm getting tired of it."

"Well, well, well; looks like the shamus is feeling under appreciated. Never mind my reasons. You want to find the mug that got the kid? I can help you with that."

"And help yourself at the same time," I replied.

"We all want something in this world, shamus. Question is: What do you want? You want to find the kid's murderer, or do you want the dame? She's a hot number; I'll give you that. But, she's trouble."

"You mean like Connie Bartlett?" I asked.

"That dame got no sense. Only thing keeping her alive is her old man's money."

"That almost changed tonight. You wouldn't happen to know anything about it, would you?"

He was quiet for a long time. Holly stood to my left, her hands curled into tight little balls. There were two games being played, and one of them was between me and the mysterious midnight caller with all the supposed answers. He was involved, and it wasn't out of boredom.

"You're quiet, mug. Cat got your tongue? You should try Scotch. That stuff will loosen those lips of yours in no time flat."

"Like I said before, shamus, you're a funny guy. One day you'll find yourself in a place where your jokes will really be appreciated, like in a cemetery."

"Either you got something or you don't. If you don't, hang up and let me get on with my life, otherwise, start talking. The games you're playing don't rate that high with me anymore. Maybe you were behind the hit. Maybe, after you were done, you might have even thought about keeping one of the slugs as a memento." The heat coming from the other end could've kept half the Bronx warmer than a five-alarm fire in August.

"It ain't important."

"Is that right? You're going to have to do better than that. I accidentally interrupted the guy before he could finish. I hated to have to take him out, but it was either him or me. Why don't you try a shot at the stiff's name?"

More silence. This cat was playing big stakes and wasn't willing to deal many high cards too soon. It made my job that much tougher.

"This isn't twenty questions, shamus," he replied. "Whoever the Joe was, he was. If you did him, he ain't worth flapping gums about anymore." For a second, the guy sounded like the gunsel that tried taking me for a ride down to the wharf. He had said Joe too. At the time, I figured he was talking about Baker. My mind was running like a mouse on a wheel. I kept talking.

"Does the name Clint Baxter mean anything to you?"

"It might at that," he replied, sounding only half interested.

"Why would Baxter want Bartlett out of the picture unless he was put to it by someone else? Someone somewhere wants Bartlett out of the way, but it ain't Big Pete. He wouldn't send a cheapie like Baxter after Bartlett. He'd send a pro so he knows the job gets done right. What do you think?"

"I think you should try finding that Schwarz fella. He might be able to help you find some answers. He's probably nice and loose by now, especially with No Shoes watching over him. You get him and I guarantee you that Bartlett dame will sing like a canary in a cage."

"Everyone tells me he's dead, but you know he's alive. Maybe what he knows could put Big Pete in the big house, but the wizard in the big white castle knows different. The only smart play would be to put him six feet under."

"Don't believe what you hear about the kid. He's still alive and he can still talk, but for how long is anybody's guess. No Shoes is about as patient as you are. There's no telling what he may do to the kid."

"You got an address?" I asked.

"Try the oyster boats near the Manhattan. Big Pete owns a big part of that neighborhood. Schwarz is nothing more than bait. What he knows couldn't fill a kid's teacup," he said. "Maybe he knows something that can nail the dame or Big Pete to a pretend murder rap that'll stick about as well as class would to you, but that's about it. Once the trap springs, the kid's a goner."

"Mugs like you make me want to hurl myself into the East River. Life is cheap, easy to buy and sell, and even easier to waste when it isn't your own. Schwarz probably isn't a picnic, but he's still deserves his day."

"It don't matter if he does or not. The sooner you realize that, the sooner we can all get on with our lives. There's too much heat on. Baker could've been somebody if he wanted to, but couldn't keep with the program. His old lady went nuttier than a fruitcake every time she sees him with the dame, see? In the end, any mug that goes crazy for a dame always buys it because of that same dame. It's sad, really."

"Stop it, will ya', you're breaking my heart," I said, trying to mimic some of the best theatre talent on Broadway. "The only person that really loved that kid was his old lady. As for the dame, I'll find her and get the truth, with or without the gat." I slammed the phone down so hard it hurt.

"Well, the Schwarz kid is still alive. At least this mug says so," I said anti-climactically.

"You think Schwarz had something to do with it?"

"I don't know, but I'm going to find out."

"What if the guy you're talking to is in on it? If this really is a setup, you might be the first one to go."

"I can't worry about that now. I think he's involved somehow. He knows too much to be an outsider. Everything about him tells me he's muscle. Probably some low-level dope Big Pete's got working for him. He could've been working with Kelly, or against him. Either way, I'd like to know who he is." I swiveled back and forth in my chair like I had a thousand times before. It felt good to be back in my office. Everything looked real. In the larger world things looked made up, like a mannequin in a department store window. The goons and Canaries behaved like characters from a bad detective novel, with accompanying music that was harsh and out of key. My world was small and dirty, but it was tangible. I could feel the dust and dirt if I stretched my hand out. I could feel the rough edges against my skin. Those things let me know I was alive. But I was beginning to realize that as real and as tangible as they were, those things, like me, looked and felt used up. Holly's concern felt fresh and new, like a tear from a newborn baby. I found myself wanting to dive in.

I stood up. Holly moved from the front of the desk to the side. Her eyes were dark, conveying a sense of depth that could challenge any ocean. Her expectant stare poured through me. We both realized a long time ago moments like this would come, but how we would deal with them was anybody's guess.

She looked fresh, like a fighter in the first round. Thin slivers of light passed through the half-open blinds and into the room; small rays crossed her face at horizontal angles. She had the kind of face a mug could die for. Her cheekbones were sharp and distinct; each line exactly where it should have been. Her lips were big and full, the ruby-red lipstick shining through the darkness like a flashlight in a darkened room. Each splinter of light flying through my office avoided me, instead choosing the lesser of two evils. There was no one to blame. It was what it was.

I closed the gap between us. She didn't move away. I wasn't at my best, but she didn't seem to notice or to care. I pulled up close, real close. Her perfume caressed me softly, clouding over the pain and hurt. I was only inches from her. She still didn't move. She just stared at me with a calm that was like looking at the surface of a still lake. There wasn't time for this and we both knew it.

We were wrong for each other right from the start. She was on the right side of things and I was all wrong. For me, every dame was wrong; it was like trying to mix oil and water. Every time you did, you started sparks that burned through the skin and into the soul.

I remembered myself and began turning away. She grabbed me. "What is it? What's wrong?"

I looked at her again. I saw no trace of my past in her eyes. I saw only me. "We've fought every step of the way since we first met. Every time I wanted to smack you, I wanted to kiss you. Every time I thought about shooting you, I wanted to hold you and never let you go. You remind me of all the good things I've never had, and all the bad things I don't want. I wonder where you and I rate in the big picture."

"We're only two people. Between you and I are a lot of things. Things I can't explain. Things I don't want to explain. It would be like trying to explain away a shadow or a trick of light that's there, but not really there. We're a moment, you and I."

The words weren't really necessary. We both knew what we were going to say and do before we said or did it. She was right, but I didn't want her to be right. I wanted her to be wrong, just like I had been wrong about so many other things. I'd put my life on the line for people that meant as much to me as an empty bottle or a bum on the street. This time things were different. The dame was different.

"Look me in the eye and say we're just a moment, sweetheart." She looked at me, but said nothing. She couldn't say it anymore than I could. They were just words, empty and lifeless. What I saw in her eyes and in her heart was real. It was tangible and it scared me to death. "Were we just a moment back at Mahoney's dive? The way you looked at me when I was on the phone before; were we just a moment then? I got news for you, sweetheart. Life is full of moments. It's what makes life worth living. Some times I hate you, but I'd also hate to lose you." I pulled her close until her breath mingled with mine, her perfume mixing with my pain until one masked the other. Her stare pierced through my heart. Her eyes were narrow slits of hazel, only partially visible against the thin streams of light that entered through the window. I felt her hands against my shoulders, resisting slightly, but not too much.

We'd been on the run so long we forgot what we were running from. Baker brought the past back to life. Through him, I also saw what Holly was running from, and it wasn't Big Pete or his boys. She was too tough for that. She was running from a picture. A picture that saw dames like Holly living on three squares a day and all the booze they could handle. She was looking for something more. I had pushed that timetable forward considerably, forcing her to confront the fact she needed someone as badly as an old man needs rest, or a dog a bone. I wasn't the most perfect mug in the world, but I'd never leave her. She knew it and I knew it. Maybe that was the problem.

With rage in my heart and murder on my mind, I kissed her. She didn't resist.

CHAPTER 17

The night felt much colder than the one o'clock indicated by my watch. It was a pressing night, with large patches of semi-opaque mist drifting between the grimy streets and rust-covered alleys. Together, the entire scene reminded me of a baby's womb with barely enough elbowroom to breathe. I could almost taste the vaporous air with each breathe. It tasted like a decomposing corpse.

Holly had said little since we left my office. Part of me wanted to believe it was exhaustion, but I knew better. It was the kiss. It felt good and it felt right. But somewhere deep in my mind, I wondered whether it was wrong to feel these feelings when the only real friend we had was death.

She continued staring solemnly out at the city. I wanted to say something, but the kiss seemed to have said it all. I don't know why I wanted it, and I don't why I said what I said. I could see death standing around the corner, a lit cigarette dangling from an ugly carcass of a mouth, a sly grin stretching greedily across, and a guarantee as fresh as a new bullet sitting comfortably in his bony palm. With that kind of guarantee just waiting to be collected, maybe I should have said more, done more. Maybe Holly was expecting more. I don't know.

Holly finally broke the silence with thoughts that had nothing to do with stolen kisses. I was glad for it. "I'm trying to work things out in my mind, but I keep coming up with zeros. Other than Connie, nothing else makes sense. She's at the center of everything. My mind knows it. My heart knows it. I think even her father knows it."

It seemed the right thing to say, but something didn't feel right. A small part of the puzzle was missing; the one piece that could complete the entire picture. "You might be right, but it's too simple to blame her, too easy. She's too dumb to be that smart. She might like to think she's the boss, and maybe Schwarz and Baker were just dumb enough to believe she was in charge, but I don't believe it for a second."

"Then what?"

"I don't know, but something just feels wrong. Something is staring me in the face. Something I missed." I pulled a cigarette out of the crumpled pack that was in my jacket pocket, lit it and took a deep drag. I passed the pack over to Holly. She ignored it, reaching instead for the cigarette in my mouth. She opened the window on her side and flicked it out into the cold night. I could still feel my gat, each cylinder loaded and ready for action. I looked at her one more time and decided it wasn't worth the trouble. I drove on.

"For starters, the mug that keeps calling me wants something. He isn't just calling because he likes the sound of my voice. It's like he's getting a nickel every time someone bites the dust." I gave up on the thought for a moment as the Manhattan Bridge rose suddenly and silently above the night like a steel monster. I saw Big Pete and Bartlett's soiled intentions everywhere. They resembled a bad paint job that wouldn't go away. As easy as it was to see the corruption, it seemed just as hard to see the truth. It remained elusive, ducking and dodging in the darkness like a rat fleeing the pied piper.

The place Schwarz was supposedly being held was only minutes away from Henry Street, minutes away from the beginning of everything. It was too close for me to call it a coincidence. Maybe this was someone's idea of a joke.

The scene before me was one I'd seen before. The streets looked abandoned. Along both sides were row upon row of filthy tenements that resembled wash lines hundred of years past their prime. A thin ream of cement tried in vain to resemble a sidewalk with cracks skittering from building fronts toward the street like chicken scratches in mud.

The Trigger Method

I stopped the car on Pike. The motor chugged nervously for a few seconds before dying. I turned to Holly. Outside, a steady breeze thumped gently against the side of the Plymouth creating a thin whistling sound. I studied the area for a few moments like a guy putting off the inevitable. Holly sat quietly observing me, wondering when I would speak and what I would say. When I finally said my peace, it sounded more like a recording played at three times the normal speed than a sensible sane statement.

"I'm going to walk the rest of the way. You stay here. If I'm not back in twenty minutes, go to the precinct and ask for Detective Miller. Don't trust anyone but him. Tell him everything. He'll know what to do." I started to turn away when she gently grabbed my wrist.

"Why are you telling me this now? You are coming back. Do you hear me? You promised to put my life back in order and I'm holding you to that promise." She leaned over and kissed me, gently. I was walking into something I didn't understand. Everywhere I looked, I saw shadows hurling questions at me like Christy Matheson hurling fastballs at a minor leaguer. In the middle was Holly. She was different. I knew that right from the first moment I saw her standing in the doorway at the Lounge. I hoped I wasn't realizing it too late.

"Listen, baby, I don't plan on dying just yet. But, I'm going to get at the truth. I've looked around corners, under shadows, behind doors and found lots of facts, but nothing that gets me any closer to discovering what happened to the kid. I've got my gat and it's loaded to the gills. I'm going to start pulling the trigger and not stop until someone tells me something. If I've got to kill every last one of those mugs it'll be worth it. Big Pete and Bartlett may own this town, but they don't own the truth. They don't have a lock on that. As long as we're alive, the truth lives." I pulled her close to me. "Have you ever seen Central Park at night, I mean really seen it? I know a place where the moon is so big you can almost reach out and touch it. When we're done with all of this, I want to take you there and kiss you under that moonlight."

"You've got yourself a date, Mr. Dixon," she replied.

"Call me Dix."

Her eyes warmed over like freshly baked bread. She wasn't tough for those few seconds. She was just a dame with love in her heart. "Okay, Dix."

I kissed her one more time before walking into the night.

CHAPTER 18

It was a quiet walk to the pier. A few solitary souls trudged back and forth along Pike, but they seemed more like empty shells of people than actual people. The night always brought them out. They were vampires, feeding on the night like a hungry dog scavenging a dead animal. If you looked into their eyes you might see a tiny flicker of light, but mostly all you saw was a deep, dark emptiness that seemed to go on forever.

I felt for my gun as a cold fear quickly snaked through me. It was the kind of feeling I got when I knew I was headed for trouble. I felt like a toy in invisible hands, thrown back and forth and almost strangled into submission. Off to my left, a pair of lean eyes, belonging to a crumpled old paper of a man, stared mutely at me. I stared back, saying nothing.

A few minutes later I was on the slip; in front of me, the houseboats bobbed silently in the river while the Manhattan strangled it, and everything else, in its murky grip. A slow-moving winter fog moved along the slip like a ghostly corpse; semi-transparent fingers held everything in a chilly embrace.

There were only two houseboats moored on the slip, and as far as I knew both were owned by the city. They leased them out to those choosing to live there, but if Big Pete and Bartlett owned the city, then who was fooling who? It wasn't the first place I would have figured for a hideout, but then I'd seen worse dives. Back in the day, oysters would have been piled sky high in front of the boats moored under the bridge. Now, the place was almost deserted, with only rats to keep the people company.

The occasional fist-sized lamp scattered thin streams of light across the slip, but for some strange reason avoided the boats altogether. I hoped it wasn't an omen. I stuck close to the darkness, scanning the slip for any signs of life. I absently caressed my piece. It felt warm against my skin, the metal smooth and clean.

Lonely, detached structures dotted brief stretches of street across from the boats. Each one looked like a steak that hadn't gone down too well. They were a dirty rust color; bits and pieces of them fell away like teeth from an old man's kisser. It wasn't pretty, and it didn't have to be, as long as it offered me enough shelter from anyone peering out from the boat or anywhere else. The fewer eyes you had looking out, the less you had looking in. I was betting on those odds like an ugly sailor betting on his chances with Dorothy Lamour.

Past the boats the East River was a dead calm. The normally busy expanse of murky water sat silent and still, almost catatonic, watching events unfold with clogged eyes. I looked away from that blackness and toward the two houseboats.

My heart continued pulling me back to Holly. I wondered if she was safe. I wondered if leaving her was a good idea. I wondered if loving her was a good idea. A quick sharp noise brought me back to the slip and the two boats nudging against the pier. The noise had come from the boat closest to me; the one swathed in darkness. It didn't sound like a scream or a gunshot. It sounded more like an argument. Above me, cars passed across the Manhattan, their ceaseless bumps sounding like an out-of-tune bassoon. I listened closely, unsure whether the noise was real or just a figment of my imagination.

I heard the noises again, this time more distinct. They were voices; people arguing over something or someone. Mixed in between those harsh tones was an urgency I had heard and seen before. It was the sound of men trapped in a moment.

I stared across the deep blackness. The distance between my hiding place and the houseboat was the distance between the Earth and the Moon. The space between us seemed like a minefield. Eyes were like machine guns, lights my enemy.

No guts, no glory, I thought to myself.

I bolted across the slip like a crazy man trying to leap frog the East River. I held my gun low and to my right. A window on the bottom half of the boat faced out onto the slip. I could see nothing within. They reminded me of the eyes I had seen on the old buzzard I had passed on my way here. They were cold, dark and full of a haunting despair that belonged only to the loneliest of men. In some ways, it was like gazing into a mirror. A pair of old, wooden double-doors stood on either side, and just above were more windows and doors. Nothing but darkness stared back.

Each step forward felt one step closer to a bullet or beating. Each step back was another nightmare. I felt as vulnerable as a newborn baby. The cold of the night bit ravenously into my cheeks like razor-sharp daggers. Still, despite the pain and the trepidation, I continued forward. I needed to know and right now Schwarz was the best clue I had to what was going on, if he was here and still alive.

I made it to the houseboat, clinging to the side like a fly on a wall. The sounds I heard just seconds before were indeed coming from within. The words were spoken in quick measures as if language were a priceless commodity used only during the rarest of occasions. I couldn't distinguish between voices, but I was sure there were at least two, maybe even three or more, inside.

I didn't think it necessary to go for a swim, and climbing up to the second story was out of the question. The front door was my only option. I leaned forward a few inches and looked inside, the blackness of New York visible from one end of the boat to the other. There were no visible signs of life. That meant if Schwarz was here, he was being held upstairs. If he wasn't here, and this was one big mistake, then Schwarz was dead and I was right back where I started.

I reached the door and turned the handle gradually. It was unlocked. I nudged it open a few inches and listened like a mouse listening for a cat. Words, like leaves, fell from the floor above. I nailed No Shoes' voice right away. The other was a stranger; maybe Schwarz.

I opened the door wider and scurried inside. The light filtering through from the rear windows highlighted nothing of interest. A narrow set of stairs led up to the second level. A small desk sat before me. It wasn't big, but it was big enough to hide me. I slid in front and waited.

The air inside was warm, as if it had been lived in for a long time. I could hear footsteps shuffling slowly and carefully toward the stairs. I closed my eyes and listened intently. I heard more footsteps near the front window. Getting inside had been easy. I hoped getting out would be just as easy.

"Maybe it's…" a voice started.

"Shut up, you moron," an angry voice interrupted. It was Jimmy alright. I'd dealt with him before, but this time things were different. This wasn't about dames or drinks; it was about concealing secrets so big you could drive a hearse through them. I was sick and tired of secrets. They examined me like spotlights during an interrogation. Behind every smile; behind every handshake, secrets dragged good men down to the level of common street thug. I saw dames that could've been the kind of girl you took home to your old lady turn into leeches willing to sell their souls for kicks. Knowing this didn't make me any smarter, it just made me that much more determined to stop Big Pete, Bartlett and the rest of the jokers involved in this sad little play.

A small part of No Shoes might have thought I was just some bum looking for a warm place to sleep. A large part of him probably thought I was trouble wrapped in a hat and overcoat, and loaded with enough lead to fill a landmine.

"Stick close to the kid. If anything happens, drill 'em," Jimmy barked. He started down the stairs. I couldn't see him from where I crouched, but I knew he was there, waiting for my next move.

I looked to my right. A wall of darkness stared back. I slid over a few feet and moved along the sidewall. Each step sounded like horses at a racetrack. I had to close the distance between the stairs and me without alerting Jimmy. He was one of Big Pete's best, ready to kill on a dime. He talked sweet, but would kill for something as small as a case of bullets. It would mean bonus points with the boys in blue if I could take him alive; unfortunately, I wasn't big on good graces.

The light filtered down from the second story in slanted arcs, barely illuminating the narrow staircase. The only way for me to see anything was to stand up, giving No Shoes the target he needed. I couldn't do that. Between Jimmy and I were crates and old boxes; however, there wasn't enough around for me to successfully get a bead on Jimmy and protect my keister at the same time. Jimmy and I both knew that.

I would have to make the first move.

"Well, well, well, Jimmy No Shoes. How long has it been, Jimmy? You trying to get the mug-of-the-year award or something?" I kept my voice low, trying not to give away my position.

"Just keep talking, shamus. It'll make my job a lot easier." Knowing he expected my arrival didn't help chase away the jitters running through my body like wild horses. Jimmy was real good at inspiring fear in others. He didn't have to do anything. He just had to talk. The killing part was just an added bonus.

"Both of us got something to say, Jimmy. Let me talk to the kid for five minutes. After that, you can do whatever you want with him. You'll get no squawks from me."

"No dice. I ain't making deals with some ginned-up shamus that don't got enough sense to mind his own business. You could have stayed away, peeper, but you didn't. Say your prayers, and while you're at it say a few for the dame because she's next."

"You talk tough, Jimmy. You talk this tough to Big Pete when he let you live?" I closed the distance between him and me. I was on my knees, the dust from the floor rising in small vaporous clouds that almost brought on an uncontrollable bout of sneezing. I held my breath in hopes of stemming the tide. I was able to hold my breath long enough to hear footsteps slowly descending the stairs. Jimmy was taking the bait. I still couldn't see him, but I knew he was moving down, slowly. He would be keeping his rod low, aimed toward the darkness, toward me.

"When I get my hands on you, you're gonna cry like a baby, kid. You're gonna buy a ticket to a place you can't afford. You hear me?" Jimmy screamed.

He was mad and that was good. Mugs like Jimmy are always good when they're calm, but get them mad, and they're like a raging bull with blinders on.

"It wasn't me that cried like a baby to Big Pete. Come on, Jimmy, wise up." I managed a few more feet. I could see him now. Through the darkness, thin bits of light exposed a crouching Jimmy, his face twisted by rage. I didn't need a flashlight to see the anger he was throwing out.

"You wise up, mug! You think you're something? You're nothing. Its guys like me that make this world. We got the guns and the brains to make things work while suckers like you slave away for nickels and dimes. We got the kid, and now we got his buddy. You want 'em, come get 'em, but come with a coffin because you ain't getting out alive!" The first shot sounded like cannon fire. The echo bounced murderously off the thin walls, literally exploding inside my head. I kept my cool. Firing would do little except give away my position, and judging from the angle of Jimmy's shot he had no clue where I was.

"Nice try, Jimmy. You're aim is as bad as the job you and the rest of Big Pete's boys did on Kelly. You snuck up on him like a coward. Only a bum with a yellow streak a mile long goes down that road. You're nothing but a two-bit thug in fancy clothes, Jimmy. When you go, no one will remember you." He fired again. His aim was getting better. Small splinters cracked off a wooden crate to my left.

"One more move, shamus, and the kid buys a bullet he can't afford," Jimmy yelled. "Big Pete controls everything. He tells you things when he wants you to know. You're only here because he wanted you here. You can watch the kid die. After I finish you off, I'll find the dame and finish her off too. After that, things go back to normal." He fired again, missing by a mile.

I moved forward cautiously, this time arcing to my right, away from the stairs. Jimmy moved down another step. His gat was still in his right hand, his left clinging to the railing. I was only a few feet away. All of a sudden the windows behind me showered too much light on my back, giving away my position too soon. I cursed the mug that invented glass.

I kept my eyes focused on Jimmy. He scanned the lower floor from left to right. He hadn't seen me, but it was only a matter of time before he did. The space between the boxes and crates was getting wider, my sanctuary becoming increasingly scarce. I had to make my move, now.

The seconds between thought and action seemed stuck in time, like a broken clock fixed on a solitary moment. Between those clustered seconds, Jimmy and I caught each other's glance. I could see him. I could see him swinging his arm toward me. I could even see the bullet entering the firing chamber as he pulled the trigger like he had a hundred times before. I started to do the same.

The air became like a moist, warm blanket. I wasn't just hot; I was sweating like a plant in a greenhouse. My hands felt slippery, my grip on my gun tenuous. Everything seemed wrong somehow, as if I'd played the wrong card in the deck and realized it too late. I closed my eyes.

The houseboat crackled with the noise of angry gunfire. The space Jimmy and I occupied became a giant cloud of impenetrable smoke; my eyes burned from the flash of the gunpowder in the hot, dry air. My senses felt like they had taken a vacation as the noise from our guns filled the small houseboat. I could hear and feel gunshots bounce around me like drunken baseballs. I felt something fly past me, a scream like an angry housefly spitting through the air, but I continued firing my .38 even as a scream as violent and insane as ever erupted from a man roared above everything. It was a scream of pain. I continued firing until my gun was empty. The shallow click of an empty chamber brought me back to reality.

What seemed like hours was over in less than three seconds. I fell back against one of the crates that huddled next to me. I felt the emotion drain from me like water from a glass. I looked down. I knew I had been hit.

CHAPTER 19

Blood was everywhere. It was splashed like an art-deco painting against the wall. It was on the coat and the pants. Lucky for me I wasn't in them. Unfortunately for Jimmy No Shoes, he was.

Two of the shots I fired hit Jimmy square. One hit him high in the chest while the other decorated a spot just below his hairline. His head hung at an odd angle against the far wall. I didn't have time to examine the rest of him since there was one more thug above. I reloaded the chamber, popping in six bullets as I scanned the stairs. If he knew Jimmy was dead he would kill the kid.

I needed to close the distance before he figured out which one I was.

I just finished reloading and had climbed the first two steps when I heard faint shuffling sounds above me followed by a muffled voice. The voice didn't get me so much as the fear that punctuated it did. I gathered my strength and quickly took the stairs two at a time, angling back toward the front of the boat, toward the muffled voice.

The second story was empty, filled only with two small lamps and a few scattered bits of furniture. Large windows looked out onto the East River. I couldn't see anyone ahead. I squatted just before reaching the landing. Between the banister and the railing I saw a young kid, probably Schwarz, hog-tied in a chair with bruises the size of Kentucky decorating most of his face. It was like looking into a mirror. Obviously, Jimmy and the boys had substituted the kid for a piñata, smacking him around until something came out. Were they looking for information from him, or was it just a case of boredom?

I heard sound coming from below. I caught a brief glimpse of the second goon race through the door I had come in and aim up toward me. I didn't have a chance to turn around and aim so I quickly dived across the floor like spilled milk. He was a good shot, firing in the direction I had been in just a second before. I stood up and fired through the thin veneer of ancient plywood that made up the flooring. It was a long shot, but I couldn't risk playing peek-a-boo with the mug. I pulled the trigger three times.

A thin audible moan broke the silence followed by one shot. This time, the shot was wild, haphazard, smashing through the floor and into the ceiling allowing little chips of wood to fall to the floor.

I heard something heavy hit the near wall followed by a slow sliding sound. I edged toward the railing and peered into the deep darkness. I could just make him out. He had slid a couple of stairs below Jimmy, his carcass lying flat against the wall. He moved, but barely. His chest rose and fell like an out-of-control piston. I slowly walked back down the steps until I was face-to-face with him. He didn't make any fancy moves and neither did Jimmy. I thought I heard Big Pete laughing somewhere beyond the East side.

The guy was young judging from his pock-marked face and slicker hairdo. A small pair of sensitive-looking eyes peered dimly out at me like half-covered windows waiting to be shut. His suit was the usual grayish-black mobster three-piece that probably cost more than my entire wardrobe put together. His shoes had a thin sheen of dust on them, but had about twenty to thirty bucks on mine. Everything about him screamed new and ready for action. Unfortunately, the only thing he was properly dressed for now was his funeral.

I looked over at Jimmy, scooped up his piece and put it quickly in my overcoat pocket. I looked for the second guy's gun, but his hands were empty. I hadn't heard it drop, and the gloom obscured my vision enough that searching for the thing was impossible. I checked Jimmy and found his pulse as active as a centenarian at a Burly-Q. The second mug looked up, his eyes darkening with each passing second. My luck had held up while his bought him an early ticket for the midnight show. One bullet hit him in the abdomen while the other pierced his ticker. Blood spread quickly from the once-white, now-crimson shirt.

"What's your name, mug?" I asked.

"G...Go shine s...some shoes, s...sh...shamus." He was hurting worse than me after a hangover. I placed the muzzle of my gun deep into his abdomen and pushed. Blood trickled out in small rivulets. He screamed.

"Talk or it gets worse."

"B...Benny," He cried. I could see a thin trail of tears marking a path down his pale cheeks.

"All right, Benny. Why hide the kid? Why not just kill him? What's he mean to Big Pete?"

Benny's head lolled to one side as if ready to fall off. Talking seemed to take every bit of energy he had left. "It don't matter now. I...I'm a g...goner. I Should've listened to my M...M...Ma. S...Sh... Should've gone s...straight."

"Yeah, kid. You still got a chance to do right. Tell me about Schwarz and the dame?"

"He's just b...bait. He's t...the web to c...catch the fly. Sure h...he knows a l...little about t...the b...bi...big man's setup. But B...big man still needs t...to know who is on what side. Besides, l...lots of p...people go d...down i...if he squeals."

"People like Bartlett and his daughter?" I asked.

"B...B...Big Pete ain't too w...wo...worried about him. H...He's soft. T...The dames a r...real peach though. Big Pete's sweet on h...he...her, b...b...bu...but so are s...some of his h...hi...hired b...boy...boys." The words were fewer and far between; the stretches of silence became longer.

Benny's gaze stretched across the room. A few seconds later he closed his eyes. I couldn't let him do that. Not yet. The muzzle of my gun found its way into his gut once again. His eyes suddenly opened and his mouth contorted into something resembling an exploding volcano, only without the fireworks. It was like listening to the radio with the sound off.

"Not yet, Benny; not until you tell me what I need to know."

It took a few seconds for him to work through the pain, but once he did, what came out might make the last page of the classifieds, if he was lucky. "T...There ain't m...mu...much to tell, sh...shamus." Benny's eyes rolled into the back of his head like fruit on a slot machine. I let his body fall clumsily toward the base of the steps. Benny went still a few seconds later. It was a quiet death. One he probably hadn't counted on. They were all big talkers when alive. But when they died, it was like watching paint dry.

I stood up and started for the stairs when I heard more movement behind me. I turned and aimed, my finger gently squeezing the trigger. I could almost see the shot as it burst through the glass and struck the target. In front of me, a graceful cat-like shadow hugged the doorframe. Long hair draped gently over curves I had seen a lot lately. It was Holly. I could've killed her, should've killed her. I don't know why I hesitated. In this business, the slightest hesitation means you're standing at the pearly gates begging your way in. My hesitation saved Holly's life.

I eased off the trigger. The shadows eased off my back a little. She opened the door slowly, a scratchy creak echoing through the rest of the lower floor. Anything I said now would probably be defined more by the colorful metaphors I used than what the words actually meant. I took a few seconds to try and calm myself before I spoke.

"I told you to stay in the car. I almost shot you, baby." I gritted my teeth, allowing the anger to slip through in pieces rather than in one big explosion. She walked in slowly, a mute stare aimed directly at the two bodies lying on the ground. I swung my gat lazily in Jimmy's direction and said, "Let me present, Mr. Jimmy No Shoes, and his pal Benny. Schwarz is upstairs. He's bruised, battered and generally not looking too presentable, but he's alive."

Her stare stuck to the corpses like flypaper. I walked over and gripped her tightly, hoping the pressure would shake her out of the state of shock she was in. No dice.

"Listen, baby, those are the bad guys. Bad guys aren't the nicest of mugs. That's why we call them the bad guys, see?"

The Trigger Method

She didn't respond. It was like talking to a statue in Central Park. I shook her, at first gently, but then harder when she wouldn't snap out of it. I finally reached out and slapped her. That did it.

"I…I…I got worried when you didn't show up. I had to come. I had to see if you were okay. I had to know if you were still alive. You promised me. You promised me." There was little emotion in the words, no sense of feeling. She spoke in even tones, no one word emphasized more than the next. She was swimming in a sea of fear, attempting to span a distance so far that her arms could no longer continue. I could see her sinking quickly into that darkness like a weighted down body. If we got out of this alive, she would need a lot of hours of peace and quiet.

"Holly, I need you right now." I gazed into her eyes. "I need to know you're here, with me. I can't do on this on my own." The sound of her name brought some life back into her eyes. I could see a small flicker where moments before was only emptiness. I fed off it. "Little Benny here said Big Pete is sweet on Connie. He also said some of his mugs were sweet on her too. More than likely he was talking about Kelly. But she would need more than just Kelly to make it work. What say you and I go up and ask Schwarz?" I stood so close I could feel her breath against my face.

"Shouldn't we take him somewhere? Someone's bound to have heard the shots and called the police," Holly said slowly.

"I doubt it. In this part of town, nobody wants a part of nothing. They'll make themselves think it was back-fire from a car, or some liquored-up gutter rat throwing bottles through a window. We got time." I turned around and started back up the stairs.

I reached the top and turned to study the face I'd been chasing for the last two days. Behind the bruises was a kid. His black hair looked like an overused mop with pieces of it going off in all different directions. He had a forgettable face. It mixed easily in a mob until it ceased to exist. He had beady little eyes that were stuck close together like tiny grains of rice in a soup bowl. It was easy to see what Connie saw in this guy: nothing.

I walked over just as Holly reached the top. Schwarz looked past me, toward Holly. A look of utter confusion decorated his bruised and battered face. He looked like a jigsaw puzzle put together with all the pieces in the wrong place. Shades of red and black mixed with lighter shades making his face appear more like that of a clown than a victim. He reminded me a little of Baker's body, only without the bullet holes.

I removed the tape from his mouth. He didn't say anything. He just stared wildly at me, then at Holly, then back at me again. He was close to losing his marbles. I just had to figure out how close.

"I've been looking for you everywhere, Schwarz. Aren't you just a little happy to see me? After all, I did just save your life."

He remained quiet. Holly hovered above me, studying Schwarz with an anger that felt like a machine gun.

"I talk now, I'm dead," he cried.

"You don't talk, you're dead," I barked. I wiped the end of my gun against Schwarz's mottled shirt until small red streaks appeared. "Say hello to what's left of Jimmy and Benny. You want to join them?" Seconds passed and still nothing. "Come on, kid, you're part of something. Big Pete knows it, Connie knows it and I know it. It was big enough to get Kelly and Baker bumped off." I stared into Schwarz's eyes and said, "Joe's death is on your hands. You better talk before it's too late."

He wanted to spill everything. He also knew talking would mean signing his own death warrant. He was sitting in the middle of a rabid group of wolves with any one of them ready to take a sizeable bite. Either way, Alfred was going to walk away with more than a few scars. It was up to him to decide how deep the scars were going to be.

"Al," Holly started, "I know what these people can do. They ruin lives because they can. They take lives because they can. You think Connie loves you, but she doesn't. She loves money. She loves any guy that will buy her the time of day. Her kind of love will do nothing but get you killed. You're close to the edge now. One push and you're gone. No one will care. Is that how you want to go out?"

The words came from the heart. They were sincere and right on the money. Problem is most kids don't listen until it's too late. I hoped it wasn't too late for Alfred. It was for Baker, but maybe there was some hope for Schwarz.

"I...I... don't know what to do." He started to cry. He was just a poor schmuck from the wrong side of town. He dreamed of catching a falling star. He caught one: Connie Bartlett. She was his ticket to a better life. He was her ticket out of boredom. It was enough to make a guy laugh himself to death.

Holly got to her knees. "Tell us what you know, Al. Mr. Dixon knows people that can keep you safe, but you have to tell us the truth."

He kept crying. The tears fell like hard rain. His head bobbed and jerked with each wave. He was sorry for what happened. We all had ghosts to deal with. Some were bigger than others, but for Alfred Schwarz the death of his friend would haunt him forever. I suddenly felt very sorry for the kid.

"B...Big Pete hired us to be runners. We weren't good enough for the big time, but if we did enough we'd get bigger scraps. He had lots of stuff going on, but we weren't in on that stuff. Kelly and Baxter knew, but they were big time. S...She said no one would get hurt. I...It was just a small racket. She said we would make a lot of money and no one would get hurt. She said there was no way Big Pete would find out, but he did. Someone talked."

"What kind of racket?" I asked.

"Connie came up with a protection racket. Joe and I knew the area. We knew the people and we knew the way they thought. Most of them are always scared. The old ones will jump at their own shadow. Kelly knew some freelance guns that would work for scraps. You know, take names and numbers, but ask no questions. Connie would organize the whole thing from the top, getting enough information from her old man and his playmates to keep us in the chips. Big Pete and he had lots of stuff going on. There was no reason to think any of 'em would care about one little part of the city. We would collect the toll, and no one would be the wiser. Only problem was someone knew and ratted us out."

"That's got to be the dumbest plan I ever heard of. No one does protection in this city without Big Pete's say so," I laughed. "No one blows his nose in this city without a permit from Big Pete. Old man Bartlett probably figured that one out the hard way. He must have known what Connie was up to and tried to warn her. She probably didn't listen, forcing Bartlett in a corner. Now he has to decide whether to back his daughter or his business partner? That might explain the fear on his face when we went to see him."

"What are you saying?" Holly asked.

"I don't know. It's just that there's something we're not seeing. Connie couldn't hope to sneak one out from under Big Pete without him knowing. Kelly was good, but even he had a big mouth. Any one of the mugs he tried to hire would go straight to Pete if they thought they could get more ratting Kelly out."

"No loyalty among thieves," Holly stated.

I turned back to Alfred. "The old man must have known what Connie was up to. Did you ever meet him?"

"No. He came by the club a few times, but Connie always said to avoid him. We only ever got to talk to Kelly a few times. Not that it mattered. He just saw us as meat."

"Where does Baker fit in?" I asked.

"He was supposed to go around and talk to some of the people. Let them know what was what. He had a problem with it right from the start. He told me we were wrong. He said we were spitting on everything we'd known. I didn't believe him. I just thought he wanted Connie for himself."

"So you took him out." I didn't really believe it, but anger has a way of letting the true mug out.

"He was my friend. No matter what happened between us, I would never, I could never kill my own friend! He was the only guy I could trust. He was straight about everything. He said we were doing wrong. He told me he felt dirty because he couldn't stand lying to his old lady anymore. He said he couldn't even look her in the eye anymore because he figured she knew what was going on. I thought he was just going soft, but he was the only true and honest guy of all of us." The sobbing didn't stop, it just became heavier. I tried looking past the tears, but they were hard to ignore. For a second, I thought I was looking into Baker's eyes again.

"So, if you didn't kill him, who did? Big Pete? Why would he kill one mug and leave the other alive?"

"I don't know. All I know is I didn't kill him." He kept his head down, as if afraid to look up. It wasn't a lie that kept his head bowed, it was guilt.

"How long have you been here?" Holly asked.

"A week, I think."

"You've been here the whole time?" I asked.

"They wouldn't let me leave. They kept telling me my number was up. Every day I thought they were going to just pick me up and throw me out the back window into the river, but they didn't. It was like they were waiting for something. Being so close to home made it even worse. I felt like they wanted me to die here, close to the place I tried to destroy. Sometimes I used to run into Joe's mom at night. She would go around collecting stuff for the war. If I ran into her tonight, I would even be able to look her in the eye. Because of me, Joe is dead."

Schwarz kept talking, but I could hear only some of what he said. I thought about the voice on the phone and everything he had told me. If he was working alone or for one of Big Pete's rivals he wouldn't be using mind games on Big Pete, he'd be using bullets. That option would take the big guy out fast and easy, but not without causing more than a few ripples.

No. This was someone with a personal grudge. Big Pete had wronged a lot of people. Many would love to take him out back and put a bullet in his skull, but most didn't have the guts.

"You're bait and we're the catch of the day. Someone wanted us to find you. It's one big frame, and right now we're the picture."

CHAPTER 20

There are a thousand different reasons to kill a man. Some guys do it for dames and other guys for dough. Some mugs will do it for both. It's a game with no end unless you have a conscience. It becomes a mirror, exposing a hard, awful truth that rests at the heart of all things.

I saw the truth in Albert's eyes. He was no killer. He was just a dumb kid yearning for something better. Working for Big Pete was like finding the key that opened the door to everything big and shiny. But having the guts to walk through that door was an entirely different ball of wax.

Baker recognized the setup for what it really was and didn't want any part of it. Maybe he went along for a little while. Maybe he even scared a few people, but you can't bury the good for too long. It washes over you, gathering strength with each successive wave. Joseph accidentally looked into a mirror one day and hated the person that stared back. I know the feeling. Albert, on the other hand, saw the person that stared back and fooled himself into believing he was working toward a higher purpose: Connie Bartlett. All he had to do was make her happy and she would sing to him like Judy Garland singing to Mickey Rooney. Too bad people don't act in real life like they do in the movies.

The arrangement was gradually becoming clearer. Connie and Kelly set up a smalltime protection racket. She milks the people on one end while Big Pete smashes them aside on the other. Baker and Schwarz sit in the middle like pawns; they shuffle from one square to another while Connie looks on. Her old man must have known, but probably didn't know how to deal with it. Maybe he figured Big Pete did. Big Pete, on the other hand, saw her as a pretty toy, worth keeping around. As dames go, she was nice to look at, but nice things never last. Baker and Schwarz both realized that. Unfortunately, Baker realized it too late.

There wasn't much more I could ask Schwarz. He didn't kill Baker, and he didn't know Big Pete's master plan, or how it connected with Baker's murder. He knew what Connie was up to, but then so did all of Times Square. It was no big secret.

I walked quietly out, crossing over the living and the dead. A cold breeze floated in off the East River sending deep chills up and down my spine. The slip was still deserted.

"So we just leave him there to get shot by one of Big Pete's boys?" Holly asked angrily.

"No. Big Pete isn't going to take a chance on plugging the kid now. Plus, if he wanted him dead, he could've done it long ago. Jimmy No Shoes was good, but sitting in one place that long can make a mug go colder than frozen meat. The kid might know some of Big Pete's plan, but not enough to prove anything. Don't forget, a lot of this city is mortgaged to that fat slob. It doesn't matter what the kid knows. If he tried to sing, he'd be dead before the first chorus."

"But we can't just leave him there. I'd like to slap him around some, but he's still just a kid."

"Don't worry, baby. I'm going to call Pete at the precinct and get his boys to baby-sit him," I replied.

We walked back to the car and drove away from Henry Street. The side streets and dirt-filled empty lots we passed were littered with bits and pieces of unwanted memorabilia. Twisted and rusted metal and broken plastic shards lay scattered here and there like monuments at a cemetery. Obviously, Baker's old lady hadn't done her nightly rounds. There was at least a buck lying here just waiting to be claimed.

I slowly drove past the decrepit buildings and dirt-filled lots. I wondered why Big Pete and Bartlett wanted the land. The place stunk like stale fish; the buildings were about as level as me after a night at Mahoney's, and the people were about as willing to leave as the poverty that followed them there.

I drove a few more blocks before pulling to the curb. "I'll be right back," I said.

"Where are you going?" Holly asked.

"I'm going to call Pete and tell him about Alfred."

A few moments later, Pete picked up the phone and after his usual tirade over rules and regulations asked me how things were going. "I'm still alive, Pete. So is Schwarz for that matter."

"You found him, didn't you?" Pete asked.

"Yeah, he was being forced to baby sit some houseboat under the Manhattan. Make sure you take a couple of body bags down there and pick up Jimmy No Shoes and some small-timer named Benny."

"Are you trying to set a record or something? You know, you can't keep killing people no matter the reason."

"Someone points a gat in my face and all you want me to do is smile and say 'cheese'? Pete, someone's using me as bait."

"Bait for what?"

"I'm not sure. What I do know is someone is pulling our strings like puppets. The guy that keeps calling me has gotten everything right. He knows dates, name, and places like they're yesterday's news."

"He's probably an inside man," Pete replied.

"He's too smart to be anything else. I can't help thinking that at the end of this crazy ride is a picture of me with egg on my face."

"What do you mean?"

"Enough people saw Kelly and Connie Bartlett together for me to guess, and most likely be right, that they were involved. They were probably using each other for the big payoff. Schwarz said he and Baker went around scaring the locals into buying protection against Big Pete and Bartlett. What they didn't tell them was that the protection lasted about as long as it took to walk out the door. If you believe in Chinese puzzles then it all makes sense. They know the neighborhood and the people. It doesn't explain why Big Pete leaves one alive if he did kill the other one."

"What if he was looking for something?"

"Like a rat?"

"Could be," Pete replied. "Maybe he's looking for the guy feeding you information. You're job on Baxter was nice. It means one less rat to worry about. No one will say anything because there'll be no way to prove he had anything to do with any of the murders. You go around and clean his house for him leaving him looking like an angel before the baptism. With his house back in order, it's business as usual again."

Pete focused on something that I couldn't quite get my head around. This land deal would be big, real big. Everyone who loves dough would want in on it, including the Connie Bartlett's of the world. It was well known Big Pete was having employee problems. More than once he'd doled out permanent cures for headaches to his unruly goons. With so much going on and the death of the kid so fresh on everyone's mind, Big Pete couldn't afford to off someone right now. It was too risky. And in the world the big guy traveled in, one mistake was one mistake too many.

"What did old man Bartlett say to you when you got to his place?"

"Not much. He told us you were there with the dame, but that was about it. When we asked him why Baxter wanted him dead, he said he didn't know. He figured the guy was drunk. I think his daughter was playing around with Baxter as well as Kelly. It could be the old man didn't approve so Baxter came around to show his appreciation. Unfortunately, I haven't been able to track down the dame to get her side. On the plus side, we know the kid was killed nearby. The dirt on the bottom of his shoes matches dirt in a lot pretty close to his apartment. I checked with the log books from a title company and found that the lot belongs to a company called 'Benson Properties'. Sound familiar?"

"That's too much of a coincidence to be a coincidence," I replied. "What else did you find?"

"We also found traces of dried blood plus a bunch of bullet casings, shoeprints, a small ring and some other odds and ends. We even found a couple bullets that missed the mark. They came from a .22 caliber. The bullets the coroner pulled out of the kid were from

The Trigger Method

a .22. The boys at the lab say the blood matches Baker's blood type. The size of the bullet casings also match the entry and exit wounds on the body. We haven't been able to find the murder weapon yet, but you put all that together and we got part of the mystery solved."

"What did the ring look like? Maybe it belonged to the murderer. If it did, we might be able to track him down through it."

"Not likely, unless the murder happened to be a pigmy with hands smaller than a rag doll. Besides, this ring is about as fancy as your wardrobe. I think it's just a piece of junk someone lost."

"Does it look a man's ring or a woman's ring?"

"I'm not much on rings, Dix. It just looks another piece of junk. Why?"

"It was just a thought. If they did kill him nearby, they wouldn't have had to carry him too far. Still, climbing up the side of a building with a hundred and fifty pounds strapped to your back would be tough for anybody, even Fats Kelly."

"Well, someone did it," Pete replied.

"Someone singular, or someone plural?"

"It would've taken at least two guys to get him up there. Plus, someone had to be on the lookout from below. I figure at least two, maybe even three goons."

"Yeah, then again maybe he flew up there with wings strapped to his back." I shook my head in frustration. Only having part of the picture was like driving with both hands strapped behind my back. "Obviously, some hired mugs did the dirty work. They beat him up until he looks like an overripe tomato, dump him in an empty lot then shoot him. Why not shoot him then dump him in the lot?"

"It could be he tried something and left them no other option," Pete offered.

"I don't know, Pete. It seems logical, but something is still missing. Someone is standing over everything pulling the strings and singing the chorus. Maybe it was a warning to his old lady, or to Schwarz. Either way, someone in this little game did it, and for reasons that will probably make about as much sense as a three-dollar bill."

"I'd like to get my hands on the dame and find out what she knows. Maybe some hot lights and a few rubber hoses might do the trick," Pete replied sarcastically.

"You tried the lounge?" I asked.

"Not without a warrant, I haven't. I still have rules to follow, Dix."

"I don't. I have a feeling the big guy will be more forthcoming with me. I'm his made-to-order patsy. His trail to the rat goes cold without my services. With me around, he's that much closer."

"What about the dead kid? You haven't forgotten about him, have you?"

"He's right here in my back pocket, Pete. The other one is all yours. I don't need him anymore. I'm after bigger game now." Schwarz was already beginning to fade like an old photograph. I had spent so much time looking for the guy only to let him fall into someone else's lap. I can't say he was all that useful, but then I'm sure Connie thought the same thing. Of course the kid wasn't all to blame. He was an easy mark. She recognized fresh meat better than most broads with too much money and too much time on their hands. She wanted an escape from the boredom of a pampered life, plus some dirty dough earned with her own twisted and warped mind.

"You might also get a bullet for your troubles. Have you thought about that, or is that just another illusion running around blindly in that thing you call a brain?"

"I see everything. I just see it when I want to. If Big Pete wanted me dead, he could've nailed me anytime. Instead, he lets me live. I run around and bother anyone remotely associated with him, shake them around until a few truths and half-truths fall out. Then I let them beat me over the head just before shoving them through brick walls or through the end of my gun. He wouldn't let me do all of that unless he wanted me to. Pete, my idea of charity only goes so far."

Pete went quiet. We were having another one of our philosophical differences. It was one of the biggest reasons I left the force. I couldn't take the moral nonsense that spread through the department. It was like watching the 1919 White Sox teach children about honesty and integrity. I helped whoever wanted it, and was willing to pay. I did the kid for free because he was like me. He died alone and afraid. Did he know the person that killed him? I didn't know the answer to that, but he did.

"Dix, I'm going to go down and pick up the kid as well as any dead bodies you left on the menu. After that, I think I'll go home and kiss Wilma, say hi to the kids, then pray for your soul. You're lost, Dix, and you know it. You used to have some sense of right and wrong, but you don't even have that anymore. You don't know love because you're too angry. You don't know light because you're always in the dark, and you don't know right because you're always doing wrong. I pity you, Dix."

"I hope that's not what you plan on saying at my eulogy. Mix in a few dame stories. That way you can keep some of the rummies from falling asleep in the back row. Actually, you better do it at Mahoney's. That way some of them will be able to cry in their beer."

"You're lost, old friend." Pete hung up the phone. I placed the receiver back in the cradle, stepped out of the phone booth and looked at the cracked and broken pavement. It was like staring into a mirror.

Pete's reaction was no surprise. I was playing for big stakes and having Pete and his boys hanging around watching my every move wouldn't just cramp my style, it would kill it. If Pete thought I was motivated by dough he might back off leaving me to deal with the big guy and his goons in my own way.

I put another dime into the phone and dialed the Lounge. It didn't take long for some guy with a voice laced in honey and a British accent as fake as a wooden nickel to answer.

"Yeah, tell Big Pete his favorite shamus wants to talk to him, now."

The voice sounded startled. "Excuse me, sir, but I believe you have the wrong number."

"No, I got the right number. Tell your boss Dixon is on the phone. If you don't get him on the line now, you'll be serving customers from ten feet under." The line went quiet. I could hear an odd assortment of noises in the background. It was the sound of music and laughter. Those sounds seemed far away.

A few seconds later another voice came over the line. This one was as sweet as stale beer and as smooth as raw leather: "Yeah?"

"Get me Big Pete. We got a lot of talking to do; mostly about dames, dough and east-side goons that just won't go away."

"There ain't nobody here by that name."

"Quit stalling, mug. Get him on the phone or it's your funeral." The voice sounded strange. It seemed muted, like it was funneled through an oil slick. I had heard the voice before. In the back of my mind I could feel something begin to stir, but before I could open that door another voice boomed over the line. It was one I hadn't heard in a long time. It was big. I suddenly thought about barrels of molasses swishing back and forth on a barge.

"Mr. Dixon, it's been a long time. In fact, the last time I saw you, you were mixed up with Faletti and some stupid broad. This time things are a little closer to home. I don't like it that way, shamus. I get real uncomfortable."

"A small chair makes you uncomfortable. Besides, Faletti is a joke. I'm not calling to talk to you about Faletti. I'm calling you about information."

"What kind of information?" He asked.

"The kind that makes ordinary guys nervous and their bosses real happy; the kind that deserves a bonus, considering you've had me doing you're dirty work for over a week."

His laugh sounded like a cow in pain. It was enough to make me want to hang up the phone. I stayed on, for Joseph's sake. "You're an okay kid. Too bad I couldn't get you to work for me."

I bristled at the thought. "I got expensive tastes. I think Connie Bartlett is more in your league."

He wasn't laughing anymore. "She's a good kid, shamus. She means well and that's all that matters. You keep disrespecting her and I might start to get angry."

"Don't sweat it. I'm just overdue for a drink. My nerves are all shot. Maybe once this whole thing is over, you and me can split a bottle of rum and laugh about the whole stupid mess. I'm sure her old man will do the same." It was a shot in the dark, but my aim seemed to place pretty well.

"Why you bustin' my chops, shamus? What did I ever do to you?" He asked.

"Don't make me answer that one, bud. I need information. I personally don't care what you and the old man got going on. This is about a kid that didn't deserve what he got. You want answers, and I got questions. Seeing as how Benny and Jimmy No Shoes are never going to bother you for their wages ever again, why don't we call it even?"

It was like playing cards with a mortician. You didn't know if the hand he was throwing out was full of Kings and Aces, or spades to bury you with. I wasn't sweating, but it was safe to say I'd need a bath after this was over.

"Who's going to pay me for Baxter? He was a useful guy to have around, even if he was chewing on my fingers a little."

"It's self-defense, Petey. I can't let some stupid gee just shoot me full of holes, can I? Plus, it was dark. There was a big mansion in my face and thoughts of dames running through my mind. You can't really blame a mug with all of that going on."

"Maybe not, but cheap names have bitten the dust for less. By the way, how's the brunette? She was kind of nice to look at. It'd be a shame if something happened to her." He spoke casually, like a guy sitting in an art galley admiring a painting. He made it sound harmless, almost witty. I knew better.

"She's got nothing to do with this. Listen, people are already beginning to think you're human. You keep wasting time, and that itch in the small of your back is going to become a knife pretty soon. I know you don't want that. I'm small potatoes. What you want is the big fish. Call off your dogs for a few hours. Dane and Connie Bartlett, Benson Properties and a few inside men are all that's keeping me from the truth. I'm sure even a mug like you can appreciate the truth."

"You're a smart man, shamus. I knew you were. I knew I picked the right bastard for the job. See, in my business, smart guys are good to have around. But, you got to watch them every second, otherwise they get to thinking that they are smarter than you are. One day you'll get too smart for your own good. I'll give you a free pass, as long as you get the goods. But remember this. You're one joke away from singing to flies." The phone clicked like a gunshot.

I swallowed, hard. He wasn't kidding. At least I could say I'd been threatened by the best. When you get threatened by Big Pete, you know you've arrived. I'd arrived. I just didn't know where I was going.

Big Pete had to know I was alone. He had to know I didn't care who got what, as long as I got what I wanted. If one of his boys saw me parading Alfred up and down the police precinct sidewalk, he'd know which side I was playing for and drill me before I got a chance to open my mouth. I dropped Benson Properties into the mix to see how he would react. He hadn't expected it. Most people in Big Pete's circle would know any land deal would have to be washed through some legal ringer. Big Pete should have expected me to know, but he didn't. His anger told me as much. He was hiding something. It was the kind of something that told me if I got too close I'd find myself gazing up at the stars from six feet under.

I walked slowly back to the car and slid gingerly into the driver's seat. It was still warm, but I felt colder than ice. Holly must have seen the look on my face.

"What's wrong?" She asked.

"I just shook hands with the devil, baby, and he may come around to collect, real soon."

Holly placed her arms around her chest and stared out the window. I started the car and headed into the bleak darkness. It would be a long night.

CHAPTER 21

An icy chill snaked up and down my spine as I thought about the empty lot where Pete said the kid was murdered. I had walked by it a few times and thought nothing of its importance. At the time, it was nothing more than an empty lot with bits of dead grass and weeds and filled with small piles of other people's garbage. Now it was a place where murder and youth stepped over each others' shadows.

"Something is bothering you. What is it?" Holly asked.

"I feel like the last guy in a conga line. I'm walking in everyone else's footsteps, chasing shadows that are gone before I get there."

"You've done more than I ever thought you could. Not too many people could've done better. At least that's what I think," Holly said in a hushed tone.

"Thanks, but until I find out exactly what happened I haven't really done anything. Pete told me the kid was killed on some abandoned lot close to his old lady's apartment. The kicker is the lot is owned by Benson Properties. That's another link back to Dane Bartlett and through him to Big Pete. Someone is trying real hard to bring down the fat buzzard."

"You mean he wasn't killed on the boat?"

"I doubt it. Big Pete and his boys aren't much on cleanliness. If they shot him there, the place would have looked like a slaughterhouse. Pete says the traces of blood they found on the lot matched the kid's blood type, and that the bullet casings match the size of the entry and exit wounds. That means he was shot there. It still doesn't tell us why, but if he was shot that close to the boat, any one of Big Pete's thugs could've pulled the trigger. Too bad they weren't very neat about the whole thing."

"We're right back at the beginning again." Holly sounded dejected. I felt the same dejection, but I wasn't about to let Holly know that. I played it cool, if not for my sake, at least for hers.

"I've got promises wrapped around my neck and it'll only take one slip for those promises to tighten like a noose. The only person that can help me now is the same guy that seems to have the playbook to the whole picture. I think he'll be willing to help me out one more time, especially if he hates Big Pete as much as I think he does."

I pulled away from the curb slowly and into the forlorn traffic. The peculiarity of the scene before me rested in the normalcy of the moment. I hadn't lived normal in a long time. The last week had been proof of that. The minutes, hours, and days expanded like a rubber band until the only thing worth remembering were the dark moments. With Holly around I could live a few peaceful moments, but sure enough, a bullet or dead body barged in and frightened the feeling away as quick as it arrived.

"I'd ask you how we're doing, but the look on your face tells me everything I need to know," Holly said, as if reading my mind. "It's bad, isn't it?"

"It's always been bad. It's just now we're really in no man's land. If I don't deliver, either Big Pete roasts me alive or the cops take me in for murder, times three."

"They can't do that. Not only were you defending yourself, but you also saved that kid's life. The city should give you a medal," Holly cried.

"Big Pete and Bartlett are the city. They probably have more on the D.A. and the judges than God. If they say I'm guilty, nobody is going to sit around and debate it."

Holly said little after that. She understood the truth as well as I did. Without solid evidence my goose was cooked. Even with solid evidence I could wind up in sing-sing on a three-to-five. I was caught between what the truth was and what it could do to me. There were some in this little drama that couldn't afford to let the truth get out. And then there were some for whom the truth mattered about as much as a wooden nickel. I figured the mug on the phone was the former.

I took my time getting back to the office, but the familiar inevitably budged its way back into my mind. My office building unceremoniously appeared above the horizon. A few minutes later we walked through the proverbial rickety door with its proverbial rusty hinges and almost working doorknob and into the dusty and dank foyer. The same bleak shadows and cobwebs clung to the same areas, as if waiting for something to happen. Holly stayed close, her perfume a welcome change to the usual sour smell of booze, rats and dust. I glanced quickly at my watch to see if I had timed it right. I hoped I had.

The elevator was working for a change. That seemed to be the first thing that went right for me all week. Sure it wasn't much, but I'd take what I could get.

All the way up I could feel Holly looking at me. I didn't look back. I had no explanations for her, or any truths to dole out like desert. All I could do was sit and wait for something to happen.

A deep, dark shadow chased me into the deepest recesses of my mind, watching me, waiting for the moment when some little truth or revelation was almost ready to jump forth before pulling it back like a ship sinking in the ocean. Coming back here again was a stab in the dark, just like the voice on the phone. I had my suspicions, but they seemed to contain as much solidity as a ghostly apparition.

I walked onto my floor like I had a million times before. The doors stared silently back at me. Peering down the hall, I saw the same fly-by-night businesses with their assorted devious intentions spewing out rusty-colored lights from windows so old they talked. Down the other end rested more darkness. It was only as I reached for the knob to my office that I felt an odd change in the air. It was like some strange sixth sense nudging me toward the newness of the moment. I pulled my gat out and slowly opened the door, the muzzle gently nosing through the gap. Holly stepped back against the far wall.

I opened the door only a few inches. The unmistakable scent of pine trees hit me like a beer truck. It was the smell of cheap cologne mixed with a cold, calculating fear. I knew the scent. I had smelled it on more goons than I cared to remember. Little Benny from the slip wore the same scent. The only difference: this mug was still alive.

I opened the door all the way. A long, gaunt shadow hung near the back of the room by the window. A thin trail of cigarette smoke twisted in the breeze that snaked in from the open window. He was scared, but he was also good at hiding it. He gazed out the window at whatever might be waiting beyond rather than notice my gat. He was either brave or stupid. I was about to find out which.

I went to turn on the light when he said, "Leave the light off, bud. We don't want anyone to know we're here, do we?" His voice sounded rough, like a badly idling engine.

"That depends," I replied.

"On what?"

"Who you are, and what you want," I said bluntly.

He took one last puff from his cigarette then flicked it to the floor as if he was standing on some street corner waiting for good luck to stroll by. I ignored the cigarette.

"Why don't you come in? After all, it is your office." I walked in, motioning for Holly to come in as well. He looked in my direction, then past me, noticing Holly for the first time. "The dame's still alive. You done real good, shamus."

I couldn't tell if he was carrying, but mysterious goons never come empty-handed. I kept my gat out and visible.

"Glad you approve. Now tell me who you are and what you want."

"Telling you what I want is the easy part. The question is how much would it be worth to a smart guy like you."

"It's only worth dust until you tell me. After that, I'll decide the payout."

He finally looked at me, but I couldn't see his face. He seemed like the no-nonsense type. He spoke in a calm, cool voice that hinted at something more. I liked the guy right away. Don't ask me why. I just did.

"Don't have much choice. Things are too hot for me here. I got to get out of this city. The heat is burning inside me like a forest fire. You know what that's like, don't you, shamus?"

"Yeah, I think I do."

"My name's Puccino, Marco Puccino. You might have heard of me."

The name wrung a bell. "You were one of Faletti's boys."

"I was once," He said, turning back to the window. He was looking for something. I didn't need a spotlight to figure out what it was. "Faletti was a good mug, but he didn't have the guts to take the action into the big time. I think Big Pete scared him too much. Now he just sits around and waits for things to happen."

I put my gat back into my holster and pulled out a cigarette. I took a few long drags. It felt good, like silk.

"You're obviously in a pinch. It doesn't take a professor to see that. But what I want to know is what it has to do with me. I'm not a charity for wayward gunsels. You got street problems, go to the cops. I'm sure they'd love to hear you're story."

"What I got to say is worth more to you than to the cops. Besides, once I'm out of this stinking city, everything I know goes with me." He continued his vigil by the window. He seemed scared, but I couldn't tell of what. His hands had a life of their own, moving slowly one minute then twitching nervously like a fish out of water the next. For a brief moment, I thought I was witnessing a guy go slowly insane.

"All right, Puccino, what do you want to talk about, and what does it have to do with me and the dame?" I threw a wayward glance toward Holly.

Puccino turned to me with a scheming gleam in eyes set deep into a narrow, boney skull. A thin flash of light emanating from outside sliced his face in half, highlighting a furrowed brow and prematurely aged stubble that wouldn't have made the cover of Gentleman's Quarterly anytime soon.

"I need a hundred bucks to blow town. Give me that, and I'll tell you everything I know about Fats Kelly, Big Pete and the whole East Side thing." There was a quiet confidence in the guy's voice; a certain something that told me he wasn't fooling around. The only problem was I didn't have a hundred bucks.

"I don't have a hundred bucks. How about I give you an I.O.U instead?"

He laughed for a few seconds before looking out the window again. It was the kind of laugh that said 'now or never'. I looked over at Holly who seemed to understand perfectly. She stepped forward.

"I have a ring. It's worth almost three hundred. You could get at least a hundred for it." She took it off and slowly handed it to me. I studied it for a second. It wasn't big, but the diamond sitting serenely in the center was real. Even in that stifling darkness the thing shone brighter than the sun. It was a perfect golden circle. One side met up with the other creating something as beautiful as anything one might see in any fancy shop window. Life seemed to move the same way: in circles. The smoothness of its sides coupled with its beauty and elegance seemed much like Holly. I swallowed hard as I passed the ring over to Puccino. I didn't need to look at her to see how she felt.

He played with it in his fingers for a few seconds then shoved it rudely in his pocket. "You got yourself a good dame there, shamus. Keep her closer than you keep your enemies. I'm learning that business a few lifetimes too late."

"You're talking crazy, Puccino. Why not check out of the loony-bin and into sanity central?"

He laughed harder this time. "I knew you were funny, shamus." He didn't look at me, but continued staring out the window like a guy searching for a lost love. After a few moments he started talking again. "The problem with people in this world is they don't know how important it is to be funny. It's like a lost art or something."

"How about getting to the point before I get bored and throw you to the wolves?"

"I worked for Faletti. This you know. But, what you don't know is that I freelanced as well. I got wind of a big job going down on the East side. I go to this warehouse and meet Fats Kelly, Clint Baxter and a couple other boys. And I do mean boys. They was so young, they should've had suckers in their mouths. There was also a dame, a real fancy type, but she didn't say much. Baxter did most of the talking with Kelly pulling up the rear. I think Baxter likes thinking he's in charge, but he has more water than blood in his veins."

"Yeah, I remember the guy, but that's old news."

"Yeah, well, Kelly was the set-up man in the job. We all knew there was someone bigger, besides Baxter, but as long as we got paid real dough we didn't care who was pulling the strings." He pulled one out and lit it as he looked down toward the floor. He was quiet for a long time. I didn't interrupt. After blowing a small line of smoke at the ground, he looked up again. "See, there were only a couple of us, but we'd been around the block a few times and knew what was what."

"Besides you, who else was there?" I asked.

"Kelly wanted to keep things quiet so he kept things small. There were only two others on the payroll: Benny Righetti and Al Schwarz. The kid knew the area. He knew who to tap hard and who to tap soft. It was good at first, but somehow Big Pete found out." Grayish-white smoke curled in thin turbulent clouds between us. To me, the guy looked like a ghost. Maybe he felt like a ghost; it might explain the confessional.

"I heard some kid named Joseph Baker was also doing some heavy pushing."

"He was there, but he was about as useful as a married dame. The kid and Schwarz were always at each others throats. Schwarz liked money and guns, and the power that came with it. Baker didn't like what was going on, but once you're in, you're in. Anyway, Benny and me got no squawks. We was paid good dough. See, we got ears on the inside making things easy for us. It was a good setup with all the angles worked out perfectly. We was making so much dough, it was like Christmas every time we turned around. But it didn't take long before we figured what kind of dopes we really was. First the Baker kid gets bumped off, then Big Pete decides it's time to clean house. He starts with Kelly, and thanks to that rat Falletti I'm next."

"Just for kicks, let's say I believe you. Baxter is a bad boy, and thanks to him Kelly is dead which makes you next up on the menu. Why wait this long to act? Why wait until the coppers know everything before doing anything about it? Every dead goon is a trail leading right back to Baxter. If he was smart, he'd make it so someone else could take the fall."

"Baxter and Kelly are real tight. They went into this thing together. Baxter knew if he tried two timing Kelly, it would be the last thing he ever did. Like I said, we all knew there was someone higher, but we never questioned it. Kelly had some power, but still had to answer to someone else. We just figured it was Baxter or the dame, but we was never sure. Like I said, we was in the chips so we didn't care too much. Kelly would tell us what area to work and when to work it. See, we had to time it so that we got there while the fear was still fresh in people's minds. We offer to protect them for a small fee. When they refuse, we rough them up a bit. Next thing you know, they're paying us good dough. The kicker was we don't do nothing. We just sit back and let Big Pete steamroll over everything."

"If Baxter and Kelly were making most of the decisions then…," my mind drifted into the past, into a moment when things were young and fresh. I could see Baker lying dead on the floor of his old lady's place, a pool of blood spreading from the center, from the heart. I remember the dirt and the look of anguish in the eyes. I also remembered the clothes that were two sizes too big for him. They had to have belonged to someone bigger, more muscular, like Kelly. Why would he put his own duds on the body, unless of course, he hadn't? I was starting to see the setup for what it really was. Puccino remained by the window dressed in a smile that didn't belong.

"Gabriel?" Holly asked, "What is it?" "He's thinking, sweetheart. You know, putting two and two together," Puccino laughed.

I couldn't give too much away, not with Puccino in the room. I thought about the voice on the phone. I thought about the textures; the inflexion; the tone; the pitch. The mug had sounded regular enough, but underneath the words was something else. He spoke like a guy hiding something. It was like trying to disguise a fleabag mutt as a prize-winning poodle. In this case, the mug was definitely south side. A lot of guys hated Big Pete. Some of them could even hate him enough to try and bump him off, but very few would try a frame like the one that was currently in the works. The only way to make something like this work was to have someone on the inside. It seemed too obvious to think Baxter was the inside man. Like Puccelli said: there was someone higher up. One or both of the Bartlett's could pull it off, but for what reason? The old man was already raking in the dough so would have no reason to stab Big Pete in the back. Fear would keep him in line. Beyond him, beyond Connie's own selfish desires arose one other with reason enough to try something this crazy. Big Pete thought he had kept a close eye on the smart ones. He was wrong. We all were.

"Gabriel?" Holly called. I looked at her with a mixture of confusion and wonderment.

I paced back and forth in front of my desk with frustration and anger etching deep lines into my bruised mug. "The whole thing is all wrong. I've been wrong," I said.

"What do you mean?" She asked.

"I've been thinking in terms of dough. If someone did all this to get a bigger piece of the pie then it would make sense, but most of those mugs are already dead. This thing is still going on. This mug," I said as I pointed to Puccino, "is proof of that. Add Connie's disappearance into the mix and suddenly nothing looks settled. If you push all of that to the side, the only other motive left is revenge." I could feel Puccino's unwanted curiosity worming its way into the back of my mind, attempting to decipher what I was really getting at. I felt like I was on Broadway acting in a play without lines. "Most of the suits on Wall Street and in City Hall would laugh anyone trying to take control of Big Pete's rackets right into the poor house or into a pine box. They can't be after Big Pete's businesses. Money would be the obvious motive. They knew I'd bite so they threw me a piece of cheese the size of Long Island." I gritted my teeth in frustration. "There aren't too many guys that work for Big Pete with enough brains to try something like this? Most of them just live for the paycheck and the dames. Baxter has some brains, but he couldn't hope to pull it off on his own. He's too close to Big Pete. Guys like Paul or Jimmy maybe, but even they would have to have a good reason."

"Baxter is nothing more than a yes-man. He does what he's told, especially where dames is concerned. Mind you, he never did get involved in the dirty stuff. He always got me, Kelly, or No Shoes to take care of them things. The skirt was always pushing him hard, like he was some kind of cheap mutt or something, only he was to dumb to see it," Puccino laughed. "One day someone will learn him real good."

"Baxter is a door stopper in a hundred-dollar suit. It would be too obvious to point the finger at him and say he's behind it all. I bet if I took the clothes the kid was wearing and put them on Kelly they'd fit like a glove. Kelly had no problem killing anyone, but I don't think he would kill someone then put his own clothes on the dead body for good measure. It's a frame and not a very good one. That explains the card in Kelly's pocket pointing straight at Bartlett. I think someone wants us to see it. It's like someone is trying to deliberately be sloppy."

"Most of the mugs on Big Pete's payroll have one-track minds. No Shoes is a primo example. He has the moxy, but not the brains. If Baxter got scared, he could've easily sold Kelly down the river before Kelly got wind of it. With him out of the way, anyone thinking about thinking wouldn't even need to think once about hurting Baxter, especially with Big Pete acting as bodyguard." He glanced casually out the window. His hands were still now, his eyes a picture of calm.

"Where would you meet the others?"

"Down by the Manhattan. On the East side, you'll see a building called 'Cordage and Cable Company'. It's another one of Big Pete's little hideouts." He replied, turning his attention back to me.

"You guys got something against meeting in a bar?"

He laughed, quieter this time, like he was afraid of being heard. He quickly glanced at his watch.

"Yeah, well, you got everything I could give you, shamus. I'm heading away from here, and I ain't coming back for a long time. If you know what's good for you, you and the dame will kick your heels back and make tracks before Big Pete gets his mitts around your throats." He looked out the window one last time. Before he walked out, he turned and with a smile as big as the moon said, "Don't take any wooden nickels." He tipped his hat and left. The door closed quietly behind him. I listened for his quickly-fading footsteps.

I walked over to the window and looked out. Nothing appeared out of the ordinary. The cold breeze from off the river crafted a kind of mild claustrophobia that gently, but stubbornly, enveloped all the open spaces until all that remained was a sort of raw tightness. I could feel that same tightness wrapping itself around my gut. I could see another circle, and wrapped within that was another lie. This time, however, it was a lie of my own making. I had played it out this far and would have to see it through to the end, even if it killed me.

I turned and sat down in my chair. I opened one of the lower drawers and pulled out a half-empty bottle of scotch and swigged it straight. I didn't stop until it was empty. I felt like a jalopy, my tank wavering between empty and so empty that even flies stayed away. Holly slid elegantly over to the desk and watched.

"I'm sorry about your ring. One way or another I'll get it back."

"Don't worry about it. Some lush of a banker gave it to me. It probably belonged to his wife anyway. We're going to that rope place, aren't we?" She asked.

"We sure are. I still got a couple of hours before Big Pete decides to use my skull as a room ornament."

"Might improve your demeanor," she laughed. It was a reassuring laugh. The kind you throw out as a lifesaver to a drowning man, or to warm someone when they're cold.

"It might at that. It might even improve Puccino's ability to tell a good lie."

Holly eyed me inquisitively. "If you thought he was lying then why'd you let him leave so easily? Why not just shoot him or beat him up or something?"

"He won't get far. What's more important is how he couldn't decide whether to think of Baxter as alive or dead. He must have forgotten the script he memorized."

"Wouldn't that be old news by now?"

"This guy is on the run for his life. The last thing he would do is keep in touch with anyone who would know anything about Baxter,

Big Pete, or this whole case. He'd run, and the only person he'd keep in contact with was his bartender. He was just wasting time for someone else, and I'm pretty sure we'll find out fairly soon who that someone else is."

I tilted my head back until my hat hung at a King-Kong-on-the-Empire-State-Building kind of angle. I put my feet up on the desk and relaxed for a few seconds. It only lasted a few seconds, but those few seconds were perfect. The phone rang unceremoniously.

"It looks like my friend, the phone, wants some company. Listen, answer it for me, will you?"

She picked it up and without missing a beat answered, "Gabriel Dixon Investigations, how may I direct your call?" It was a good moment; one that seemed as natural as watching the sun rise. Watching her answer the phone, her voice as smooth as silk and as fresh as a garden of roses, renewed me. Sometimes, a moment is all it takes to get a man back on his feet again. I glanced at the empty bottle. There was nothing there anymore. I took it and threw it in the garbage. The glass made a muffled clang against the hard metal of the garbage can. I looked up at Holly. She smiled for a second before saying, "Just one moment, please." She handed me the phone.

"Dixon, here," I answered.

"Looks like things are looking up for you, shamus. Now you got dames answering phones for you. You should think about hiring a whole chorus line of girls to dance up and down the street advertising for you. You'd be amazed at the amount of business that would draw."

"I'm not worried about the amount of business I get, only the kind of business. That's probably why I would never take your dough."

"Oh? And why's that?"

"You're as yellow as they come. It doesn't matter if you killed anyone or not. The fact you stand by and let innocent people die is more than I can take; innocent blood that never had a chance. I'm going to make sure when this is all over you get what's coming to you." I wasn't mad, just angry. I knew he would call, like I knew they'd make another bottle of Scotch, or more guns. This guy was as predictable as a drunk on the bowery.

The Trigger Method

"I'm no murderer, shamus. I provide a service for those that want information. I'm a messenger trying to do the world some good. The Big Pete's of this world have had it too good for too long. If someone doesn't stop them now, more innocent kids are going to die." He spoke differently this time, a distinct bitterness embedded in each word. This went well beyond public duty. It was personal.

"What do you got to tell me now? Make it good. I don't have a lot of time. I have an appointment at the beautician, and she hates it when I'm late; something about not leaving enough time for the really important stuff."

"You find the Bartlett dame? Word on the street is she's hiding. Big Pete's had his goons searching the whole city for her, but so far, zip. She didn't know about the hit on her old man until a little while ago. Now that she knows she's scared. With Kelly out of the picture and her old man almost in the grave she thinks she's next. Big Pete likes her, but not enough to bet his whole business on her life."

"You're telling me she had nothing to do with Baxter's botched up hit on her old man?" It had been my guess all along, but I pretended to be surprised. I couldn't afford to give anything away, especially with the tab being what it was.

"That's exactly what I'm telling you. Baxter had a thing for the dame, but didn't like the old man or his ideas about who should and who shouldn't see his daughter. He figures he's good enough for her, but the old man figures different. Baxter don't like that so goes and tries shooting Bartlett only to have you show up as a surprise. They say there wasn't much left after you got through with him. Think Big Pete will give you some extra dough for taking care of that little bit of fun?"

"I did what I had to do. You can ask No Shoes and Benny the same question."

"Those mugs got what they deserved. Now, there's only one left. That's the mug you need to find."

"Who's that?" I asked.

"His name is Marco Puccino. He was muscle for Kelly and the dame. When Baker started getting yappy, the dame told him to take the kid out. He shot him a couple times then dumped his body in the old lady's apartment. You'd have to be pretty cold to dump the carcass of someone's son in their own living room. Mind you, from what I hear, that old lady was plenty tough on that kid. Maybe the dame did him a favor." I had been living variations of that nightmare every night for a week. I could envision the act in my mind. The only problem was it was a fiction of my own making. At the edge of my vision lingered the real truth. I could see his death; however, the moments before and the moments after were a blur. Sure he was toying with me, but part of what he said not only had to sound like the truth, it had to be the truth. He had to keep dangling the carrot in front of my nose to keep me going. I ignored the comments about the old lady.

"Why didn't you tell me this a week ago? You could've saved a lot of lives, and me a lot of grief. Schwarz could've come in handy a week ago."

"You're in the middle of a big game, shamus. Those at the top want to keep things rolling, but can't trust the grease-grinders they got now. That means going outside of normal channels to keep things quiet. Tapping the loose screws is getting harder and harder. Nobody wants to talk because they know what'll happen if they do. The Baker kid learned that lesson too late. He couldn't keep his yap shut about Bartlett's setup and bought a dirt-nap for his troubles. It's a game an honest mug like you needs to understand. It'll help keep the doctor away."

"I don't like games. And I especially don't like thugs that play games with other people's lives. People are dying all around me, but all you can think about is the next move in your little game."

"Easy, shamus, or you'll burst a blood vessel. I know what I know because I keep my ears to the ground. I listen real good and I keep even better notes. That's the problem with Big Pete. He don't know how to retain information, only the fat between that thing he calls a skull." He was on a roll now, talking as if he were running for president. He was on the top of the world, and the rest of us schmucks were nothing more than fodder for his field of dreams. He was also giving himself away.

"All right, so you're another Falletti. That only makes you yellow."

"It ain't like that. I'm a shadow. I make moves no one can see. I'm here, I'm there; I'm everywhere. The big man himself should fall at my feet." It was like listening to a preacher on a greasy pulpit. I was waiting for the 'amen' to shriek across the crowd of one. "The only reason you're still alive is because Big Pete wanted you alive. He could've taken you out at Bartlett's place, or at that crumby place you call a bar. He could've shot your can off in broad daylight at the dame's apartment a few days ago, but he needed you. He needed you because he's too fat and stupid to do anything on his own. Sure, he's got rats, but only because he keeps feeding them."

The wheels in my brain turned faster and faster creating a whirlwind of thoughts I could barely comprehend. I closed my eyes on a headache and hoped for the best. On the outside, I could hear him reciting more words from the dirty mug's holy prayer book.

"What the kid told you only makes sense if you know what that fat pig is planning. It's big enough that the Bartlett dame knew only didn't do right by the information. She got greedy and stupid. When Big Pete finds her, the only place she'll be parading her new dress is at the funeral home."

"You're all heart, but you can't really expect me to believe she's behind the whole thing. Somewhere there's a name that carries a lot more weight than hers. I've got a few running through my mind, but only one voice to match. Do you want me to tell you which one I'd pick?" He didn't seem offended by my accusation; in fact, he seemed to relish the words, like a fighter just before he delivers the knockout blow.

"I'm not in this for dough. I just hate to see a good kid taken out like that. That dame is colder than ice. If she had it her way, even the old lady would have chewed on a bullet by now. What they don't realize is that cold only gets you so far. Without brains, you're nothing. Puccelli's a mug what looks out windows too much. And Baxter, he was so dumb he thought he could take out Bartlett and walk away without any repercussions. You took him out, but there was a bullet out there with his name on it, I guarantee it. There ain't nothing worse than a mug in love. It makes them weak and pathetic."

He was right there. Baxter became a corpse long ago. Cutting in on the big man's business was a sure death sentence, but cutting in on the big man's girl, that would be worse. Mobsters love their dames. The guy on the other end of the phone knew that better than all of us. Connie's old man also knew that. He tried to rectify that situation and ended up with a bullet in his gut as a 'thank you' present.

"I guess love tore a hole through Baker's heart. At least he was dressed nice when they killed him. The brown shoes and gray slacks matched the drapes real good, but the two bullet holes ruined the shirt. I think strangling the kid's neck like a chicken was a bit too much. Still, he was a good-looking mug when he went. Bruises would've really ruined any chance of an open casket funeral."

"There ain't no law that says they can't look bad when they go, is there?"

"No. No law at all. It just seems wrong somehow. Out of curiosity, how did you know the kid was dead? I mean, maybe you did it and now you're trying to frame someone else. It has happened before, you know."

"I could at that. But, you'll have to believe me when I tell you I actually liked the kid. Killing him wouldn't have done anything for me. It wouldn't have done anything for anybody. Well, almost anybody. See, somebody wanted him dead and I think you know who that somebody is. You just don't want to believe it."

"Is that right?"

"Find the dame, peeper. She'll be dying to tell you the truth. With her and Puccino behind bars, you'll get the goons and that good night's sleep you've been looking for. So far I've been on the level about everything. There ain't no reason to believe I'd lead you wrong now. It's all about motive, peeper. The person with the strongest motive for killing Baker is either Schwarz or the Bartlett dame. Schwarz could've done it, but mostly he's just a schmuck. That only leaves the dame. You've seen her; you know what she's like. Killing the kid would be a great way to show anyone willing to look how serious she is about making money and a reputation. Oh, and one last thing; the .22 she's got might be of interest to you and the coppers. If you're real nice, she might tell you which dead mug she lifted it from." He hung up as quickly as a bullet being fired from a gun. He was trying to give me an out. It was a nice neat package with all the bad guys in one little basket. Only problem was I didn't go for nice and neat. I never did. When anything comes out looking that clean and respectable, check your drawers because somebody probably just stole your life.

"This guy is more than just an innocent bystander. He's probably some sort of low-level thug under Big Pete's umbrella."

"Well, whoever he is, he's starting to work on my last nerve," Holly said, exasperatingly.

"At least we can count him out as a suspect in Baker's murder." Holly gazed at me with an expression of outright surprise. The look didn't last long; maybe because disappointment was something we had learned to live with in the last few days. Either way, I knew what she was thinking and spoke before she could.

"For one thing, Baker was wearing a white shirt with black shoes, and he was shot so many times only his ghost would recognize him. This guy didn't know that. Either he's playing stupid or he really doesn't know. Plus, Baker was worked over pretty nicely, maybe by Puccino, maybe by Kelly. I don't know for sure. But, beating him up then dumping his body in an empty lot would be enough to warn any mug to play by the rules, but shooting him after that would only be a crime of either passion or revenge. It wouldn't do anybody any good from a business viewpoint."

Every suspect I came across could have killed Baker, but each seemed to have very little reason to do the deed. I was beginning to think Joseph Baker had been killed by the invisible man, or gremlins, or little green men from Mars. Mugs like No Shoes and Kelly had the roscoe and the guts that came along with the territory but lacked a motive. The most likely of suspects was the one everyone pointed the finger at, and the one suspect who had the least to gain from such an act: Big Pete. He could've ordered the hit, but knew it would bring down more heat than it was worth. Still, the few clues I did have pointed to a murderer, someone close; someone who knew what the kid's death would mean for the mob.

"Tell me something. Who did the guy sound like to you? Have you heard his voice before?"

"It sounded familiar, but I can't exactly place it."

"The problem is a lot of mugs sound the same on the phone, but this one sounded real familiar--almost too familiar. Think real hard. If Brutus was in the room, would he sound like the mug on the phone?"

"Paul Brutus? You think he's behind this whole thing?"

"I'm not sure. It's just a hunch. First time I ran into him was at your apartment. He said Big Pete could've taken me out anytime, anywhere. He even got as specific as saying at your apartment in broad daylight. The only way he would have known that was if he was there. He could've easily phoned Baxter who then called you. Brutus could've told Baxter you were talking to me and telling all. It didn't matter that you didn't know anything. Baxter, probably thinking his number was up, called you thinking Brutus was still outside. He probably thought Brutus would get me when I got to my car. He could've had someone take you out after you got off work then dumped us both in the East River. He could spin the rest anyway he wanted with us gone. He probably didn't figure on Brutus playing his own hand, though. Now, think hard, did the voice sound familiar?"

"It's hard to say." She wrinkled her face into a half-smile, as if ready to sing a duet with Bing Crosby. "It was almost as if he was trying to talk polite. He was hiding something, that's for sure."

"That's why I wanted you to answer the phone. Maybe you might recognize the voice. If it was Brutus, he was probably trying extra hard to not let you recognize him. I didn't pay attention to the south side in his voice before, but I could hear it now. It rang as clear as a church bell."

My next destination was a no-brainer. I knew what I would find when I got there. I also knew each tentative step taken toward the truth would mean taking two steps away from the truth. Where that would leave me was anyone's guess.

CHAPTER 22

My mind drifted between the voice on the phone, Connie Bartlett, and her old man with the bullet holes for a chest. The land deal Bartlett had going on with Big Pete was big. A lot of private handshakes, and even more private I.O.U's, would be passed around before either man got what he wanted. In some cases, promises made with a gat in the hand meant dollars in the pocket. In the middle of it all was Joseph Baker. It didn't matter rich or poor, young or old. His death sounded an alarm bell that rang across the underworld like shockwaves from an earthquake.

The murderer's intentions seemed clearer with each passing second. It was an extreme act, but extreme situations sometimes require extreme acts of both courage and cowardice. All of a sudden bodies were falling like ducks during a big-game hunt. In life, Baker was as important as a spent cigarette; in death he was as dangerous as a loaded gun. Suddenly, the guilty and the innocent ran for the shadows faster than an old biddy trying to avoid the rain. Mobsters were making paranoia their best friend because it was better than having flowers sticking out of your gut. The truth wasn't important anymore. Maybe it never was. The voice on the phone understood that better than any of us. So did the murderer.

Mahoney's bucket of bolts swung easily from side to side as we drove back toward the river-- toward the heart of the matter. No matter how far I tried to run from the place it kept pulling me back. There were ghosts there; I could feel them.

"Gabrielle, I've been thinking about a few things and something still doesn't make sense to me," Holly started.

"What's that?" I replied distractedly.

"Why go to all this trouble to get back at Big Pete? If he wanted revenge why not just shoot him, or hire someone to shoot him? Why do all of this? Wouldn't he want to keep it a little quieter?"

"Maybe that's the point. With everyone pointing their flashlights in a hundred different directions, Brutus could slip out from under everyone's nose like Houdini. Who would notice a guy like Brutus when you have Big Pete on the menu? There's more to Brutus than most of us give him credit for."

"You mean besides money?" Holly asked.

"Power isn't what Brutus is about. The more I twirl it around in my mind the less it makes sense. That's why killing the kid doesn't make sense, it's not Brutus's style. It would also be too easy to pin the blame on Connie. Baker's old lady had seen her in the apartment at least once. She had motive and opportunity. She would be doing a pretty good job of setting herself up if she was the murderer. That's all the cops would need to bring her in for questioning, her old man notwithstanding."

"Would Big Pete even let it get that far?" Holly asked.

"He's trying to get at the truth just as much as I am. He knows who Baker is now, but a week ago Baker was nothing but a shadow to him. Big Pete is after bigger game. That's why Kelly's gone. Baxter might have easily tried giving him up to save his own skin. And even if he didn't, there'd be enough word on the street that Kelly would've been gone sooner or later anyway. Puccino is another Kelly, only not six feet under yet."

Holly looked at me curiously, "What do you mean?"

"He's a messenger for somebody," I replied.

"You mean Brutus?"

"We'll find out soon enough."

"Alfred is guilty of more than he's letting on."

"The only thing that guy is guilt of is stupidity. I could see them fighting, but Schwarz doesn't have the guts to kill anybody. If there was a little love triangle going on between those three, it might get them mad at each other. They might even sock each other around a little bit, then go to some cheap gin-joint and apologize over a few illegal shots of orange juice and vodka. But to think one might kill the other is a stretch. I wouldn't worry too much about him anymore."

I stopped at a light. A tough-looking kid of about nine crossed the street with a fleabag mutt on a rope barely held together by bands of filthy translucent tape. His bumpy, jerky stride seemed better suited to a drunken nag. In some ways I envied the kid. At least he didn't have to worry about guns, bored dames, or mobsters too lazy to do their own dirty work. I watched silently for a few more seconds until the picture lost its magic. I pressed on the gas and breezed through the intersection leaving him and everything else behind.

Holly directed her gaze toward a spot near the steering wheel. It was a faraway look, the kind one gets when serious thought is on the menu. It was tough to say whether Holly was being serious or if she was just tired of our little question and answer period. She let out a short-sighed: "No one seems to worry about anyone anymore; at least not enough to get anything right."

It was a strange thing to say, but she had a point. It didn't seem important to get names or locations right when you considered the number of dead bodies popping up throughout the city. People wanted a murderer, or a stooge to pin everything on. The fact someone may not be guilty would mean little. People died everyday. The reasons are as varied as a restaurant menu. If you looked hard enough you'd probably find someone who knew someone who was murdered. Some probably even saw someone get murdered. Did that make them guilty of anything? My answer shifted uneasily between yes and no. I shifted uneasily along with it.

I glanced at my watch; the hour hand crawled, sloth-like, a couple of minutes past three. The numbers didn't really mean anything. The darkness did. It penetrated my mind like a knife, cutting apart the facts until only their essence remained.

"After the last few days I don't know what a kid is anymore," Holly said exasperatingly.

"I don't think I know either, but whoever dumped Baker's body must have known the area well enough to know where he lived and how to get into his apartment without anyone seeing anything. Connie had been there at least once that I know of. She probably knew the layout just as well as Alfred."

"Puccino's going to get away with everything. It's not right. Someone should do something," Holly cried.

"I wouldn't worry about him. He won't get far. In fact, I have a feeling I'll be seeing him real soon. These mugs are all guilty of one thing or another. If I got mad at them for every little thing they did, I'd probably hate myself until doomsday. Besides, he did give me some good information."

"How do you know it's on the level? He could've been throwing you a curve."

"Even if he was lying, some of what he said had to be the truth. Puccino isn't very good at lying, so whatever he says has to have some portion of truth in it, otherwise, I'd just blow him right off. Whoever sent him knows that. They want me down at the warehouse for a reason, and I'm not about to disappoint them. On the other hand, he could be throwing me a curve, in which case someone will probably be waiting for me with a roscoe and a story that could make me a millionaire."

I could feel Holly's stare like I could feel a baseball bat against my skull. Either she was impressed and I had nothing to lose, or she was unimpressed and this night would never end. Or maybe she was a little bit of both, in which case I was probably just thrown out at first. It was a terrible truth, and a terrible lie to tell, but I needed her confused and angry; otherwise, the next few hours would add up to nothing more than my funeral.

"Do you have to take everything like a joke? We've been lucky so far. Now you're going somewhere because some guy told you to. You might find nothing but a few bullets for your trouble. But you laugh like we're going on a Sunday afternoon picnic. Isn't your life worth anything to you?"

I rounded another corner, the jalopy pulling a little to the right as I did. Returning to the slip might mean running into some of Pete's buddies from the precinct. That wouldn't be good, especially if some of those guys were also getting paychecks from Big Pete. It was hard to tell how close the fat guy would let me get before he put up a big red light. Holly was right about one thing: walking into the lion's den was a dangerous move, but it was a move that had to be made. I had to know why they wanted me involved. There were a lot of other private detectives in the city. They could have easily called one of them, but they didn't. They called me. Or, more specifically, he called me. The mug was not only spitting on Baker's grave, but also on the grave of my brother and a thousand other kids that never had a chance. Holly could never, would never understand. I continued driving, ignoring Holly's questions. The answers would only make her angry.

I found myself in the middle of a cluster of ancient buildings that opened onto a sprawling view of the city. I pulled up close to the side of the building I had been told about. On the north side, in large faded white letters were the words: 'New York Cordage and Cable Company'. It wasn't a big place during the daytime, but in that deafening darkness, the place looked bigger than all of the districts put together. The dusky blacks and grays and the ancient smell in the air reminded me of the nightmares I suffered through as a kid. I didn't like it here. I never did.

The silence was the first thing I noticed. It was like being in a cemetery. I could feel a thousand pairs of eyes boring into Holly and me like nails being driven into wood. It was an inescapable feeling that both frightened and excited me. All the paths I'd traveled over the past week ended here. It was here a poor kid from the wrong side of the tracks watched his life come close to the end. It was here that a dame with a silver spoon in her mouth and time on her hands went one step too far in her chase for something more; all the clues, all the evidence, pointed to this place and this moment. I would go in ready. She would expect no less.

I turned to Holly. "This is it, sweetheart. It all ends here, in that building," I said as I studied the building carefully.

"You're sure this is the place? And what if you're wrong? What if Brutus did kill Baker? All you'll get is a bullet for your troubles while that woman laughs all the way to the bank." Holly was a study in contrasts. She was no longer calm and cool, but a lady on the verge of an emotional breakdown. I remained calm.

"I don't know. I don't play maybes. I play for keeps. I think she's here and I think Big Pete knows it. He's too smart to get his own hands dirty so he gets me to do his dirty work for him. Either way, I'm going in." I turned to Holly and with words as emphatic as words on a tombstone I added, "Everybody's got the score to the game except me. I'm tired of it all. I'm tired of the facts being pushed in my face. I'm tired of guns. I'm tired of secrets with no punch line. I'm tired of mobsters with too much time on their hands. It's time it all ended." I looked straight ahead. It was hard to describe my thoughts at that moment, but they weren't thoughts of cute green teddy bears or fruit-filled baskets. My head was filled with thoughts of anger and betrayal. I was sick of dames that figured they could get their way by dropping a handkerchief to the ground or by blowing kisses in the wind. "Go find Pete and tell him where I am. Tell him to bring a couple of body bags."

Before she could say anymore I got out of the car and started for the building. Along both sides, ancient-looking structures mixed with the black of the night to craft a kind of rotting death shroud that enveloped everything. Beyond the crunching sound of my shoes against the gravel pavement, all else was quiet. The street narrowed along the far end. The buildings that lined both sides looked tilted, as if one light breeze might blow them into the center. The bridge's shadow fell in a north-south direction. The little revealed by what meager light there was looked disinterested, like an old dog waiting for the right moment to die. A small parking lot hung to one side of the building. The front looked like any other. Two small doors sat below three rows of windows above. A Packard and a gray coupe were parked in front. I thought about looking in, but realized that would only confirm what I already knew.

I walked toward the door and tried the knob. It opened easily. I pulled out my .38 and went in.

CHAPTER 23

The place was old and dirty. Primordial lights hanging high from the ceiling barely illuminated the ground floor while two sets of old wooden stairs led to a second floor with large sprinkles of dirt and mud dotted throughout. That didn't surprise me. I had seen that kind of dirt before. Swinging my flashlight from one end to the other illuminated a warehouse full of twine, rope, and cable of all shapes and sizes. I had also seen the rope before. The rest of the place was filled with a kind of raw, stale air that made me want to sneeze with each breath.

I heard voices further back in the warehouse. One of them sounded sweet. I had heard it before. The surroundings were different, but the smooth softness was something I could never forget because it reminded me of a cat just before it reached out to cut you with its claws.

I moved past the old wooden crates and piles of dirty rope and into the back of the warehouse. I saw a small office, brightly lit and filled with two arguing voices, huddled against the back corner. I listened for a moment before making my presence known.

"…before they figure something out." It was a man's voice. I could sense the fear and mistrust in each syllable. I didn't recognize the voice, but figured it must have been some poor young sap looking for a way out of something that was too big for him. The next voice was easy to identify.

"Stop sniveling. You knew what you were getting into." She tried sounding tough. Apparently, the whelp on the receiving side was having none of it.

"Maybe it's easy for rich dames like you. All you gotta do is sit back and look pretty while guys like Big Pete clean your messes for you. All I'm gonna get is dead. And that's if I'm lucky. I ain't waiting around for Big Pete to turn me into dust. I ain't yellow, but I ain't stupid neither."

"That's exactly what you will be. If you run, he'll find you and kill you. If you listen to me…" Connie began.

"That's all I've been doin' is listening to you. Kelly listened and it didn't turn out so hot for him. Just because you know some people doesn't mean my keister is covered. If that loony, Baxter, did try to kill your old man, then we're all in trouble."

"There's no way of knowing what happened." Her voice edged beyond frustration and into the realm of insanity. It seemed Connie was attempting to hold something together with smoke and mirrors when what she really needed was the truth. I had heard enough.

I strode casually out of the shadows and into the small arc of light that spilled out from the small, dusty office. Connie was pacing back and forth while the help-I didn't recognize him-sat hunched in a corner like some deformed rag doll. The two of them together looked like a couple of caged rats. I smiled.

I moved slowly, but steadily; my feet felt like they were walking on clouds for the first time in a week. They didn't notice me until I was almost in the doorway. The gee stood up. He reached for his gun.

"I wouldn't try that if I were you, buddy. I'll put more holes in you than a cheese-grater." I turned to Connie. She looked surprised. A few seconds later, that look was replaced by a smile as big as Yankee Stadium. I decided to play along. "Hiya, sister; it's been so long I almost forgot what you looked like. It's good to see your curves haven't gotten lost along with the rest of you."

Her smile morphed into something Eve probably saw just before biting into the apple. "Mr. Dixon, I'm a little surprised to see you, but since you're here, how about we come to a little understanding?"

The Trigger Method

"You mean the kind of understanding you had with Kelly, Schwarz, Baker and the rest of your merry gang? By the way, what made you think you could actually pull off this little caper of yours? You're dealing with mugs that would sell out their own grandmother for a buck. What made you think you'd be any different?"

"I really don't know what you're talking about." She turned away from me and sauntered casually toward the desk. A rock the size of an apple sparkled like a firecracker on her right hand as light from above danced across her fingers. It was like Holly's, only twice the size and probably worth five times the dough.

"You take another step and I'll forget my manners." She abruptly turned back to face me, her eyes as thin as a sheet of paper. When you pushed a dame hard enough, the canary usually turned into a snake. In this case, the canary turned into an eagle. She could have scratched my peepers out had I given her the chance, and from the look on her face, it was obvious no one had talked to her that way lately and still kept their job. The mug in the corner wanted to move, but all of a sudden decided it wasn't worth the effort. My reputation must have gotten here ahead of me. "Just stay right where I can look at you, hands and all."

"I'm not half as bad as you think I am, Mr. Dixon. I liked Joe. He was a good kid. Him and me, we could have gone places. But, as they say, three's a crowd."

I discerned movement to my right. Connie's button-man tried for his gat, again. I turned and fired a warning shot off his bow. The mug, more than surprised by my action, stood shaking like a tree in a stiff breeze, a petrified look of horror sketched haphazardly into every feature.

"That's the last time I miss on purpose. You move again and I'll make you a permanent part of the wall." I turned my attention back to Connie. She held her hands to her face, a rush of horror passing through her like the uptown special. She had been around guns-that much was clear-but she hadn't been around ones that actually fired. And she hadn't been around one owned by a guy who was working his last nerve like a crazy Italian working over pizza dough.

"You had a nice setup going, doll, but you loused it up. The first mistake you make is hiring Big Pete's own guns to do your dirty work. Gunsels like that always have big mouths. That's probably what got Kelly done in. Never hire from inside. Always get the freelancers. Second, you tried scamming the biggest cheat in the city: your old man. He's about as strong as a paper cup in a stiff wind. Once Big Pete found out, you had to know that he'd sell you down the river to save his own skin. Baxter found out what he did, and to make it right with you, tried to force-feed him lead for dessert. Baxter was sweet on you. He figures with your old man out of the way, he'd have clear sailing. Only problem is, the only thing Baxter knows about lead is that it hurts when it hits you. That's why he's lying on a slab in the morgue. Thirdly, you tried to swindle the biggest, fattest swindler in town: Big Pete. Nobody robs from Big Pete. I was rooting for you, but you just weren't game enough for the big dough. You got sloppy, baby. You let a kid die that didn't deserve it." I leaned against the doorframe and watched as Connie stare coldly back at me.

"You keep swinging for the low ones, don't you, Mr. Dixon? You can try and put the pinch on me, but I'm not talking unless it's to my lawyer."

I laughed as I spoke. "The only person you'll be talking to is the undertaker if I let Big Pete have his way. He's smart enough to connect Baxter to you. That's why he gets me to do the dirty work; that way if something nasty happens to you, he doesn't take the blame and lose your old man as a partner. Besides, he won't like someone taking potshots at his golden goose. It don't matter how much jive you got in that swing of yours, sister, he'll bounce you harder than a football in a mud pit."

"What about me? What's gonna happen to me?" The guy was skinny, small and hopelessly hopeless, and that made him dangerous. It was like cornering a monkey; you didn't know what would happen.

"You made your bed, brother, now lie in it. I can respect guys like little Benny. Sure I took him out, but at least he didn't cry like a little baby. Make a deal with the D.A. and maybe he'll be able to keep you alive." I turned back to Connie, "If you can be straight with me and tell me all you really know about Baker, maybe I'll forget I ever saw you. Sure, Big Pete will find you and make you beg for your life, but that's your problem."

Nobody had to hold up a neon sign in front of her that read 'dame in trouble'. Her choices for survival were thinning out fast. She would have to give with the truth if she wanted to live to spend her inheritance. Even if she told me the truth, I was far from certain the big guy would leave her untouched. He had allowed me to go this far, but then I was just a patsy, a pawn in a game far beyond my pay grade. Connie had her looks, and that might buy her some time, but even as a Bartlett her future was far from secure.

"Come on, baby, you got one chance to tell the truth. You pass it up, I'm gone. And my offer goes with me. You can take your chances with Big Pete on your own after that."

She kneaded her fingers nervously in her palm all the while staring at the wall in front of her. Her brilliant blue dress made a gentle rustling sound as she paced. She finally turned back to me and spoke with gentle, elegant tones that would've been better suited to an opera or a piano recital. "All right, Mr. Dixon, but what I have to tell will not be much. In fact, you might already know most of it."

"Humor me," I replied.

"Hold on, sister. You ain't saying nothing unless my can is covered too. I can make any deal you can only I'm ready to spill the truth." The little rat turned to me, "Listen, shamus, you want the truth? I'll tell you everything I know. But, you got to guarantee my safety out of town, see. I'll tell you all about Kelly and the kid, and about how sweet Baxter was for this dame," he said, pointing toward Connie. "They were going to take out her old man then spend his dough like it was play money."

"Shut up, moron! I'll decide what's best for us. If you want to get out of this alive you'll do what I say, understand?" Watching her lecture the little rat was like watching me try to preach sobriety to a priest. She seemed to treat everything like a mirage, believing that things existed only if she said they did. The rock and the hard place that was Big Pete and the cops existed firmly in the here and now. I knew it, and somewhere in the back of her deluded mind, Connie did to. Still, she tried to manage the situation to her benefit, thinking that a few carefully chosen words could keep the deck from falling on top of her delicate and curvy frame.

I stood back and took in the show. It was like watching a bad detective movie.

"I've listened to you for too long, doll. You're history." The little rat turned to me, his eyes shining like a smudged nickel. A thin, greasy smile dripped off his lips. "You want something, shamus? You want to know about the kid? She set the kid up. He was getting cold feet so she tells us to rough him up; you know, get him shaking so he'll do whatever we say. We did a good job on him, but she says it's not enough. Even his buddy didn't like it, but he was too scared of her to say anything. He knew he'd be eating a couple of knuckle sandwiches too if he squawked." He gave her another menacing look before saying, "It was just like her to give orders and not get her hands dirty. Her and Baxter was the same that way. They never did want to see what us hard-working mugs had to do for a living." A quick laugh, like a pig-snorting, burst briefly in the air. "They didn't even have the guts to stick around and watch the kid take it. They just kept giving orders like they was the President or something."

Connie looked on, her eyes transforming from blue to red in seconds. It was hard to concentrate on the moment with so much falling around me. Somewhere between everything lay a hint of the truth. I wanted to step outside of the situation and turn my eyes to the apartment and to something Pete told me, but the rat's screeching voice pulled me back in. I cringed slightly.

"Ha, ha, ha, you're a swell dame, but you're on your own, baby." He turned back to me and opened his mouth to say something else when I noticed Connie reach inside her purse. My mouth went dry. It was like watching Mahoney pour a good bottle of Scotch down a drain. I could've done something, but after a bullet is fired it's too late to warn the mug on the receiving end.

He was hit mid-laugh, his face contorting into a grimace of pain I usually felt only after a heavy binge. His eyes went small, the light I had seen earlier dimming as if he had forgotten to pay the bill. My gun suddenly seemed heavier than the fat lady at Barnum's freak show. I couldn't raise it; I couldn't shoot it. In fact, I couldn't even feel the trigger.

Connie was angry, yet, despite the anger, she still managed to nail the little rat square. Two subsequent loud pops burst through the room like rampaging elephants, piercing the rat's delicate frame like scissors cutting through paper. The impact sent him crashing back against the glass. I didn't race over to see if he would live.

The image of the rat in that dirty office brought back an image of Baker lying dead in his old lady's apartment. Joseph Baker had been worked over good. Large bruises, like a checkerboard, marked his entire face. His body had also been riddled with enough bullets to create a lead shortage. In contrast, the rat's body was fairly presentable. I thought about what I had seen and remembered that night. I also considered what the rat had said. I had seen Baker, Pete had seen Baker, and so had the coroner who took away the body. Fortunately, only a few other people had seen the body and even fewer knew what it looked like. It wasn't the kind of thing you showed off like a present, especially to the next of kin. I looked past those thoughts and toward the rat. He lay in the corner moaning like a dog. I glanced at Connie as she held the gat firmly in her hand. It was a snub-nosed .22 that looked well taken care of. I suddenly thought about the scene that must have played out here a week ago. It seemed that my friend on the phone had come through again.

"I hope you have a permit for that sucker, otherwise, the fine on something like that will be a killer." She was in no mood for my jokes. She pointed the gun right at me. Had she really been insane, she probably would have fired at me after bumping off the rat. As it was, the look in her eyes told me she still had most of her marbles. The gun itself looked good and clean. It wasn't big, but no gun ever had to be too big to kill someone. If the weapon really was the one that had belonged to Baker, and the same one that was used to kill him, I'd need to work my act perfectly. I wouldn't be able to fire back, although, judging from the rats' moans and groans it might not be too much of a problem.

"What do you think the fine will be for killing a no-good private dick? Maybe they'll give me a medal or something. You know something, Mr. Dixon? You're as dumb as Alfred and Joseph were. In my books, dumb is dumb no matter what kind of suit you where or what kind of gun you carry. It's a tough world where only the strong survive. Baker died because his head was as empty as the gun he carried. In fact, the only good thing he was good for was taking a bullet." It was like listening to a sermon on a tired Sunday morning. The tone of her voice was somewhere between Librarian and shy Sunday school teacher. She twirled the gun playfully in her hand as she spoke.

"Listen, baby, we could sit here all night and throw the weight of our rods around, but that won't get either of us anywhere. I'm just here to find out who killed Baker and why. Whatever you had going on with Kelly, Schwarz, or Big Pete means nothing to me. I made a promise to his old lady and I intend on keeping that promise."

"She doesn't want to know who the murderer is anymore than she wants a hole in her head. Nobody does. Don't you get it? Baker, Schwarz, Kelly; they were all left out to dry; even you. Maybe even Big Pete. This isn't about money or land schemes. It's about ego. Someone wanted more without having to pay the toll." She was talking fast now, her words hurtling forward like a freight train bound for hell. I was listening, but a large part of me was outside that warehouse, away from the heat of the moment and edging toward a shadow that haunted me from the beginning. I wondered if the death I had seen that first night was my fault. Had I let the game go on too long?

"What's wrong, Mr. Detective? Cat got your tongue?" She was playing with me now, like a cat playing with a mouse. I played along, one last time.

"You're singing, baby, but the tune is a little out of key. Maybe I believe you. Maybe we are being toyed with. But for a simple mug like me motive is everything. Sure you could've helped set things up to frame Big Pete or Kelly, but what do you get out of it? What does Brutus get out of it?"

She blinked. She didn't expect Brutus's name to land in the middle of our conversation. The first time I'd seen him, I thought he was there to knock off Holly and me. What I didn't realize was that he was there to complete the picture. Brutus's presence made everything look the way it should have.

Connie regained her composure, laughing like a dame lost in the moment. She held the .22 tighter, the barrel aimed directly at my gut. Her eyes were a mystery, her intentions darker and more mysterious than my dreams after a night of Scotch and giggles.

"Come on, sister. What does Brutus get out of it? He's too dumb to run things on his own. Who'd back him up? You got too much smarts to want to volunteer for that job. Or, do you?" It was a question that had only one answer.

"You really think you got things figured out; you and that dame of yours?" She backed up. "You don't know the half of it. One day, maybe, you'll figure it out, but I seriously doubt it." She backed up a few more steps.

"Don't take another step, doll." We stared each other down until there was nothing left but sinister intentions. We were seconds away from something I might never be able to take back. Connie wasn't ready to die anymore than I was. It was all one giant act with me as the sucker. I knew it the moment I saw the look pass between Connie and her old man. I knew it the moment Clint Baxter lay sprawled on a cold, hard piece of dirt with his guts spilling out into his hands waiting to die for a dame that cared about as much as an out-of-control machine gun. I had seen the pieces tumbling around in front of me for a week. Only now did I realize the truth of it all.

"Ha! You're nothing." She backed up another step. The cold air of the warehouse became hot with an eager anticipation, like a bull just before it enters the arena. If the mug on the phone played his cards right, I'd shoot the dame. That's why he sent me here. That's why he wanted me to see her. It all made sense, in a crazy kind of way. Thing is, I wasn't ready to play things that way. Too many dead bodies had kissed my gun in the last couple of days. I was tired of death, like a man tired of the monotony of dreaming about a life never lived. Calling her bluff was the only option left.

Her eyes were a mixture of anger, confusion, and sadness that mixed well with the opaqueness of the moment. I almost couldn't see what she was thinking. I played along to the same tune, only I danced a few steps slower.

There was little upside in leaving me alive. All she had to do was pull the trigger. The first two shots weren't bad. The next few would surely be as mean as a junkyard dog. If I replied in kind, the wizard behind the magic curtain could successfully eliminate anyone who knew anything about the grand plan. The whole thing had been pulled off magically. If he believed I was playing by the rules, things would work out just that way. Unfortunately, gun shots and bullet holes don't always add up to a long cold night in Hell. The rat in the corner was proof of that. He became increasingly quiet. The moaning I heard earlier had subsided to a dull wheeze. It didn't matter. He didn't exist for me anymore. Connie was my game now.

One thing was for sure. I wasn't about to take any more lives. I had lived next to death too long. Its shadow hung like a bat over me, sucking all the life out of my soul until I was nothing more than a lukewarm body living on borrowed time. It was time to start living again.

"Listen, baby, we don't need to do this. You shoot me; I shoot you. That's what they want. I can protect you, if you'll let me." Her eyes remained transfixed upon me and the gun in my hand. My intentions remained transfixed on the moment and what it would mean a few minutes down the road.

"I want to believe you, I really do. Nobody can protect me and you know it." She was a dame caught in something she thought she could control. But the dog she thought she could tame reared its sharp teeth and bit back. The look on her face showed the scar, but the scar went only so deep. "He knew that the whole time. That's why he was so nice to me. He knew I'd bite. Now, it's too late. If Big Pete doesn't get me, he will. He can do things like that, you know." She held the gun up again, but there was no strength in it. She moved in brief spurts, as if her mind and her body were two different people headed in two different directions. I threw a cursory glance over at the guy sprawled against the side wall, bits of glass splashed across his chest and face. He still looked dead. I looked back at Connie.

"You still got a chance in all this. It isn't too late. Sure, we're dogs on a leash, but dogs can bite back. That's what he did. Big Pete is so big he can't see what's going on under his own feet. You're old man may have sold you out, but it's tearing him up inside. He was probably happy to see Baxter when he came to visit. He was facing ghosts he hadn't faced since that first day I came around calling. You knew it and ran. But you don't have to keep running. Most of the mugs that run get nothing but wooden coffins for beds. Don't make the same mistake. Let me help you." My rod hung weakly by my side. It was a risky move, but I had to show some faith. "Let me protect you."

Connie shook her head side to side in frustration. "I don't know anything anymore. My world is spinning out of control. I don't know what to do. He just made it all sound so easy." She looked at me with pleading eyes, "Raise your gun, Mr. Dixon, please." I could see shallow tears running down her face. She didn't want to die. I felt like a man who wanted to die because I was too afraid to live. Connie wanted to live. I could see it in her eyes like I could see dice go snake-eyes before it landed. She had turned again, this time before I could figure my next move.

"Don't do it, Miss Bartlett." Holly walked up slowly behind me. "You're in a jam, sure, but let Mr. Dixon help you. Don't give them what they want. Can't you see? They want you gone. It makes there job that much easier. Don't give them that satisfaction." Holly stood next to me then walked past until she was face-to-face with Connie. "If it wasn't for him I'd probably be dead right now. He's a good guy, even though his mug looks a little like a bag of bad meat." Connie laughed in between the tears. It was a good sign. She walked a few steps closer to Connie. "One dame on her own might have problems, but two of us, together; well, two of us together will be a handful for any number of Big Pete's goons. What do you say?" She reached out with one hand and gently brushed Connie's arm. Connie started crying like a baby. I leaned heavily against the frame. Suddenly, the worst was yet to come.

Holly held Connie close, soothing her the way a mother soothes a child. She pulled the gun out of her hand and tossed it on the table. I walked over, , pulled out the magazine then shoved it into my pocket. The grandeur of the moment almost overwhelmed me, but the image of Joseph Baker kept me from forgetting why I was here, and, more importantly, where I was going. The good thing was now I knew where to look.

Holly turned her head slowly and said, "Go. Do what you have to do. I'll take care of things here." I turned around and walked out. Outside, the night felt slightly warmer, subtle shades of gray looming over the blackness. I hoped Holly would be okay. I crossed myself then walked away.

CHAPTER 24

I stopped at a phone booth and made a couple of quick phone calls before heading back to my office. It was a long, slow drive; the traffic on the streets was light. I felt like I was the only one in the world with problems the size of Babe Ruth's gut. The only good thing was with Holly out of the way I could afford to take a few more chances.

The last few blocks seemed to take forever. I passed the time smoking a cigarette and listening to the radio. The music and the laughs were part of a foreign language that I could only barely comprehend. I finally shut the radio off and opened the window. I listened to the dull breeze wheeze past like a stranger in the night and wondered silently if I had the courage to go through with the rest of the play. The familiar image of my office building appearing ahead of me made the decision an easy one.

I parked my car and walked inside. I climbed the stairs, ignoring the elevator this time. Each step was more painful than the last. The bruises and cuts on my face throbbed in sharp notes that on paper would have sounded like a C sharp. I ignored the pain and continued up slowly. I pulled out my .38 and checked the bullets. I also had Connie and Joseph's gun, but knew it would do me no good here.

I thought about the same journey a lifeless corpse named Fats Kelly had taken not so long ago. He didn't have to worry about joint pain or cuts and bruises getting infected. He didn't have to worry about anything anymore. He had paid the toll; the price had been his life. Jimmy No Shoes and little Benny were also paid-up members of the club. They were all just forgettable statistics in a long list of statistics that Big Pete kept in his back pocket. He chewed them up and then spit them out like poppy seeds. He also tried to keep a mug named Clint Baxter, but kept mugs never stay kept. They become hungry mutts looking for the next meal. If they get hungry enough, they'll eat anything at any price. Connie Bartlett had helped name that price, but she was just the middleman in a deal that was meant to go wrong right from the start. Everyone was out for the double-cross. Only one face had the cheat sheet for the play. He'd been there the whole time, like the inevitable shadow that stuck like gum on the soul of a shoe. The accidental collision of greed, murder and vengeance formed the perfect foundation for a double-cross of epic proportions. It seemed everyone knew what the kid's murder would mean in the long run, only no one had possessed the kind of motive necessary, except one person. And only one other person knew that well enough to take advantage of the opportunity.

 I walked up the last flight of stairs. I stopped for a moment when I reached the top. I took a deep breath then slowly opened the door. The place was dark as usual, except for one light at the end of the hall. I had ignored that door more than a few times. At the time it meant as much to me as a cockroach crawling across my shoe. This time things would be different.

 It was a door, no different than mine, yet different in so many ways. Behind were the answers to all the questions that had dogged me right from the start. I expected this moment to rear its ugly head for some time. I knew it would come when I saw Baker's riddled corpse bound in rope tighter than that which bound me. I knew it would come when Dane Bartlett walked back into a room, into a lie, of his own making. I knew it would come when a soft mug named Clint Baxter decided to put his own neck on the line for a dame that probably didn't care two-bits for him. I knew it would come when a dame as cool as ice shot a mug clean and as clear as an empty shot glass. I knew it would all come raining down on me like phony tears.

 The numbers '407' beckoned me forward. He would probably be waiting for me. There was no doubt of that. He might even have a gat or two leveled at me as I walked in. I breathed evenly between each stride, my headache disappearing for the moment. My steps were measured in those same steady rhythms, not slow or fast, but even. I looked up for one brief second. I prayed one more time, hoping the man above was listening. Finally, I knocked on the door.

"Come on in, Dixon. I've been waiting for ya'."

I opened the door and stepped inside. Paul Brutus sat behind a desk similar to mine. The only difference was the submachine gun that rested comfortably in his lap. He had been expecting me. I wondered if the mug ever slept.

His eyes seemed better suited to an executioner, and the slick grin that stretched serenely across his face looked as black as a preacher's suit. I lowered my gat a little, if only to show him I wasn't scared.

"Long time no see, Brutus." The words slid out of me like a walrus trying to skate on ice. I was tired and it wouldn't take a magnifying glass to recognize it.

"It hasn't been that long, shamus. It wasn't more than an hour ago we talked on the phone. You seemed kind of grateful for my help, as it were. I hope you haven't changed your mind since then." The same smile decorated a pockmarked face that, at one time, made ten-to-one look like a cakewalk. After Big Pete got his clutches on the mug, Brutus turned into a second-rate stumblebum with a few fancy moves and a weak left hook.

"I figured I'd go and see whatever it is you wanted me to go see. Now that I've seen it, I can safely say I've seen everything."

"I didn't really expect her to shoot you," Brutus laughed. "If Big Pete's dogs couldn't kill you, there was no way a stupid dame like her could take you out. Let's face it, Connie had some guts, but when it really counted that dame was strictly amateur."

"Funny, that's what they said about you, wasn't it?"

"Them days is long gone, shamus. I'm just a man of business now."

"Whose business might that be?" I asked.

"Does it really matter? One's the same as another? Besides, you ain't going to live long enough to worry about it anyhow. And thanks to you and Big Pete, a lot of others aren't going to worry about it either; hats off to you for a job done well, shamus."

"You're playing with fire, Brutus."

He patted the gun as he spoke. It was like watching someone pet a dog.

"That fat slug is the one playing with fire. He's riding high now, but it won't be long before he's sitting in the chair up at sing-sing cooking like a duck. I've been waiting a long time for this moment. That fat bastard thinks he owns me, you and everything else in this town. He's just starting to see now what his world is really about. It's nothing but smoke and mirrors, shamus. All you got to do is wave a few dollars around and his whole organization falls like a house of cards."

"You're just a cheap hood who couldn't hack it as a fighter. Big Pete might be a fat slug, but at least he earned his name. You got nothing but weak knees to your credit. You should take that and blow before he gets his paws on you."

He laughed like a man ready for the nut-house. "Big Pete is nothing more than a fat fish in a fancy suit. I had a chance once, but he took that away. I'm gonna make sure he gets what's coming to him." A malevolent fury worked its way to the surface. I was starting to see the real reason for this whole charade. It had come down to ego. The last week had all come down to one man's tiny, fragile ego.

"You took those dives, not him. But, if you want to ruin his breakfast go right ahead. It's no skin off my nose. But why hurt the kids? What'd they ever do to you?" I asked.

"They were just warm bodies; mugs that could do a job without asking too many stupid questions. But that Baker kid just wouldn't shut his yap. Connie kept telling me he was having problems dealing with his conscience so I told her to teach the mug some manners, the hard way. I didn't tell her to bump the kid off, though. It ain't my fault she got an itchy trigger finger. It's too bad. I think she was sweet on the kid." He laughed like it was the funniest thing he'd ever said.

"No dice, Brutus. I know you killed the kid. No one else had the motive or the opportunity. Connie had the kid roughed up some, but you saw the numbers in killing him. Big Pete's whole setup starts to shake from the ground up with the kid gone. You take the gun and give it to Kelly or Connie. Then you call me and get me to do the job of pinning Baker's murder on Connie. She gets nervous enough to louse up anything her old man and Big Pete might have on the cooker. You know Baxter is hot for Connie and might do anything to help her. I was just the handy trigger man mad enough to blow Connie to smithereens. After that, you just sit back and smile. And the cops, well, they can only ignore so many dead bodies, even with Big Pete's dough lining their pockets."

"It's a nice tune your singing, shamus, but the words don't jive with reality. I had no reason to kill the kid."

I ignored Brutus's words and marched forward with more angles. "Sure, Puccino and Kelly hurt the kid some, but they left him alive. They dumped his body in a field close to his place. They figured he'd just drag himself home, but you had other ideas. Kelly would have gladly handed Connie over if it meant saving his skin, but somehow he found out about you. Maybe your mouth is bigger than that pumpkin you call a head, or maybe you whisper one too many sweet nothings for Connie to pass on to her new friends. Either way, he knew and threatened to haul your can in along with his, so you told Big Pete about Kelly, making him about as valuable as a plug nickel. Buying off Puccino was easy. You get him to call on me and give me all the information I need to hang myself in exchange for a piece of the dame. He's also a good stooge to keep me occupied until you showed up ready to call. That's why he kept eyeing the window while he was talking to me." He sat quietly. The look on his face didn't change. I felt like I was talking to a wall, but I kept on talking, kept reaching for a truth I knew was there. "With Kelly gone and the Baker kid dead, the only thing left was to find yourself a couple of patsies to take the fall. Connie was one; Schwarz was the other. You knew Baker and Schwarz were fighting over Connie. Maybe Connie even set it up that way. Either way, that would have been a perfect way to set Schwarz up just in case he got difficult. He had no way of proving he didn't do it, and with Big Pete on your side, all you'd have to do is step back and let the blood flow. After all the bodies were in the ground, you set Connie up as the evil canary and then had me kill her to prevent her from telling the truth about you. That would all but destroy any allegiances her old man might have with Big Pete. Pretty soon, everybody would be out looking for their own slices of Big Pete's pie, including the cops, the judges and the Falletti's of the world."

"Your good, shamus, but there's one thing you got wrong. Schwarz wasn't in town two weeks ago. I sent him and No Shoes off to Jersey to take care of some business for Big Pete. He didn't get back until a couple of days before Baker died, and even then, they didn't see each other. Kelly didn't think it was a good idea, and Connie seconded that. As for me, well, I'm as pure as the driven snow. Big Pete, that fat mug, trusts me so much he's even got me guarding the contracts for his land grab." He reached over and threw a thin ream of paper onto the desk. 'Benson Properties' was written on one corner in bold. "I hate to burst your bubble, shamus, but you're barking up the wrong tree. I'm innocent, and everything else you're babbling about makes about as much sense as a Jap fighting for our side. Now that we got everything straightened out, how's about Pucky and I take you for a little ride?"

Puccino's gat nosed into the small of my back. I knew he'd be around, and I knew he'd be carrying. I looked back over my shoulder and smelled Puccino. I turned back to Brutus. A tiny fragment of something whizzed through my mind. It was as small as dirt but became as big and hot as a spotlight. Connie had mentioned it once and only once. As philosophy goes, it wasn't much worth worrying about, but, as a clue to the identity of a murderer, it was off the mark by quite a bit. Brutus had been especially picky when it came to his victims. That's why Baker didn't fit. It still didn't fit. I was starting to see why.

"How's about I ask you one question? We can still be friends if you tell me the truth; otherwise, I'll have to turn you over to Big Pete."

He laughed again, Puccino joining in this time. "Ha, ha, ha! Sure, shamus. Go right ahead. I'm all for last wishes!"

"Why pick me when there are so many other private dicks in this city?"

"You're a smart mug. Smart mugs are hard to find in this town."

"I've got a gun to my back so how smart could I really be?" I smiled.

"A smart man knows when he's had it, and in my book that's you. Pucky might have the drop on you, but one-on-one, I'd give odds on you any day. Besides, you were one up on Connie, Baxter and Big Pete. That tells me I picked the right sucker."

I laughed along with him, if only to delay the inevitable. "And here I thought Big Pete and Bartlett were the suckers. I guess that goes to show you what I really know. I guess in the end it didn't matter who I was. A suckers a sucker in your book, isn't it?"

"Don't worry too much about it. Like I said before, things happen for a reason. Connie knew that better than anybody. That's why she was into me. I'm an action man. I'm not like Big Pete or Dane Bartlett. They're too soft for the big time. It's my turn and I ain't stopping for anyone, especially no half-wit loony dame with more money than sense." He kept smiling as he talked, all the while slowly stroking the gun in his lap. "And as for the dead kid, well, I can't say as I care that he's dead, but the man above must have been looking out for me, because it sure put everyone in a bind."

"That's a good speech. Maybe you can tell that to his old lady some day."

"That kid was just in the wrong place at the wrong time. He's a statistic, shamus. He didn't need to die, but he did. I'm pretty sure you understand." Brutus said.

"Yeah, I think I do," I replied.

"Not that it's gonna do you any good, at least not where you're headed. If your dame is still alive, we'll find her and take care of her, permanently." With Puccino standing behind me grinning like a ghoul during Halloween and Brutus loaded to the teeth, anyone with brains would have thought my goose was cooked. I knew better. I still figured I had the upper hand even after the phone rang. Brutus grabbed it with hands as big as bear claws and fingers that looked like sausages in a meat store. I waited for the inevitable.

Puccino offered an eloquent, "Your numbers up, shamus. Only a lame brain would come here lookin' for trouble."

"We'll find out soon enough."

"What's that supposed to mean?" I didn't have an answer to his question. I was in extra innings now where runs would be counted by the number of body bags that littered the field. If the game didn't play out the way I hoped, I might never get a chance to answer Puccino's question.

"I'm proud of you, baby!" Brutus exclaimed. "Put her on the phone." He turned to face me with a smile better suited to a crazy mutt than a man. I could tell he was disappointed. "Why don't you listen to your pretty little canary sing now, shamus?"

I walked the few steps to his desk and grasped the phone. I waited for what I already knew was happening. "Gabrielle? It was all a setup." Holly spoke calmly, her voice almost reassuring. I hoped I was doing the right thing. I was no longer playing with my own life, but with Holly's life as well. Before she could say anything else, Connie's devious voice crawled across the receiver.

"Hello, Mr. Dixon. I wanted to like you. We could have made some sweet music together, but Mr. Brutus can give me things you can't. Plus, he's smarter than you could ever hope to be." It was like listening to some cheap hood brag about the candy store they just ripped off. It was all I could do to keep from blowing the whole thing to smithereens.

"We'll see, baby." I threw the receiver on the desk and turned to see Puccino smiling like a clown at a circus.

"Listen, sweetheart, you know where to take her. Tell Cozy to lay low. I'll get Puccino to take care of him. Okay, doll, I'll see you soon."

Brutus examined me for a few seconds before speaking again. I pretended to be angry. I didn't have to try very hard.

"What made you think you could come here and take me down? I figured you for a smart guy, but you really let me down, shamus. I guess I'm gonna have to find someone else to do my dirty work, won't I?"

"You're a heel, Brutus. Mugs like you will never last. You're a death just waiting to happen. Big Pete knows it and I know it."

He laughed hard enough to split the seams in his trousers. "I'm not afraid of that fat slug. I know you talked to him. I was there listening to the whole thing. After it was over, who do you think he turned to for advice? I'll give you two guesses, but you'll only need one."

"Maybe I called him before I came here and spilled the whole works to him. What would you say to that?"

"I'd say you were lying. You see, shamus, I've been studying you."

"I'm honored," I replied.

"You should be. You ain't no ordinary mug, shamus. You got pride, probably more than most mugs in your line. You don't take charity and you don't give it. That's probably why you're still alive. The only reason you'd call that fat, greasy butterball was to beg for your life, or trade someone else's for it. And honestly, shamus, I don't see you doing either. It makes you a tough mug, but it also makes you a sucker. That's why I don't think you called Big Pete. How does that sound to you?"

"It's a guess, and a good one, but since my number is up how's about you answer one last question for me?"

"Go ahead, I got a few minutes." He looked like a guy waiting for the winning numbers in the lottery to come strolling through his door. His smile got bigger by the second. The more I stared, the more I wanted to punch his lights out. But my sense of the moment got the better of me. I wanted to hate myself for what I was thinking. Standing in front of Brutus, watching him smile like some nut in the loony bin made me want dive into a bottle and never get out. I finally understood why, for the murderer, death was so bittersweet.

"Who took the body up to his old lady's apartment? Was it you or one of your hired goons? I mean it would have been tough to see anything with the lights off, no?"

A look of confusion etched deep X marks into his battle-scarred face. It was the first time I'd seen him confused about anything, and the last. After a few seconds of indecision he waved one of his meaty digits at Puccino and said, "Why don't you ask Marco?"

I turned and faced Puccino. A smile, like a thick string of overworked taffy, stretched across his face. He held the gat firmly in his right hand.

"What about it, Puccino?" I asked.

"All right, shamus. I went back to Henry to make sure the kid understood we meant business. Kelly really worked him over but good. Still I had to go and put a little more scare into 'em. I see the kid lying in the middle of the lot, still tied up. I pull up a little short and look things over. The place is deserted so I get out and see what's what. It's dark, but not too dark for me to see the kid ain't gonna be asking for seconds no more. His roscoe is just lying there so I pick it up. I head to a phone and tell Kelly. He says he don't know from nothing, but tells me to dump the kid in his old lady's apartment. You know, for laughs. It's kind of spooky, but I got no squawks. He ain't too heavy so I carry him up the trellis so no one sees me. He's leaking like a hose, but I make it up. I jimmy the window open and carry him inside. The old lady ain't home. I dump the kid inside and high tail it out. End of story."

He grinned the whole time he talked. He found funny what I found extremely sad and pathetic. It never failed to amaze me how mugs like Puccino laughed through life, trying to get by playing angles and gimmicks the way kids play marbles. Sometimes, I could see the dark clouds hanging over these goons, like a knife, ready to cut away the last remnants of honesty that might still remain.

"And nobody saw you, not even the old lady?" I asked.

He looked at me like I had two heads. "The whole place was deserted. It was like someone pulled the plug out of the wall or something."

"The lights were all out?"

"Yeah, the whole place was lights out."

"And the gun you found, what did you do with it?"

"I gave it to the dame. You'll have to ask her in the afterlife what she did with it."

"I told you she'd have something interesting to show you," Brutus laughed.

I turned to face Brutus. I took the .22 out of my pocket and threw it on the desk. Brutus didn't even flinch. He didn't have to. "You have one chance. Go to the cops and tell them everything you know. You're in hot water, but at least they won't decorate the East River with you. You go to Big Pete and he'll turn you into duck soup."

"Nuts. It's time for you to go nighty-night, shamus." He waved at me like a kid waving good-bye to his mother. I looked down at my watch; the long hand was quickly winding its way toward zero-hour. I could make out the sound of footsteps above me. Brutus was too busy smiling to notice those sounds. Maybe he put it off to cockroaches or some fancy new typewriter. I recognized those sounds and knew why they were there. I also knew that I was no longer on the side of truth and justice, but swimming in the same murky water that Dane Bartlett and all the other Dane Bartlett's swam in. I had called in Faletti as my insurance policy, hoping his aim would be good enough where my killer instinct wasn't. If I survived, my guilt would be the premium.

Suddenly, a sound, like bursting balloons, filled the air. I had to make my move now before Brutus managed to save his own bacon and cook mine. I pushed back with all my strength, thrusting my weight into Puccino so suddenly that all he could do was fall backward with me. Brutus tried to raise his Tommy-gun in my direction, but it was too late. The plaster from the ceiling fell all around the desk, the floor, and over Brutus, turning his expensive suit into something resembling painter's coveralls. The roar of gunfire was matched only by the screaming of my own rapidly-beating heart. I didn't have time to check the number of bullets that washed over Brutus, but the bright red spots that suddenly appeared were more than enough to tell me he'd probably never see the light of day ever again. My bones, meanwhile, managed to keep time to a fancy hypnotic rhythm that was playing for one night only to a captive audience of three. In front of me, Brutus jumped up and down in his chair like a half-drunken puppet whose strings had suddenly come to life. Bullets rained down from the ceiling in a thundering shower of lead that seemed to have no end. His arms and legs flew about uncontrollably like the arms of a drug-crazed octopus, and his head jerked from side-to-side in ragged spasms, his once perfect hair now a jumbled, tangled mess.

The dizzying heights of insanity that exploded in those diminutive confines sounded like Times Square on a massive bender. In between the falling plaster, the hailstorm of bullets, and the screams from Puccino and myself could be heard the beating of my own heart.

I screamed a thousand pains and cursed a thousand heartaches in those few moments, each time wondering why I hadn't hit the ground yet.

In the end, what seemed liked hours took only a few seconds. Puccino and I fell out into the hallway with me on top. I didn't know where his gun was, but I wasn't going to give him time to think about the answer. I immediately thrust my elbow into his ribs quick and hard as I landed. A barely audible grunt rose above the angry din. The gat slipped out of his right hand and skittered across the grimy floor like a crab racing toward shelter. In front of us, Brutus continued to shudder wildly on the chair. Countless bullets penetrated every part of his body; blood was everywhere.

Puccino lay dazed beneath me. I shoved another heavy elbow into his side. He grunted a little louder this time. I turned over and with all the strength I had left smacked him in the kisser. He was out for the count.

I felt a throbbing pain working its way down my arm and into my hand. I tried shaking it off, but it stuck to me like flypaper. I stood up slowly and peered into the office Brutus had sat in for more than a week. The phone he used sat on the desk, the receiver resting at a crooked angle. The hail of gunfire had finally stopped. Everything was quiet, especially Brutus. I examined him briefly. He seemed to be spilling out of his chair. Only gravity kept him from completely falling out of it. I'd never seen so much blood before, and hoped to never see so much ever again.

His story was over. Mine was just beginning.

CHAPTER 25

Faletti and his guns hastily exited the building before Pete and his boys descended on the scene, for the second time. I wasn't sure how he would take things, but I was sure it wouldn't be with a smile.

I sat in my office, door open and feet up on the desk, waiting for Pete to arrive. I thought about pouring myself a glass before realizing the necessity for sober thought for the next few minutes. I didn't think, or care, that there was a dead man in the office down the hall. I cared even less that I was responsible for it all. I had secrets, both past and present. Some were secrets to no one. This time, I would have to take things to my grave, for Pete's sake and my own.

Outside my office window, the light of morning rose solemnly out of the ashes of the quickly-fading night; a steady drifting fog undulated slowly through the street below. It was strange to see that sight so deep within the city. It hid much of the decay.

It wasn't long before Pete arrived on the scene. I could hear cars brake and doors slam; orders were given to secure the area. I tilted my head back, blowing smoke up into the air until it filled the upper reaches of my office. Gazing through that haze reminded me of the haze that surrounded Brutus after the firing stopped. All I could see was the vague outline of a mug that tried to beat the odds and failed.

I was still trying to figure out my story when Pete came drifting into my office like the second coming of Dick Tracy. His features were marked by a kind of vivid, raw anger that I was, by now, more than familiar with. I could hear the blue boys drifting through the hallway, a smattering of conversation punctuated by words you wouldn't want a kid to hear. I managed to finish my last cigarette just as Pete entered the room. He couldn't decide whether to pace back and forth, or just stand still and yell at me. I waited for him to make the first move.

He opened his mouth to say something then stopped. He turned from me and began pacing in front of my desk. When he reached the corner of the room for the third time, he turned and stared at me like a bull staring at a red cape. I waited for the charge.

It wasn't half as bad as I thought it would be.

"You want to tell me about the piece of dead meat just down the hall?" Pete asked quietly.

"Did you find Holly?"

"She's fine," Pete replied exasperatingly. "She was pretty broken up at first, but she's in good shape now. She's a tough kid, Dix. If we hadn't gotten there when we did, there's no knowing what kind of condition we would have found her in." I tried ignoring the images, but they kept flying at me like angry bats in a cave. As if reading my mind, Pete added, "Don't worry, Dix, she's okay."

"It's been too many hours between my last life and this one, Pete. I feel all stretched out. Funny thing is it's not over yet."

"I don't get it. We got the dame, and the mug that was with her. Presumably, the corpse down the hall and the unconscious mug on the floor are their companions. Add that to Kelly, No Shoes, and the other dead gangster at the slip and you got yourself a nice, tidy ending."

"I got one more thing to do. I can't tell you what it is, but you'll find out soon enough."

Pete's eyes went as big as watermelons. "Oh, well, there's a big surprise. You have to go and do something and not tell me. You're treating me like a mushroom, Dix, and it's starting to get real tired. How's about telling me something before you do it? I might be able to actually help you for a change instead of having to cover for you all the time."

"I'm too tired to argue you with you, Pete. I have to do this. I owe it to someone. I made a promise and I intend on keeping it even if it kills me inside." Pete went quiet for a few seconds. He didn't know what I knew. I can't say he would have thought differently had he known, but I had to give myself the benefit of the doubt. "I've asked a lot of you, Pete, but this time I'm asking you as a friend, let me do this my way. It'll be hard enough on my own, forget about doing it with a bunch of police standing behind me. After I do this, it's all yours."

Pete shook his head in frustration. A quiet moment passed between us. It was uncomfortable, but neither of us seemed to know how to start. We were both stubborn as mules and hated to admit when we were wrong. In this case, we were both on the wrong side of the ledger. Finally, as if sensing my thoughts, Pete asked, "Were you right about, Brutus?"

"Yeah, I was. He put the Bartlett dame up to the whole thing, although, she was probably willing to take the ride anyway."

"A bored, rich dame with nothing but time on her hands; is that the way you see it?" Pete asked.

"That's the picture I kept getting. She's got guts, but not enough to put together the kind of circus they had running. Brutus makes it look like Schwarz took out Baker because of the dame. Maybe they both figured they had dibs on her, and anyone on the outside might figure Schwarz killed Baker because of it. After all, they both had the same gun: a .22 caliber. Big Pete doesn't know who is on what side and can't risking killing Schwarz without bringing a lot of heat down on himself and scaring old man Bartlett into the retirement home. So, he uses Schwarz as a target to find out who's playing by what numbers. Only he doesn't realize Brutus is the one lighting the fire under his feet. Schwarz could say he didn't do it, but who would believe a poor schmuck like him when Big Pete and Dane Bartlett are on the other side pointing their fingers. Had they got him in that position, they would have made sure he copped to the whole thing."

"So, Schwarz becomes the dope to draw you in," Pete replied.

"Brutus figures I'll want the kid bad enough to risk a showdown with the dame. Maybe he already knows I've figured out most of the angle, maybe he doesn't. Either way, he knows I'm at the breaking point. At least, that's what I thought most of the picture looked like."

"What changed your mind?"

"I made her mad when I got the mug with her to sell her out. She 'supposedly' shoots the guy in a fit of rage. Only problem is she used blanks. I knew that because the guy she shot couldn't play dead to save his life. I've seen guys who've really been shot and he wasn't even close to the real thing. I had to get her to believe that I believed she had killed the mug. Brutus figured I'd be crazy enough by now to shoot the dame once I'd gotten what I needed from her. Once she's gone, then I make for Brutus's office and have a showdown with him. He doesn't think I've figured out the angle between Puccino and him. Once there, he can get rid of me anyway he wants. After that, he frames Big Pete for my murder and for Connie Bartlett's. Connie's old man gets mad enough to spoil Big Pete's ideas for the East side, or maybe just gets scared enough to run. Either way, things go real bad, real fast for Big Pete."

"If Brutus had you all set up to shoot the dame, then why did she take Holly hostage?"

"I made Holly think I was a little crazy and willing to shoot anybody for anything. I also knew she'd probably follow me in and probably try and stop me from doing something she figures I might regret later. Meanwhile, Brutus tells Connie to play out the scene so that I'll see her as nothing more than a desperate dame looking for a way out. He also probably had her believe I wouldn't shoot her. Meanwhile, he keeps tabs on me, giving me just information to make me want to use him, and anyone else, as the ball just before the bat hits it."

"He plays both of you against each other, then sits back and watches while we shake down Big Pete. With us keeping Big Pete occupied, Connie wouldn't have lasted two minutes had Brutus taken you out."

"With her out of the way, there's one less witness to worry about. He could've easily spun the rest of it anyway he wanted with her gone. And Big Pete would've been dumb enough to believe it. As it was, she played her part perfectly, making me believe she was sorry for everything, and that she wanted another way out. But Brutus didn't figure on me not shooting the dame. I knew that from his reaction to her phone call. They take Holly as a prisoner in case I decide to play tough with Brutus. With both of us finally out of the way, everything else falls exactly where it should. The way he saw it, he had everything covered."

"That still left Holly in a dangerous position."

"Sure it wasn't the smartest move leaving Holly there, but they wouldn't kill her until they got word from Brutus. She was probably safer there than with me. If Brutus got his mitts on her, there's no telling what he might've done. Oh, and you might want to check the .22 against the bullets you found. It's probably the murder weapon."

"I'll do that." Pete was quiet for a moment. It was a queer silence that seemed to stretch on for hours. He finally broke the silence, the tone in his voice taking on an almost motherly quality. "You put the dame in a tough spot. I don't know if she'll forgive you for it." Pete was right. I felt like a heel leaving her there. She might understand, but not before belting me hard enough to hit a home run. Thing is, I could deal with the physical stuff; it was the emotional part I had a problem with.

"I'll deal with that when I have to."

"How about telling me how Brutus got all the holes?" Pete asked.

He eyed me suspiciously, like a mouse eyeing a snake just before it says goodnight for good. I caught myself sinking between an illusion and the truth. I could've told him what happened, but then where would that leave me? I had promises to keep to others, not to mention those I made to myself. I wasn't sure Pete would understand. I don't know if anyone would, or could, ever understand.

"They were waiting for him, one floor up. One minute I'm talking to the guy, the next minute he looks like a cheese-grater. What can I say?" It was weak. Pete looked down; his eyes looked as sharp as knives. He worked through my words carefully, attempting to discern the truth lurking behind it all. It wasn't the kind of truth that gave you warm feelings in the middle of the night, and it definitely wouldn't put an end to the images of death that danced like wild demons in my head.

"What about the guy on the floor? How did he get the broken nose and the busted ribs?" Pete threw an uncomfortable stare in my direction. I stared back, half-heartedly.

"I tripped on him when I accidentally kicked him in the head. It could happen to anybody." There was no real logic in any of my answers, but in a faraway place called dreamland everything made sense.

"Go home, Dix. Get some sleep. Come in tomorrow afternoon and we'll get your whole story down on paper. That way I can hold it against you outside a court of law." Pete smiled for a second. I smiled back.

I got up out of my chair and looked around. With all the death outside of my office, things were still the same inside. My body felt like a pincushion, every joint and muscle screaming pain in a thousand different languages. I didn't need to look at my face to know that it couldn't look any worse unless I was a badly burnt steak. I also thought about Holly and whether she would ever talk to me again. I could get by if she didn't, but it wouldn't make things any easier.

"Is she somewhere safe, Pete?" I asked sheepishly.

Pete glanced at me reassuringly. "Yeah, she's with Wilma." As if reading my mind, Pete added, "Don't worry, Dix. She's mad, but she was also worried about you. I like her. She's got spunk. She's definitely tough enough to beat some of that bull-headedness right out of you."

"Thanks, Pete." I started for the door when Pete asked me one more question. I had hoped to get out of the office without having to answer any more questions, especially this one.

"Who killed the kid, Dix?" Pete asked reluctantly.

I didn't turn around. "I'll tell you soon enough." I walked out the door, out the building and into the brisk winters chill.

CHAPTER 26

I didn't go back to my apartment. The miles that stretched between home and me seemed too simple, too easy. I could have pointed my suspicions in any number of directions, like a mug shooting a roscoe in a dark room, but I'd still be living with the truth.

The early morning cold bit deep into my chest, infusing me with a deep sense of sadness. I'd hoped for something different from this case, but it hadn't worked out that way. My brother was still dead, I was still a physical wreck, and I was still living for the next drink. In the middle of it all stood Holly. I was half-dead and she was so alive. She deserved better.

Sliding into the driver's seat of Mahoney's car was like sliding into a coffin; only the coffin was more comfortable. I peered out the window at a scene I'd witnessed a thousand times before, but never really examined until now. For most, it was something they'd seen in every corner without stopping to appreciate it for what it really was. I called it life.

Outside of my own selfish concerns the city continued moving like an assembly line without end. The frail pitter-patter of feet echoing off the crumbling, soiled sidewalks slowly brought light back into that faraway realm I had called life for almost a week. It was an okay feeling as feelings go.

I started the ignition and pulled out of the parking lot. I headed back in a direction that felt as comfortable as a bullet in the head. I couldn't quite place my finger on what it meant; however, the feelings it inspired reminded me of those days when I could pass by a street without thinking about how many sorry mugs had died there. Before this case, it was just another part of the city. Now, it was something else.

It didn't take me long to get to where I was going. I pulled to the side and turned off the ignition. The bridge beyond was a steel gray, its tentacles reaching deep into the river. Beyond its grasp lay the rest of the city.

I got out and looked up at the building. It all began here. A slow, tentative building reaching up toward the grayish sky, any opulence it once harbored long since departed. I crossed the street and quietly entered. I shuffled up the stairs until I came to the old lady's floor. The light directly in front of the apartment was lit. A faded yellow glow swam sluggishly through to the far end of the hall. The old, wooden floor creaked with each successive step.

Each step took me further away from the kid, away from reality, and away from Holly. I began to realize why I wanted this case so bad. It wasn't about the truth. It wasn't even about my past. I had made many mistakes in my life. Some had come at a very heavy price; some I could live with, and some I couldn't. It was the latter that had haunted me the most.

I wondered if Shanny Warchinski slept with the same troubles. Her adopted son was a kid looking for something better. He didn't find it. He only found death at the end of a gun. It wasn't pretty, but then death has never been confused with a fashion show. I've always believed that most kids looking for the big easy see a gunsel's life as something glamorous, something worth celebrating. It means fast money and a good time. The ones left with the truth are always those that have to bury the remains. The old lady understood that and accepted it.

I wondered, however, if she really thought things through before shooting her son. I wondered if she thought about the price of such an action. In the darkness of the night, it's easy to kill when you don't really see the truth behind the person your killing.

I wondered about a lot of things in those few minutes I stood outside her door. The working light told me she was in. It would be an easy thing. I could knock on her door and ask her. What would she say? What could she say? In her mind it all made sense.

Not even the gangsters could figure out how many times the kid had been shot, but she knew. Pete never showed her the body before I talked to her; yet, she knew he had been shot multiple times. I think part of her wanted to tell me, wanted to share with someone who also harbored a deep pain. The dirt on the floor that matched the dirt from the empty lot, the faded area on her finger where a ring should have rested, the raw tension in her hands, the averting eyes, the late nights; it all seemed like a surreal sort of reality that belonged in a fairytale. She had wandered through that lot, saw her beaten and bruised son; saw him for what he'd become. For her there was only one solution. She could shoot him and have his murder pinned on those responsible for turning her son into something evil, something shameful. Her anger and disappointment had been clearly marked into every awkward bullet hole. She wasn't an expert shot, not like Connie. Even angry and insane, Connie could still make the shot count. Kelly's gift to the kid ended up being his goodbye present.

I scanned my left, the window where Puccino carried the kids body in, dragging it like a sack of potatoes in a grocery store. The kid had made a choice, and all it got him was a one-way ticket to the morgue. His old lady was alive, but she wasn't too far behind.

She meant it when she said she wanted me to find the men who killed her son. She just didn't phrase it properly. She meant find the people responsible for killing her son's honesty and integrity. Find those people; make them pay. She had gotten her wish. Most of those mugs were either dead, or knocking on death's door. The rest were just waiting their turn.

I turned around and walked away.

CHAPTER 27

The cold breeze buffeted my face as gentle as a shovel digging into hard dirt. I would've pulled out a smoke, but remembered that I'd eaten the last one back at my office.

I was about to walk to the car when a long, sleek Rolls Royce pulled gently to the curb. I didn't need a score sheet to know who it was. Big Pete rarely gave personal interviews so I should have been flattered. Strangely enough, I wasn't. Nevertheless, I walked forward and waited for the mug that got out and stood near the back door to do something.

"Someone would like to talk to you, Mr. Dixon." It was the doorman from the Lounge. Big Pete must have been shorthanded.

"My old lady told me to never get into strange cars. If he wants to talk to me, tell him to open the window; otherwise, I got things to do." The window rolled down and a face as big as a twenty-pound omelet examined me through eyes that looked like marbles owned by a pigmy. He wore a large, black fedora with a white ostrich feather sticking out one side. His suit was a mixture of purple and black with a green tie that could have looked at home on a clown. His skin was a creamy pink tone that offset the purple from his suit the way a kid's balloon would offset the weight of an elephant. It seemed to cap things off just perfectly.

"You did okay, Dixon. I just wanted to stop by and offer my congratulations on a job well done. Not only do you get to enjoy the rest of your life, you get to do in style." He reached into his pocket and pulled out a small, white envelope. Both his hands were gloved.

His right handed me the envelope. "You earned it, shamus. Go out and enjoy yourself. I wouldn't worry too much about that Bartlett dame. Things like that always get squared one way or another."

I took the envelope and said, "Save it, bud. I'll take the dough because I earned it, but I didn't do it for you or to save your business. The sooner you understand that, the sooner we can part ways." I opened the envelope and pulled out five one hundred dollar bills. There was at least two thousand in there, but I didn't want it. I took only what I earned. I folded the envelope up and handed it back. "Keep the rest. I'm only asking you for one thing."

He took the envelope and without hesitation asked, "What's that?"

"Leave my friends alone."

"You're sweet on the broad, aren't you?" I kept quiet. I wasn't about to spill out my feelings to a gangster with a heart as big as a pea.

"Do we have a deal?"

"I didn't realize we were negotiating. You made good on the delivery so I can let it pass, this time. But, don't let it get around; otherwise, everybody'll want a handout."

The words came out cold, like a block of ice. I didn't know whether to be grateful or angry. I had been used like a handkerchief. Events twirled around me, and all I could do was sit back and watch. Mugs shot at me; dames played with my past, and the people I most cared about couldn't go anywhere without looking over their shoulder. For all of that, what did I get?

I wanted to lean into the car and kiss Big Pete with my roscoe. Instead, I said, "Thanks, now, how's about you let me get on with my life?"

"No problem. Just answer me this. How did you know it was Brutus killed the kid?"

I thought about the truth and the lie that sat next to it. So far, only two people knew what really happened, and it was up to me to keep it that way.

"He told me he did it." It was a simple answer to a simple question. It didn't have to matter that it was the wrong answer. It was the one that he wanted to hear.

"It's too bad about the way he bought it. All them holes ruined a damned nice suit." Our conversation ended with those words. He smiled one last time then rolled up the window and drove away. In some ways it was like watching a mirage pass before my eyes. I blinked just to make sure it was real.

CHAPTER 28

I didn't see Holly again until two days later.

I spent a whole day just sleeping off the last week. When I woke up, night was pressing down on me like two pieces of bread on a slice of turkey. My first thought was to reach for the phone and call Holly. I quickly realized that the memories of the past twenty-four hours were too fresh, and sharing them with Holly right now would be like dropping a brick on my foot. The pain wasn't about to go away anytime soon.

I showered, shaved and dressed the part of a private dick, making my way slowly back into a world I had all but forgotten. My mug still looked like a cross between Frankenstein and the Hunchback of Notre Dame, and my body ached as if I'd just been used as a tackling dummy, but those pains were nothing when compared to what I'd left behind on Henry Street.

I stopped feeling sorry for myself long enough to get to the precinct and give my account of the story to Pete, editing some parts for personal reasons. The facts painted a picture of Paul Brutus as a scheming and jealous mug out to pay back Big Pete for ruining his prize-fighting career. Everything else was just a matter of arranging the facts in a way that suited Pete's notebook. Brutus took the fall for Baker's death; Connie took the fall for kidnapping and attempted murder while Schwarz got off with a smack on the wrist for telling all. I was sure it wouldn't be long before her old man or Big Pete got her out of that jam. Dane Bartlett, meanwhile, kept the bullets

Baxter fired at him as well as his relationship with Big Pete. Big Pete wouldn't have had it any other way.

The only question remaining was whether I could face Baker's old lady ever again. I had made her a promise and in some ways I kept it, but did that mean I kept the promise to myself, or my dead kid brother, or to my parents? Some things in my life still lived in the shadows, waiting to come out another day.

I was still unsure about seeing Holly after everything that had happened, but something Pete said just before I left made me think. Pete wasn't exactly the poet for the ages, but as a married guy, he had the business on things I had no clue about.

"I've been talking to her a little, Dix," Pete started, "and she's all right. Women like Holly get mad for a lot of reasons. It isn't up to us to explain it. All we can do is try to make things easier for them, mostly because it makes things easier for us. Dix, you need to tell her about Allen, and I don't mean just say it in a few words. I mean, tell her everything, Dix. You got to tell someone, and I have a feeling she's exactly the kind of woman that will listen. Give yourself a chance."

I thought a lot about those words after I left the precinct. Faith was a rare commodity in my world. It was as rare as a rich detective, and as hard to hold onto as a ten-dollar bill. For a lot of years I took the fast way around faith, living for pain instead, because at least I was feeling something. That all changed when I met Holly. She knew pain. She had lived through it for a long time. I didn't need to know her whole life story to notice the pain she harbored inside. I knew it because I hid the same pain. It was the reason I took so many chances. Standing in the doorway looking at Brutus was like peering into a mirror, only dirtier.

"A penny for your thoughts, Mr. Detective." The voice was smooth, soft, and right in so many ways. It was also a voice that I wasn't ready for. If it didn't work out, I would ensure the rest of Pete's days were filled with pain, lots of it.

I turned to Holly slowly, a cigarette hanging off the corner of my mouth like a life preserver. Holly looked good, refreshed, like a dame ready for a fashion show. The last few days didn't show on her.

"You look good, sweetheart."

"You look all done in."

"I've looked worse." The bright yellows and reds of my cigarette contrasted magically with Holly's dark hair and mesmerizing gaze. I looked past the flame and toward her, a subtle breeze brushing past like a stranger in the night. Her dark eyes cut through the cold and into my heart.

"Pete told me they found Honey. She's okay, just a little shaken up."

"I'm glad to hear it. I know you were really worried about her." It felt like a stupid thing to say. I was in the middle of a conversation that could have been as casual as talking about fine China or travel plans. Holly seemed to take it all in stride. A few tense seconds passed before Holly spoke again.

You were right, you know," Holly said.

"Oh?"

"Your friends are real nice. They took real good care of me. Pete's wife is a nice lady." She suddenly looked like she was a million miles away.

I walked up to her, head down, my hands stuffed deeply into both pockets. The air turned a little warmer as I inched closer to Holly. Looking at her took all the strength I had. "They're good people. They deserve better than me as a friend, but they won't give up on me. I don't really know why."

"It's because they love you. Pete would never admit it. I guess guys are like that. But Wilma told me all about you two, and the bond you have. Reminds me a little of what Schwarz and Baker had before Connie got her mitts on them. It's strange what a woman can do to men."

A few seconds of quiet descended upon both of us. It felt like hours. "I didn't want to leave you there, but I had no choice. I couldn't afford to have you with me when I faced Brutus. I had to do it alone. You were never in any real danger." The words came out in a rush. I wasn't sure if it was the right moment or not.

"I know that. When the police came, the first thing I wanted to do was hit you. I hated you for leaving me there. I suppose I panicked, but after awhile I realized you had to do things your way. I just hope things worked out for the best."

"Brutus is on his way to meet his maker; Big Pete is pleased with my work enough to let you and me live a while longer and the cops got their man, or woman."

"What about Baker's old lady? Does she get what she was looking for?"

It was a strange question to ask in the middle of a busy street. I suppose death was a strange topic anywhere.

"I know and that's all that matters. In the end, the score winds up even for everyone. Everyone got what they wanted out of this whole crummy deal."

"What's that supposed to mean? Who killed Joe?" Holly asked.

I was quiet for a long time, letting my eyes wash over everything until it all became one living thing. I blew a long thin strand of smoke up into the air until it blistered into fragments and disappeared. I turned to Holly. "You sure you want to know. I sure don't. Not anymore."

A haunting look plunged deep into her eyes. She held herself tight. "What scares you so much about the answer, Gabrielle?" She looked deep into my eyes. "You're the bravest man I've ever met. You went to bat for me when you could've just left me to rot. You took beatings, bullets and everything else these people could throw at you and survived. But, for all of that, you're still as fragile as China."

"I've seen things and done things I'm not proud of. My life isn't the kind of romantic thing you see in cheap movies or read about in dime-store novels. It's a life covered in shadows and dirt. These bruises," I said, pointing to the still-fresh bruises on my face, "These are what I bring home every night. Two nights ago I saw something, a truth; a truth that scared me more than anything else I'd ever seen before."

"What is it that scared you so much? Gabrielle, please tell me?"

I suddenly realized I couldn't do it. Speaking through my soul was something I had never done before. I stepped back. "It's all wrong. This is all wrong." I turned and looked at her, really looked at her. I finally took her by the hand. "I want you to do me a favor.

Meet me tonight in Central Park by the fountain. Can you do that for me?"

She looked into my eyes, confusion and uncertainty seeming to hold domain over her. She took a deep breath and replied, "Yes, if it's that important to you."

"It is." I kissed her once then walked away.

CHAPTER 29

The lady was in magnificent form. Her fluid grace hadn't been diminished by the years, the countless storms, or the roughhouse hooligans that patrolled the place. She stood in the center like she always had, her hand gently blessing the water at her feet. It had been like that for me ever since I first saw her. She was more than just the 'Angel of the Waters', she was a second chance.

Up above, the moon shone brightly. It was like the perfect night. A few others walked past, most of them caught in their own time, their own moment.

I suddenly thought about Holly. I wondered if she would show or whether I had just set myself up for another big fall. She had reached out and tried to listen, wanted to listen, but something about the moment felt wrong, unclean. Paul Brutus, Big Pete, Connie Bartlett and the rest of the cast were still fresh in my mind. It felt wrong talking to Holly about the present, or even the future, when the past was still so fresh in my mind. I stared at the statue some more, hoping to get lost in the moment.

I heard the click of shoes behind me. I turned to see Holly slowly striding toward me with a brand new dress on, new shoes and a smile that looked brighter than ten suns put together. I suddenly felt like a kid on his first date.

She glided up to me like an expensive yacht. Each step was perfect. Watching her was like watching the perfect homerun, or listening to the perfect Tommy Dorsey song. She was elegance in A minor and I was just a dope from the slums who thought he had a chance. I watched her for a long time. I suddenly wished I hadn't bought the suit or shaved or done any of the things it took me all day to do.

The first thing that hit me was the perfume. The second thing was the hug. It was good, it was long and it made everything else disappear.

I looked into her eyes like a man possessed. "I guess I should have gotten you something. That probably would have been the right thing to do."

"It's all right. I got everything I need right here," she replied.

I reached into my pocket and pulled out a small box and handed it to her. She looked at me with tears in her eyes as she slowly opened the box. Inside was a ring, her ring. She looked up at me again with enough tears to sink a battleship.

"I promised I'd get it back for you, didn't I?"

Between tears she replied, "Yes, you did." She slipped the ring back on her finger then kissed me. It was another perfect moment.

"I promised you the moon as well. What do you think?"

"It's lovely. Everything is lovely. I even like the suit."

"What about the scars? They kind of scream a little more without the stubble, don't you think?"

"I wouldn't recognize you without them. I like them just where they are." She took a few seconds before speaking again. "Pete said you had something to tell me. He said you could probably tell me now that it was all over."

I looked at Holly anxiously, like a man on the edge of something he doesn't quite understand. I finally said, "His name was Allen. He was my kid brother. He died without ever knowing anything about life. My parents never blamed me for it, but I always got the feeling they wanted to. They pampered me, giving me just enough room to let his ghost into my subconscious. Seeing Baker reminded me of him, just a little. I've been living that nightmare for a long time. Every dead mug I see reminds me of Allen. I've tried to forget through booze, guns, dames and whatever else I could find only to find myself in the same mud-pit along with all the other crazies. Even in Brutus I saw my guilt. He's dead, but I know his death is on my conscience and probably always will be."

"He was a bad man who did bad things. They were all bad people. They tried to hurt innocent people and get away with it. If it wasn't him, it would have been you. You can't take the blame for that. You deserve a medal for what you did."

I can't say that she was right, but I couldn't stand there and say she was wrong either. I figured my shadow stood somewhere in between it all. I took a deep breathe then asked, "Can you accept that Joseph Baker's murderer will never be caught?"

"I don't understand. I thought Brutus..." Holly trailed off.

"In the end, he's the one responsible, but not the one who pulled the trigger. Can you accept that the real killer might never be caught?"

She was quiet for a long time.

"I don't know," I said in frustration. I looked up at her until I saw her and nothing else. "Peace and quiet would be real nice right about now."

"You once said life is full of moments. Some of them are good and some are bad, but that's what makes life worth living. Did you mean that or was that just a line?"

"Yeah, I meant it. If I hadn't, I wouldn't be standing here in this monkey suit trying to win over a dame that's way too good for me."

"And I wouldn't be standing here in this bath-towel of a dress trying to get you to tell me you love me." It was what I wanted to say for a lifetime. I felt it every time I looked at her. Something pinched inside of me like a needle against a bruise. It was painful, and it was real. I finally realized it was love.

"Can you love a man that makes fifty dollars a day plus expenses?"

"Can you love a dame that does the hoochie-coochie better than anyone else?"

I laughed until it hurt. I laughed until the tears streamed from my eyes like a mad rain on a warm summer night. I cried until Big Pete, Connie Bartlett, Paul Brutus and the rest were purged from my soul. I cried until I felt all right again. Holly cried because I cried, and when it was all over I kissed her. I told her I loved her and that I would always be there for her.

I also told her that I loved the hoochie-coochie and that if she could dance it to some mean Count Basie, I'd marry her. She said she could.

About the Author

Ivan Narayan was born November 1970 in Vancouver, Canada. He published his first novel, The Big Fall, in 2006. Besides obtaining a B.A. in English Literature from the University of British Columbia, Narayan has edited numerous financial manuals for internet marketing companies as well as written several unpublished short stories. He is currently at work on his next novel.

Printed in the United States
131859LV00002B/16/P